THE

HOUSEKEEPERS

THE
HOUSEKEEPERS

A NOVEL

ALEX HAY

GRAYDON
HOUSE

GRAYDON
HOUSE®

Recycling programs
for this product may
not exist in your area.

ISBN-13: 978-1-525-80500-4

The Housekeepers

Graydon House
22 Adelaide St. West, 41st Floor
Toronto, Ontario M5H 4E3, Canada
www.GraydonHouseBooks.com
www.BookClubbish.com

Printed in U.S.A.

For my mother, for getting me started.

And for Tom, for cheering this book every step of the way.

THE

HOUSEKEEPERS

The House of de Vries

REQUESTS THE HONOR OF YOUR COMPANY AT A

COSTUMED BALL

ON MONDAY, THE 26TH OF JUNE, 1905

NINE O'CLOCK

PARK LANE, W1   FULL DRESS

AN ACKNOWLEDGMENT IS REQUESTED,
ADDRESSED TO THE LADY OF THE HOUSE

POST OFFICE TELEGRAPHS

HANDED IN AT 11:02   CHARGES: £0.0s 0d. PAID

BE ADVISED MARKET IS OPEN   [STOP]

TAKING BEST BIDS ONLY   [STOP]

FELICITATIONS ALWAYS   [STOP]

THE HOUSEKEEPERS

1

Friday, June 2, 1905
Park Lane, London

Mrs. King laid out all the knives on the kitchen table. She didn't do it to frighten Mr. Shepherd, although she knew he would be frightened, but just to make the point. She kept good knives. She took excellent care of them. This was her kitchen.

They had scrubbed the room to within an inch of its life, as if to prevent contamination. The tabletop was still damp. She could feel the house straining, a mountain of marble and iron and glass, pipes shuddering overhead.

She reckoned she had twenty minutes until they threw her out. Madam was awake and on the prowl, up in the vast ivory stillness of the bedroom floor, and they were already late with breakfast. It was important that Mrs. King didn't waste time. Or endanger anyone else. She didn't care what they did to her—she was past caring about that—but troubles had a way of multiplying, sending out tendrils, catching other people. She moved fast, going from drawer to drawer, checking, rummaging. She was looking for a wrinkle in things, a missing piece, something out of place. But everything was in perfect order.

Too perfect, she thought, skin prickling.

A shadow fell across the wall.

"I'll need your keys, please, Mrs. King."

She could smell Mr. Shepherd standing behind her. It was the odor that came off his skin, the fried-up scent of grease and gentleman's musk.

Breathe, she told herself. She turned to face him.

He made an excellent butler. But he'd have done even better as a priest. He had that air about him, so tremendously pious. He stared at her, feasting his eyes on her, loving every minute of this.

"Good morning, Mr. Shepherd," she said, voice smooth, same as every morning.

Mrs. King's rule was: choose your first move wisely, and you could steer things any way you liked. Choose it badly, and you'd get boxed into a corner, pummeled to pulp. Mr. Shepherd pursed his lips. He had a strange mouth, a nasty little rosebud.

"Keys," he said, holding out his hand.

Straight to business, then. She circled him, making her approach. She wanted to capture a picture of his face in her mind. It would be very helpful later, once things were properly underway. It would give her all the encouragement she needed.

"I'm still doing my rounds, Mr. Shepherd," she said.

He took a tiny step back, to preserve the distance between them. "No need for that now, Mrs. King," he said, eyeing the door.

The other servants were eavesdropping in the kitchen passage. She could feel them, folded just out of sight, contained in the shadows. She placed them like chess pieces in her mind. The chauffeur and the groomsman in the yard, the housemaids on the back stairs. Cook in the pantry, entirely agitated, twisting her handkerchief into indignant knots. William, sequestered in Mr. Shepherd's office, under close guard. Alice Parker upstairs, keeping well out of trouble. Each of them watching the clock. The entire house was waiting, motion suspended.

"I never leave my work half-finished, Mr. Shepherd," she said as she slid around him. "You know that."

And she made for the door.

She saw figures scattering, ducking into pantries and offices. Her boots echoed hard on the flagstones. She felt the cold, damp breeze coming down from the back stairs and wondered: *Will I miss it?* The chill. The unforgiving scent of carbolic on the air. It wasn't nice, not at all, but it was familiar. It was funny how you got used to things after so much time. Frightening, even.

Mr. Shepherd followed her. He was like an eel, heavy and vicious, and he moved fast when he wanted to.

"Mrs. King," he called, "we saw you in the gentlemen's quarters last night."

"I know," said Mrs. King over her shoulder.

A steep staircase ran from the kitchen passage up to the front hall. She kept her eyes fixed on the green baize door at the top. It was a partition between worlds. On the other side the air thinned and the light became frosted around the edges. *"Don't go up there,"* called Shepherd.

Mrs. King didn't care for this. Being ordered about by Shepherd made the inside of her nose itch. "I've things to check," she said.

He continued to follow, sending a tremor through the staircase.

Come on, thought Mrs. King, *chase me.*

"You stay right here," he said, reaching to pull her back.

She stopped on the staircase. She wouldn't run from Shepherd.

He got her by the wrist, his stubby fingers pressing into her veins. His breath smelled stale, but she didn't recoil. She did the thing he hated most. Looked him straight in the eye.

He said, "What were you *doing* last night, Mrs. King?"

Shepherd had begun balding over the years, and all he had

left were scrubby little hairs dotted right across his brow. Yet still he slicked them with oil. No doubt he waxed them every morning, one by one.

"Perhaps I was sleepwalking."

"Perhaps?"

"Yes, perhaps."

Mr. Shepherd loosened his grip slightly. She saw him calculating. "Well. That might change things. I could explain that to Madam."

"But, then again," she said, "perhaps I was wide-awake."

Mr. Shepherd pressed her wrist to the banister. "*Keys*, Mrs. King."

She peered up at the green baize door. The house loomed over her, vast and unreachable. The answer she needed was up there. She knew it. Hidden, or sliced into bits, but *there*. Somewhere. Waiting to be found.

I'll just have to come back and get it, she thought.

She took him to the housekeeper's room, her room, and he stood guard in the doorway, blocking the light. Already it seemed to belong to her past. It wasn't cozy, just cramped. On the table was the master's present to her. Four weeks before, she'd marked her birthday, her neat and tidy thirty-fifth. The master had given her a prayer book. He gave them all prayer books with gilt edging, satin ribbons.

She held her head up as she handed Mr. Shepherd the keys.

"Any others?"

She shook her head.

"We'll see to your personal effects. You can come and collect them in…" He considered this. "In due course."

Mrs. King shrugged. They could inspect her bedroom and sniff the sheets and lick the washbasin all they liked. Even give

away her uniforms, if it pleased them. Serge dresses, plain ribbons, tight collars. You could construct any sort of person with
those. "Best to choose a new name," they'd told her when she'd
first arrived, and she chose King. They frowned, not liking it—
but she held firm: she chose it because it made her feel strong,
unassailable. The *Mrs.* came later, when she made housekeeper.
There was no Mr. King, of course.

She kept her navy coat and her hatpins, and everything else
she folded away into her black leather Gladstone. There was only
one more thing she needed to remove. Pulling open a drawer
in the bureau, she rummaged for a pack of papers.

She threw them on the fire. One neat move.

Mr. Shepherd took a step. "What are those?"

"The menus," said Mrs. King, all the muscles in her chest tight.

The packet was held together with a ribbon, and she watched
it darken on the fire. Red turning brown, then black.

"The what?" His eyes hurried around the room, disturbed,
as if he were looking for things he'd missed, secrets stuffed and
hidden in the walls.

"For Miss de Vries's ball," she said.

Mr. Shepherd stared at her. "Madam won't like it that you
did that."

"I've settled all the arrangements," Mrs. King said with a cool
smile. "She can take it from here."

She studied the ribbon on the grate. It was satin no longer,
simply earth and ash. How quickly it changed, dematerialized.
How completely it transformed.

Shepherd marched her through the servants' hall to the mews
yard, but he didn't touch her again. They passed the portrait of
the master hanging above the long table. The frame had been
draped with black cloth. She wondered when Shepherd would
replace the portrait, now that the funeral had passed, now he'd
been buried. Would he put up one of Madam instead, something
in soft oils and lavender? It would give everyone the willies if
he did. That girl's eyes were like pincers. She guessed Shepherd

would delay as long as he could. He'd be mourning his master longer than anyone.

I hope you're watching from heaven, she said inwardly, looking at the portrait. *Or wherever you've landed. I hope you see it all play out. I hope they pin your eyes open so you have to watch what I do to this house.*

The *house*. She'd admired it, once. It was bigger than any other on Park Lane. A sprawling mass of pillars and bays, seven floors high from cellars to attics. Newly built, all diamond money, glinting white. It obliterated the light, shriveled everything around it. The neighbors hated it.

Had any house in London ever been decorated in such sumptuous and stupendous style? Miles of ice-cold marble and gleaming parquet. Walls trimmed with French silks and rococo paneling and columns. Electricity everywhere, voltage throbbing through the walls, electroliers as big as windmills. Enormous gas fires. Acres of glass, all smelling wildly of vinegar.

And everywhere, in every room, from floor to ceiling, such *treasures*: stupendous Van Dycks, giant crystal bowls stuffed with carnations. Objets d'art in gold and silver and jade, cherubs with rubies for eyes and emeralds for toenails. The zebra-hide sofas in the saloon, and the baccarat tables made of ivory and walnut, and the pink-and-onyx flamingos outside the bathrooms. That library, with the most expensive private collection in Mayfair. The Boiserie, the Red Parlor, the Oval Drawing Room, the ballroom: all dressed with peacock feathers and lapis lazuli and an endless supply of lilies.

They didn't impress Mrs. King at all anymore.

⟶

She didn't shake hands with Mr. Shepherd. "I shall keep you in my prayers, Mrs. King," he said.

"Do."

She supposed the upstairs servants were already clearing out her room. The girls would be scrubbing the floorboards with boiling water and soda crystals and taking the bedsheets to be laundered, eliminating any trace of her.

It was important that she didn't look over her shoulder on the way out. The wrong look at the wrong person could betray her, spoil things when they were only just underway. A pigeon landed on the portico of the gigantic marbled mausoleum as she crossed the yard. She didn't give it a second glance, didn't dip her head in respect to the old master. She marched straight past instead.

She stepped into the mews lane, alone. Heard the distant rumble of motors, saw a clutch of wild poppies growing out of a crack in the paving stones. They were being neglected, trampled, yearning upward to the sky. She plucked one, pressed a fragile crimson petal in her palm, held it warm. She took it with her.

Her first theft.

Or, rather, the first correction. It wasn't simply *stealing*, not at all.

2

Indoors, upstairs, in the fortressed silence of the saloon floor, Miss de Vries inspected the invitation list for her ball.

The preparations had been in motion for weeks. The date had been set: the twenty-sixth of June. Three weeks and three days, and she was counting every moment.

Truthfully, of course, it had been conceived months before, the very moment Papa set sail for the Continent in search of spa cures and the best gaming tables, entirely distracted from home affairs. *He* would not have held any sort of party. No breakfasts, luncheons, high teas or dinners were permitted at Park Lane. Those things would put Miss de Vries entirely on display, up for auction on the market. He refused to countenance that.

Papa went *out* into the world: to the Royal Regatta, and the diplomatic dinners, and the Queen's Drawing Room, and the gymkhana. He wore his yellow-spotted neckerchiefs and his most vulgar waistcoats, and spent lavishly on the charity dances—and people roared for him. They feasted on anecdotes of his extravagance and lowborn manners and brilliant buttons.

She remained home: preserved, contained, scratching at the walls.

After Papa's funeral, Miss de Vries had summoned Mrs. King. The housekeeper entered the room quietly, smoothly, already wearing a black armband. The sight of it sent a shiver through Miss de Vries's chest.

"I'm minded to hold a ball," she said.

She expected astonishment, demurral, doubts about propriety. Or better still: a rebuttal. Loyalties to Papa were shifting and eddying: things felt febrile. Certain members of the household might be reconsidering their options altogether. Miss de Vries welcomed some aggression, even insolence. It would provide a reason to give certain people their notice.

"Have you considered a date, Madam?" asked Mrs. King, unruffled.

It was already high season: Miss de Vries had missed the private view at the Royal Academy; she had no costume for Ascot Week. "Before the end of June. No later," she said, knowing what a strain it would cause for the household. A ball was an entrance, an entrée: it had to be enormous, gargantuan, the best in the calendar.

"I quite agree," said Mrs. King, in an obliging tone. She took on the whole operation, almost as if it were of her own design, startling Miss de Vries with her efficiency. She worked up the menus and managed the worst negotiations with Cook. Ordered the flowers, new linens, fresh crystal ware, waiters, tents and tarpaulins, entertainments. Listed out the necessary staff: new house-parlormaids, daily women, even a *sewing* maid to help with the costume. Closed off half the rooms, opened up others, rearranged the furniture, clearing drawers, putting things in packing cases.

"You can leave all that to the girls, Mrs. King," Miss de Vries said, uneasily, seeing her rifling through one of the closets. "You shouldn't exhaust yourself."

Mrs. King had given her a steady gaze. "I'm never exhausted, Madam," she said.

It was Mr. Shepherd who brought the news. He'd come at dawn this morning, flustered, wearing an entirely disagreeable expression.

"I thought I'd better tell you at once, Madam," he said. "The lamp-boy caught Mrs. King entering the gentlemen's quarters. We think she was planning an *assignation*."

Miss de Vries had dressed in deepest mourning, no jewels, her hair concealed beneath Chantilly lace. Entirely modest, virtuous.

"Which footman?" she asked.

He paused, just a half second. "William," he said.

"How disgusting," Miss de Vries said, without emotion. "Do the other servants know?"

"I fear they may, Madam."

"Then we need to set an example. She must leave today."

She could feel pleasure tingling in her veins. *One by one*, she thought. *I'll get them out one by one.* Shepherd's eyes flickered in their sockets. Ever since she'd left the schoolroom and Papa had given her charge of the housekeeping, Shepherd had been chasing her for decisions. Appointments, expenditures, complaints, approvals. He came through the door every hour, bringing cards, notes, tea, messages, deliveries. It was as if he had leashed himself to her leg, spying on her. Miss de Vries sometimes wondered what he would do if she lifted a hot poker from the hearth and pressed it to his skin. Would he sink to his knees, would he scream, would he beg her to do it again?

These people, Papa's people—Mrs. King, Mr. Shepherd, the lawyers, the rest—they simply wouldn't *do* anymore. Of course Papa had done his best. Furnished her with nannies, ayahs, everything one could pay for. But that only took you so far in life. She wished to operate at the very top of the ladder, right up in the heavenly heights of society: among cabinet ministers, earls, dukes, princes. She just needed to leverage herself properly. Clear out the deadwood. Build on clean, fresh ground.

Mrs. King was out of the house by breakfast time. Miss de Vries came down for luncheon at noon, studied the invitation list, making corrections. The lawyers arrived at two o'clock, per appointment. Mr. Lockwood led the pack, silver-haired and perfectly groomed, concise as always. She ordered him to stay for tea.

"I'd like you to open negotiations for a marriage settlement," she said, pouring the tea, playing mother.

He took the saucer from her, eyes narrowing. "Mr. de Vries always headed off those discussions. I don't know that we have any takers in mind."

That didn't seem like a particularly agreeable response. "Perhaps we might set out some attractive terms," said Miss de Vries.

He considered this. "What is your objective?"

She smiled, adjusted her voice down a notch. "Love," she said. "What else?"

What couldn't she achieve, once she sold off Papa's positions? A first-rate alliance, a title, installation at a house on Berkeley Square, or any address equal to it. She hated this place, the stench of motor oil, its shiny newness. She wanted to live somewhere ancient. Sink her roots into lovely old ground. Papa's address book repulsed her. Steel merchants and newspaper proprietors and *Americans*. She was after eminent men. Blue blood.

Mr. Lockwood had summarized their trading position. His assessment infuriated her. "Overextended," he'd said. As if the de Vries empire had eyes bigger than its stomach.

"I'm not sure the accounts will bear close scrutiny," he said. "Better to wait a year or two."

A year? Another season? Six of those had passed already. And clearly, he was talking nonsense. The household bills were always paid on time, weren't they? Loans came in, payments went out. Of course a fortune fluctuated, when it was as colossal as hers.

Confidence, she thought. *We must project wealth. Splendor.*

She was her father's daughter, after all.

"I'm holding a ball, Mr. Lockwood," she said. "Did I mention it?"

The lawyer seemed smooth, but he only *seemed* it. Really he was serrated all over, knicked and ridged from top to toe. You could prick your skin if you got too close.

"I'm not at all sure about that," he said. "It hardly seems— proper."

"I'm in mourning, Mr. Lockwood," she said. "Naturally the arrangements will reflect that. You needn't be alarmed. I won't be dressed as a chorus girl."

"But aren't *you* alarmed?" He was giving her his usual look, implacable and unrelenting. "By the risk?"

A motor engine coughed outside on the road.

She gave him a level stare. "What risk, Mr. Lockwood? A ball in this house has been long expected. I am *pressed* for one, day and night."

"By whom?" he asked, dubiously.

"I have already commenced the preparations. It would be a great inconvenience to cancel it now."

"You know it's my duty, Miss de Vries, to give you good counsel," he said quietly.

"*Legal* counsel, Mr. Lockwood," said Miss de Vries. "I didn't have you down as chaperone."

"A young lady's reputation," he said, with that same fishlike smile, "is a fine and delicate thing."

"It is immeasurably precious," she agreed. "Of near-incalculable value. It should be burnished, brightened, properly displayed."

Something flickered in Lockwood's eyes, a flash of—what? Recognition? Papa would have said, *Do what I want—make it happen.* He made himself *especially* vulgar for Lockwood, wore his biggest gold rings, placed gigantic fuchsias in his buttonhole. He liked battering the man over the head.

"Modesty," said Mr. Lockwood, "is the most bewitching virtue in the world. It has enormous currency in these affairs."

"Affairs?"

"In the conveyancing of a marriage."

He studied her mildly, one hand in his waistcoat.

The motor outside barked and roared to life.

Of course it wasn't *proper* to hold the ball now. The notion that this hadn't occurred to her, made her stomach churn with anger. It *was* improper. That was precisely the *point*: she needed to stand firm, deviate not an inch. No bets came without risks. They gave a game its dimensions, its oxygen. She needed to catch the world's attention. Now was the moment. Now, more than ever, while her power was still fresh and newly minted.

Mrs. King had said as much herself when they'd first discussed the arrangements. "You've only got one life to live, Madam. Don't spare any expense. Best put on a good show."

After Lockwood had gone, Miss de Vries went up to her own rooms. They had once belonged to Mama, but carried no remnants of her at all, sparked no memories: she died before Miss de Vries had even reached the schoolroom. This suite was perfumed the way Miss de Vries liked it: violently and completely of orchids. She breathed it in for comfort, for surety. It wasn't easy, maintaining the scent. In this house foul odors rolled in from every direction: the pavement, the cellars, the city.

They reminded her that she was making entirely the right decisions.

3

Twenty-four days to go

Petticoat Lane. Mrs. King felt the sun on her neck. She'd walked all the way from Mayfair to Aldgate to save the twopence on the Tube. She had to jostle her way with the crowd, but it was worth it, a necessary investment. There was one person she needed to see. Not an easy person to manage. Not someone who liked surprises. You didn't charge into Mrs. Bone's territory without due preparation, and a good reason to call. But Mrs. King was nothing if not prepared, and she had the best proposition in town.

The heat gave the lane a whirring, jangled energy. It smelled like old things, manure and wrinkled fruit and drains. Everyone seemed dislocated, running in packs, a sea of flat caps. Mrs. King heard the distant *dandle-dandle-rum-tum-tum* of music, spied a fiddler balanced on a stool. It gave her a queer twist in the chest. She always felt it, coming home.

Concentrate, Dinah, she told herself.

She pulled out her purse, flipped a coin between her fingers.

Studied the market stalls, separating herself from the crowd. The stallholders clocked her. Eyes swiveled sideways, nostrils flared.

Mrs. King raised her hand, shielding her eyes from the sun. She knew she looked strange to them. Not a lady, not a school-mistress. Not a nurse, not a cook. An anomaly. Tightly buckled, hat tipped low over her eyes. A touch of stain on her lips—red, the color of garnets. Armored.

She folded her arms.

And waited.

It didn't take long. The message must have been transmitted through the walls; it must have gone rippling down the back al-leys. The door to the pawnshop opened with a bang. It startled the stallholders, the bell clanging in the air. A woman wearing widow's weeds emerged squinting into the sunlight.

Mrs. King straightened. "Mrs. Bone," she called.

Mrs. Bone was strong, compact, cunningly built. Perhaps fifty years old, at a guess. Sunshine didn't suit her. It drained her, made her look as if she'd been hiding in the cellar. You'd overlook her altogether if you didn't know any better. Which was just the way she liked it.

Her eyes narrowed, and Mrs. King saw her mind working: the *click-click-click* of the gears.

"Well, well," Mrs. Bone called back, voice hoarse. "Aren't we highly favored?"

The stallholders repositioned themselves. Casual, heads turned, gazing up at the sky as if it fascinated them.

Mrs. King crossed the street. Followed the old rules. Ducked her chin half an inch. Scraped one boot behind the other. Kiss to the cheek, kiss to the hand. "Good day, Mrs. Bone."

Up close Mrs. Bone carried the same scent as always: rose water and hair that smelled of wood shavings. "How can I help you, dear?" she murmured into Mrs. King's ear.

Mrs. King didn't fall for that. Whatever your trouble, whatever the jam, you didn't ask Mrs. Bone for *help*. Help was for the birds. You presented her with a proposition, nicely packaged, nothing else. Mrs. King straightened up, assessed the terrain. There was a skinny-looking chap leaned up against a lamppost, head buried in his newspaper. Frayed cuffs, bare ankles. Not a detective. A scout, a lookout. And not employed by Mrs. Bone. *Her* men didn't dress like scarecrows. Mrs. King scanned the street. Another lad at the corner, by the pub. A third under the guttering.

Mrs. King considered this with interest. These were Mrs. Bone's stalls, and that was Mrs. Bone's house. She'd drawn and quartered and marked this part of the street as her domain. Her territory ran from here to Docklands, a snaking line of enterprises, legitimate and not so legitimate. Nicely demarcated ground. You didn't play on Mrs. Bone's turf if you didn't want trouble.

And yet there were men playing all over it.

"Busy out here today," Mrs. King said.

Mrs. Bone tutted in irritation. "Get inside."

But she glanced over her shoulder as she closed the door.

Mrs. Bone's pawnshop was a legitimate business. A humble one, too. An entirely sensible place to hold a meeting. Mrs. King's eyes adjusted to the dull and respectable shimmer, the brass and silver and gold.

Mrs. Bone turned the sign on the door to Closed and dissolved into the gloom, scuttling behind a gigantic desk, grabbing a pile of receipts pinioned to a nail. "This your afternoon off?"

"No."

"You've come shopping, then."

"Not exactly."

Mrs. Bone rifled through her receipts. "You're in trouble."

"No trouble. I'm on a leave of absence."

"Oh, lovely."

"Yes."

"Must feel marvelous."

"Yes."

"I'm not one for taking holidays myself. Not got the time."

Mrs. King smiled. "You should treat yourself."

"And I should call myself Princess Do-As-I-Please, but I can't always have my way, now, can I?"

Mrs. King raised an eyebrow and unbuckled her Gladstone bag. She pulled out a copy of the *Illustrated News*, held up the photograph of the old master. The image flashed and winked at them. That famous spotted neckerchief. His teeth bared and gleaming. Black scrolls at the top of the page: "Wilhelm de Vries. Born 1850. Died 1905."

"Yes, yes, I heard," said Mrs. Bone, voice tight.

Mrs. King tilted her head. "And?"

"I'm a Christian lady. I don't gloat about nobody's passing." Her eyes darkened. "They're calling him that *name* in the papers."

"You still don't care for 'de Vries'?"

Mrs. Bone began shredding receipts. "He was Danny O'Flynn when he was born. He was Danny O'Flynn when he died." She sniffed. "*If* he died. If it's not a great prank. If it's not an almighty tease."

Mrs. Bone's personal feelings about Danny O'Flynn, the man who transformed himself into Wilhelm de Vries, were well-known to Mrs. King. They were among the category of sensitive things, topics avoided.

"No, he's gone, Mrs. Bone."

"And what's he left behind?"

Mrs. King glanced down at the paper. They'd printed a photograph of Madam, too. "A fair flower in bloom, Miss de Vries in her winter garden…" She appeared in a cloud of chiffon, blurry, hard to pin down. Innocent looking.

Mrs. King had been present when they'd taken that photograph. They did it in the winter garden, the conservatory overlooking the park. They made the photographer stay all day, long after the light had faded. Madam faced the window, eyes flat and unreadable, telegraphing a silent order through the air. *Get it right. Make it perfect.*

"The daughter."

Mrs. Bone's gaze tightened. "And?"

"And nothing."

"*Were his affairs in order?* That's what I want to know."

Mrs. King sighed. "I've no notion, Mrs. Bone."

"Then what are you *here* for?" Mrs. Bone replied, snapping her fingers. "I'm a busy lady. I don't have time for nonsense conversations."

She's rattled today, thought Mrs. King. *Combing the newspapers, picking over old ground.*

"Perhaps I just came to say hello," said Mrs. King calmly.

Mrs. Bone's eyes flew upward. "You're up to something."

"Am I?"

"You've got something cooking up here." Mrs. Bone tapped the side of her head. "Not a nice thing. It never is."

"Heavens," said Mrs. King. "*You* taught me everything I know."

Mrs. Bone's mouth thinned. Evidently, she didn't like that: she saw it as an aspersion on her character. And Mrs. Bone took good care of appearances. Gave generously to the church collection, kept an entirely dull front parlor, still wore mourning clothes for her long-departed Mr. Bone, erstwhile husband and ironmonger. Her jet ornaments clanked every time she moved.

"They gave you the shove," she said, "didn't they?"

Mrs. King inclined her head. "For a minor indiscretion."

"What did you do?"

Mrs. King told her. Mrs. Bone raised an eyebrow.

"You were visiting your fancy man?" she asked.

"It was all a great misunderstanding," said Mrs. King smoothly.

"You've got *something cooking*. I can smell it!" Mrs. Bone sighed. "Come on back."

Mrs. Bone's private office was behind the shop, far away from the street. The windows faced another dirty courtyard where young men stood smoking. Mrs. Bone banged on the window. *"Company,"* she shouted, and they started like pigeons, scattering, disappearing into the shadows.

The front of the shop was gloomy, shabby, full of cheap rings and watches. The private office was different altogether. Here Mrs. Bone kept her fancies, her shiny things. Queer inventions, oddities, curios. Mrs. King knew she had other secret houses, scattered all the way to Essex, full of machines and portraits and furs and looking glasses. Exotic artifacts, paid for on credit and imported from across the empire. Mrs. Bone darted around, dodging footstools and side tables, armoires and escritoires.

"How's business?" said Mrs. King courteously.

"Splendid," said Mrs. Bone.

It didn't look splendid. Mrs. King picked up a silver bowl, gave it a quick once-over. Painted tin. She could have peeled the skin off with her teeth.

"Were those Mr. Murphy's boys, hanging about in the street?"

Mrs. Bone grimaced. *"Murphy.* Don't mention him."

"He's not tried intimidation before, Mrs. Bone. What's changed?"

"Intimidation? Who's intimidated? He can send his little goblins to leer at me anytime he likes. I'm hardly ever in. I'm rushed off my feet."

Mrs. King smiled. There was some truth to this: she was lucky to have got hold of Mrs. Bone herself, for she never stayed for long at the pawnshop. She had the factory out by the docks. Warehouses all down the coast. Plus a whole line of cigarette shops and barber shops and ironmongers and the rest. Plenty of street work, too. Though Mrs. Bone didn't sell dirty daguerreotypes, she ran no bawdy houses. She engaged in elegant, *use-*

ful trades. A neat bit of housebreaking. Some calculated affray. She'd taught Mrs. King nearly all of it herself. Always kept an eye out for her. "Somebody has to," she'd said, fiercely. "Your ma hasn't even brushed your hair."

"So, what have you got, then?" Mrs. Bone asked. "A bit of business?"

"Always."

The air smelled as if it were ripening, as if the whole house were on the turn. Mrs. Bone looked out of the window.

"You've been casing a place?"

"Yes."

"Where?"

"Park Lane."

Mrs. Bone's expression changed. "Eh?"

"Interested?"

Mrs. Bone propelled herself up and out of the chair. She picked up an empty dove cage. Swung it back and forth. "Don't," she said.

"Don't what?"

"Don't tell me you're that *foolish*."

Mrs. King said nothing.

"Park Lane." She made a *tsk* sound. "Dinah. You never, *never* do a job when it's personal. I taught you that myself." She rubbed her chin again. "Park Lane?"

"Yes."

"You beggar belief. Marching in here, without a by-your-leave or word of warning..." She straightened. "I know my patch. We don't do anything west of Gracechurch Street, for God's sake. I'm not tripping up to town for any geegaws on *Park Lane*."

There were a dozen clocks piled on the mantelpiece, ticking furiously, all out of time.

"Perhaps it's time to branch out, Mrs. Bone."

"I don't need to branch out!"

Mrs. King softened her tone. "It's a big house. Bigger than anything. Marble like you've never seen before. Chairs from Versailles. Silks. Jewels the size of goose eggs."

"You think I don't know all that? You think I don't know what sort of palace Danny built for himself?"

Of course she knew. Diamonds made Danny O'Flynn. Gave him a fortune beyond all comprehension: stockpiles, monopolies, loans even governments couldn't win. He made his whole new life on the back of them, a whole new name. *Mr. de Vries* had a fierce, white-hot sort of wealth, the kind that stopped your heart in your chest. Millionaire, they called him. *Millionaire.*

Mrs. Bone never forgave him for it.

"Well, then," said Mrs. King, spreading her hands.

The clocks shimmered, bright and angry.

Mrs. King reached into her pocket and drew out an object wrapped in a handkerchief. She lifted a silver watch into the air, dangled it by its chain. It turned in the light, revealing little engraved letters: WdV.

"How about an advance?" she said. "Against services rendered?"

Mrs. Bone looked at the watch, the swiftest possible glance. The silver reflected in her eyes. "I *told* you. I don't do jobs when it's *personal.*"

Mrs. King doubted that very much. Mrs. Bone's whole operation was personal. It had been formed out of a hundred thousand tiny chain links, a whole line of gifts given and received, favors sought and granted, enmities formed and settled. Mrs. King had been counting on this. Her motives were personal, too, although they had their own secret, slanted edges. They were driving her brain, her blood, every muscle in her body. It had taken her the best part of a month to put this plan together, but really it had been building for years. It must have lurked in Mrs. Bone's mind, too. The kind of thing you dreamed of doing, the kind that took everyone's breath away. All those treasures, sitting idly in that house. Mrs. King intended to take them all.

Calmly Mrs. King said, "If you're not interested, I can go elsewhere."

Mrs. Bone's face did something curious then, a puckering of the mouth. Not annoyance, exactly. A flash of hunger.

She sniffed, and studied the watch. "What services do you need?"

"Funds, principally."

"Everyone always wants my funds. Have you got *people*?"

"The principal players, yes. Naturally we'll need more. Alice Parker is in residence already."

"Alice *Parker*? That odd little fish? Now, I don't like the sound of that at all. Who's acting aide-de-camp?"

"Winnie Smith."

"Never heard of her. Namby-pamby sort of name. You won't get me backing strangers."

Mrs. King handed over the watch. "I'm holding a meeting on Sunday to go over the details. Come and inspect everybody then."

"Sunday? *This* Sunday?"

"No use hanging about."

Mrs. Bone's eyes widened, and she began to chuckle. "I'd need to see your numbers."

"Naturally." Mrs. King reached into her coat pocket, pulled out a slim envelope.

Mrs. Bone snatched it up. "Bottom line?"

"Lucky Sevens," said Mrs. King. "My favorite split."

"*Sevenths?*" Mrs. Bone held the watch up to the light, let it spin slowly on its chain. "You've got seven fools lined up for this job?"

Mrs. King went to Mrs. Bone and kissed her gently on the cheek. "I've got three, besides myself, if you're in. Why don't you have us over on Sunday, and tell a couple of your best girls—I need a pair of sturdy types for the indoor reconnaissance."

Mrs. Bone bristled. "Oh, I see. You think you can come marching in here, frazzling my nerves, spoiling my afternoon, giving *me* orders…"

Mrs. King drew back. She fixed her coat, adjusted her hat. "Sunday, Mrs. Bone. You say where. You say when."

Mrs. Bone folded the envelope into her sleeve, twirling the silver watch. "I am *not* in," she said, eyes sparkling. "Not yet. Not even a little bit."

4

To Spitalfields, and a cloud of dust was rising high into the air over Commercial Street. Mrs. King perched on the edge of a fruit barrow, munching an apple, waiting for her aide-de-camp. She had her eyes pinned on the hat shop across the road. The sign sparkled in the sunlight: Mr. Champion, Milliner. In normal circumstances she would have found it very disagreeable, wasting time like this. But of course she didn't *have* chores anymore. Her objective for the day had become altogether more interesting. There was something very *particular* she needed.

Nobody noticed her waiting there, except for a little girl in a mud-spattered pinafore who watched her hungrily. Mrs. King flicked her a sixpence.

"That's for good observation," she said. The girl leaped for it, scrabbling on the cobblestones, and hurtled away.

Mrs. King didn't need to check her pocket watch. She knew exactly what time it was. She crunched apple pips with her back teeth, counting seconds in her head.

It was another five minutes before her quarry appeared. Winnie Smith came lurching around the corner with her gigantic perambulator, heading for Mr. Champion's shop. That pram carried hatboxes, not babies, stacked in teetering, dangerous piles. Mrs. King felt a familiar stirring of affection. Winnie: trussed up in a violently mended purple dress, hat pinned at a hopeless angle, steering the perambulator as if it were a tank. Something snapped, the suspension or a spoke, and she staggered. *Oh Lord*, thought Mrs. King, and closed her eyes.

She finished the last of her apple, licked her fingers, and sauntered across the road.

Winnie was wrestling the pram over the curb when she spotted Mrs. King. *"Today?"* she said, disbelieving.

"No time like it," said Mrs. King with a wry smile.

Winnie sucked in all her breath, straightened her hat. "I've an appointment to keep," she said, frowning.

Mrs. King remembered the first time they'd met, twenty years before, in the kitchen at Park Lane. She'd sensed then that Winnie, five years her senior, would make the perfect elder sister. Someone fierce, someone reliable, someone you could trust right down to the bones—even at her most harried, as she was today. Mrs. King nudged her.

"Hang your appointment, Win. We've got bigger fish to fry."

Winnie hauled the perambulator up onto the curb. She shook her head, stubborn. "Ten minutes. Then I'm all yours."

Winnie was raised very nicely, very properly. She had such *enormous* scruples. It made Mrs. King click her tongue in impatience. She peered into Winnie's perambulator, flipped open one of the hatboxes. A squashed, queasy-looking article gazed back at her. It had taken on the shape and color of a blancmange, festooned with ghastly brown ribbons.

"Lovely," she said.

"Don't touch it! I'm calling it the Savoy." Winnie stroked it.

"Champagne satin, chocolate velvet. And silk-finished braid, do you see? It goes right under the brim."

"Is that hair?"

"It's *braid*."

"Whose hair is it?"

Winnie batted Mrs. King away, rammed the lid back on the box. "It's what they're showing in New York."

Mrs. King put her hands behind her back. "How much are you charging for it?"

Winnie hesitated.

Mrs. King smiled. "I'll help you negotiate." Winnie was stolid, steady, the most industrious person Mrs. King knew. But certain things needed to move with a clip.

Winnie looked annoyed. "Dinah…"

"Don't worry. It'll speed things up."

"I don't need you to *speed things up*."

Mrs. King simply raised her eyebrow at that. She kicked the shop door open, the bell pealing in alarm, and Winnie sighed, battling with the pram. "Dinah, *go easy*…"

The light inside the shop was clean, the shelves stacked with eggshell ribbons and bolts of satin. Mrs. King disliked dainty things. Muslin made her teeth ache. "I'm on my break," said a voice from the back of the shop. "Come back later."

"But it's your lucky day," said Mrs. King.

"It's just Winnie Smith, Mr. Champion," called Winnie, colliding into everything. "We have an appointment!" She gave Mrs. King a warning glance: *Not another word.*

Mr. Champion sat in his office like a ham stuffed into a picnic basket, pink-cheeked and glistening, surrounded by wicker and wires. The air smelled of dried fruit and vinegar. He started, spectacles quivering on the end of his nose. "No, no, *no*," he said. "*Not* you. I've told you already. I ain't buying any more *tat*."

Winnie grabbed one of the hatboxes, knocked the lid to the floor. "Just a moment of your time, Mr. Champion," she said,

planting her feet firmly apart. "Have a look at this one. I'm calling it the Navy. Blue rosettes, do you see? I've dressed it with
heliotrope flowers, and of course I could do white ones, too…"

Mr. Champion pointed at the perambulator, neck reddening.
"Get that great heaving article *out* of here!" He addressed Mrs.
King. "And who are you?"

Mrs. King smiled, cracked her knuckles. "Her agent."

"A trial offer, Mr. Champion," Winnie said quickly. "How
about that? Your customers might *like* to try something new."

"My customers," said Mr. Champion, "buy *quality*." He looked
Winnie up and down—and Mrs. King knew what he saw. A
faded dress, skin gray and saggy under the chin. Nothing to respect, nothing to worry about. "Now, clear off."

"Did you take her last delivery, Mr. Champion?" said Mrs. King.

His eyes swiveled to meet hers. A sneer. "I doubt it."

Winnie appeared troubled. "That's not correct, Mr. Champion. I gave you my very best stock."

"I daresay you might have off-loaded some old handkerchiefs
on me. I really can't recall."

"I'm sure you have the receipts," said Mrs. King.

"I'm sure I *don't*."

He looked like suet, a sick-making color. "Might I check?"
she said.

"Might you…" He paused, taking a breath, reddening further. "No, you may *not*. You can show yourself out." His eyes
rattled back and forth between them. "Here, what is this? Some
job you've worked up between you? I said to *clear off*!"

Winnie lifted her hands, alarmed. "Mr. Champion…"

"Five guineas, Mr. Champion," said Mrs. King.

He stared at her. "What?"

"Five guineas for the Navy. Or I want to see your order
book."

Mr. Champion let out a scornful laugh. "Don't make me send
for the constable."

"Be my guest," Mrs. King said in a congenial tone. "I'll re-port exactly what I can see occurring here. You're cheating la-dies out of their dues."

"Say that again," he said, voice dropping, "and you won't be able to sell a stitch to any living body in town."

"Order book, please," said Mrs. King, pressing her palms to the table.

There was a long silence. Winnie was holding her breath.

"Three guineas," Mr. Champion said.

Mrs. King sometimes wondered, *How do I do it?* How did she get people to capitulate, to bow? She didn't exactly like it. It made her feel chilly and contemptuous of the world. But of course it was necessary. Somebody had to put things right in life.

"Done," she said, keeping her distance from Mr. Champion.

He made a lot of noise, a lot of fuss, counting out the change. "You're nothing more than a thief. You won't be coming around *here* again. They'll lock the doors on you two, that I can tell you for sure and certain—"

But they got their three guineas.

Winnie shoved the pram out into the road. "For heaven's *sake.*"

Mrs. King closed the shop door with a bang. "Here," she said gravely, counting out shillings.

Winnie gave her a long look, as if deciding whether to say thank you or not. She pressed her lips together. "I need a sherry," she said.

"Lead the way," said Mrs. King, reaching for the perambu-lator. "I'll mind Baby."

They quick-marched to Bethnal Green, the perambulator list-ing and keeling all the way, men throwing them filthy looks as it ran over their toes. Mrs. King watched the sky changing.

The sun drained away, as if giving up. It stirred her, the dusk: it put her in the hunting mood. And she was hungry for a very particular object. Mrs. King wasn't the only housekeeper ever employed in that house on Park Lane. Winnie had held that illustrious title herself, only three years before. And she still held a most useful item in her possession.

Winnie lived in dreary lodgings at the top of a damp and narrow building: cramped and low ceilinged and desperately well scrubbed. *So, this was freedom.* Mrs. King looked at the bleach-stained floorboards, comparing them to the gleaming parquet in the saloon at Park Lane, and felt a quick, fierce flare of anger. She refused to end up like this.

Winnie shoved the cork back in the sherry bottle. They clinked glasses, swallowed.

"Have you got it?" said Mrs. King.

Winnie sighed. "Just a moment."

She ducked out of the room, and returned carrying a large object wrapped in tissue paper. "Here."

Mrs. King felt her heart start ticking. At last, here it was. That marvelous leather-bound book, those gray-green covers inlaid with gold, those thick pages crackling as they turned.

The Inventory.

"So, *you're* the naughty thief," said Mrs. King, reaching for it.

"I didn't *steal* it," said Winnie solidly. "I wrote it, didn't I? It's mine as much as anyone's. I had every right to take it with me."

The Inventory had *everything* listed in it. Every painting, every chair, every toothpick in that house. The pages smelled like gruel: oaty and wet. Oval Drawing Room. Boiserie. Long Drawing Room. Ballroom. Lines and lines and lines written on each page. All the way down to the smallest pantry. "One set snuffers, tin. One pair candle molds, tin. Two pairs paraffin lamps, blue. Two pairs paraffin lamps, yellow." Mrs. King could picture them. Purple mottling, buttery tin. "Tinderbox. Three sets brass candleholders. Three sets candle boxes—dry room."

She felt her breath tightening in her throat. She placed her hand against the page, covered the words. *I can make everything disappear*, she thought.

"Good," she said, voice flat. "Thanks." She closed the book with a tremendous thump, pressed her hands to the cover, possessing it.

"You're welcome," Winnie said, giving Mrs. King a dry look. Then her expression changed, hardening. "What now? Is your woman going to pay us?"

"Don't let Mrs. Bone hear you call her 'my woman.' She'll have your guts for garters."

"But *will* she pay? We can't do a thing without funds, Dinah."

Mrs. King laughed. "Hark at you. Don't worry about funds— I'll sort those. You just worry about getting our final friend on board. We'll need everybody in place by Sunday, not a day later."

Winnie reached for her notebook, flipped through the pages. She'd already given herself hundreds of instructions; Mrs. King could see arrows and crossings-out and scribbles running slant-ways across the page.

"I hope you burn that book when we're finished," she said.

"This won't give us away. I've made up a code."

"Of course you have," said Mrs. King with affection.

It was four weeks since Mrs. King had first mentioned the plan—obfuscating at first, circling around it, looking for the subtlest way in. "Do you mean you want to commit a *robbery*?" Winnie had asked, disbelieving. Mrs. King had backed off, shaking her head: "Goodness gracious, steady on, hold your horses, Win…" But Winnie's frown had deepened, her thoughts burrowing down, down, down into the darker reaches of her mind.

"What do you think?" Mrs. King had finally asked. Winnie needed the money. That much was clear. Mrs. King remembered what Winnie had said when she'd first left Park Lane. "I've got to go my own way. I need to make something of my life." There was something desperate, hurried, inexplicable about it. Winnie was fast approaching forty: she'd been working at Park Lane nearly all her life. But it wasn't as if she had any fine prospects on the outside. She had no grand schemes. She barely made a pittance hawking those hats around the East End.

"If anyone could do it, you could," she'd said, looking up at Mrs. King. "You know all the right people." Winnie's eyes had gleamed a little. She'd started to smile.

Because it was mad, this job. Of course it was. The best games always were. They were like the illuminations at the pantomime, laid with magnesium wires and quicklime blocks, fizzing and exploding before your very eyes. They drew in even the steadiest of folk, even Winnie.

"Oh, I know all the right people," Mrs. King had said with a grin and a nod.

Winnie had always turned a blind eye to Mrs. King's *outside interests*. She was no fool: they'd shared a room, and she noticed Dinah running side jobs for Mrs. Bone—passing messages, delivering hampers. Winnie had spotted goods being sneaked in through the back door: sealskin gloves, a tortoiseshell parasol, the most heavenly emollient soaps…

"Who gave you this?" she'd asked sternly, holding up a bolt of fine lace, concealed at the very back of Dinah's wardrobe.

"I bought it myself," Dinah said, truthfully. It was a risk, taking those side jobs. But risks always paid well.

Mrs. King had never worried that Winnie might snitch on her. The bond between them was absolute. "Here," Winnie had said, rummaging inside the wardrobe, grimacing, loosening a back panel. "Hide your treasures if you must." She paused. "But you should save your pennies. You might want them one day."

Mrs. King remembered the advice. She stopped buying scent bottles and bracelets, and put her cash in old stockings instead.

"Sunday," Winnie said now, scribbling in her notebook. She bit her lip. "Awfully soon, Dinah."

"Sooner the better."

Winnie looked serious. "I suppose you're right."

Mrs. King stretched out a hand. "You'll make a terribly good thief, Win."

Winnie frowned. "Don't tease me."

"I'm not teasing in the least," said Mrs. King, with mock seriousness. "I've never met such a bloodthirsty woman in my life."

Winnie stared up at her from her chair, with an expression in her eyes that made her look suddenly much older. "And I've never met a woman in my life who decided to clear out a whole house, strip it right down to the bones, for no more reason than she *feels* like it." She studied Mrs. King. "Remind me never to cross you."

Mrs. King kept things easy. "I'm sure you don't need reminding." She tapped her pocket watch. "Now, come along. You've got a job to do, my fine lady-felon. Clock's ticking."

5

Winnie entered the Paragon through the doors on the Mile End Road. She crossed the crush room and saw herself reflected in the giant mirrors, flushed with heat. They'd replaced the gaslights with blistering new electroliers and put Chinese prints all over the walls. Everything was glazed and swagged with red velvet. She rather liked it. She took a breath and made straight for the auditorium, spying a door near the stage.

Mrs. King had given very clear instructions. "We need someone with a gift for deception, someone who knows all about *acting*."

"Who did you have in mind?"

"Who do you think?"

"You can't be serious," Winnie had said, knowing exactly who Mrs. King meant. "She's *entirely* unpredictable."

"She's perfect. And you've known her the longest. She'll do it if you ask her."

Winnie had shaken her head. "Not a good idea."

"Nonsense. I have every faith in you," Mrs. King had said. "*Off* you go," she'd added when Winnie hesitated.

Winnie hadn't been able to tell Mrs. King why she dreaded this appointment. It had depths and dimensions even she was only just beginning to comprehend. And she'd sworn to keep them secret. So she had nodded, stoically. "Very well," she'd said. "I'll do my best."

Now Winnie felt a hand on her arm. "Madam!" It was an usher, barring the way. "Have you got a ticket?"

Winnie felt his eyes assessing her shabby coat, and marched back to the lobby. She spent all the cash Mrs. King had given her on a box. *Necessary expense*, she told herself, trying not to look at the price.

They gave her a program for free, which was something. It was printed on silk, the color of peaches and cream. She ran her finger down the acts, searching for one name: Hephzibah Grandcourt. Couldn't find it.

She frowned, looking out over the balcony. There were an awful lot of shopkeepers and cutlery salesmen here. The men wore tartan jackets, luridly patterned, and left their umbrellas in the aisle. *Stop being a snob*, she reminded herself. She looked odder than they did, a lump of coal in a jewelry box, pins falling out of her hat.

Another usher peered in. "Something from the menu?"

"Brandy," she said, summoning her courage. She might as well have asked for a tankard of stout.

The usher gave her a wink. Winnie didn't know if this made her feel better or worse. Her legs were shaking, she noticed. Guilt.

Then she heard the door. The creak and rustle of silk.

"Well, they're in a wonderful flap downstairs," said a voice over her shoulder. "Some charlady's gone and pinched the best seats in the house."

Winnie steeled herself, and turned around.

Her first impression was not of the person standing before her. It was of the person hidden *within* that person. It was just about possible, if you concentrated, to see the girl who'd once worked in the kitchen at Park Lane twenty years ago. A common house sparrow concealed inside a splendid bird of paradise. Her teeth were bared in a smile, pearls choking her neck, hair gleaming and soaring into the air. But the eyes were the same. Cornflower blue, and wide open.

"Hullo, Hephzibah," said Winnie. She took care to use the new name. It seemed the least she could do.

Hephzibah Grandcourt's eyes didn't move. She was an actress, after all. She had the most extraordinary control of her face. She'd possessed that skill even when she worked at Park Lane, back in the days when her hands were yellow from the laundry soap and she always smelled of ammonia. She'd had *presence* then, and she had *presence* now, and her expression radiated anger.

"Who told you I was working down here?" she asked.

Winnie straightened. "Nobody. I guessed."

Hephzibah gave off a powerful scent of sugared fruits and almonds, sickly sweet. "I spotted *you* from behind the stage, of course." She flexed her fingers. "I simply *couldn't*. Believe. My. Eyes." She skewered Winnie with her gaze. "Did you come for my autograph?"

Winnie reminded herself to tread carefully. She had known Hephzibah half her life. And when Hephzibah left Park Lane, eighteen years before, Winnie had stayed in touch, with dogged persistence—sending humdrum letters; buying tickets to the Christmas pantomime; being entirely, perfectly, unimpeachably *good* to Hephzibah. It made Winnie redden with shame now, to think of her own pomposity, her own complete lack of comprehension.

In normal circumstances she and Hephzibah met at tearooms or by the river—on safe and neutral ground. But coming here, onto Hephzibah's own territory, was a bold move. It threatened the hard-won equilibrium between them. "I wanted to talk to you," Winnie said.

The usher brought her brandy and a glass of sherry for Hephzibah. It came on a tray with a bowl of cherries that looked as if they'd been dipped in sugar water, obscenely shiny.

"Well, here I am," said Hephzibah.

"You're not on the program," Winnie said. "Aren't you performing?"

Hephzibah skinned one of the cherries with her teeth. "I'm the understudy," she said, without emotion.

"The what?"

"The stand-in, the spare. They still pay me for that, you know."

The air had a sour-apple tint to it. Hephzibah's nails didn't stop clicking against the beading of her dress, and it pained Winnie to see her anxiety. "Perhaps I can match the fee," she said eagerly. "I've got a commission for you."

Hephzibah spit a cherry stone into the bowl. "What does that mean?"

"A job."

"To do *what*?" Hephzibah's eyes darkened.

"To—charm someone," Winnie said, casting about for the right word. She couldn't afford to be overheard. She wasn't used to this sort of business at all.

"*Charm* someone?"

"Yes! The way only you could do it."

The silence was dreadful. Hephzibah took another cherry, examined it. "Not all actresses are tarts, you know," she said.

Winnie felt herself grow cold. "That's not at all what I mean."

Hephzibah's eyes flashed upward. "I don't need money that badly. I've *got* money."

"Hephzibah…"

"I've got any *number* of jobs coming."

Winnie sat forward in her chair. "Let me explain myself," she said.

Hephzibah snatched the program, held it up to the lamplight. "It's a bad night tonight. Rough acts, top to bottom. You should've come on a Saturday. Then you'd see some talent. Not this rubbish."

"*Hephzibah…*"

"If I ran this place, it would go like a dream. I'd write the bloody plays myself. I've got a great talent."

"I know."

"A *rare* talent. It deserves proper cultivation." She sent another cherry stone bouncing into the bowl. Perfect aim. "It's pretty rich, you marching in here, out of the blue. I haven't heard from you for months."

Winnie opened her mouth. Closed it again. "I always write," she said uneasily.

"And I reply!"

"Well," said Winnie, not able to help herself, "you send me pictures of *yourself.*"

Hephzibah shot her a look. "Picture postcards."

Winnie wilted. "Yes."

"*Very* fetching ones."

Sometimes the moment was presented to you, the window opened just a crack. Winnie forced herself not to be a coward. "Hephzibah. I'm so—" The words came in a rush. "I'm so *enormously*—sorry."

That face! Immaculate, the expression smoothing out, like the tide sweeping the sands. Hephzibah said nothing.

Winnie remembered the day Hephzibah had left. Upped and vanished in the night, they said. Yet another runaway. It had infuriated everybody, Winnie included, who'd been left with the task of clearing out Hephzibah's rubbish and sad, much-mended uniforms.

Dinah King had laughed. "You know how she is," she'd said. "She's got *dreams*. She wants to be on*stage*."

They hadn't asked any questions.

Hephzibah crumpled the program in her hands, tossed it aside. Grabbed her glass of sherry, spilling a little over the brim. "If you weren't so bloody pious," she said, "and *po-faced*, then I shouldn't get so annoyed with you. Honestly, it's too bad. Every time you come plodding down to see me you just make me feel beastly. It brings everything up again. You do understand that, don't you?"

Winnie nodded. "I don't mean to."

Hephzibah handed Winnie her own glass. "Here. Put some color in your cheeks. I can't sit here and watch you sweating all night."

Winnie grasped it. "Thanks."

"So, *tell* me."

Winnie took a swig. "There's something delicate we want you to do," she said, feeling the burn in her throat.

"We?"

"Me and Dinah King."

Hephzibah's eyes widened. Winnie raised a palm. "She doesn't know, Hephzibah. On my honor, she doesn't know a thing."

Hephzibah leaned back in her chair.

"Lucky her. Go on, then."

6

Twenty-three days to go

lice Parker was running late. She tied her apron, two hasty knots. Tucked her crucifix under her collar and gave herself a quick look in the glass. One month in Park Lane and she'd grown accustomed to wearing a uniform. She'd feared she would hate it, feel pinched at the neck and the wrists. But she slipped into it so easily. This was how a soldier must feel, putting on fatigues. It made her pleasingly anonymous. She didn't look like herself—she simply looked like a maid.

She adjusted her black armband. Mrs. King had handed it to her on her first day in the house.

"We're in mourning for the old master," she'd said evenly.

They didn't seem mournful. Mr. de Vries was hardly cold in his grave. Yet the new mistress was making plans for a costumed ball, the best of the season, and was in urgent need of a sewing maid. Something about this awed Alice. It seemed like a very wicked thing to do, and that made the job rather more exciting. Was that strange? Her sister thought so. She said as much when she offered Alice the job.

"Don't be a queer fish about things, all right? I need someone sensible to keep their eyes on the mistress. Someone invisible. Got that?" said Mrs. King.

Half sister was the correct moniker. Suitable, really, since they were only really half-alike. Fourteen years between them, and the only thing they ever shared was their mother. "All right, Dinah," said Alice.

"It's Mrs. King to you," said Mrs. King. "No preferential treatment, understand?"

Alice made herself meek. "Of course not."

Mrs. King looked doubtful. "You understand what I'm asking? You do get how a big job works?"

"Perfectly," Alice said. "And I fancy a change."

Mrs. King raised an eyebrow. "Are you in trouble?"

Trouble, trouble. Alice hated the word. It circled her, snared her, followed her all the time. "Trouble?" she said. "How would *I* get myself into trouble?"

Her sister studied her without blinking, a force stronger even than Alice's own.

"Very well. Report to the house on Monday morning. I'll smooth the way for you. Breathe a word to anyone that you know me and I'll skin you alive." Mrs. King put out her hand. It was sheathed in a calfskin glove, ivory colored. It was lovely. "Do we have a deal?"

Mother had small hands, too. It had been Alice's job to button Mother's gloves, keep her tidy, properly put together. Mrs. King had abandoned those chores long ago.

Alice congratulated herself for not giving anything away. For of course she *was* in trouble, about as deep as you could get. Sometimes it made the bile rise right up in her throat. All she'd wanted was to make a decent living. Shop girls looked so crisp and composed. She'd yearned to be one. Father had trained her behind the haberdasher's bench, and she knew she was skilled with a needle, but she wasn't about to be sweated out for nothing. She could sketch a garment faster than most girls could brush their hair. Even her plain work was tighter, more delicate, more perfect than any pattern. She swiped all the illustrated papers she could find, inhaled the advertisements. Alice studied the popular fashions as if under a microscope, watching the lines shifting each season: lengthening, narrowing, tilting forward at the bust, sweeping around the hips. Secretly, she longed to design her own. But she needed to be apprenticed. And that required cash.

It wasn't hard to get a loan. She had her wits about her—she knew all about sharks. There were women in the neighborhood who'd pawned everything they owned and still couldn't pay off their debts. Alice scorned them. She went to a woman called Miss Spring, who kept a very plain and respectable house on Bell Lane. Miss Spring had a soft voice, and gentle manners, and kept immaculate oilcloths. She listened to Alice's request, took scrupulous notes, and offered an advance against future wages—calculated at seven-and-six a week, no need for sureties, all agreed on note of hand alone.

Alice spent six months as a machinist before she made it to the workroom bench, and she only made three shillings a week. Even the experienced girls were only making five-and-six. Alice watched her debt rising slowly, like a tide, pooling around her ankles. She visited Miss Spring's house and found it boarded up. But the men who took the repayments still turned up every fortnight, teeth gleaming. She met them on the lane at the end of the road, where Father couldn't see them.

"Next week," she said. "I'll catch up next week."

"Of course, miss," they said, all courtesy. "You take your time."

It would have been better if they'd got out a lead pipe to beat her, if they'd sent her screaming down the lane. Then she could have gone running for help without feeling any shame. As it was, she had the upside-down feeling of being sucked deeper and deeper into something she couldn't control, something that presaged disaster—for there was only one way things could go with a bad debt. She told no one.

The collectors gave off a strange smell: powdered chalk mixed with gardenias. The scent stayed in her nostrils late at night. She wasn't sleeping well. Saying her prayers didn't soothe her in the least.

Protection was what she needed. And Park Lane was perfect. She couldn't have hoped for somewhere bigger or more fortified if she tried. She left the department store without even giving notice. She gave the wrong forwarding address to Father. Best to unstitch herself from the neighborhood altogether until she could get her cash in hand.

"What's the fee?" she'd asked Mrs. King.

Mrs. King told her, and Alice felt her chest expand in disbelief. That was all she needed—it was unimaginably *more* than she needed. As sewing maid, all she needed to do was keep her hands clean and her mending box tidy and watch Miss de Vries. She was even given a room of her own, a tiny box in the breathless heights of the house. That first night, she went down on her knees and recited her catechism three times under her breath. She felt like a thief claiming sanctuary in a church. Ironic, really.

It wasn't hard to avoid her sister in public. There was one vast table running down the middle of the servants' hall, and Alice was always seated at the bottom end, above the lamp-and-errand boy and the scullery maids and the endless parade of kitchen maids. The air smelled permanently of boiled meat and stewing fruit, and the pipes clattered without ceasing. Above Alice sat all the housemaids, and then all the *house-parlor*maids, and then the men: under-footmen, footmen, Mr. Doggett, the chauffeur, and Mr. de Vries's valet. That wasn't even counting the electricians, and the gardeners, the family physician, a nurse, three carpenters, half a dozen groomsmen to muck out Mr. de Vries's stable of horses, the mechanics, or the French chef who came downstairs twice weekly and fought unceasingly with Cook. It was an army big enough to run a country house, let alone an address on Park Lane. The butler, Mr. Shepherd, sat at the head of the table, lord of all, with Mrs. King on his right hand.

They reconvened in secret, in snatched moments. Brisk conversation, no time for affection. It made Alice feel rather lonely.

"Here," Mrs. King said, tipping out the contents of a box. "Labels."

Alice picked them up, doubtful. Microscopic letters had been printed all over them. "Labels for what?"

"Instructions. I want them ironed into these skirts." She dumped a dozen crisp, machine-made petticoats on the bench. "We'll have new girls coming soon. And I won't be drilling them myself. They'll need the plan printed out."

Alice stared at her in wonder. "And where will *you* be?"

Mrs. King was aloof. "Never mind about that. Get ironing."

She didn't say goodbye. She didn't even give a warning that she was going. The news broke that morning as the maids were trickling down the back stairs. Mrs. King had been spotted in the gentlemen's quarters. Mr. Shepherd was having it out with her in the servants' hall. William, the head footman, was being detained in Mr. Shepherd's office for questioning.

William? thought Alice. She supposed Dinah might have held a candle for him. He was handsome, certainly—he had glorious golden eyes. He could keep up a decent conversation. She'd told him about the street on which she'd grown up, the hateful behavior of the neighbors, and he'd listened very hard while she was talking, as if what she was saying was peculiarly interesting.

Cook feasted on the scandal. "Fornicators!" she said. "That's what they were!"

Alice spotted William sitting in Mr. Shepherd's armchair, the under-footmen guarding the door, face flushed, eyes defiant. He looked puzzled, wrong-footed entirely. *It's beginning*, Alice thought, skin tingling. The petticoats were stashed in her wardrobe, the labels ironed beautifully into the hems.

Things in the household began to fall apart the moment Mrs. King left. The breakfast service ran late, the fresh flowers were abandoned in the front hall, one of the still-room shelves collapsed, the electrolier in the front hall started spitting and blinking, and someone saw a pair of rats entering the cellar. One of the house-parlormaids ran downstairs, out of breath, red in the face. "Didn't you hear the bell? Madam's asking for the sewing maid. *At once.*"

Alice glanced up.

"Me?" she said.

Alice took the electric lift. It was in an iron cage, and the other servants always struggled to close the gate, but she never did. Some people just couldn't work their way around machines. Alice punched a glass button and the cage jerked violently. She felt its teeth clenching, locking, and then it rose slowly through the house. It hummed as it went, an uneasy sound. The hall expanded and then disappeared beneath her. The air changed, grew sweeter, and Alice glided upward to a different realm altogether, one blanketed in a cream-and-gold hush.

The bedroom floor.

Alice had never felt carpets like this before entering Park Lane. They were so rich, so new. They seemed to suck at her feet. The doors were mirrored and looked as if they'd been glazed with syrup. She adored the bedroom floor. It made her teeth tingle, as if her mouth were filled with sugar. It was heavenly, the home of angels.

She waited at the end of the passage, smoothing her apron, listening to the clocks. Straightened her cap. The household machinery tensed, every clock hand poised, straining, ready.

"Wait for Madam in the passage," the house-parlormaid had warned her. "*Don't* go and knock. She hates that."

Until now, Miss de Vries had been an entirely remote figure. Nearby, certainly: really only a few feet away if Madam was in the bedroom and Alice was in the dressing room. But she was attended by other servants. Alice observed her, studied her daily movements. She didn't *talk* to her at all. The Bond Street seamstresses managed all the fittings for Madam's ball dress. Alice despised it.

It was black, per instruction, suitable for mourning. But the sleeves were fussy, heavy, and the lace looked almost antique in its design. The seamstresses worked section by section, sending parts up to Park Lane for Alice to finish. Hackwork, really, the kind of thing she could do with her eyes closed. Yet she found herself unpicking their stitches, remaking the lines, softening the gown's edges. Trying to make it elegant. Sometimes, when she was hanging about for the latest delivery, Alice would make sketches of the gown that *she'd* design for Madam. Something with a little pep to it, something with a little *go*. Something to make people stare.

Thunk.

The clocks marked the hour, and soft chimes issued through the house.

At the end of the passage there was a fan window, admitting a bright shaft of sunshine. And in it, threaded into the haze itself, she spied a figure on the approach.

A wisp of a person, a moth-wing flutter of black lace, fair hair. But there was a force around her, pressure in the air.

"Madam," called Alice, raising her hand.

The figure paused. The light shifted, dissolved, and Miss de Vries turned and looked her way.

The first time Alice saw Madam, she'd been startled. She hadn't expected Miss de Vries to be so tiny. To be such a small, delicate person. She was—what? Two years older than herself, at most? Twenty-three, and only *just* that.

Just a girl, really.

Miss de Vries was wearing mourning, black-dyed and ruffled lawn, and the lace came all the way up to her chin. Her flaxen hair was teased and curled so that just one lock fell on her forehead. She had curious features. A thin nose, and slightly protuberant eyes. Like a fairy, or a goblin. She waited for Alice to approach.

And it was the *way* she waited—patiently, perfectly, preternaturally still—that gave Alice pause. As she stepped closer, Alice felt it. Electricity crackling around those delicate hands, wrists. Miss de Vries's bones seemed miniature, like a bird's, but there was something dense, ferocious, about the way she was constructed.

"Alice, isn't it?" Miss de Vries said. Her voice was low, carefully modulated, controlled.

Alice nodded.

"Good. Come to the dressing room. I've something to ask you."

The bedroom doors were on runners, and they slid back noiselessly.

The light changed when you entered the bedroom. It was an enormous gilded box, cold and lofty and strange. There were pale pink flowers printed on the walls, and the windows were thickly sheathed in muslin, but you could still see the gray-green shadow of Hyde Park across the road. There was a bureau where Miss de Vries kept her letters and her personal papers and— Alice had squinted through the crack in the dressing-room door to make sure of this—her own personal funds. Banknotes and postal orders and petty cash tied up in silk bags.

The bed was very grand indeed. Someone had stitched words into the canopy: "If you do not rise early, you can make progress in nothing." Alice had always assumed young ladies stayed in bed till noon. But Miss de Vries got up at dawn, before her servants were even awake. "What does she *do* with her time, rising so early?" Alice had asked Mrs. King.

Mrs. King had considered this, deciding whether it was a relevant question or not. "She reads," she'd said, at last, voice stiff.

"Oh? What does she read?"

Alice had detected a tiny note of doubt in her sister's voice. "Improving texts."

"What sort of topics?"

Mrs. King had frowned. "War. Philosophy. The art of diplomacy. Chronicles of great kings."

Alice had laughed. "Not really?"

Mrs. King had been quite serious. "What else?"

Miss de Vries opened the door to the dressing room. It was a miniature copy of the bedroom, mirrored and gilded and festooned in silk. But it was much darker, and without windows. It contained only wardrobes and painted screens. Alice was here all the time, carrying bolts of fabric back and forth from the closets.

"Tell me," said Miss de Vries, and her voice lightened, as if she could talk frankly now that they were alone. She marched to the wardrobe, threw open the doors, rummaged quickly for something—and drew out a stack of papers. "Are these yours?"

Alice flushed. Madam was holding the sketches, the ones Alice had made. She raised an eyebrow when Alice didn't reply. "Well?"

Alice reached for them. "Beg pardon, Madam," she said. "I shouldn't have left those there."

Miss de Vries smiled, a cold line. She lifted the sketches into the air, out of reach. "They're good," she said shortly, spreading them out on the dressing-room table, expression unreadable. "You're a remarkable draftsman," she said. "Or draftswoman, I suppose."

Alice shook her head. "I wouldn't say that, Madam."

Miss de Vries's eyes narrowed. "Nonsense. I can't abide false modesty." She pressed a finger to one of the pages. "This one. What would it take to make it?"

Alice felt a prickle of unease. "*Make* it?"

"Yes." Miss de Vries tapped it with her nail. Alice went to the table, examined her own design. A gown with a waist strapped and laced, a fanciful and cloud-like train, shoulders that were mere skeins of thread, slipping off the skin. Something that would ripple when it moved. Something entirely unsuitable for a lady in mourning. Alice reached for the paper, to hide it. "I really shouldn't have, Madam."

Miss de Vries placed her fist on the table, holding the page in place. "Shouldn't have what? Imagined something *nice* for me to wear?"

Alice shook her head. "They're just scribbles, Madam. Silly drawings."

"My dress is ghastly. It won't do at all—I see that now." Miss de Vries stepped back. Up close, at this angle, it was perfectly possible for Alice to inspect Madam's skin, the tiny freckles and wisps of hair on the back of her neck. It made her gentler, more human. "I want something like *this*. Could you do it?"

"Me?" said Alice, in disbelief.

"They can help you down at Bond Street, I'm sure," said Miss de Vries. "I suppose it's simply a matter of stitching it all together." She nodded at the sketch. "You've got your pattern, after all."

Alice's mind started ticking, assessing this for problems, for risks. *Simply a matter of stitching it together?* A dress like that would be a mountain of work, bigger than anything she'd undertaken before. She had the urge to go and seek Mrs. King's advice.

"I'm not sure there's time, Madam," she said.

Miss de Vries looked straight at her. "You'll be rewarded handsomely for your efforts, of course."

That settled the matter.

7

Twenty-two days to go

There was a haze on the waterfront, a tissue-paper mist. The Thames smelled of brine and coal smoke. Mrs. Bone's favorite factory sat between the sugar refinery and the India-rubber warehouse, on a road swamped with mud. Men struggled through it, getting swilled like pig food. Mrs. King wondered why they couldn't take the other path. *People should consider all their options*, she thought dryly.

There was a villa attached to the factory, with high walls around the perimeter, and blood-colored glass in the windows. A wraithlike porter bolted the door behind her when she entered. She unpeeled her gloves. Better to meet this lot bare-skinned, knuckles out.

Mrs. Bone was standing in a dim-lit parlor, shutters drawn, drapes drawn, hands on her hips. "This is my inventions room," she said, raising a warning finger. "No memorizing anything. I've got patents. Don't even *try*."

Old-fashioned lamps gave the room a rum-colored glow. There were flecks of paint and varnish everywhere, and rifles holstered to the walls. Guns, in all shapes and sizes. A striking choice in decoration. Mrs. King understood this impulse entirely. Mrs. Bone was just making a point.

The women were punctual: a good start. Hephzibah raced in like an emu, feathered and beaded, wig bobbing, eyes everywhere.

"Good to see you, Hephz," said Mrs. King, going to embrace her.

"Is that a pudding trolley?" Hephzibah exclaimed, snapping her fingers. "Bring it here at once!"

Winnie steered her straight to the couch, giving Mrs. King an agonized expression. *Long day*, she mouthed.

Alice followed close behind, ducking a half curtsey and pecking Mrs. Bone on both cheeks, then kissing her hand.

Mrs. Bone had brought in a pair of housemaids in mismatched aprons. "You said you wanted my best girls. Here they are. Sisters," she said. "Useful. They come as a pair. They're called Jane."

Mrs. King eyed them. These girls weren't sisters. They were too deliberately alike, hair like broom bristles, squashed under their caps. Country girls, carted into town. They weren't called Jane, either. Mrs. Bone always reserved rights of nomenclature.

"Worked in the circus, didn't you, girls?" said Mrs. Bone. "I like my girls to have some *capability*," she said, facing the room. "You learn all about *mechanics* when you work at the fair. And they're entirely schooled—I always make sure of that. We all know our letters in this household."

Mrs. King studied the girls. Eighteen, maybe nineteen, no older. She pictured them at the edge of a field, perched on a gate, scaring villagers. She could guess where they'd have ended up if Mrs. Bone hadn't acquired them. A paid-for flat, somewhere off the Charing Cross Road, taking calls after dark. Girls like these, with no family to speak of, didn't get shop work, or secretarial positions, or positions in decent houses. They got swooped on. Everyone knew that.

"We'll differentiate between them somehow, Mrs. Bone. We can't just call them Jane-one and Jane-two," she said.

"That's what *I* call 'em."

Mrs. King raised an eyebrow. "Girls?"

They glanced at each other, a quick, uninterpretable look. "Makes no odds to us."

"Well, we're all equals here," said Mrs. King. "You can sit down next to Mrs. Bone."

Mrs. Bone's eyes narrowed. "You don't make the rules around here, my girl."

"As a matter of fact, I do," said Mrs. King pleasantly. "And that's the first. *Equals*, Mrs. Bone, one and all."

"You can eat your rules for breakfast. You're the one asking me to pay for this enterprise."

"And I'll be infinitely grateful to you if you make that considered investment, but I've got my own terms of engagement." Mrs. King kept her gaze dead straight. "Second, and to quote Mr. Disraeli, 'Never complain, never explain.'" She scanned each of them. "We will have one object, one single plan. There will be no grumbling, no discord. If you're given an order, you follow it. Additionally, all your other duties and obligations are hereby suspended. Until this job is concluded, you're answerable to the members of this group, no one else." She looked at her sister. "I am God, till July."

Mrs. Bone snorted.

"Third," said Mrs. King. "*Speak before you're spoken to.* You have a voice, so use it. See a risk? Speak up. Make an error? Confess. Say boo to the goose, if you will. Content, Mrs. Bone?"

Mrs. Bone pulled the Janes to sit down beside her on the couch. "I'm not signing up to *anything* until I hear this plan in full."

Winnie leaned in, voice steady. "We'd really better get on," she said. Agreement rippled around the room.

Mrs. King gave them a brisk nod. "Very well. Ladies, lend me your ears."

They'd gathered in a circle. Mrs. King wanted them seated where she could see them. Winnie on her right hand, positioned as aide-de-camp. Mrs. Bone, eyes glittering as she judged whether to invest. Hephzibah, restless and magnificent, concocting her stage directions. The Janes, notebooks on their knees, inspecting the engineering. And Alice, eyes wide, jaw set, the canary already in the coal mine.

Mrs. King beckoned to Winnie. "Bring out the Inventory, will you? Ladies, this is critical. We have a record of nearly every item in the de Vries house on Park Lane. *Nearly* every item. You girls—" she nodded to the Janes "—are going to need to fill in the gaps."

Jane-one raised her pencil into the air. "What for, Madam?"

"Don't call me Madam. Call me Mrs. King."

"What for, Mrs. King?"

"Because we're going to take the items listed and sell them." Mrs. King gave them a smile. "I don't intend to miss a thing."

Jane-two crossed her arms. "How much are you selling?"

"*Everything*, darling," said Hephzibah, reaching for the dessert trolley, swiping a lemon pudding. "Am I right?"

"Quite right."

Mrs. Bone rubbed her chin. "Fantastical."

"Risks later," said Mrs. King. "Maneuvers first. The job will be executed on the twenty-sixth of June. Mark the date in your diaries, ladies. Alice, tell us what's happening that night."

Alice started, but found her voice. "There's going to be a ball."

"A ball?" said Hephzibah, licking her lips.

Mrs. King opened her arms wide. "A costumed ball, ladies. The most magnificent party. The kind you'll tell your grandchildren about. It will be, I can tell you, a right knees-up."

Mrs. Bone pursed her lips. "While their precious master's still warm in his grave?"

"Life goes on, Mrs. Bone. And just *think* of the crowd that the house of de Vries could command. Americans. High rollers. *Royalty*."

Hephzibah smoothed her gown. "Royals are usually very dowdy."

"Mad," said Mrs. Bone at once.

"No, entirely sane," said Mrs. King. "We couldn't ask for more favorable conditions for this enterprise. I myself have been intimately involved in all the preparations. Half the rooms will be closed off for their own protection. A quarter of the goods can be put into safekeeping before the first guests even arrive." She nodded to her sister. "Alice won't be the only new arrival on Park Lane. They've got a big staff but a ball on this scale requires an even bigger one. I've lined up all the appropriate posts: house-parlormaids, daily women, et cetera. Mrs. Bone, if we can count on your resources, we'll be able to get people expediting our affairs on every floor of the building." She looked at Hephzibah. "And with *your* talents, Hephz, we'll be providing half the guests, and *all* of the entertainment. They'll be really rather critical: moving people around is important. Our estimates are that we'll commence the full clearance at midnight."

"Our estimates?" said Mrs. Bone, sending a piercing gaze across the room.

"I've gone over the timings, Mrs. Bone," said Winnie helpfully. "In great detail."

"Nobody knows this house better than Winnie Smith," said Mrs. King smoothly, before Mrs. Bone could speak. She patted the Inventory. "Believe me."

Mrs. Bone folded her arms. "And I s'pose you'd be expecting my fences to get the stuff moving?"

"Every van you've got, Mrs. Bone," agreed Mrs. King. "Every carthorse, come to that."

"Have some donkeys," said Mrs. Bone. "There's a few in this room." She shook her head, tutting. "You don't rob a place when there's a *party* going on. You wait till they've gone away, cleared off to the country, sent the butler down to the seaside for his week off. You don't do it in high season, for God's sake."

Mrs. King often noticed this. Other people simply didn't know how to take bets, how to set wagers. It showed such a disagreeable lack of imagination. She wondered if Mr. de Vries had noticed this shortcoming in Mrs. Bone. He'd built his empire without her help, after all.

She quashed the thought: that was a disloyal line of thinking, never to be expressed out loud.

"We want this job to have a little *fizz*, Mrs. Bone," she said. "A little get up and *go*. Imagine it, ladies: the grandest house in London, licked clean on the biggest night of the season. People won't be able to *sleep* for thinking about it. The papers will be full of it. And wouldn't *you* want something from that house? A little clock, perhaps? Some drapes? A hearth rug for the nursery? Something wicked, something naughty, something *stolen*, just for you? Don't you think you *deserve* it?" She gave Mrs. Bone a hard look. "We can add a fifty percent surcharge to the prices, possibly double, no question about it. And the best items can go straight to auction."

"Auctions?" said Mrs. Bone. "My agents need weeks to set up auctions."

"Then we'll set them up," said Mrs. King, not allowing her smile to waver. "We can get messages out to the big buyers in no time. You can pave the way for us. Let everybody know there's a big seller in town."

"I'm not using my name! I can spread the word, get my men lined up for anything I want, but I need deniability, right up until things kick off. That's *my* rules, for you."

"We'll use a code name, then," said Mrs. King. "Leave it to me."

Jane-one raised her pencil. "How many rooms in the house, please?"

Mrs. King approved of practical questions. "Winnie, bring me the soup tureen."

Winnie nodded and drew out a vast silver bowl from behind the sofa. Mrs. King opened the lid, showed it around the room with a flourish, the light reflecting in their eyes. "Schematics, ladies. Floor plans of the cellar, ground floor, saloon floor, bedroom floor, old nursery and guest chambers, servants' quarters and attics." She saw Hephzibah leaning forward, incredulous. There were delicate etchings on the underside of the tureen lid, carved in minute detail. "If you're lost, make for the dining room. These will set you straight. Winnie has made paper copies, but you'll need to burn those after reading."

"That's clever," said Jane-one, taking her pencil out of her mouth, examining the tureen.

Mrs. King nodded. "And necessary. Now, Winnie, tell us about the doors."

Winnie straightened. "There are four entrances to the property." She looked around, checked they could hear her. "Front door. Tradesmen's door. Mews door. Garden door. These doors are all double or triple locked. The front door is double bolted, too."

"And who's got the key, Mrs. King?" said Jane-two.

"I had it, once," said Mrs. King. "But I surrendered my set the day I left. Now the butler holds them. Mr. Shepherd. Until they recruit a new housekeeper, that is." She glanced at Alice. "We are going to do our level best to impede *that*, of course."

Hephzibah's glass clinked on the table. "Shepherd? I'm not going anywhere near *him*. Repulsive, odious man."

Mrs. King saw Winnie place a hand on Hephzibah's arm, whether to soothe or silence her she couldn't say.

"Does someone need to charm the butler?" said Mrs. Bone. "Get him onside?"

"There's no use recruiting Mr. Shepherd," said Mrs. King. "He was Mr. de Vries's man, utterly loyal."

Mrs. Bone scratched her nose. "But if somebody were to use a little *persuasion*..."

Mrs. King shook her head. "No knuckle-dusting, Mrs. Bone, but thank you for asking. You've brought us nicely to a central point. We will not use violence, nor any incapacitating force, on any person, in that house. We will not break or damage any lock, window, entrance, or door frame of any kind."

"It's a question of insurance, Mrs. Bone," said Winnie when Mrs. Bone scowled. "The house of de Vries holds a large policy against any act of burglary or theft. The terms of the contract are quite clear. A crime, if it has been committed, shall be evidenced by visible marks showing a violent entry to the property. Failing that, it shall be evidenced by a threat of violence of any kind against any person in the household."

Mrs. Bone rolled her eyes.

"You see our conundrum, ladies," said Mrs. King, snapping her fingers. "In either circumstance, the insurers would pay out the full portion of the policy."

Alice twisted in her seat. "So?"

"So what?"

Alice looked alarmed, but she lifted her chin. "We'll get our reward when we sell their property. Don't they deserve to be compensated?"

A clock chimed peaceably in the hall.

"They?" said Mrs. King. "Who are 'they'?"

"Well," said Alice, blinking slightly, "*Miss* de Vries."

Mrs. Bone spluttered before Mrs. King could reply. "Hang your ethics, girl. If we can't knock 'em out, can't screw 'em over, can't lock 'em up, can't break a *bloody window*, then we're not going to get so much as a teaspoon out of the front door."

"Leave Miss de Vries to us, Alice," said Mrs. King. "You watch her—that's all. We'll manage things with her when the time comes." She glanced at Winnie, who gave a silent nod. It didn't pay to reveal everything all at once. Breadcrumbs, that's what they needed.

That was all they'd be able to manage.

Alice looked uneasy, but didn't object.

"So, to the finances," said Mrs. King, knowing this would keep things moving. "Every penny made goes in a ledger. Mrs. Bone, we'll let you inspect the books and distribute the profits. An equal portion of net receipts, as discussed."

"How much in cash?" said Hephzibah.

Mrs. King named the sum.

The Janes eyed each other, expressions ferocious, devouring this.

Mrs. King fixed them all in her sights. "It'll be enough to give you a future. Enough to make your own rum luck, however you please." She opened her hands to them. "It'll be enough to be free."

A shiver passed around the room.

"Now, wait a minute," said Mrs. Bone. "Don't go playing snake charmer on me. I've seen jobs a *fraction* the size of this one go right up in flames."

Mrs. King felt a wriggle of annoyance. "I said we'd cover risks later, Mrs. Bone."

"And I say we cover the risks *now*. Janes?"

Jane-one nodded, went to the cabinet. Drew out a leather-bound folder filled with sheets of paper. "We've done our due diligence, Mrs. King."

Winnie frowned. "Due diligence?"

"Big jobs gone bad," said Mrs. Bone, eyes fierce. "You lot need *educating*." She grabbed the folder from Jane-one's hand. "Look at this. Harry Jackdaw tried a rush job in Vauxhall. Commissioned a hot-air balloon to take the silverware out of the pleasure gardens. The whole place caught fire."

Mrs. King sighed. "We discounted hot-air balloons already, Mrs. Bone."

"We really did, Mrs. Bone," said Winnie eagerly.

Hephzibah gave them a quizzical look. *"Balloons?"*

"Look at this one," Mrs. Bone went on, shoving a typescript in Alice's face. "Old Nanny March hired twenty men to dig a tunnel into Flatley Hall. What happened to them? Buried alive!"

"Did we look at tunneling, Winnie?"

"We did, naturally we did. London clay can be so unpredictable. Not at all suitable, Mrs. Bone—you're quite right."

Alice peered at the typescript. "Who's Old Nanny March?" she asked.

"Who indeed," exclaimed Mrs. Bone, triumphant. "Nanny's rotting in jail, good as dead, finished."

Mrs. King caught Winnie's eye. They'd planned what to do at this juncture. *Go on*, she mouthed.

Winnie stepped into the breach. "Now, ladies," she said. "Certain preparations and contingencies will have to be made. Some elements of the plan carry greater risks than others. I don't doubt we may need to correct course now and again."

Mrs. Bone leaned back in her seat. "You're Icarus, my girl," she said to Mrs. King. "You're flying a good deal too close to the sun."

"Then leave, by all means," replied Mrs. King evenly. "Talk to Mr. Murphy. He'll happily take over your patch."

The women grew still.

Mrs. King looked at Alice. "Or you. Go back to making cheap dresses in a department store for the rest of your days." A flush ran up Alice's neck. "Or you, Hephz. Run on down to the music hall. Let's see all your dreams come true."

Hephzibah set down her glass. It let out a high, clear ring. "Don't be beastly," she said. Then she glanced at the Janes, sitting in the corner. "What do *you* think, you little oddities?"

They had hardly moved. "We can manage risks," said Jane-one.

"I'll keep a log," said Jane-two. "Anything we need to keep an eye on."

"Hold your horses," said Mrs. Bone. "I want to do some preliminaries. I'd need to do a full survey on that house, from the drains to the bloody cock on the roof, if it comes to that. And I want to do it myself."

"*You* want to do it, Mrs. Bone?" Winnie said gently, clearly trying to work out how they could manage this.

"'Course I do! What, d'you think I'm going to sit in here with my feet up, having a little smoke, twiddling my thumbs, while *you lot* eat my dinner—" she pointed at a startled-looking Hephzibah "—take my loans, run riot around town, pricing up trinkets you ain't never even *seen* before, on *my credit*, on *my account*?" She took a breath. "Not on your life. You think I don't know how to do my own due diligence?"

Mrs. King sighed again. Best to *seem* annoyed: it paid to give Mrs. Bone the easy wins. Naturally she'd accounted for this. "We do have an opening ready, if you'd like to take it, Mrs. Bone. As I say, I cued up all the new posts before I left. We can work up some false references for you with no trouble."

"References?"

"Yes. For the post of daily woman. Does that suit you?"

"What, scrubbing floors?" exclaimed Hephzibah in delight. "Emptying piss pots? Oh, heavenly for you, Mrs. Bone!"

Mrs. Bone bristled. "*You* can give me a hand," she said.

"Been there," said Hephzibah. "Done that. Believe me."

"Mrs. Bone," said Mrs. King. "Is that role acceptable?"

Mrs. Bone folded her arms. "*More* than acceptable," she said. Her maids goggled at her. "What?" she added. "You think I'm too proud to scrub a floor?"

Mrs. King smiled. "Splendid. Then I think everything is quite settled."

There was silence. The women—her women—were pondering this.

Mrs. King raised a finger, swept it through the air, encompassing them all. "Ladies," she said. "It's time for us to get what we deserve. But be quite certain—I'll be watching each of you.

Don't even *think* about selling me out. If I hear a canary singing out of tune, I'll wring its neck myself."

"Or I will," said Winnie Smith, voice soft. Then she reddened, as if she'd startled herself.

"Clear?" said Mrs. King.

They all nodded, one by one.

She drew out her slips of paper. She'd inscribed these words herself: "I pledge allegiance to this plan, and to the bonds herein defined—with firm intent, free will, in ridicule of all doubt and fear."

They all signed it, save for Mrs. Bone. "I draw up my own contracts, my girl," she said. "You know that."

Mrs. King looked forward to that negotiation.

8

Eighteen days to go

Mrs. Bone didn't take long to make her arrangements. She started in her bedroom, her secret place, the place she called her hidey-hole. The walls were as thick as those in a strong room. The bed was piled high with cushions and feather pillows and she needed a stepladder to climb into it. The rest of her furniture was temporary. Portable. Easy to off-load. But her bed was her great luxury; it was very important. It simply had to be nice.

The windows were shuttered and bolted. She didn't need to peek outside to know there were men watching the house. Mr. Murphy's boys. There'd very nearly been a skirmish with his men behind the shop. She thanked her lucky stars it hadn't come to anything. Intimidation was one thing. Outright assaults were another. They demanded retaliation. And Mrs. Bone didn't have the resources to retaliate at present.

But soon she would, if this job were worth it, if it passed her test.

She climbed out of her black dress and put on a tea gown.

She had a fine collection of those. This one was the color of
ripe peaches, edged with ermine. She lit a cigarette, gave it a
few good puffs. It was nice to have a smoke in private. Then she
hauled open her closet and started rifling through her dresses.
"No good," she muttered. "Too nice. No, no, no."

She had to push right to the back of the closet. Dragged out
boots and stays. Found a neat, sad blouse, much mended. A long
coarse skirt of indeterminate color.

"Perfect," she said with a wry sigh. "Oh, very nasty."

She'd look just like a daily woman, wearing that. She stubbed
out her cigarette and tried it on.

Next, resources. She summoned a ragged-looking boy, who sat
before her, head in his hands, bawling with rare splendor. He
kicked his heels on the floor. Mrs. Bone counted her fingers.
"And your ma. And your pa. And your Aunt Eilidh. And your
cousin Gerry. And you, too."

The boy's howls grew louder.

"Now don't start. You know what you owe."

"I don't know nothing 'bout that!"

"Well, you'd better run home and ask your pa, then, hadn't
you? Tell him Mrs. Bone got her ledger out."

He lifted his head at the word *ledger*. Mrs. Bone opened the
book and licked a finger, keeping her eye on him. "Let's see.
Where's your name in here?"

The boy switched off his tears. She saw him calculating
whether he could run for it. He realized he couldn't. Sensible lad.

"What do you want?" he said, mutinous.

"I'd *like* repaying—that's what I'd *like*. But I'm willing to
make some alternative arrangements. For now."

"What sort of arrangements?"

"Men," said Mrs. Bone, digging a stare into him. "Your brothers. All six of them. And you. Seven's my lucky number."

"What you need us for?"

Mrs. Bone slapped the desk with the ledger. "That's for me to know, and you to find out."

The boy untangled himself from the chair. He sniffled, rubbing his eyes. "They'll ask me whether you can pay."

"Whether I can *pay*?" She leaned right into his face. "Wasn't you listening? I'll come for your *ma*, and your *pa*, and *you*, too."

He scrambled out of the chair. "I'll tell 'em," he said.

Mrs. Bone nodded, done with him. "Then ta-ta, my love, and off you tumble."

The boy wanted to know *whether* she'd pay. Not *what* she'd pay. Mrs. Bone didn't care for that at all. Her sort of business depended on everybody having *great confidence* in her affairs. She'd done the sums on this job, of course. It made her heart hammer, working out how much Danny's house could make for her. It made her hate him, too.

A few years ago she wouldn't have touched this enterprise. She'd have tested the risk, and put it back in a drawer. But big jobs had their own momentum. They'd keep Mr. Murphy and any other rival families in line. And this *was* big. This was bigger than big.

Her next chore was one she despised. She went to get a second pair of hands to mind the shop. She met her cousin Archie on a bench in the park. He'd curled his mustachio to magnificent points, and Mrs. Bone didn't like that. She didn't care for showy fashions, not outdoors. Archie jumped at the sight of her ratty skirt and blouse.

"What in the world?" he said, not able to help himself.

"Manners," she said, pointing a finger in his face.

He ducked his chin, gave her an oily kiss on the cheek, then the hand. "Is the ledger up to date, ma'am?"

Mrs. Bone didn't lower her finger. "Don't you worry yourself about the ledger. Anything tricky comes up, one of the boys'll know where to find me. I can be back in a jiffy. Believe me."

He scratched his nose. "I was thinking about going on holiday myself."

Mrs. Bone told him his fee.

His eyes popped. "Why didn't you say so? I thought business was slow?"

Mrs. Bone leaned in, gripped him by the arm. He smelled of sugar and oil, pomade and cologne. His skin was polished and creamy. He looked like an egg.

"Business is never slow," she said.

Great confidence: that's what she would *always* project.

He ducked his chin, gave her an oily kiss on the cheek, then

Arriving at Park Lane was quite something. The house was like a hotel, Mrs. Bone thought, wiping a line of sweat from her brow. Doors opening and closing, parcels and goods coming in and out. A place this big needed feeding, laundering, delivering, restocking. *Waste of money.* Of course Danny had an army of servants. Typical of his extravagant tastes. Mrs. Bone tugged her ugly hat down over her ears. *I'm a poor, humble creature*, she told herself sternly. *I'm as low as can be. I'm a rat; I'm a worm.*

She reached out and jabbed the tradesmen's bell. Heard it ring, shrilly, somewhere in the depths of the house.

She looked up. White walls, fancy pillars, windows the size of buses. So big it could squash you. "I'll tear you limb from limb," she told the house, under her breath. She corrected herself. She hadn't made *any* decisions about investing in this job yet. She was here to check the lay of the land—that was all.

It wasn't the first time she'd visited. Back then the house was only half-built. She'd seen the dust cloud all the way across the park, heard the clang and clatter of construction as she approached through the trees. The scaffolding was immense: a monstrous, sprawling mass of beams and joists and planks and cranes. There must have been fifty men employed on the site. Carts lined up around the street. White tarpaulin flapping in the breeze, a tall ship with a hundred sails. It frightened her, somewhere far, far down in her gut. It made her feel nastily tiny.

She'd seen Danny stretched out on a picnic blanket, watching the men at work. Tweed jacket, white boater tied with a yellow ribbon—immaculate silk, that. His butler had crossed the grass with a silver platter, a jug of lemonade, ice bobbing on the surface.

She'd balled her fists. "Danny," she'd called, voice hoarse.

He'd aged. Of course he had: it had been a decade since they'd seen each other. But she still recognized that quick, lethal turn of the head. That was an O'Flynn, through and through. If anyone could spot it, she could. Wealth hadn't made him soft, not at all.

She'd wanted to scare him. At first she reckoned she'd managed it. She noted the *click* in his jaw. But then his mouth revealed a Cheshire Cat grin. She remembered that, too. He loved it: the thrill of winning, of beating her, of having something over on her. It was everything, the stuff of life. He was *pleased* to see her.

"Hullo, Sister Scarecrow," he said, same as always.

Mrs. Bone had *loved* her brother. He was five years older than she was. He took her gambling when she was still a girl—only fourteen, fifteen. Dogs, fights, sometimes the races. She watched him take men out by their kneecaps. Helped him count out the returns. Went shopping with him, helped him choose beautiful things. Danny knew his silks. He had a fine collection of neckerchiefs. Yellow spotted, black fringed, always printed, never plain. He bought quality. So did she.

The diamonds had been his idea. She had to credit him with that. It was the early rush across the world to the mines in Kimberley: you had to be quick as lightning to get in with a shot. He'd brought the scheme to all the neighbors before he came to his little sister.

"You're asking me *last?*" she said. Clever of him, really. It put her in a temper. She had the cash, after all. She was already making good money, her commissions from prizefights and protection.

"You'll make it all back," he said. "And then some."

"Says you."

"Says me, exactly." He gave her a hard look. "And you can't tag around after me forever. You need a husband. You'll need a down payment."

Mrs. Bone wasn't Mrs. Bone, back then. She was just a girl called Ruth O'Flynn, from Devil's Acre, working for an ironmonger called Mr. Bone who kept a shop over in Aldgate. She was good at selling nails. She *looked* like a nail. Hard and pointed and gleaming. Her older brother was the flash one, the one with the wild schemes and reckonings. He was twenty-one and a man of the world: he was going to bend it to his will.

"Don't mess me about, Danny," she said.

He shrugged. "The risk's on you. Take it or leave it."

He called a spade a spade, did Danny. Or at least he did when it pleased him. When it suited the story. But she understood that, too, didn't she? She gave him what he needed in the end. Enough to buy his ticket all the way across the world, to the Cape Colony.

I'm on the make, she told herself, reading his letters, racing through the newspapers, waiting for him to buy his first claim, purchase his first stones, start making returns. It was very wonderful, that heart-stopping, breathless feeling. That certainty that she was sorted, that this was it, this was her made, forever. It lasted until the letters stopped. Till Danny dropped her. Vanished altogether.

At first she couldn't credit it. She went up to town, waited outside the offices of the only mining company she knew, doorstepped a clerk on his way home for dinner. There were a whole host of women on the pavement, waving billets and ticket stubs and blurry photographs, asking for news of husbands and brothers and cousins who'd gone off to the mines.

"It's about my brother," she said. "Daniel O'Flynn."

The clerk was a young man, but he had silvery threads in his hair. He smoothed them now, irritation written all across his face. "Madam. I get inquiries such as these nearly every week. There are as many as fifty *thousand* men out there. You understand? I would have—we have—simply *no way* of knowing all their movements."

She squared up to him, pressed a letter into his hand. "Put out an inquiry. That's all I'm asking."

The clerk clicked his tongue in impatience. "I see I must be frank with you. It is a hard life out there. It's been a long, taxing summer. Even when they take the greatest care in the world, men put their lives in the hands of their Maker every day." He frowned. "Is this an insurance matter?" he asked. "If so, I really must reserve my counsel."

This notion, that Danny could be *dead*, carried no credence with her. She turned her back on that clerk and marched home. There was no circumstance on earth in which Danny would have got himself killed. He was too hard-shell, too wily, for that. He would have negotiated with the boulder before it fell on his head. She pictured him in a shack office somewhere on the other side of the globe, heat raging down on him through a slatted window. Signing contracts, pondering his signature. He never respected his name. He hated being an O'Flynn, being one of a multitude, cousins crawling all over the neighborhood.

"I'd like to live forever, Scarecrow," he used to say, lying awake at night, bouncing a rubber ball off the beams. *"Forever."*

He'd return—she'd always been certain of that. The rest of the family wore black armbands and the priest came and Ma expired with grief, but *she* never went into mourning. "You wait," she said grimly. "Just you wait."

There was no satisfaction in being right. Trust Danny to return with a horde of newspapermen in his slipstream, a milksop merchant's daughter on one arm: renamed, transformed, richer than the devil. Wilhelm de Vries, he called himself. They were ablaze with it, in the old neighborhood. Danny sent a gentleman, a young clerk with silvery hair, from house to house, making arrangements. Everybody needed a little something to keep their mouths closed and their opinions to themselves. Danny—*Wilhelm*—was extravagant in his generosity. He gave a good deal more than was necessary. He could afford to, of course.

That day at the house, she'd trod carefully across the grass, stopping at the edge of the picnic blanket. He didn't get up.

She understood why he was smiling. This must have been everything he'd ever dreamed of. To lie there, basking in the ferocious heat of a London summer afternoon, his mansion springing up behind him. His own sister staring at him, goggle-eyed. He *wanted* her to feast her eyes on him. To see how well he'd done. To marvel. She understood that impulse: she felt it herself. It wasn't easy to make a name for yourself in the lanes and back alleys of Devil's Acre. You had to roar as loud as a lion if you wanted anyone to pay attention to you.

His curls had faded and he looked thinner around the cheeks—sunken, as if his back teeth were rotting. But he'd done something to the surface of his skin, rubbed it with oils or creams, made it shiny and expensive looking. He was wearing a wedding ring. He was always wearing wedding rings, she remembered. Every time he knocked up a girl he used to wear one, for the sake of appearances, to appease the neighbors. He'd yank it off five minutes later, of course.

"We hear you're not dead, then," she said tartly, trying to hide the shake in her voice.

"I'm *not* dead," he said, grin stretching, arms stretching too.

She loathed him for that. "You should be ashamed of yourself," she said.

He raised an eyebrow at that. "Don't be so pious, Scarecrow. You'd have done the same yourself." He paused. "If you could."

In the end he gave Mrs. Bone two checks. The first was a neat repayment of that original loan, plus a very fair rate of interest. Everybody in the old neighborhood heard about it. He made sure that they did. It was signed in his new name, with the most beautiful flourish, that whip-crack *W* slicing right across the paper: "Wilhelm de Vries."

She didn't cash it. She knifed it to the wall instead, to make the point.

The second check was bigger. Nobody heard about that one. It came with no terms, no parameters—without words, even. No need for explanations with a sum that size. It said, *I don't want any trouble.*

That one she lingered over, weighing it in her hands, for many months. Of course she cashed it in the end. It bought her the factory, and the villa attached to it, and her seaside place in Broadstairs, and the storage house for her favorite treasures down in Deal. It bought her evidence of her own importance, her own mark on the world. It made her feel bigger; it made her feel as if she had teeth. It didn't parch one iota of her rage against Danny. It made it worse. She yearned to crack rubies between her teeth, drink liquid gold, draw blood.

All that was twenty-four years ago. And now Danny was gone, really gone, and here she was still on the outside, gazing up at his vast and glistening house.

Nobody had answered the tradesman's door. She banged on it, hard.

"Oi!" she shouted. "Let me in!"

The kitchen impressed her—she couldn't help it. It bustled with life. Stove belching heat, tiles as white as teeth. Mrs. Bone felt stirred up by the glinting surface of everything. She eyed a line of gigantic fire irons. Mr. Bone would have liked those, she thought, with a little pang.

"Very busy, ain't it?" she said to the cook, who was giving her the tour. Clearly, the woman had schooled the new people before, had perfected her system. She described the contents of every cupboard, taking her time about it. Mrs. Bone was itching to get on, get upstairs, take a look at the good stuff. "You'll need to be patient," Mrs. King had warned her. "Don't let them know you're a little racehorse. Don't give yourself away."

"I know how to do my preliminaries, thank you," she'd said brusquely.

"What shall I call you, mum?" Mrs. Bone asked the cook now, trying humble on for size.

"Cook," said the cook. "Now, then. Here's where you empty the cinder pails. I suppose you know how to do that? You'll need to make up the housemaids' boxes, do the tea leaves for the carpets, get the hot-water buckets filled."

Mrs. Bone sniffed. "All right."

Cook eyed her, suspicious. "*You* bring the fresh dust sheets out. My girls don't do that. And *you* do the napkin press, all right? Mr. Shepherd don't like seeing no utensils out and about in the kitchen, and *nor do I*." She glared at Mrs. Bone. "Got that?"

I'm a worm, thought Mrs. Bone. *I'm a slug.* She bowed from the waist. "Oh, yes, mum. That's all most familiar to me."

Cook liked being bowed to. It showed on her face. But it went against the rules. "You don't call me mum, you call me Cook," she said. "Now, are you f'*miliar* with brushes?"

Mrs. Bone had rolled her eyes when Mrs. King lectured her

on this point. Hard brush for mud, soft brush for blacking, and the blacking went in a corked bottle. Always a *corked* bottle.

"Oh, yes," she said. "I know ever such a lot about brushes!"

"And look out—you're in Mr. Shepherd's way."

Mrs. Bone only vaguely recalled the butler. The one who'd brought out a jug of lemonade to the park, carrying his silver tray. He plowed heavily toward them, followed by a train of bootboys, oblivious to her, nodding vaguely. He smelled of camphor and oil, and he was sweating. She saw a flash of light, the bright and perfect glitter of a key, attached to a chain around his waist. *Oh, I could snap it off with my teeth*, she thought.

"We don't like *dawdlers*," Cook said, and grabbed Mrs. Bone by the elbow.

And I could snap you in two pieces and all. Mrs. Bone grinned like an idiot, and matched Cook's pace: slow, slow, slow.

"And here's your room," said Cook, banging the door open. "You'll be sharing with Sue."

Mrs. Bone could see an urchin peering at her from the shadows, wide-eyed and holding on to the washbasin for dear life. She looked pale and scaly, wracked by storms. Mrs. Bone felt her skin crawling. She hated sharing a bed.

"All right, Sue?" said Cook.

"All right," replied the girl, voice husky.

Mrs. Bone disliked the name Sue. It always made her feel edgy, as if there were static in her hair. Her own little girl had been called Susan. She tried to breathe it away.

Cook fiddled with the water jug and the pail, straightening them, then straightening them again. "It's lights-out at eleven, once you've put away the irons. Then we lock up."

Mrs. Bone frowned. "Lock up?"

Cook was serene, halfway out the door. "We'll be locking your bedroom doors at night."

Mrs. Bone banged her bag down on the bed. It managed a sorrowful sort of half bounce. "Nobody's locking me in anywhere," she said before she could help it.

Mrs. Bone could hear bodies moving next door, girls coming in and out of their rooms. The light paused at the tiny window, unwilling to cross the threshold. She looked down at the purple-stained boards and saw grooves in the paintwork, nicks and cuts and spoiled varnish, as if someone had been dragging the furniture across the floor, barring the door.

"We've had a lot of unpleasantness this month," said Cook. "And it's Madam's orders."

Mrs. Bone could feel her heart thumping slowly, steadily. *Madam.* She repeated the name in her head. It made her feel the nearness of her own flesh and blood, the presence of Danny in the walls. She looked at the door and thought, *He's got me in a cage.*

"Well," she said, with a monumental effort, "if them's the rules."

Cook wrinkled her nose. "Good. Now put your things away, and report downstairs. Any questions?"

Mrs. Bone imagined her prize, the vast booty glittering and clinking in the house beneath her. She pictured herself standing on top of Aladdin's cave, filled to the brim with treasures. *That* was all that mattered: not her own memories, her own feelings.

She sucked in her cheeks and practically curtseyed. "Oh, no, Cook," she said. "Everything's lovely."

9

On the other side of town, Mrs. King and Hephzibah were holding rehearsals. Rather, Hephzibah was holding them. Mrs. King was there to keep the doors locked and a keen eye out for blabbers. She was glad of the distraction. Knowing Mrs. Bone was inside Park Lane, poking holes in the plan, making up her mind whether to invest or not, was putting Mrs. King on edge. She didn't like loose threads.

"Thank heavens you're going with Hephzibah," Winnie had said.

"Why?" said Mrs. King. "You'd have a marvelous time. Hephzibah adores showing off for you."

Winnie had frowned. "She doesn't."

Mrs. King didn't have the time or inclination to press this. Winnie and Hephzibah had their squabbles now and then: all par for the course, nothing to fret over.

One of Mrs. Bone's men had obtained the keys for an abandoned church hall, and Hephzibah was already running lines with a motley collection of aged actresses who had once be-

longed on the curlicued playbills and picture postcards of Mrs.
King's youth. They were being herded around the hall by
Hephzibah, who had drenched herself liberally in modern per-
fume and smelled extraordinarily of lemons and spices.

"Over here, we have the countesses," she said, pointing at
one gaggle of women. "Over here, a set of ministers' wives.
A few ghastly old courtesans, just for the fun of it, you know.
Anyone else?"

"I think we'll need a few Americans."

"*New* money, how delicious. You," barked Hephzibah, pointing at a tremulous-looking grandmother with perfectly preserved
curls. "You're from New England now, all right? All right, everyone, *off* you go!"

The actresses all took a gigantic lungful of air, and began bellowing their speeches, talking over one another nineteen to the
dozen: "How do you do… What a glorious evening… Have
you seen my husband…? Didn't you go to Cowes?" The din became unbearable almost at once. It struck Mrs. King then that
she'd never been in charge of so many people before. Even on
Park Lane the final authority lay elsewhere. The proportions of
her scheme shimmered in her mind, huge and daunting, beyond the capability of anyone she knew. *Not beyond my capability,* she reminded herself stoutly. But her expression must have
revealed a sliver of doubt.

"Don't worry," shouted Hephzibah over the din. "I'll get everyone shipshape for you."

She was in a good mood. That was a relief. Hephzibah was
one of the most mercurial humans Mrs. King had ever encountered. Secretly it made her edgy, getting too close to other
people's fears and anxieties. They could be catching. She was
sure that Hephzibah felt the same. It underpinned the smooth
accord between them. She eyed the actresses. "Can we trust
them?" she asked.

"Is the sky blue? They've taken an oath of utter loyalty to our cause. I'd trust them with my *life*."

"I'd rather lock them in with a decent fee, Hephzibah."

"Well, that too, darling. I'll send you the bill."

Mrs. King had to accept this. They needed bodies in that house: roving, corralling, managing the crowds of guests on the night of the ball. "We'd better get on," she said. "We've got at least a dozen appointments to make before lunch."

She had to acknowledge that Hephzibah was rather good at this part. When Mrs. King left Park Lane, she took a copy of the invitation list for the ball, a long list of smart addresses scattered all across Kensington, Belgravia and the best side of Piccadilly. Hephzibah and Mrs. King went to nobble a footman at each one, faces carefully veiled. "When a certain invitation card arrives," Hephzibah murmured, stroking them on the arm, "you're to bring it *straight* to us, all right?"

One of the footmen studied the slip of paper. "We get a hundred invitations a day," he said, eyeing Mrs. King and Hephzibah with suspicion. Hephzibah lowered her voice. "Then *one* little card from the house of de Vries is *hardly* going to be missed, is it?" She gripped him by the forearm. "Cash please, darling."

Mrs. King got out her purse and made the necessary payment. Household by household, they managed to control who would—or wouldn't—attend the ball. Most of the footmen were entirely obliging. Some pushed their luck, of course.

"What am I supposed to do with this?" said one, peering at their bank order. He was a particularly gangly fellow managing a cabinet minister's house on Curzon Street.

"Cash it," said Mrs. King coolly.

"I'd need twice that to start interfering with the minister's post."

Mrs. King considered this. She had two options in these circumstances. Accede, and spoil the financial margins. Not a very agreeable prospect. Or she could shut it down.

"You'd only need to take half as much," she said, "for the

newspapers to come knocking on your door. I don't much like the headline, do you? Minister's Man in Bribery Brouhaha."

"Bribery *bonanza*," added Hephzibah for good measure. "Bribery *hullabaloo!*"

The footman scowled, but he took his fee.

"I *do* love men in long tails," said Hephzibah conspiratorially as they marched arm-in-arm across Berkeley Square. The motor traffic was jammed all the way around the bend in the road, and there were a lot of tradesmen roaring furiously at one another as they tried to fight their way across the junction to Charles Street. This pleased Mrs. King. She hoped the arteries of Mayfair would be entirely clogged on the night of the twenty-sixth. *Her* drivers would be taking the mews lanes and side streets, the slowest and least predictable routes, sneaking out of the city under cover. "Don't you?" said Hephzibah, jabbing her on the arm.

"What? Sorry, I wasn't listening."

"Don't you like footmen in *tails*, darling? With stockings, and bloody great big strapping *garters*. That's what I like on a man. A good bit of calf muscle."

"I prefer long trousers."

Hephzibah wriggled with pleasure at this. "*Do* you? Do tell. Have you a long-trousered beau in mind?"

"A beau?" said Mrs. King, sliding away from this. "I'm not sure I know what one of those would look like. What of you, anyhow? Where did you get your taste for a man in livery? It wasn't from Park Lane. I can't remember you mooning over any of the bootboys or footmen there."

Hephzibah's face stiffened behind her veil. "I hardly remember. And I expect you were too busy smuggling potted meat, or slipping tinned sardines onto the black market, or whatever little jobs kept *you* occupied every night."

So it always went with her women. They grew twitchy if you said something amiss. There were potholes everywhere, threatening to trip you up. It made Mrs. King almost miss dealing with someone straightforward. Someone like Miss de Vries.

The notion startled her. But it was true. Madam had always given swift decisions. She had clear opinions. Planning the ball had been almost—what? Not pleasurable. *Satisfying.*

Mrs. King remembered the precise moment the plan began to take shape in her mind. It was the day after the master's funeral, the mausoleum locked, the garden silent. Miss de Vries received Mrs. King in the winter garden, dressed in her fullest mourning, face pale and shining. There was some sort of electricity sparking off her. It sent an answering shudder through Mrs. King's heart.

Miss de Vries's voice was low, calm. "I'm minded to hold a ball," she said.

Her eyes probed Mrs. King's, searching for a reaction. At first Mrs. King didn't understand. A *ball*?

Then a thought flickered, the shapes and lights shifted. Things that had seemed scattered and disconnected now swam together. A ball was perfect. *Perfect.* Heat, light, crowds, confusion...

"Have you considered a date, Madam?" she asked, keeping her voice as low as Miss de Vries's own.

Of course, Madam needed the ball for quite different reasons to Mrs. King. To shackle herself, trade herself, hitch her wagon to the best-bidding star. Mrs. King congratulated herself on her own approach: free, clean, entirely uncompromised. They wanted the same things and different things, and this gave her a strange feeling of fellowship, a delicately ridged collusion. Heads and tails flipping over and over, spinning on the gaming table...

Footmen in tails, she thought, idly. Yes, she did like them. She did miss them. One in particular.

She very nearly—*nearly*—sighed.

"We need to get back," she said briskly.

10

Mrs. Bone spent her first afternoon on Park Lane rubbing copper pans, keeping her head down, as instructed by Mrs. King. She cleaned that copper with furious energy, and with an eye on the clock, waiting for her first break. She had no intention of waiting around. She needed to disentangle herself from Cook, and the other servants, and make an immediate examination of the house. The lower offices were sufficiently warren-like that she could sneak upstairs without being observed. She entered the front hall first. It felt satisfying to start somewhere forbidden.

There was a cathedral-like hush, light coming down through a glass dome above. Palms and ferns in great vases. A floor made of white marble. Gold on the door panels and crystal in the doorknobs. A lot of very disgusting and expensive things that Mrs. Bone rather liked: paintings of nude ladies, foxes stuffed till their eyes popped, stags screaming silently from their plinths. It wasn't exactly the size of the place that caught her breath. It was the curve to it, the way it flowed upward, all glass and iron and light. It seemed frosted, iced, a lickable, kissable house.

Her envy made her skin grow hot.

The hall was connected to the gardens by a long, colonnaded passage and several glass-fronted doors. She remembered it from the schematics engraved on the soup tureen. *Good*, she thought. *Easy access.* But she wanted to inspect the garden exits properly. Remembering the maps Winnie had drawn up for her, she crept back downstairs. She sidled through the kitchen passage, passed the sculleries, pantries, laundry rooms, larders, still rooms, dry rooms, inched around the edge of the kitchen and into the mews, and scuttled straight for the mews door.

She tested the handle. Not locked. She glanced back at the house. This was a clear run from the gardens. Helpful.

Gently, keeping her eyes peeled for onlookers, she opened the mews door, and backed out into the lane.

"Mrs. Bone."

Mrs. Bone's heart jumped. "Christ alive."

Winnie Smith was hidden in the ivy. "I beg your pardon. Did I startle you?" Winnie peered at her, her cabbage-colored dress covered in detritus from the wall.

"Nobody startles me," said Mrs. Bone, catching her breath. "What d'you want?"

"I come here to collect Alice's daily report. I thought you might wish to share your first remarks."

"Oh, it's *remarks* you want, is it? Heavens, let me just fetch my magnifying glass and look at my notes." Mrs. Bone tutted. "I've only been here five minutes. Give me a whole day at least."

Winnie frowned, and Mrs. Bone sighed, lowering her voice. "Look, the way I see it, I'm going to be cooped up in the kitchens, shoved up the back stairs, or locked in the attics. If I'm going to assess this place, then you need to find me a reason to get into the *good* part of the house."

Winnie hesitated. "I'm sure you'll find a way," she said.

Mrs. Bone gripped Winnie's wrist. "I'm not going to be

boiled like a load of old petticoats in the laundry room. *You* can find the way."

Winnie shook her off. "Very well," she said, voice hardening. She paused to consider it. "They'd allow the daily woman upstairs if there was a cleaning job that the other girls couldn't manage. Rough work, you know."

"I'm not doing anything with blood. And nothing in the privy. Don't even ask."

"Look in the dining room. It always gets the worst of the grime—the motor cars are parked right outside the front windows. Find something filthy, and then tell them you'll clean it."

Mrs. Bone sucked in her cheeks. "Simple as that, is it?"

"It'll work, Mrs. Bone."

"Hmm. Now, you can do something else for me. Have you got the local bobby's name?"

"What do you need that for?" asked Winnie, dubiously.

"Have you got it or not?"

Winnie frowned. "Not his name. But naturally I've kept his beat under observation." She hesitated, then drew out a notebook from her pocket. Flipped the pages. "He comes around at these times, without fail." She tore out the piece of paper for Mrs. Bone.

"Hmm," Mrs. Bone said, approving. "You're on top of the detail, I'll grant you that."

Winnie looked pleased, but made her expression grave. "You really oughtn't to see a policeman by yourself, Mrs. Bone. Something might go seriously awry. Alice can keep an eye on the mews yard, if you like. The second you go and see him, she'll hurry down and give you some support. Will that suit?"

"Support? I don't need support from the *sewing* maid." Then Mrs. Bone pondered it. "Scrap that, she'll be very useful. Tell her to bump into us in the yard." Mrs. Bone waved Winnie away. "Now, clear off before they see you."

She hurried as fast as she could back across the mews yard. She was preoccupied, and so she didn't notice a weaselly little face watching her from the staircase that led to the cellars.

"Whatchoo doing?" it said. "You're not allowed out there."

A boy peeped up at her. An errand boy or kitchen boy, she couldn't remember which.

"Ain't I?" she said. "Well, what*choo* doing?"

"Nothing."

"Well then, I'm doing nothing, too, and you can go on doing nothing before I come down there and box your ears."

He muttered something.

"And I'll knock your teeth out for good measure," she called after him.

Little runt, she thought, but she knew a rogue element when she saw one. She could hear the patter of his footsteps all the way down the stairs and away through the cellars. She stopped and paid attention to them, the beat and the rhythm and the direction as he traveled through the foundations of the house, and committed them to memory. Rats always had hiding places. Best not to forget about them.

Mrs. Bone never slept soundly at the best of times. And in this place she feared she'd be lying awake for hours. Sue was tiny, but she was still a whole breathing creature taking up space in the bed. Mrs. Bone's leg throbbed. The routine here was going to be torture. She was the one doing all the rough work through the dinner service. Cook watched her like a hawk, firing orders every moment.

Mrs. Bone's mind blinked and flickered, and she tried not to pine for her hidey-hole. Where had Danny slept in this house? Growing up, he had a mattress that was laid crossways to hers. She remembered the smell of him at night: stale breath on the air. Rafters, low beams, sackcloth over the windows...

She must have dropped off, for when she opened her eyes the light outside had shifted, darkened—and someone was knocking softly on the door.

Mrs. Bone sat up straight. "Who's that?" she said, her body alerting.

Sue lay beside her in the bed, motionless, pressed so low she seemed to have sunk into the bedsprings.

The air whistled faintly up there in the attics. If there had been more light, Mrs. Bone would have got up out of bed and gone to the door, poked her eye to the keyhole, hissed, *Go away.*

But she didn't. For reasons she couldn't explain, her body told her to stay where she was, to be still. Sue didn't move, didn't snore, didn't seem to be living at all. She must have been holding her breath.

Mrs. Bone studied the darkness. *What's this, then?* she wondered. A girl from the room next door, after a spare blanket? Someone feeling unwell?

Her skin prickled.

The moment lengthened. There was a tiny noise, the softest footstep, or a breath—and then silence.

In the morning she counted the faces around the table, trying to keep hold of the numbers. Five kitchen maids. Sue. Five under-footmen. The chauffeur, Mr. Doggett. The boy with the face like a rodent had vanished, and the house-parlormaids were on active maneuvers upstairs. There were entirely *too many* people here. They couldn't possibly all have enough chores to do. Yet they were in constant motion, coming and going. It made it nigh on impossible to track them.

"Sleep all right, my girl?" she asked Sue.

Sue nodded, eyes down. "Yes, thanks, Mrs. Bone."

"Here," said one of the under-footmen, depositing another pile of pans on the table with a clang. "Look sharp."

My poor hands, she thought gloomily, looking at the polishing rags.

"Hark at you," said Cook.

"Eh?" Mrs. Bone said.

"*Mumbling* to yourself."

Mrs. Bone flushed. Reporting to Cook was going to be a very disagreeable experience. *Choose your words carefully.*

"Now, Cook," she said. "I've been meaning to ask. I saw a lot of dirty picture frames upstairs. Very greasy. Someone ought to take a look at them."

The head footman caught her eye. "And what were you doing upstairs?" he asked.

His name was William. Very handsome. Maybe thirty-five, thirty-six. Dark hair. Long nose. Out of his liveries he could've been a forester, a woodsman. There was something wild in his gaze, something golden and jaguar-like. She'd heard the others whispering about him and Mrs. King over supper the night before. *Good for you, Dinah*, she thought, approving and disapproving all at the same time.

Cook spoke before she could reply. "And what are you telling *me* for? I don't take care of upstairs chores. I take care of the *kitchen*, that's *my* job, and we've *more* than enough work already. *You're* the bleedin' daily woman, for heaven's sake…"

Mrs. Bone raised her hands for peace. "I'll make up some soda."

Cook snapped her fingers to her girls. "Fetch three ounces of eggs, some chloride of potass, and someone give her ladyship here a *mixing* bowl." Her eyes glittered. "Dirty *frames*. I ask you. I'd like to come and look at those myself!"

Mrs. Bone fetched a bucket. "You rest here, Cook," she said. "No need to trouble yourself in the least."

The bucket was full of foaming liquid, and she had to grit her teeth, concentrating, to make sure she didn't spill any and stain the marble. She slid the dining room door open with her foot.

The room loomed large around her, the mirror big as a church window. The dining table irked her. It was octagonal, and very small—*tiny*, really. She felt a nasty snag of recognition. Like brother, like sister. She always positioned her desk far away from the door. Made people walk miles to approach her.

Mrs. Bone set the bucket down gingerly on the carpet. She had a good eye for carpets, and an even better one for chairs. She knew Louis Seize when she saw it. The chair legs created a bowlegged shimmer across the room. The walls rippled with tapestries, Gobelins, and they seemed almost flimsy up close. But they'd fetch a good price; that was for sure.

She began to feel better.

Working quickly, she shuffled around the room, opening drawers. She found plenty of silverware, just the third-rate stuff.

"Lovely, lovely," she murmured to herself, dropping knives and spoons and their accoutrements into the deep pockets of her apron. She was glad to be wearing such a thick, coarse skirt. It muffled the clanking and jangling sound she made when she moved.

"You in there?"

She turned with a start, scurried back to her bucket, whipped a brush from her pocket.

The door slid open.

Cook appeared, arms crossed. Peered at the frames. "These don't look any cleaner than before. You've got some nerve."

Mrs. Bone abased herself. "I ought to have asked your opinion first, Cook."

Cook's eyes narrowed. "Yes, you *ought*," she said. But her chest swelled all the same.

This lot, thought Mrs. Bone, rolling her eyes inwardly. *They're easy pickings*.

She corrected herself. Presume nothing. Disaster lurked in every corner. Fate was waiting to crush her pride. But she liked the odds. She wouldn't have admitted it to Mrs. King. But she liked them a lot.

The next day she went to snare the policeman with her stolen goods. Mrs. Bone *never* took on a job without compromising the constabulary. No use launching a burglary if you didn't have a bobby up your sleeve. The chauffeur, Mr. Doggett, and two of the under-footmen were sitting in the mews yard, playing cards. Mrs. Bone dropped them both a free cigarette in exchange for their silence. "You're like a bloody chimney," the chauffeur said.

"I've got bad nerves," Mrs. Bone replied, and slipped out to the lane.

Oh, there was a lot of waiting around in this place. It was going to make her back ache, standing up for hours and hours, for days on end. She was keeping a list of pros and cons in her head. That went firmly under Con. Mrs. Bone heard the clocks chiming distantly from the house.

At last, the bobby lumbered around the corner of the mews lane, following his beat. He spotted her and frowned. She gave him a wave. "No, you don't know me," she called, scrunching her nose, tipping a curtsey. "I'm new."

"They let you have cigarettes here, do they?" he asked.

Mrs. Bone wagged a finger at him. "Don't tell." Extended her hand. "Want a puff?"

The constable laughed. "Nasty habit on a lady."

Mrs. Bone winked at him. "A lady's got to pass the time. I've been waiting for you."

"Waiting for me?"

"I thought you might want a bit of business."

The constable's face went blank. "I don't know about that."

"About what?"

Mrs. Bone knew that the thing to do in situations like this

was to stay extremely still, be extremely careful, send out all the right signals.

"Oh?" he said, at last.

"Oh, yes," she replied.

A long moment passed. And then she saw a grin tweak the edges of his mouth. "Give me a puff of that, then," he said, beckoning for the cigarette.

Mrs. Bone handed it to him, pinching her fingers so their hands didn't touch.

"Now, have a look at this."

She glanced down the lane, checked they weren't being observed, and planted her legs firmly apart. The constable raised his eyebrow.

"In my apron. Go on, have a look."

He leaned forward, whistled. "You left them *something* to eat with, didn't you?" He cleared his throat, leaned back. "Oh, I see. You've brought me the cheap stuff."

Mrs. Bone cocked her hip. "Don't be difficult. Which bits d'you fancy?"

The constable may have been crooked, but he knew his business. "I'll give you a guinea for the lot."

Mrs. Bone was civil. "I don't deal in guineas. And we'll discuss things piece by piece or we'll not discuss them at all."

He shrugged. "All right. What'll you take for the teaspoons?"

"Two pounds three and six."

He sucked his teeth. "I'll give you thirty bob. And you know that's more than they're worth."

Mrs. Bone closed her apron. "I see. You want knock-offs. I don't trade in those, Constable."

He stepped back. "I didn't know you was in trade at all."

Mrs. Bone clicked her tongue in impatience, rummaged in her apron. "Fancy a saltcellar? Egg cup? How about a muffineer?"

A shadow moved in the distance, and the constable stiffened. "Someone's coming."

Mrs. Bone held up the saltcellar, gave it a little shake. "Now, thirty bob for this I *will* countenance."

The constable put his hand over hers. "Put that away."

"One pound ten and I'll throw in a spoon. What d'you say?"

Yes, there was a figure coming through the mews yard. A woman, making for the gate.

"I said put that *away*," said the constable, trying to block Mrs. Bone from view.

"And the muffineer?"

He glanced at her, looked over his shoulder, shuffled notes and coins in his pocket. "One pound six. But tie your apron up, for Gawd's sake—there's someone coming."

"One pound six? Oh, you're a thief, Constable. You're a regular padfoot." But she lifted the articles from her own apron, taking his money. "You're running rings around a poor widow."

She slipped a silver spoon in his pocket, in full view of the woman approaching them from behind.

The constable lurched. "Morning, miss."

It was Alice, slightly out of breath. She eyed the constable, and then his pockets, and he reddened.

Mrs. Bone whispered to the constable: "I think she saw you. Naughty rascal. We'd best keep this between the two of us."

His eyes flashed with worry.

Alice glanced at him, then back to Mrs. Bone. "We haven't met," she said stiffly to Mrs. Bone. "I'm the sewing maid."

Mrs. Bone looped her arm around Alice's shoulders. "Oh, I've ever such a lot of mending for you, my girl." She sent a brilliant smile over her shoulder. "Good day to you, Constable!"

They sped up the garden. "Got him?" Alice whispered, anxious. "What d'you think?"

This could work, Mrs. Bone thought. She could almost feel

Danny watching her, fury sizzling on the surface of his skin. *Pro*, she decided, marking up her list.

"Don't be nosy," she said, not uncheerfully, and linked her arm through Alice's. She was feeling better and better about this.

———

11

Fifteen days to go
3:00 p.m.

Sundays were the dullest day in this place, thought Alice. In the morning the servants went to church, traipsing down to St. George's in two neat lines like schoolchildren. Madam didn't accompany them. She said her prayers in her private chapel, a turreted and curlicued box suspended over the garden, or else went to the Church of the Immaculate Conception on Mount Street. Alice asked Mr. Shepherd if she might be allowed to do the same.

"Certainly not," he answered, as if she were launching a papist plot. She kept her rosary beads out of sight.

After luncheon, the servants were dismissed for their afternoon off. Alice stayed behind, to catch up on Madam's dress.

A stillness descended upon the house. Sometimes Madam was the only person left in the building, save for the under-footman on rota. She didn't keep a personal maid, Alice noted. She simply rotated through the senior house-parlormaids, getting them to button her into her dresses and carry out menial tasks. It was as if she preferred to keep herself unconstrained, aloof: when she grew bored of one girl, she simply moved on to another. At present she was attended by Iris, who was hotel trained and impressed Alice immensely. She had blueish lips and curls done with hot irons so that they looked like bedsprings. Alice stayed in the dressing room, per her instructions, eyes peeled to the crack in the door. "You're our canary, remember," Mrs. King had said. "If something smells off, start singing." But working on Madam's new costume made it difficult for Alice to keep her eyes peeled. It took every spare moment of the day, and she was already sewing long into the night. It was an assignment beyond anything she'd encountered before.

"I was thinking Cleopatra," Miss de Vries had said. "In mourning colors, naturally. Can you draw something up for me?"

Alice had no idea where to begin. Her sketches had always been her own flights of fancy. "Help," she said when she crept out to the mews lane to make her report to Winnie Smith. "You'll need to get me a pattern."

Winnie looked troubled. "I don't like it," she said, standing amid the ivy, concealed from both the road and the house. "Madam shouldn't be talking to you. We didn't account for that at all."

"I shan't breathe a word," promised Alice, impatient. "But *please*. I haven't the foggiest idea what she'll care for, and I need to show her a dummy version by Sunday."

Winnie rummaged in her bag. "Here," she said reluctantly, drawing out clippings from the *Illustrated News*. "Pictures from the Devonshires' ball. They might help."

"*Thank* you," gasped Alice, and hurtled back inside.

She had mountains of fabric to work with, all ordered from Worth of Paris at quite extraordinary expense. Black crepe de Chine, and delicate ostrich feathers, and black-dyed gauze. She pored over the photographs of Mrs. Paget and Countess de Grey in the *Illustrated News*, and gathered Madam's ropes of jet jewelry into the best headdress she could muster.

I can do it, she thought. I *must*.

Now Miss de Vries came through from the bedroom. She was carrying a paper in her hand, a letter, from the look of it. She screwed it into her sleeve.

"Take my measurements again, will you?" she said.

Alice set down her needle. "Things can't have changed much in a week," she said. And then, remembering her manners, added, "Madam." Mrs. King had been very clear about this. *Keep her on side. You need to be as meek as a mouse.*

"I need everything to fit perfectly." Miss de Vries studied herself in the looking glass, expression sharp. "Dresses get so baggy."

"Of course, Madam," said Alice.

Miss de Vries's eyes changed in the light, Alice noted. Grayish some days, greenish others. Her gaze swept Alice from top to toe, running right through her. In those moments Alice felt uneasy. She didn't exactly care to be scrutinized with such intensity. Alice fetched the measuring tape, crouched beside her. "Stay still, Madam." At length she said, "There. Just as I thought. No change." She rolled the tape away. "Perfect."

Miss de Vries thinned her lips at that. "Very well." She sighed. "Show me how you're getting on."

Alice took a breath and fetched the beginnings of the costume. It was littered with pins and pieces of tissue paper, a fragile, half-formed thing. Alice could feel the ridges and sore parts between her fingers where her hands had been pressed to the needle.

Miss de Vries smirked at her. "You carry it as if it's about to disintegrate."

"It's at a delicate stage, Madam."

"Hmm." Miss de Vries stepped forward, let a tentative finger touch the black-crusted beading on the bodice, the silk. "Who taught you to sew?"

"My father," Alice said. "He's a haberdasher."

"Haberdashers can't make gowns like this."

Alice was pleased, but she tried to hide it with a frown. Pride always came before a fall.

"Have I offended you?" said Miss de Vries.

"No, Madam." Alice hesitated, holding a pin in her hand. Miss de Vries looked at it, the glint of metal, the sharp edge. Alice threaded it carefully into her apron.

"Are you close to your father?"

That was a courteous enough remark. But Miss de Vries had never shown any special interest in Alice's circumstances before. Alice shook her head, treading carefully. "Not in the least." She didn't wish to think about Father, or their grim front parlor, or his prayer books on the mantelpiece. At home the floorboards were coated with cheap red stain and covered with frayed carpets. Up here in Madam's rooms things were soft and luxurious, downy and pure. They were immeasurably nicer.

"How sad."

There: Miss de Vries was looking straight at her. The ironic smile had disappeared. Her gaze was fierce and penetrating, picking Alice right down to the bones. Then she unscrewed the letter tucked into the cuff of her sleeve. "Put everything away. And when you go downstairs, tell Mr. Shepherd to come and see me." She raised the letter. "I have a visitor coming tomorrow. I need to change the menus."

Alice was relieved. Standing near Miss de Vries was dangerous: she was altogether too observant. "Yes, Madam," she said, retreating. And then, to be obliging, "Should I tell him who's expected?"

Miss de Vries was scanning the paper, mouth moving silently with the words. She spoke offhandedly, but there was something in the ferocity of that gaze that held Alice's attention. "Lord Ashley, from Fairhurst. Mr. Lockwood will accompany us."

The names meant nothing to Alice.

"Very good, Madam."

She began to carry the fabric away.

"Oh, Alice?"

Alice turned. Miss de Vries's eyes were on her again. The light had changed, grown yellowish. It made Madam look softer, gentler. "You're doing splendidly," she said.

It was so unexpected, so entirely unlike Madam's usual cool, disinterested tone, that Alice felt wrong-footed. She didn't think anyone had praised her handiwork before. They paid her wages—that was all. Even Mrs. King never said *well done*. Alice didn't mind being buttered up a little. She rather felt she deserved it. "Thank you," she said in reply, and she was startled to hear the catch in her voice, as if Madam's good opinion mattered to her more than she had realized.

12

The same afternoon

Hyde Park. Winnie was studying her wristwatch, concentrating, her notebook open on her knee.

"How's the timing?" asked Mrs. King.

Winnie held up a finger, waited. Then took a breath. "By my calculations we'll get those crates from the dome to the floor in less than a minute."

"Well, crack a smile, then, Winnie. That's good news."

Winnie lifted her head. The sun slanted across her face, drawing out the lines around her eyes. Neither of them had slept properly in days. Their list of tasks seemed to grow longer by the hour. So did their debts. Winnie had just returned from an appointment on Curtain Road, bringing back a bill of sale for three dozen Parenty's smoking machines. She'd looked flushed, pleased with herself.

"Not a bad price," Mrs. King had told her encouragingly.

Of course she could have got them a better deal herself, buying on credit as they were. But there was no need to upset Winnie. Mrs. King had spent the night going through the Inventory with two monocled gentlemen brought in—and paid for—by Mrs. Bone. They smelled extraordinarily of fox fur and cheese, and knew everything about art. The prices they quoted made Mrs. King's heart expand.

She decided she and Winnie deserved a treat.

"I'm buying you an ice," she said to Winnie.

"I don't care for ices."

"I'm paying," Mrs. King said.

"Fine."

Now they sat together near the bandstand. Park Lane glistened between the trees, tantalizingly close. Mrs. King licked her ice cream with relish.

"How's Hephzibah getting on with her stagehands?" she said, rubbing her mouth with her hand.

Winnie rolled her eyes. "You know Hephzibah."

They'd put Hephzibah to work on Mrs. Bone's men: training their accents, fixing their manners, straightening their posture. She would be responsible for directing them through the house, on the night of the ball.

"Is she terrifying everybody?"

"She's terrifying *me*. She thinks she's Sarah Bernhardt."

"Perhaps she's better."

Winnie lowered her voice. "This is a robbery, not opening night at the Coliseum."

"It could be both."

"I'm serious."

"And so am I. Hephzibah's good at her job. And she can get close to the action."

"I'm good at *my* job."

"Sewing, you mean?"

"Yes."

"We've got Alice for that."

"That's not the point."

Mrs. King sighed. "Actually, that's entirely the point. I need you by my side."

Winnie shuffled in her chair. "D'you think I'm lousy at needlework?"

Mrs. King saw her worried little expression, and felt a burst of affection. "Not lousy, no."

The crowds were moving in gentle waves across the park. "It's horribly tiring, all this," said Winnie.

"Have a nap."

"I don't have time to have a nap."

"Then have another ice."

Winnie inspected her ice cream sadly as it dripped relentlessly onto the bench. "When did you become such a brute?"

Mrs. King dug her gently in the ribs. "When did you become such a goose?"

There was a long silence, but for the shushing of the trees overhead.

Winnie wiped her hands. "Dinah," she said. "Is there any more to this?"

Mrs. King licked her fingers. "More to what?"

"All this." She met Mrs. King's gaze. "This job."

"You mean beyond earning a fortune greater than our wildest dreams?"

"Yes."

Mrs. King finished her ice. "Why do you ask?"

"Because I know you. You're a proud woman. But you're not *that* proud."

"What's that supposed to mean?"

"You lost your job. Bad luck, poor you. But you're not struggling. You've got your wits about you. You'll be fine." Winnie looked contemplative. "One doesn't tear a house down every time she grows tired of gainful employment."

Mrs. King laughed. "Oh, *doesn't* one?"

"No," said Winnie stubbornly. "So I'm asking: is there something more going on?"

Sometimes, in the dark of the night, Mrs. King thought about the one thing that frightened her about her plan. Other people. All their strange little fears, their jealousies, their persistent needs. Animals didn't buck authority this way. Birds didn't. They flew in perfect formation, a powerful confederacy.

"Oh," said Mrs. King, "probably."

Winnie's eyes narrowed. "Tell me."

There were times when a titbit, a tiny particle of information, soothed her fine band of women. It was like training dogs, feeding birds. She swiveled position on the bench. "When I first came to Park Lane, Mr. de Vries made me a promise." She stretched her legs. "Two promises, actually."

Something darkened in Winnie's eyes. "Mr. de *Vries*?"

"Yes. First: that people wouldn't ask me where I came from. Second: he'd pay my mother's hospital fees."

"Hospital?"

"Yes. I don't know what you'd call it. A workhouse. An asylum."

"I understand."

"Do you? I'm not sure I do."

"I'm sorry," Winnie said.

Images came into Mrs. King's mind, the old ones. Gray light. Mother's stare, growing stranger. "They promised me I wouldn't have to talk about it. I could put everyone behind me. Mother. Alice, too."

Winnie said slowly, "We've never discussed this, you know. In all our years together, never. I always thought it was a strange thing."

"What was?"

"You. Coming to Park Lane. Right out of the blue. No family, no papers. You didn't even know how to tie your apron properly."

"Well," said Mrs. King, "I had you to teach me, didn't I?"

Winnie tilted her head. "We know what sort of girl arrives in a house without a character."

Mrs. King laughed. "I wasn't in that sort of trouble, Winnie."

"No?"

"No."

"Then *why* did Mr. de Vries hire you?"

Mrs. King had been asked that question before. "Old friend of the family."

Winnie let out a short laugh. "An old friend. I see." She shook her head. "Good *Lord*. When I think about the way we bent over backward for you, made exceptions for you. Changed breakfast time, suppertime, gave you the nice chores, extra candles, extra sugar, more tea. A bed by the window, a room of your own, new caps, free mending..."

"You didn't do so badly by him yourself."

"I *worked*. I worked my fingers to the bone. I've never worked so hard in my life."

Winnie's face glimmered with something hard to read. Mrs. King had to allow that it was true. Winnie had plodded through that house like a shire horse: inexhaustible, determined. She'd gone from kitchen maid to between-maid to housemaid to house-parlormaid. When she made housekeeper, they gave her a round of riotous applause. Even *Cook* had been decent about it. Five years and then—she left. No farewells. It took Mrs. King months to even find her, selling tatty ostrich feathers to a milliner in Spitalfields.

Winnie took a breath. "What was he to you?"

"What do you think?"

"What do I *think*? I think you were on a pedestal the moment you arrived. I think you had protection. I've no notion why. That's what I'm asking."

Mrs. King concentrated on keeping her face smooth. "Heavens, Inspector."

Winnie raised a finger. "Don't do that."

"Do what?"

"Manage me."

Mrs. King felt her patience thinning. She caught it before it snapped. "It's my job," she said coldly, "to manage you. I'm managing everyone. That's what I'm here for."

Winnie was calm. "Dinah. Tell me."

They'd come right up to the brink of something.

"You're barking up the wrong tree," Mrs. King said. "Really."

"What tree? I don't even know what I'm asking."

Mrs. King rose. "We've got work to do. I need to talk to Sanger about the camels."

"No."

Winnie didn't move. If it had been Hephzibah asking, or Mrs. Bone, or Alice, it never would have come out. They were easy to sidestep, divert, deflect. But Winnie simply sat there and waited for the truth. She expected it of Mrs. King. She deserved it.

Mrs. King felt a queer sensation in her chest, the fear that she couldn't control her face.

"He was my father," she said.

Winnie wondered later if she'd looked like a fool. She wondered if she'd paled, gasped, done any of the stupid things. A child came tearing past, balloon in hand, shrieking with laughter. Mrs. King put her hand to her cheek.

At last, Winnie spoke. "Your father?" Confirmation seemed necessary; it seemed absolutely vital.

Mrs. King dragged her gaze up to meet Winnie's. "I didn't know at first. They never told me."

"Then how on earth…?"

She spoke in a strange, flat voice. "I worked it out."

Winnie said, tentatively, "You mean, he never *told* you? You just…wondered…"

"No, he told me." Mrs. King folded her hands. "In the end."

Winnie suddenly wished very badly that they were not sitting in public. The day felt too hot and too glaring, and there was a weakness in her chest. It was shock, she supposed.

"Did you know for a very long time?"

Mrs. King nodded.

"And you didn't—*say anything?*"

Mrs. King's voice came out low, quiet. "You *don't* say, when it's something like that."

Winnie's stomach clenched. "Come," she said. "Let's walk."

She linked arms with Mrs. King, pulled her away from the bench. They moved away from the broad paths, away from Park Lane.

"Do the others know?" she asked.

"They won't care about this."

They would care—they would care a great deal. "It might do you some good to tell them. It would help them understand. It must be the most dreadful burden, keeping such a secret."

"*I'm* not the one keeping it a secret. Everyone else has been doing that."

She really believed that, Winnie thought. She was holding on tight to it. "Well. Better to get it out in the open now, then."

Mrs. King's arm went rigid. "Mrs. Bone knows," she said. "She's known from the start. She's as much connected to him as I am. She's his sister."

Winnie halted. This time the shock felt like pain, not like weakness. She drew her arm away. Mrs. King at least had the grace to look uneasy. "It was best you didn't know," she said.

Winnie felt as if she'd like to scream. "For heaven's *sake,* Dinah." She put a hand to her head, feeling an ache starting there. "You should have told me. You should have told me *years* ago."

Mrs. King just shook her head.

Winnie sighed. "This discussion has unsettled us both. Let's go back."

And so they did, not speaking. Winnie gave full but silent vent to her feelings. It was unpardonable that Dinah should have kept so great a secret from her. But that question nagged at her. *Didn't you guess?*

She pictured Mrs. King, that playful, sideways tilt to her expression. It was so entirely like the old master that it made Winnie's legs feel weak.

She understood quite clearly what must have happened. Mr. de Vries had got himself a bastard. Most gentlemen would have sent the mother a stipend, or at any rate a warning letter, or simply run away. He had gone one better. He had hired the child on as his housemaid. It astonished her, the audacity of it. It was the kind of breathtaking self-assurance that made her burn with envy.

Here, then, were the secret things of which she could never speak. Mr. de Vries was brutal, he steamrollered people, he was unendingly brash, twisted up in his crimson silks and canary-yellow buttons. But he was gentle with Winnie. He treated her with courtesy. "My dear Winnie Smith," he used to say, grinning at her. "The cleverest person in this house." For clever she was, clever she dubbed herself, so well educated and reliable and nicely spoken. She spent hours in Mr. de Vries's company, taking dictation, acting amanuensis. He gave her little gifts, an allowance, he even had her mother over for tea when Father died. His charm was extraordinary. And she thought she'd deserved it. She devoted her soul to that house. She'd admired Mr. de Vries tremendously: of course he was vulgar, but at least he was honest about it.

Her shame hardened in her gut.

She linked arms with Mrs. King. "I'm sorry I never guessed," she said.

Mrs. King turned, face drawn. She looked almost scared of

what Winnie might say to her. It twisted Winnie's heart, made tears prick in her eyes.

"I didn't *want* you to guess," Mrs. King said. "I wouldn't have *let* you." She squeezed Winnie's arm. "Don't mention it to the others," she added.

Winnie let out a breath. "We oughtn't to be keeping secrets, Dinah."

The anxiety left Mrs. King's expression. It was replaced with something harder, grimmer. "That's an order, Win," she said.

13

Later

Mrs. King met Mrs. Bone on neutral ground, in Kensington Gardens. They met by appointment, as arranged. It was time to receive Mrs. Bone's assessment of the risks—and her funding.

It reminded Mrs. King of the old days, of being schooled in her trades, learning how to pick a pocket. Mrs. Bone used to truss herself in her vulcanite and black bog oak beads and sit on a bench in Regent's Park, going over and over the process: *Gently, girl, like your fingers are made of air...* She always said she had great expectations of Dinah. She said she knew a sharp eye and a good temper and a strong character when she saw one. They shared good, quick-moving O'Flynn blood, after all.

"Don't get up," Mrs. Bone said, and pressed both hands to her thighs. "Gawd's sake, I'm puffed."

The nursemaids were out in force, pushing modern perambulators with wheels that wouldn't go amiss on an omnibus. The scene looked tranquil, but it wasn't. Mrs. King had seated herself on a bench facing the palace and the sheep, and counted the men. One on the Broad Path, unmoving. Three under the parasols by the tea tent. Two more on the water, gliding past in a boat, very upright. She knew what that meant. They had pistols strapped to their ribs.

Mrs. Bone had brought reinforcements for this discussion. Mrs. King was inclined to take this as a good sign. She knew her aunt. This meant she was in a negotiating mood. She was ready to buy in.

Mrs. King rebuttoned her gloves. Smoothed her skirts. "Good afternoon, Mrs. Bone," she said pleasantly.

"Yes, yes, how d'ye do, splendid to see you. I've only got chilblains and blisters and bleedin' *corns* popping up all over my feet, tramping around that great blooming place for you." Mrs. Bone sat down with a thump, the vibration passing through the bench, and stretched her legs. She'd picked up the aroma of the back offices already. Stewed gammon and carbolic. It gave Mrs. King a strangely homesick feeling. She brushed that away at once: that sort of sensation was extremely dangerous, not required, not to be repeated.

"Well?" she said, awaiting Mrs. Bone's decision.

Mrs. Bone breathed out. Closed her eyes. "I don't like the odds."

Mrs. King nodded her head at that. She'd expected that response. "I appreciate your candor."

"Well, *candidly*, duck, the plan's a load of balderdash."

"Balderdash?"

"Hogwash. A load of old bull. I've looked around. I've sneaked into every nook and cranny I could find. You've got umpteen floors to sweep, a garden lying crossways to the house, a backyard in full view of the lane, and motor traffic the likes of which you wouldn't see at the gates of *hell*, not even when they're sending the pimps and whores and *fornicators* down for their just desserts…" She paused to take a lungful of air. "I mean for heaven's *sake*, girl. You can't give me one reason the whole thing won't fall apart in five seconds."

"Certainly I can."

"Go on, then."

Mrs. King gazed out at the water. Watched Mrs. Bone's men paddling slowly by. "Because I'm running it."

Mrs. Bone smiled sadly. "You've a good fire in your belly, dear. I'll grant you that. But that's all. You do my small jobs. Side stuff. You always have. Cheap soap and silk handkerchiefs." She raised a finger. "Don't get me wrong. I'm much obliged. You keep things ticking along nicely. All my men think you're nice and prompt. But this is too big, even for you."

First move. Clear as day.

Mrs. King thought about it. This job *was* big. It was huge, glittering, the sort of thing nobody in the world expected someone like her could pull off. It was exactly the reason she adored it. "Fair enough," she said. "I can't fault that. Thanks for giving it your consideration, Mrs. Bone." She stood up. "Shall I walk you to the station?"

"Walk?" said Mrs. Bone. "Walk one more step and I'll keel over. I'll be lamed. I'll be turned into glue."

But she got up all the same, not hesitating, and linked arms with Mrs. King, her bony fingers digging into Mrs. King's coat. This was a signal, too.

Mrs. King knew where to go for the next stage in the negotiation. There was a cigarette shop on Queensway, humble as anything, that would be waiting for them. Mrs. Bone swore she didn't operate east of Cheapside. But even she kept a little outpost or two up in town. Mrs. King knew this. She had studied every inch of Mrs. Bone's estate over the years.

"Mind if I pop in for some fags?" she asked when they reached the Bayswater Road.

Mrs. Bone chuckled under her breath. "Good girl. I guessed you knew about my little shop."

"You know me," said Mrs. King, giving her arm a squeeze. "Always got my eye on the side jobs, the small stuff."

The bell clanged furiously as they entered the shop. Mrs. Bone was serene, flicking dirt off her filthy overcoat. The man behind the gargantuan cash register opened his mouth. Closed it again. Jars of sweets lined the counter, a radiant, marbled profusion of striped and glistening treats. Mrs. King lifted one of the lids. "Fancy a gobstopper?"

"Humbugs for you, dear," said Mrs. Bone with a thin smile.

Mrs. King shoveled a stack of lemon sherbets into a paper bag. "Be an angel," she said to the shopkeeper, "and give us a moment, would you?"

She could see shadows forming on the wall. Men in the street, men in the next room. A creak overhead. Mrs. Bone's men were already upstairs. That meant Mrs. Bone had planned all her moves.

Another good sign.

The shopkeeper looked at Mrs. Bone, paled, nodded, and backed out in a hurry.

Mrs. King popped a sherbet on her tongue. Sucked. Felt the juices zinging on the roof of her mouth. "Tell me," she mumbled. "If I could change one thing, what would it be?" Best not to circle around things with Mrs. Bone. If there was an objection lurking somewhere, Mrs. King wanted it out in the open.

Mrs. Bone put her hands behind her back, expression angelic. "Good Lord," she said. "It's not for *me* to say."

"The date?"

"Any day's a bad day for a bad job."

"The time?"

"No."

Mrs. King transferred the sherbet to the other side of her mouth. "The crew?"

Mrs. Bone shook her head. "No, they're all right. Not an inch on my Janes, mind you."

"I can't change your fee."

"Can't you?"

Another figure appeared on the pavement.

Mrs. King offered the bag. "Sherbet?"

Mrs. Bone batted her hand away. "You've got dirty fingers." She rummaged into a jar of pear drops, drew out a fistful, shoved two in her mouth. "Go on."

"*You* go on."

Mrs. Bone stared at her, eyes bright, sucking hard. "I want an advance."

"You've got an advance."

"No, I've got one of Danny's trinkets, which you *stole* from him, at no cost to yourself, bearing no value at all."

This was a bit rich. "It doesn't have symbolic value?" said Mrs. King. "I chose it rather carefully."

"These aren't the Hanging Gardens of Babylon, my girl. We aren't in the pyramids. I ain't painting *symbols* all over the walls. I don't need *gestures*. You're doing this whole job on credit. Good for you, I'd do the same. But then I've got decent lines. You want to spend on my account, on my good name, then I need cash up front, to cover my risks."

"Yes," said Mrs. King, crunching her sherbet. "You do."

Mrs. Bone looked annoyed at that. "Well, then, you understand, don't you?" she said. "I can't be making big investments until trading gets a bit brisker."

Second move, thought Mrs. King.

"Your trade's not about to get any brisker," she said.

Mrs. Bone took another pear drop. "Says who?"

"I've got eyes."

"And?"

"I can read accounts."

There it was: a streak of anger. *Startled you, didn't I?* thought Mrs. King. She felt almost sorry, prodding Mrs. Bone. Her aunt was the only person who'd ever kept an eye out for her when she was small. Gave her clean pinafores, sturdy boots, fresh stockings, when Mother couldn't manage. But this wasn't a time to be softhearted.

"Not your accounts," she added smoothly. "I never pry into a lady's affairs. But I've paid a call on Mr. Murphy. His books are looking *splendid*, Mrs. Bone. Heaving with orders. Whereas all I smell around your place is a pile of old debts."

"Is that so?"

Mrs. King nodded. "Debts and debtors, crawling all over your patch."

Mrs. Bone said nothing. The flesh around her neck was taut, as if she were holding her chin up with great effort, as if it were costing her dearly not to backhand Mrs. King. Then she mastered herself. Smiled, put the other pear drop into her mouth. "Shall I name the sum, dear? Or shall we bully each other till sundown?"

Mrs. King crossed her arms. "You may name the sum."

Mrs. Bone did so.

The light outside was strange. Not stormy, not like the week before. But weak willed, almost slippery: grayish. Mrs. King disliked it. It depressed her.

She sighed. "Payable against what?"

"Two-sevenths of net receipts."

"Two?"

Mrs. Bone nodded.

"I'd have to give up my own share to pay you that, Mrs. Bone."

"Or someone else's." Mrs. Bone shrugged. "They're not my people."

"Alice Parker is my sister."

"Lucky you."

"Winnie Smith is my oldest friend."

"So chuck the other old tart, if you must." Mrs. Bone crunched her own pear drops.

Mrs. King held her gaze. "I'm not chucking any of them, Mrs. Bone. We're all equals in this. I've made that quite clear."

"I'm offering fair terms, my girl. You give me an advance against future earnings, and I put up the rest of the credit you need to get this thing moving. I mean *properly* moving."

"I thought you said the whole plan was a load of nonsense."

Mrs. Bone smiled, beadily. "It may well be, my dear. But that's on you, not on me."

Mrs. King considered this. She *could* pay Mrs. Bone's advance, of course. In cash, too, just as Mrs. Bone would expect. It equaled almost everything she had saved, in a whole lifetime at Park Lane. She didn't have any more than that. No backstop, no surety beyond it, at all. But if this job failed, a loss of savings would be the least of her worries. Mrs. Bone never loaned capital without expectation of full repayment. The cost of a default was an unspeakable punishment, whatever the family connection.

Mrs. King didn't believe in God. Logic followed that she didn't believe in the Devil, either. But she felt the presence of something then: a power greater and darker than her own. Her shadow loomed monstrously on the wall. She felt the presence of Mr. de Vries, his roar of laughter, lost in the air.

"Deal," she said. She'd decide how to make it work later.

Mrs. Bone grimaced. "Not in here. I want it signed and witnessed. Two-sevenths, in black and white."

She rapped loudly on the counter. A door at the back of the shop opened. "Through there," she said, scratching her nose. "My boys will take care of you."

Mrs. King looked through the door to the yard beyond. Those men weren't the same as the ones in the street. They were heavier: older, denser and entirely impassive. They looked as if they were made of granite. They were carrying knives.

The chap nearest the door was smoking a pipe. He stepped to one side, making way for her. She looked through the door and saw a small table. Pen and ink. A contract, crisply minted, ready to sign. The walls in the next room had no windows, no escape routes at all.

Third move.

Mrs. King took one last lemon sherbet for luck. It left powdered sugar all over her hand. She licked it off, eyes on Mrs. Bone. "All right," she said. "I'll finish up here. Back to the house you go."

Mrs. Bone was already adjusting her diabolical hat, racing for the door. "Ta-ta," she said, and the bell clanged on the way out.

Honor thy family, thought Mrs. King wryly, as she went to sign the contract.

14

Two weeks to go

Lord Ashley was coming for tea. Miss de Vries had invited him to dinner, and Lockwood had negotiated with the Ashleys' agents for hours to make them take the bait. But the diktat came down from the mother: it was tea or nothing; they could take it or leave it.

"Lady Ashley is giving our matter her close attention," said Mr. Lockwood. He'd come over first thing in the morning to set the plan.

Miss de Vries sniffed. She'd been up all night, on edge. "A doting mother. How charming."

Lady Ashley. A name that would come to her if this went through. It had something, a certain swing to it. She rather liked it.

Mr. Lockwood itemized the Ashley portfolio. They kept a lofty black-bricked house on the smartest end of Brook Street. Fairhurst, their country seat in Surrey, had been in the family since the seventeenth century—lots of pale stone and gracious lines. Their place in Scotland was built in a violent shade of terra-cotta, decked with flags and ghastly turrets. It was a brutal, hideous house, and it made her heart start ticking with pleasure.

"Tell me their weak spots," she said to Mr. Lockwood.

He spread his hands. "One sees it so often. Old money, locked up in land. They're simply gasping for something liquid."

Miss de Vries nodded. "Tea it is, then," she said.

Lord Ashley drove himself to Park Lane in a Victoriette two-seater, one-handed, elbow resting on the crimson side panel. Papa would have hated that little motor carriage, Miss de Vries thought. He would have coveted it for himself. She stood by the window above the porch and watched his lordship arrive. The carriage rattled up to the pavement just after four. She went to the top of the stairs, placing herself behind one of the marble pillars to observe him arrowing into the house. Young—or at any rate not much older than she was—twenty-four at most. Not tall. In photographs, his face looked delicate, with pointed eyebrows that could have been drawn on with a brush. In the flesh he appeared denser, harder. He had a lantern jaw with a vicious heft to it.

His voice carried up the stairs. "God, the smell," he said, flicking a silk scarf from his neck, holding it out for the foot-man. "It's putrid."

That sort of voice came from the back of the throat, lazy and clipped. Miss de Vries envied this. She had trained her own with enormous care, with exceptional discipline, in order to make it *work* for her. But the more she spoke, the more tired she became. What freedom it must be, to simply talk without caring, with no worry about where your words might land.

"And the drafts," he said, frowning upward. "This place is ghastly."

Miss de Vries grew still. She agreed with him entirely. But she resented him for saying it. By any measure her house was immense, beyond splendid, constructed at unimaginable expense.

"My lord?" Mr. Lockwood had gone downstairs to greet him.

"You must have rats in the house. Can't you tell? It reeks. Something must've crawled into the walls and died."

This remark irked her, too. Naturally they had mice. Even Brook Street had them, surely. They crammed their little bodies into the crevices beneath the floors, and there expired. The smell they left behind was almost familiar now—oozing, stinking, mingled with vinegar and rose water. She hardly noticed anymore. Perhaps she was missing things.

Lord Ashley came up the stairs, taking them two at a time. Miss de Vries had to back quickly into the saloon.

By the time they rolled open the double doors she had gathered herself. "Lord Ashley," she said, modulating her voice down a notch, to freeze him to the spot, to set the tone. "Good afternoon."

He marched straight in, already talking. "...*and* the windows are facing full west—it's absolutely *scorching* in here. I don't know how you can stand it..."

Her voice had no effect on him at all.

Lord Ashley sat with his back to the window. *A boy, really*, thought Miss de Vries, the longer she looked at him. Ugly or handsome, she couldn't decide. He had a mean face, and his hair ended in a curl that seemed to be slicked to his forehead. He stretched his legs out wide, heels scudding the carpet.

Mr. Lockwood managed the conversation, and Miss de Vries had to give him credit: he knew what he was doing. The topics seemed disconnected. Lord Ashley's stables, his judgment of the railways, the expense of motoring, the vulgarity of Americans. But Lockwood knitted them together neatly, making an occasional jotting in his notebook, smiling throughout.

"I agree," said Miss de Vries at intervals. They'd agreed she would say nothing more. Modesty, moral rectitude, dignity—

she radiated these virtues, unrelentingly, unendingly, maintaining perfect posture.

"But you can't care for town in the summer," Lord Ashley said to Lockwood, but his eyes were on Miss de Vries. "You can't possibly intend to keep this house."

There was a silence, a stretched-out moment. That was an opening gambit.

Miss de Vries put down her cup. "I…"

"And you know we don't like the look of the books. You're vastly overextended. Has your man told you my view?"

Miss de Vries saw Mr. Lockwood's face go taut. It was the impertinence of it. That the house of de Vries was considered so vulgar, so lowborn, that it was perfectly reasonable to debase it. That you might eschew good manners, cross your legs and slurp your tea, and simply haggle without any hint of compunction.

"I don't have a head for business," said Miss de Vries, making her voice gentle, "but I know my father left his estate in perfect order." A little white lie, an entirely fair one.

Lockwood said quickly, "We have a most extremely rigorous handle on the household's affairs."

Lord Ashley shook his head. "But you're still in gold! You should get out of that, for a start. And the loans are a joke. They should be axed at once."

Miss de Vries sipped her tea.

"By the way," added Lord Ashley—and something twisted in his tone. "What's all this talk about your old man's funny business?"

Mr. Lockwood went still.

"Talk?" said Miss de Vries. She studied her fingers.

Mr. Lockwood cleared his throat. "People say all sorts of things."

Lord Ashley was watching her. It was the first time he'd looked straight in her direction. "I'm not necessarily objecting," he said with a testy laugh.

Miss de Vries pushed back her chair.

In this house there were all sorts of boxes. Drawers and vessels and canisters and cases beyond counting. They contained all manner of things. Some were left unlocked. Some were soldered with lead, encased in marble, locked up behind bars, buried in the ground. What Lord Ashley was discussing belonged to the category of untouchable, unknowable things. Miss de Vries knew the rules: she hadn't made them; they had never been spoken aloud; they were things you intuited, just like breathing. You didn't hesitate in these circumstances—you didn't speak a word. You simply turned around and got out.

She rose.

"Lord Ashley," she said, "I must bid you good evening."

Later, Mr. Lockwood came up to see her.

"Well?" she asked. She disliked asking Mr. Lockwood his opinion on anything. It made him more self-congratulatory than he already was. But she had no other counselor to whom to turn.

Lockwood scratched his chin. "He's a curious mixture of parts. A fearful snob, of course, but determined to cut his own path in the world. His grasp of economics is dismal, I mean really *dismal*. We'd have to be mindful of any undue interference. But he wasn't rattled by any of the things that have troubled us before."

Miss de Vries said coolly, "What troubled us before?"

Lockwood examined his notes. "Gracious, where to start? Wrangling over the jointure, election of trustees, talk of thirds and dowers. His sort have been negotiating marriage portions since Magna Carta. But Ashley's brisk, and not worried by the detail." Lockwood sniffed. "Perhaps he doesn't understand it."

"Mr. Lockwood," said Miss de Vries, "you forget yourself.

You are speaking to the future Lady Ashley." It paid to keep Lockwood in his place.

Lockwood raised his eyebrows, not daunted. "The *current* Lady Ashley *is* worried by the detail. Her people will spin things out as long as they can afford to. Their pride will see to that, I can assure you. We'll have several rounds of negotiation, assuming we're minded to even accept an offer."

Miss de Vries felt her heart skipping with impatience. "Then go and turn the screws on *them*. You said it yourself: he doesn't care a jot for detail. If the Ashleys are so desperate for cash, then they can stump up and sign for it. Bring them to the ball. Let him see the rest of the world at my door. Someone else will put in an offer if they don't."

Lockwood sighed, his expression signaling his disapproval. "This *ball*."

Miss de Vries regulated her voice. "You take care of your business, Mr. Lockwood. I'll take care of mine."

Afterward she went upstairs and inspected the invitation cards. She'd discarded several designs. This was the best one. She felt the thickness of the paper between her fingers, the delicate ridges, the gilt edging and black scrolls. Gold for grandeur, black for propriety.

"Fine," she said, and the servants began stacking them up, shoving them into envelopes. Hundreds and hundreds of invitations.

She closed her eyes, pictured them vanishing into the postal system, wheeling out across the city at dawn. Hurtling up South Audley Street, along Piccadilly, across Cadogan Place. Skittering, leaping, glittering. Caught on silver platters, handled with cream gloves, sliced open with a sharp blade. A hundred eyes taking in the request—then two hundred, five hundred, a thousand eyes more: *The House of de Vries requests the honor of your company...*

It was time for her to be noticed.

Across town, Mrs. King and Winnie sat stuffing envelopes of their own. Short letters and telegrams, going out to the names supplied by Mrs. Bone. Agents in Paris, Hamburg, Naples, St. Petersburg, Philadelphia, all receiving notice of an imminent movement in the market for luxuries and rarities and impossibly splendid things...

"What name shall we use to sign them?" asked Winnie, taking a breather. The pages were teetering in piles, spilling all over the floor of Mrs. Bone's house in Spitalfields. They worked in a room with bars on the windows, Mrs. Bone's men standing guard in the passage.

Mrs. King's concentration broke, and she accidentally gave herself a paper cut, a fine, long trail across the tip of her forefinger. She sucked it quickly, and left a stain on the letterhead. A pale, pinkish watermark. Signed in blood.

"You're the cleverest," she said. "What do you think?"

Winnie's eyes brightened. "It should be something grand, something with meaning. What about the Fishwives of Paris? Or the Monstrous Regiment? Or the Army of Boudicca?"

"We're not fishwives, we're housekeepers."

"We *were* housekeepers," Winnie replied, hotly. "We're not anymore."

"You shouldn't forget where you come from," said Mrs. King thoughtfully. She took out her pen, signed the first letter with a flourish. "*The Housekeepers* will do nicely."

At sunset they carried the sacks to the postbox, frog-marching the postman down the lane with one of Mrs. Bone's stony-faced guards.

Winnie patted her sack as it was borne away from her hands. "Godspeed," she murmured.

Mrs. King glanced at her. "You're enjoying this."

Winnie considered this seriously. "I am," she said.

"Come on," Mrs. King said. "Let's have a drink."

She felt it then: that burst and tingle of pleasure, that thrill of surety. She had her funds, her women, her plan. She pictured the messages flying out into the night, lifting off like starlings in flight: looping and undulating and gathering force like a storm cloud. To Europe, to America and beyond. Spreading the word: there was a big job on the horizon, bigger than all imagining, a fortune to be made…

Godspeed, she said to herself—in private, deep inside.

Alice came downstairs while the other servants were managing the dinner service. She'd been at her worktable nearly four hours, mouth parched, eyes blurring, and there was an intractable ache in her neck. Madam's costume was at the stage where it controlled her, not the other way around. Unpicking one thread meant unpicking a dozen more. The shoulder seams were immensely delicate, spun as finely as silkworm threads, and they needed to carry so much weight: the rich lining, jet ornaments, the far-reaching acreage of the train. The dress seemed to unspool every time she looked at it, growing uglier, wilder, blacker. She hoped never to see crepe de Chine again.

Miss de Vries hadn't sent for her all day. Alice hounded the other servants with inquiries: had Madam given word as to when she next wanted to be fitted? Had she left any message, any instructions for Alice at all? She needed some assurance that she was still doing well, that she was excelling, that she was safe.

The weaselly-looking errand boy was lugging a bucket of coal in for the range. "Whatchoo asking so many *questions* for?" he said, staring at Alice without compunction.

Alice rounded on him. "Bugger off, little rat," she said, showing her teeth.

His eyes widened, startled, and he scuttled off across the yard, his ragged coat flapping in the breeze. Alice had startled herself. She put her hands to her crucifix. By any measure it was too late for Miss de Vries to still be eating her dinner. Evidently, she was preoccupied, absorbed in business.

Alice lingered in the front hall, trying to invent excuses to enter the dining room. William, the head footman, came out and spotted her. "You'd better make yourself scarce before Shepherd sees you," he said, eyes narrowing. And then, voice gentle: "What's got you in a twist?"

"Nothing," she said, anguished.

"Hmm," he said, turning his gaze away from her. "Do I sense a tragedy?"

She blushed at that and scurried outside, crossing the garden, then the yard. Mr. Doggett and his boys were playing Racing Demon outside the mews house, flicking cigarette ash behind the ornamental urns. They didn't notice Alice, or else she supposed they didn't care to acknowledge her presence, taking her to be a plain and stupid girl, with no purpose in this house, nothing at all to recommend her. The dress was calling silently to her, summoning her back. She wanted to avoid it. She needed a *break*. She marched to the mews door, as if she had an errand to run, as if she were on a mission of great import. As the clocks chimed the quarter hour she stepped out through the mews door into the lane.

She froze.

Two men, wearing rich, silk-lined overcoats, were standing under the streetlamp. The air smelled of gardenias. She recognized the scent, and then their faces, at once.

They came to the gate. The taller of the two lifted his hat, tilted it toward her, perfectly courteous. He had a smile on his face that Alice knew by instinct, that she would have known even if she were a babe in arms. Danger, danger, danger.

The debt collectors had found her, after all.

Perhaps they didn't think she was going to run. Or if she did, they didn't care. They continued to smile at her, eyes steady, as if to say, *We'll track you anyway.* They had one message, and they handed it over on a piece of paper.

She opened it once she was inside the house, in the kitchen passage, back to the wall. Breathing hard, she made out the words under the flickering lamplight: *One week.*

15

Twelve days to go

It was time to get some more skin in the game. Mrs. King had gone over the calculations with Winnie. They needed enough hands to manage the pulleys, set up the winches, pack and wheel the crates, dismantle the runners and the slides, lift the heaviest articles of furniture, and more. Mrs. King went to Mrs. Bone's villa on the docks to start hiring men. The wraith-like porter eyed her with suspicion from the second she arrived.

"Mrs. King?"

She glanced up and saw the Janes peeping around the door to the inventions room. The girls were in starched collars, fierce frills on their aprons.

"They're here," said Jane-one.

There was a vast warehouse on one side of the yard. Jane-one dragged the door back on its runners. Jane-two handed Mrs. King a piece of paper. "Names," she said. "Burn it after, please."

Casting feeble light, the electric lamps sputtered as she entered the vast space. The whole warehouse smelled of sulfur. The cobblestones had been swept, scrubbed, rinsed, and swept

again, and half a dozen men stood waiting underneath a gigantic set of metal beams.

"Where are the others?" she murmured to the Janes.

"Mrs. Bone says to buy the foremen," Jane-two replied.
"They'll recruit the rest. Go on."

Mrs. King kicked herself: she should have known that. She
approached at an easy pace, felt the men examining her. One
of them looked ancient: sun beaten and resplendently wrinkled.
The others were enormous, brutal-looking men—built like shire
horses, and lavishly perfumed.

"Let me talk about the fees," she said, not wanting to beat
about the bush.

They frowned. Their eyes flicked sideways, seeking consen-
sus. The old man shook his head. "We know the fees."

They took a step forward, then another. Tiny, fractional
movements, so small you almost didn't notice them.

"Risks, then?" she said.

The old man shook his head again. "We've looked at those,
too." He smiled, showing an enormous set of teeth. False, she
guessed, and bought at tremendous expense. His breath was
meaty and dry.

Mrs. King smiled back. "Then shall we discuss *your* credentials?"

They shifted a little at that, scratched themselves.

"Clever girl," said the old man, nodding. "Aren't you?"

Mrs. King sighed. "Aren't we all?"

The old man's eyes sparkled. They were small and depthless.
"You should make more of yourself, dear," he said. Reached
out. Ran a finger down the seam of her blouse. "If you want
to make your mark."

Mrs. King didn't flinch. "I don't need to make my mark,"
she said.

The man retracted his finger. "Do you not?" he said. "'Cause
here we are, dragged down here to pay our respects and show
our credentials, when we ain't never negotiated with you in our
lives before." He tilted his head. "Where's Mrs. Bone?"

Mrs. King spread her hands. "Mrs. Bone is otherwise engaged."

"No, I won't allow that. My boys run Leman Street to Tower Hill. Joey here takes anything north of the Crown and Shuttle. Walter Adlerian's tucked up nicely in Limehouse. And so we talk to one another. We compare notes, dear. And what do we hear? Nothing but talk, dawn till dusk, of a nice young lady pottering around Mrs. Bone's estate. A mere wisp of a thing, no meat on her, hardly any references—entirely in charge."

Mrs. King laughed at that. She liked a negotiation. It made her nerves go away. "I have references."

His smile widened, showing the outer edges of his dentures. "For side jobs. Skimming. Shifting ostrich feathers and cans of potted meat. Nothing wrong with that. Everybody has their level. Rich man in his castle, poor man at his gate—nice and tidy." He studied her again. "But you coming along gets us all to wondering."

"Wondering what?"

"Whether there's a storm coming."

Mrs. King considered this. "Check a barometer," she said.

He bowed his head a little. "I do, dear. I check it every morning. I don't like getting caught in the rain. I don't care for nasty surprises. None of us do."

He raised a finger.

"We can do what you need. We can do it with our eyes closed. Our boys are top notch—you know that. So don't ask me about my credentials." The teeth glinted at her. "But let me give you a warning. We keep our eyes on Mrs. Bone's enemies, same as you do. We know Mr. Murphy. A proud man. A good family. Loyal. Very *careful*. He doesn't move if there's a risk. And they're moving on Ruth Bone. I can smell it."

Mrs. King said nothing.

"Our men are loyal, too. Been loyal to Mrs. Bone for twenty years. But we follow the wages. If there's any risk to Mrs. Bone, we've got to consider our options."

Mrs. King understood the sentiment entirely. "There's no risk to Mrs. Bone," she said, at last. "She'll be here forever."

"That's as may be. But someone new might be putting big ideas in her head. Over-extending her. Spending on her credit." He frowned. "It's a finely balanced thing, this web. Delicate. We don't need no other spiders coming along, messing it up."

"I'm not a spider," said Mrs. King coolly.

"Then you're a fly," said the old man. His eyes scurried all over her. "And that makes you somebody's lunch."

"Hired," she said to the Janes when she was safely indoors.

"Were you satisfied?" said Jane-two.

"Have I got a choice?"

The Janes considered this.

Mrs. King sighed. "Never mind."

They brought her tea and cake on the dessert trolley, wheeling it in at top speed. The teapot rattled alarmingly.

"Sugar, Mrs. King?"

"Two," she said. She wanted something sweet, something comforting. It surprised her. Perhaps she was feeling the tiniest bit lonely, kicking her heels out on the docks.

I can live anywhere I like when this is done, she mused. But where would that be? She didn't allow herself to think too far ahead. It led to complacency. She had no tolerance for that.

Jane-one dragged a pair of ropes across the floorboards. They hissed as they came. "This is our swing," she said. Mrs. King studied it. Four ropes, four handlebars, two wooden bars. They looked fearfully delicate. "You need a good, solid hook when you're doing trapeze," said Jane-one. "Will we have one?"

Mrs. King thought about it. "We can get the chandelier out of the way for you. Use the hook on the dome in the hall."

"What sort of dome?"

"Glass."

"Reinforced with?"

"Steel, I suppose."

"Very well." The Janes nodded.

Mrs. King felt, not for the first time, that they were school-ing her in this job, not the other way around. "Good. Alice can make sure you get a look at it."

A spark of something crossed Jane-one's face. Jane-two closed her eyes.

"What?" said Mrs. King.

"Nothing," said Jane-one.

They folded their arms, inscrutable.

Mrs. King laughed. "Don't tell me you've formed an enmity against my sister."

"She strikes us as a changeable sort of person," said Jane-two.

"Moony," said Jane-one. "A milksop."

"That's hardly fair," said Mrs. King. "You've only met the girl once."

"We have eyes," said Jane-one. "We have our instincts."

"We're using our *voices*," added Jane-two, witheringly, "as *in-structed*, to indicate a *risk*."

"No use putting a canary in the coal mine when it doesn't have a nose for gas," said Jane-one. "Alice Parker's got eyeballs as big as saucers. You could run rings all around her, easy as pie. I know the sort."

"Nonsense," said Mrs. King, laughing again. "Alice has a good head on her shoulders. Trust me." She steered the Janes out of the room. "Back to work."

***

But later she pondered it. She remembered carrying her sister in her arms as an infant. Alice used to turn so red, cry so much.

Mrs. Bone had been the first one to clock it, years before. "Is Baby running a fever?" she said once.

"Don't think so."

"Then what's she working herself up about?"

Alice had been beating the air with her little fists, pulsing with energy, lolling and struggling. It went on forever. When she finished, she looked gray and wan and spent.

"Like a weather vane," said Mrs. Bone. "Doesn't know which way she's blowing."

Mrs. King had hated looking after Alice. It made her long to climb the drainpipe, scale the roof, run and hide. It had felt wicked and marvelous when she didn't have to do it anymore, when she left Alice and Mother and Mr. Parker behind, and entered Park Lane.

She recalled the day she left home so well. Mother was in her chair by the mantelpiece. There was a fierce buzzing coming from the corner of the room, a wasp trapped in spider threads, trying to escape. The dust on the hearth had congealed, growing sticky. Mother's expression was worse than usual, frayed around the edges. A man with a shiny coat and silvery hair was sitting in Mr. Parker's chair. He had his hand pressed on Mother's wrist. It wasn't a friendly gesture.

"You should find yourself under *no* anxiety," he said.

Mrs. King had been standing in the doorway. She raised her voice. "What are you saying to her?" she asked. She felt afraid, but she put it in a box.

The silver-haired man turned. She remembered the look. Long, frank, disinterested. "Many things, young lady," he said. "And not for your ears."

"Dinah…" Mother said.

It wasn't an instruction, or even a plea—but Mrs. King came in, arms steady, and lifted Alice from Mother's lap. She averted her eyes. She didn't want to see the vacant parts of Mother's expression.

"Your daughter will find herself in an excellent position," said the gentleman. "A *privileged* position. She will earn a very comfortable wage. She might be able to send something home."

Mother faced the grimy window, and she took the daylight with her, sucked it into her skin. "I don't know," she said.

Mrs. King remembered the feeling in her gut, an understanding that she was being discussed. That something was being arranged on her behalf.

"Splendid, Mrs. Parker," said the gentleman. He released her wrist, and examined his nails. "We'll send a man to fetch young Dinah tonight."

Mrs. King remembered shifting Alice in her arms. "Why?" she asked.

Nowadays she'd demand an answer. By any means necessary. It would be inconceivable not to get it. But back then, when she was only a girl, it wasn't inconceivable.

The gentleman looked at her again. "Hold your tongue," he told her.

Mother didn't admonish him. She didn't seem to hear him at all. Alice grizzled, as if she couldn't decide whether to start crying or not.

Changeable, Jane-two had said. Mrs. King didn't like that word, in relation to Alice. Of course there would come a moment when Miss de Vries would try to befriend her. Mrs. King had seen it happen to girls before: the lazy, sideways nature of it. Almost like an alligator yawning, catching flies in its mouth. Madam liked to make alliances below stairs, circumventing the natural order of things: bypassing the butler, housekeeper, the senior servants, anyone with their wits about them. There was no particular *harm* to it. She just liked to have one humble little person up her sleeve. No doubt it made her feel a little bigger than she was.

Alice might fall for it, she thought.

She closed that thought away. Not likely. Alice possessed Mrs. King's own blood. Of course there were girls who would have weakened themselves for Miss de Vries. Indulged all sorts of fantasies—mooning over her, adhering to her, wishing to possess all that *she* possessed. But Alice wasn't a fool. She knew which side her bread was buttered. She wanted her fee.

She'd said so, only the day before, when Mrs. King went to get her report.

"Look here. I don't suppose I could get some of my payment up front, could I?" Alice had asked.

This annoyed Mrs. King. First Mrs. Bone, now the rest of them. "Certainly not," she said. "I can't show special favors to you—I told you before."

Alice looked uneasy. "I was only asking," she said.

Mrs. King softened her tone. "Why?" she said. "Is something the matter?"

She watched Alice's expression harden. Mrs. King recognized that demeanor. It was her own.

"Not in the least," her sister said quietly. "And I've nothing to report."

16

Nine days to go

Miss de Vries heard William and the under-footmen sorting the post in the front hall. They were fetching extra platters. She knew what this meant. The responses were arriving. It put her on edge.

"Alice?" she said, calling through to the dressing room.

The girl appeared, eager faced but tired, hair scragged back, skin gray. She tucked her needle into her apron pocket, wiped her hands. "Yes, Madam?" Her throat sounded dry.

"I'm running late. Iris has the afternoon off. Bring me some afternoon dresses to look at, will you?"

Alice's eyes widened, and Miss de Vries understood why. Sewing maids sewed. They didn't do any more than that. The rules below stairs were rigid, unbending. She always enjoyed this, sending them scrambling. It settled her own nerves.

"Certainly, Madam," Alice said, and hurried out of the room.

She was keen to impress, and that pleased Miss de Vries, too.

Alice returned with two dresses. "Perhaps these, Madam? The plain crepe or the crepe with jet."

Miss de Vries opened her arms. "You choose."

Alice hesitated. "Plain," she said. And then, with a little flush, as if testing herself, "It suits you better."

Miss de Vries laughed at that. "You ought to tell me they suit me equally."

Alice reddened. "Beg pardon, Madam."

Miss de Vries put out her wrists to be unbuttoned. "I suppose I shall have to give up the jet, then." She met Alice's gaze. "You have it."

Alice dropped her hands. "Me?"

"Certainly. It'll get moth-eaten otherwise. I can't possibly wear it now."

Alice took a step back. "I didn't mean to speak out of turn," she said, frowning.

Miss de Vries studied herself in the glass. "You didn't. You have a good eye, as well you know." She adjusted the lace around her neck. "Iris could take a lesson from you."

She didn't look at Alice. She knew what effect this would have. It happened the same way, every time. A blush, a demurral, a lot of pretty confusion. They were such adorable playthings, the junior maids. Pet them long enough and they gave up all kinds of gossip. The house-parlormaids were machine-made, perfectly trained, more inscrutable. They'd waited on grander ladies in even bigger houses than this one. Sometimes they even unsettled Miss de Vries herself. But Alice was timid, mouselike. She'd gobble up nice treats.

"I oughtn't to take this, Madam," said Alice, voice serious. She held the dress at arm's length, as if she were afraid of it. "It's too generous."

Miss de Vries turned, surprised. Evidently, *this* mouse had more strength of will than she had expected. "Whatever do you mean?"

The girl's face looked grave. She hesitated, as if searching for the correct response. "You might want to keep it for yourself," she said.

Miss de Vries considered this unlikely. Black dresses already bored her to tears. Six months to go till half mourning—it was an intolerable wait. "Suit yourself," she said. "I'll know not to spoil you next time."

At that moment William knocked on the distant bedroom door. "Post, Madam," he called.

"Enter," she replied.

William left the silver platter by the bedroom door. The male servants never entered her inner sanctum.

"You open them," she said to Alice, her stomach tight with anticipation, her tone careless. "Tell me who to expect."

She went to the window, concentrating hard on the muslins.

"Very well, Madam." Alice began opening the envelopes. A minute passed.

"Well?" said Miss de Vries.

Alice glanced up. She gave Miss de Vries a furtive look. "I've put the declines on this side, Madam."

"Declines?"

"Acceptances, too, just here."

"Who has accepted?"

"The general manager of the Quaker Bank. Mrs. Doheny and her son. Charles Fox and Mrs. Fox."

Bankers. Americans. *Industrialists.* "And the declines?"

Alice was threshing the envelopes like a machine. "The Marquess of Lansdowne. Lord and Lady Selborne. The Gascoyne-Cecils. Lady Primrose."

The best neighbors. "Stop," said Miss de Vries. "I shall go through them myself."

"But there are dozens, Madam."

"I said to leave them."

Alice put the envelopes back on the tray. "Very well," she said, voice serious again.

Miss de Vries turned to look at her properly. The girl was staring at her and there was something in her eyes that Miss de Vries didn't exactly like. Not derision, not judgment. A tiny flare of sympathy. "Do you still want to be measured today, Madam?" she said, with care.

It wasn't a barb. But Miss de Vries took it as one all the same. What use was it to be measured, to be fitted into her gown, if she were only to be seen by fishwives and bankers? Anger fizzled in her skin.

"No," she said, voice sharp. "Certainly not."

There was a flash of resignation in Alice's expression, and she turned to go downstairs. It was as if she knew not to press things. It gave Miss de Vries the sensation of being managed. Of being ever so slightly *cared* for. It was a peculiar feeling.

"You can go," she said quickly, to make sure that Alice was leaving because *she* had ordained it. "I'll send for you if I need you."

Afterward, Miss de Vries went to the winter garden and ordered a pot of tea. She drank it in the corner seat, by the window, concealed behind the ferns. She studied Stanhope House, just down the road. Of course *they'd* come. Soap manufacturers were no trouble at all. Her teacup burned her fingers.

Should she cancel the ball? No, impossible. The ball was like a storm, gathering strength all of its own. She felt its pressure in her skull. It was a bet, and she never feared taking big bets. She'd taken the biggest risk of all already. Of that she had daily proof.

She blew on her tea—cooling it, controlling it, forcing it back into line.

Beneath her, on the pavement, Jane-one and Jane-two were moving in quickstep down Park Lane. They were playing their game. One of them sped up, then the other. You had to be alert; you couldn't blink. If you did, you'd fall out of step—you'd lose. They ducked and wove their way down the street.

Jane-one rang the tradesmen's bell. Jane-two slipped a wrench from her pocket to her bag. "Ready?"

She hardly needed to ask. Jane-one nodded. "Ready."

The butler interviewed them in his office. He smelled of gas lamps, and sweated incessantly. There was a general sense of disorder and confusion in the servants' hall: the Janes had picked up on it immediately. There were tradesmen waiting at the side door, boxes piling up in the passage outside the kitchen, kitchen maids scurrying around in hectic, directionless circles. This house had lost its circus master. Chaos was creeping in, chuckling all the way.

"We're presently seeking a housekeeper," Mr. Shepherd told the girls. "And *she* would do the interviews. But we've yet to find a satisfactory candidate…"

The Janes knew that already. Mrs. King and Hephzibah had paid a call on Mr. Shepherd's preferred agency. His letters requesting fresh applicants kept going missing. The Janes had snaffled one or two themselves.

Shepherd peered up at them. "You've got glowing references. You served a… Mrs. Grandcourt? Correct?"

"Yes," they said.

"Yes, Mr. Shepherd," he corrected with a sniff.

"Yes, Mr. Shepherd."

He scratched his nose. "Hotel trained, are you?" he said.

Jane-one felt him assessing her like a butcher, checking her parts: neck, chest, thighs, waist.

She kept her face blank. "Yes, sir."

"Thought as much. But you haven't worked in a big house before?"

"Not as big as this one."

"Well, that's quite understandable. Few have, my dear. Are you good Christians?"

They stared at him.

"Well?"

"Yes," they said in perfect unison. Mrs. King had instructed them in this, too. Mr. Shepherd liked clean, scrubbed-up voices. It indicated a desire for self-improvement.

"Mr. Shepherd is a great advocate of self-improvement," Winnie Smith had said flatly.

"Show me your hands."

They shoved their fingers right in his face, making him jump, giving him a whiff of carbolic soap and chemicals.

"Well, very clean. Good nails." He shuffled his papers again, and Jane-one waggled her fingers. "Yes, that's fine." He thought of something. "You know there's no allowance for sugar or tea in your wages?"

"We don't drink tea," said Jane-two.

Mr. Shepherd liked that, too. "Very good. Most economical."

"We *are* economical." Jane-one pressed her palms to his desk again. "We'll split our rations between us."

"Two for the price of one, ha-ha," said Mr. Shepherd, plainly ready to have this business over and done with. "Well, consider yourselves on trial."

They nodded, stepped back. "We'll meet the mistress now, then," said the Jane-two.

"Meet the… No, you certainly will not. Madam has delegated all downstairs matters entirely to me."

"But engaging domestics is one of those duties in which the judgment of the mistress must be keenly exercised."

"Indeed it is, indeed it is," Shepherd said. And then, with more strength, he added, "And I am most *extremely* observant of Madam's strictures on these matters." He straightened in his chair. "So there won't be another word about it, Miss…" Clearly he was struggling to remember their names. "Miss…"

"Jane," they said, in tandem, with force.

It wasn't easy, hiding everything. The extendable poles, the rope swing, the breakaway ladder, the nets, the winches, the braces, the platforms, the joists. All those had to be stored in the attics. They were cavernous, and accessible by drainpipe, and you could winch things up from the garden if you were quick about it. Winnie had given them detailed instructions.

"You'll find porthole windows here, here, and here." She'd pointed at them on the map. "You can easily get pulleys down to the garden."

Jane-one had thought there was something fishy about her expression. "You love this place, don't you?" she'd said.

Winnie had seemed startled by the idea. "No," she had said, grave faced. "But I know it very well."

They began operations on that first night. The odious cook informed them that they were to be locked into their bedroom at night, which necessitated an immediate survey of the drainpipe and the guttering. They were pleased with the results. Jane-one loved modern houses. The dimensions were hopelessly vulgar, of course—everybody knew that—but the craftsmanship was tip-top. They waited until the house started to still and settle, and then they inched out of the window.

They had to pause on the way up to the roof. Jane-two dug her foot into Jane-one's shoulder.

"What is it?"

"Shh."

"Is it *him*?"

"I said *shh*."

They'd clocked *him* at once: a gerbil-faced lamp-boy who ran errands all over the house. He was staring out of a window on the fourth floor, nose pressed to the glass, gazing up at the sky. Jane sighed inwardly. This was no time for stargazing.

At last, Jane-two kicked her again. "He's gone. Come on."

Jane-one took a breath. It had been a long time since she'd been up this high. That was the trouble, working for Mrs. Bone. It made you soft. Forget your training. She closed her eyes.

"Are you experiencing a crisis?" whispered Jane-two.

"No, I'm just experiencing your great blooming arse in my face," muttered Jane-one.

Up they went.

Once they got the pulley in place, they had to lay padding to muffle the attic floors. They couldn't allow anyone in the servants' quarters to hear any creaking footsteps overhead. Winnie had purchased an enormous number of Turkish carpets, which some of Mrs. Bone's men delivered at night by vaulting over the walls. The tallest gave Jane-two a wink when he landed at her feet.

"You did that rather well," she said, appraising him.

"I do lots of things rather well," he replied, appraising her right back.

"Moira," gasped Jane-one, staggering under the weight of the carpet rolls. "For pity's sake."

They were nearly caught the following night, lifting crates up to the attics, ready to be packed up on the night of the ball. Two of the under-footmen were still awake long after lights out. They'd cracked open their window, smoking contraband cigarettes, talking in hushed tones. Jane-two had to make a low whistle, her best impression of an owl. By then at least two dozen of the hired men were already crawling over the roof of the mews house to gain access to the garden and the eastern side of the house. They froze on their haunches, not moving until the footmen blew their lights out and the window juddered closed.

But otherwise the servants paid the Janes no mind. Cook had a good deal of violent and offensive opinions, but the Janes knew their rights: they'd been hired on as house-parlormaids—they sat outside her jurisdiction. The under-footmen were either too superior or too gauche to talk to girls. The head footman was very beautiful, but the Janes were never swayed by beauty. The other housemaids smoked, monitored their tea rations, took in the illustrated papers and avoided their chores when they could get away with it. A bevy of new servants came in daily, in expectation of the ball. Waiters, clock winders, glass cleaners, mechanics, a man with a splendid toupee who specialized in topiary. In other words, the Janes blurred entirely into the background.

"This is going to be easy," said Jane-one.

"Too easy," said Jane-two. "And note that down in the log. An assumption made is a day's delay."

Jane-one rolled her eyes, but she complied.

They only encountered Mrs. Bone when they crossed the kitchen. She was always caught in some degrading position, struggling with a mop and bucket, usually on her hands and knees, utterly subjected to the tyranny of Cook. "Cup of tea, girls, I beg you," she whispered when they found her scrubbing the pantry floor, hands blistering from lime solution, eyes wild and bloodshot. "I'm gasping."

"Sorry, Mrs. Bone," they said. "We can't be seen to be fraternizing with you."

Alice Parker was permanently ensconced in Madam's rooms, sewing all day.

"Now, girls," said Winnie, when she sneaked around for the daily report, "Mrs. King says you have an objection to Alice. Tell me what the matter is. We can't have discord in our ranks."

"We do not wish to mistrust Alice Parker," said Jane-two gravely, "but we do."

"But it's illogical. She's done nothing wrong."

Jane-one sighed. "She never comes down for dinner. She stays upstairs, mooning over Madam all day."

"Those are her instructions."

"We've all had our instructions," said Jane-one witheringly. "But there's no need to go off the deep end."

Winnie shook her head, as Mrs. King had. "No complaining, girls," she said. "You know the rules."

They shrugged at that. No use banging the gong if nobody wanted their dinner. Miss de Vries, meanwhile, they rarely came across at all. This relieved them. You couldn't trust a girl who'd clearly spent so much time drilling herself, manipulating her voice, her movements. People in this place talked of her as though she were remarkable: preternaturally calm, wise, serene. But the Janes just thought that Madam was a bully. She liked it when the under-footmen dropped things. She winced when they opened their mouths, as if their breath stank. She isolated people, gave them pointless tasks.

"There's a piece of paper I need," she said to Jane-one. "A letter. I've no notion where I put it. Find it, will you?"

A single piece of paper, in a house as vast as this, with countless drawers and closets? Jane-two marked it in her logbook of risks that very night. "She's always inspecting things. She'll know if we move something. This could cause a grave problem."

Jane-one was practicing her handstands. It helped her concentrate. She could ponder the house's tiniest parts, its atoms. She could picture millions of threads, long strings of numbers. Drapes and blinds and bulbs and figurines and carpet grips and candles. "You worry too much," she said from the floor.

17

One week to go

Mrs. King had left this chore for as long as she could, but it could wait no longer. There was only a week to go. It was time to see William.

Certain appointments thrilled her. Some of them amused her. Some of them were tedious but necessary. This was quite different. It involved the digging up and dusting off of feelings.

Winnie eyed her from the other side of Mrs. Bone's inventions room. "Something's put you out of sorts," she said.

"Not in the least," said Mrs. King briskly, fastening her gloves.

"*Who* did you say you were going to see?"

Best not to obfuscate. "William," she said.

"You're not serious."

Mrs. King buckled her belt, gave it a fierce tug. "It's about the tiniest little thing. I wouldn't even have mentioned it if you hadn't asked."

Winnie's hackles were up in seconds. "Tell me," she said.

Her temper was growing frayed. She'd been quick to anger ever since she'd discovered Mrs. King's secret. Trust was such a precious thing. It broke so easily. There was no neat mending of it.

"No," she said firmly. "I won't."

If she'd been sleeping properly, she might have kept her own cool. She might have taken Winnie further into her confidence. Winnie of all people would have understood. She was sympathetic to affairs of the heart. But Mrs. King was growing tired and edgy and she was running out of time.

Winnie stood aside to let her pass. What else could she have done? Wrestled Mrs. King to the ground? She'd never win in a struggle, and they both knew it.

"Good morning, then," she said, voice tight.

"Good morning," Mrs. King replied, voice tighter.

Mrs. King stood outside the garden door on Park Lane. The heat was rising, scorching the door handle. Around here, in the shadow of the house, the world had grown quiet, as if it had run out of breath. The cypress trees sagged, quite still. The sky seemed bigger than ever, the color of dust.

Mrs. Bone had been watching, and had reported back: he went out for a smoke at two thirty. Every day. Like clockwork.

Her eyes had narrowed. "Visiting a fancy man at night, were you?"

"Don't listen to gossip, Mrs. Bone," Mrs. King said.

Her affairs were hers alone. She reminded herself of her resolve: this wasn't a romantic rendezvous. She was taking care of loose parts. This was all about business.

Right on cue, she heard footsteps on the other side of the wall.

The scrape of a match, the sound of the flare. He was lighting a cigarette. Why? To calm his nerves? Buck himself up?

There followed a long, suspended silence. He was taking a drag.

She stood outside the garden door and took a long, deep breath—and listened.

He was pacing. She could hear his footsteps circling, slowly, around that quiet shady spot behind the shrubbery.

Now was the moment.

"Got something on your mind?" she said through the door.

A pigeon rose from the wall above, a nervy wingbeat, breaking the stillness. She sensed, rather than heard, his tiny intake of breath. "Dinah?"

"Open the door," she said.

Another pause. She put her hands behind her back, looked up at the house. When she was a maid, less encumbered by her own dignity, she used to open the attic window at first light. She'd creep out onto the balustrade and walk slowly, coolly, along the whole length of it. Training herself to walk faster, then run, without fear. Will had once spotted her from a window ledge in the men's quarters. He'd raised an eyebrow, tipped a finger, a gesture that said, *Nice work*. He was new then, and the same age she was: twenty-one, with his whole life ahead of him.

From the other side of the door, she heard him mutter below his breath. "For God's sake." And then she heard the scraping of the bolt.

She passed out of the world and into the garden.

"Hullo, you," she said with a smile, and she kicked the door closed behind her.

The air changed as she crossed the threshold. Thickened. She saw the rush of paving stones, their jagged lines, the ferns.

William stood there, tall and dark, watching her. Flies made low, lazy loops around his head, and he dashed them away with his hand. "What are you doing here?" he said.

"Just visiting."

He was incredulous. "Visiting?"

"Thought I'd say hello to you."

She saw the flicker of something in his eyes. *Hurt, hurt, hurt,* she thought, *and not even nearly ready to forgive.* She put a hand out, touched him on the arm. He was burning underneath his jacket. She could feel it even through that thick navy cotton. Hot flesh and sinew, tightly wound.

His arm jerked. "You should clear off," he said. "You don't want to be seen down here."

"No harm if I am."

"*I* don't want to be seen with you. I've enough work already just trying to get my reputation back."

He looked weary. He wasn't much of a sleeper. That's how things began, between them. He'd said one evening, "Fancy a stroll?" It had been a damp and cloudy night. "Yes," she'd said, and they'd scaled the wall as if it were a normal thing to do. They'd walked for miles. Deserted roads, church spires white and ghostly in the mist. A city entirely their own. And when they'd come back, Park Lane seemed even smaller than before.

"Look," said Mrs. King, "I've come to make amends." She perched on the low stone bench, beside the pool. The trellis managed to obscure her from the house, but only just.

"Amends?" He stared at her. "What were you *doing*, Dinah?"

She kept her face expressionless. "I told you. I just needed to look for something in the men's quarters. I didn't know anybody would be keeping watch for me."

"Look for what?"

She didn't do what she'd have done with Winnie, or Mrs. Bone, or the others. She didn't wag her finger, give him a teasing smile. She said, serious, "I can't tell you. So don't ask."

He let out an angry breath. "I don't believe this."

"It's a fine life on the other side, Will. You should think about getting out. Reassess your prospects. It might be time to try something new."

"Oh, really?" he said, in a withering tone.

"Really. You could learn to drive a motor. Become a chauffeur. It pays well. Easy hours. You could get a room in a hayloft for your trouble." She grinned. "Just think what you could get up to in a hayloft."

He was quiet for a moment, as if trying to read her. Then he said, "And what about you?"

"What about me?"

He tilted his head. "What's your plan? Become a seamstress? Open a greengrocer's? Set up a knocking shop?"

"In this neighborhood?" Mrs. King leaned back, letting the house loom dizzy and white overhead. "Why not? I'd make a roaring trade."

William squeezed his cigarette. "Well, I'm fine as I am, thanks."

She noticed something inside her chest: a little flare of disappointment. She studied William. The neat, clean ridge to his forehead. The wide-set slope to his eyes. She knew his shoulders, his chest, the cords of muscle around his rib cage. She knew what his shins looked like underneath his long socks, hairy and nicked and bruised.

She took a risk, against her better judgment.

"I've made plans, you know," she said, in a low voice. "You can get in on them."

William laughed, a husky sound. "Plans?" He shook his head. "You don't have any plans. You're done for. There's no luck to be had around you. Not anymore."

Mrs. King knew better than to react. "Steady on."

His jaw tightened. "Why not? It's the truth. They gave you the sack."

"And now I'm free."

"They gave you the *sack*, Dinah. They nearly gave it to me. I only got out of it because Shepherd decided to tell everybody you were bloody *sleepwalking*." He took a breath, eyes fierce. "Nobody *knew* about us. Now they do. And you've made it look..." He was testing the word in his mind.

She could guess what it was. Tawdry. Cheap. Meaningless.

"Never mind," he said, heavy. "You don't understand."

It was infuriating sometimes, managing people. Accounting for their feelings. When you were on the same page then life was easy—it was like breathing. But the second she broke things off with William she had felt the change. *Break* wasn't even the right word. A break was a clean thing. And this was different. She felt him twisting away from her.

"I just need a little time," she said. "To put some affairs in order. It's not that much to ask."

He shook his head, disbelieving. "You broke things *off* between us, Dinah."

"For heaven's sake." Mrs. King governed herself. "I said we should wait. That's all."

"We aren't people who *wait*. *You* don't wait." His voice was low. "I bought you a ring."

"Oh, enough," she said, rising to her feet.

Mrs. King felt her anger burst through, breaking its bonds. She'd proposed a pause, a temporary suspension of things between them, just until this business was concluded. She needed to *concentrate*. And to him this represented a schism, a betrayal, an irrevocable parting. It was so completely *foolish* of him.

Her rage passed as quickly as it came, and left the usual shame behind. He was right to judge her. She hadn't been straight with him; she hadn't shared one iota of the truth. She would have been furious at him if he'd done the same to her. "Look," she said. "I've got plans. Come with me—if you like."

A long moment passed. William was silent. Then, slowly, he said, "Miss de Vries's new girl. Alice."

Mrs. King felt her skin tightening. "Who?" she said.

Those eyes shimmered. "Don't 'who' me. What's the connection?"

Mrs. King was caught off guard.

"Well?" And then, impatient, "She told me she comes from up your way. Same neighborhood. That doesn't seem like a coincidence to me."

Mrs. King shut her eyes.

"Dinah?"

"How do you remember which neighborhood I come from?"

"You told me."

She frowned. "Ages ago. Years back."

Some understanding crossed his face. "I remember everything when it comes to you," he said.

Mrs. King remembered how it used to be, when she was a house-parlormaid, back when William arrived. Of course the girls went mad for him—half of the men, too, come to that. William knew this, and he handled it gently. He didn't let it turn his head. He kept himself to himself—he was hard to read, same as she was. The first time their hands touched, they were both buttoned up in their gloves. He'd taken a breath, a deep one, as if steadying himself. They kept it secret, whatever it was between them. They didn't even call it *love* for years. It was their thing, theirs alone.

On their night walks they skirted Whitechapel, and he pressed her, curious: tell me who you are, tell me where you come from. "Who cares?" she said, laughing. "Let me be a mystery." She led him down the old street, right past Mr. Parker's house, in silence. Yellow-gray brick, and a broken lamppost, and a shadowy boy flipping ha'pennies at the end of the lane. She must have gone silent, fretting, remembering Mother. He'd clocked it, yet he didn't say anything; he didn't want to cause her pain.

I remember everything when it comes to you.

Those words made her throat dry. "Don't repeat that to anyone."

He stared right back. "Which part?"

"Any of it." She closed up her face, turned her back on him. She could feel it: danger, pulsing through the garden.

18

Tilney Street, Mayfair. Mrs. Bone had rented lodgings for them on a side road off Park Lane, in order to maintain the closest possible presence to the de Vries residence.

"Can she afford it?" Mrs. King murmured when they first inspected their new lodgings.

"Why couldn't she afford it?" said Winnie.

Mrs. King's expression smoothed out. "No reason."

Now Winnie sat in the parlor with a mountain of fabric, sewing tunics. She frowned, struggling with the machine, which whirred and rattled and threatened to destroy her faith in herself. She wasn't making nearly enough progress. They needed to dress at least sixty men. She was barely a third of the way through.

She called through to the bedroom. "How are you getting on in there, Hephzibah?"

Hephzibah's voice came back, rich and imperious. "Call me Lady Montagu!"

Mrs. Bone had sent one of her own gigantic-looking mirrors to Tilney Street, and they'd propped it up at the end of the bed. Winnie peeked around the door. Hephzibah was examining herself, ruffled and rippling, awash with pink silks. A hat triple-barreled with roses floated merrily on her head. "I'm *radiant*," she said.

"You look like a regular Venus," said Winnie, with care.

Hephzibah eyed her beadily. "Because of the pink?" She sniffed. "Yes, I like that."

Winnie approached carefully. She touched Hephzibah's neck, checked the buttons on the back of the dress. Studied the photograph they'd pinned to the glass. The real Duchess of Montagu stared back at her. Strong oval face. Fine, long nose. She looked at Hephzibah. The resemblance was remarkable.

"Have you been learning your lines?" she said, trying to be cheerful.

Hephzibah's hands seemed jumpy. "There's more to this job than *learning lines*."

Winnie made herself smile. "You're every inch the duchess."

Hephzibah let out a breath, flexed her hands. "I'm a terrible ham, aren't I?"

"You're magnificent," whispered Winnie, and squeezed her arm.

Hephzibah picked her way slowly across the room and Winnie reminded herself, she won't spoil things; she won't mess it up. She kept smiling, to be encouraging, to hide her doubts.

Mrs. Bone had hired a Daimler for them at further eye-watering expense. It had a bright blue body and button-leather seats, slick and black as tar. Hephzibah held her parasol over her head and tried to stay cool. Winnie passed her a box of visiting cards, marked the top one with a *PPC*. "Keep the rest. But don't you *dare* pay any other calls."

Hephzibah felt hot and clammy, sweat running down her

back. She prayed it wouldn't stain the satin. The motor ground to a halt and Winnie flashed a nervous smile as she slipped out. "Good luck."

Hephzibah concealed her expression, and her trepidation, with her parasol. "Talent does not require luck," she said, in as frosty a tone as she could manage.

They'd hired the chauffeur with the car. He didn't know Hephzibah from Eve. "Here, m'lady?" he said.

Hephzibah peered out. She hadn't planned for this moment. The house was still so extraordinarily *big*, so white—like a wedding cake, many tiers high. The park was a desert, all baked earth and scrub grass. Dust came in great billowing clouds from Rotten Row. It was desolate, a dreadful place.

I'm not equal to this, she thought.

"Yes, here," she said to the driver, and he got out to deliver her card. Her own self vanished. She sank into her silks and ruffles, and became the Duchess of Montagu.

The head footman ushered Hephzibah through the hall. Servants paused in their duties and huddled behind pillars. The staircase was still tremendously ugly. She'd forgotten its recesses, those blocks of black and blood-red marble. They looked like gravestones, signposts on the way to hell. How many times had she cleaned the banisters, rubbed them with blacking, cracked her nails on their grooves and whorls?

The footman gave Hephzibah a wide and courteous berth. "No more visitors," he murmured to the under-footmen, and they closed the doors.

He was enormously good-looking. Stony faced, dark haired, terrific eyes. He was something to focus on, to occupy the mind.

"This way," he said, extending a gloved finger.

"Oh, I can guess the way," said Hephzibah. She needed to

warm up, to test the voice. "People only move in one direction when they build a house like this." She held out her parasol, and he took it. "Up."

His eyes flashed, a single golden gleam. Amused. *Good*, Hephzibah told herself, *that was a clever line. Well judged. Nice and rude.* She wondered, *Would a duchess speak to a footman?* Perhaps there were no rules for duchesses.

She tried to quiet her mind. It was too easy to lose a character, just by listening to all the chatter in one's head. She eyed the footman's calf muscles, the hard curve of his arse underneath his tails. *Lovely*, she said to herself, trying to cheer herself up. She could smell beeswax: there was parquet upstairs. It made her dizzy, the memory of all those tiny pieces of wood. It took hours and hours to polish every block.

The saloon doors slid open—slowly, slowly. She spied a small figure on a couch, far away in the center of the room. Great slanting shafts of light came through the windows facing the park. Hephzibah shaded her eyes with her hand.

She had tried to cast her mind back to the old days, to remember the child who'd lived in the nursery. A snowball creature, with yellow-gold hair done up in ringlets. More like a pet than a person, a fluffy thing fed and watered by the senior servants. Hephzibah had hardly thought about her, had hardly imagined her living or breathing or existing at all.

This woman—straight, thin, upright, alert—was different altogether. "Don't let her hook you," Mrs. King had warned her. "Whatever you do."

Hephzibah paused at the threshold. She could leave, right now. Claim another appointment, feign illness, call the whole thing off.

Slowly, Miss de Vries rose to her feet. "Your Grace," she said, in a voice that startled Hephzibah. It was low and calm. Hephzibah longed for a voice like that herself.

She studied Miss de Vries. Something was working furiously

in the girl's mind. Surprise, delight, fear. "The other neighbors are cutting her," Winnie had told her earlier, per Alice's regular report. "It's got her right in the neck. She's desperate for a lady to come calling. A real *lady*. So do your worst."

"Miss de Vries," Hephzibah said, in a thrilling voice of her own, and extended her gloved hand. She wanted her fingers to be touched reverently—to be kissed, as if she were a queen.

Inside Hephzibah was the creeping, shrunken ghost of a scullery maid, shaking violently, but the Duchess of Montagu had a steady hand.

Miss de Vries extended her own. "How do you do?" she said.

Hephzibah smiled. *Curtain up*, she thought.

They drank tea. Hephzibah remembered the advice Mrs. King had given her.

"Don't aggravate her. At least, not straight away. Her father trained her well. She's his perfect creation. She'll observe etiquette."

"So what do I do?"

"Tickle her. Give her a little fight. It'll make her feel like your equal. She'll like the game."

Easy, Hephzibah told herself, fingers trembling. Miss de Vries's skin glistened as if someone had rubbed it with oil.

"*Do* sit down," Hephzibah said, indicating Miss de Vries's own chair with a careless toss of her hand.

Miss de Vries's gaze tightened. Her nostrils flared, just a fraction, as if she could smell blood on the wind. "Thank you." She ignored her chair, the plump-cushioned, gilt-framed seat in the middle of the room, and perched on a humble stool, back as straight as a soldier's. "Ah," she said. "Refreshments."

Hephzibah turned, fast. A milky-looking boy in dark tails

was carrying an enormous tea tray through the door. "Madam?" he said.

"Yes, perfect. Do bring it in." She smiled as she said it. And her smile wrong-footed Hephzibah. It was gentle.

"I'm parched," Hephzibah said. "Don't spare the sugar."

Miss de Vries bowed her head. "I never would."

Her wrists were small and faintly blueish, as if the veins ran close together. She wore no jewelry, no ornaments of any kind. She looked like meat that had been well wrapped in muslin, to keep her fresh and away from flies. The water poured out scalding hot, steam rising in a vicious cloud. Hephzibah thought, with sudden conviction, *I don't want to stay in this room a moment longer than I need to.*

"Miss de Vries," she said, summoning her courage. "I come to you today as an emissary of the royal household. I received your letter of invitation. The private secretary passed it to me. I'm sorry it's taken us such a terribly long time to respond."

"Not a terribly long time at all," said Miss de Vries, passing a cup and saucer.

"We've been quite run off our feet. We've any number of engagements. You *know* how it is."

The boy took the tea tray and began backing out of the room.

"I do," Miss de Vries said. Her eyes were lizard like, unreadable. Then she added, with a tiny twist in her voice, "Was it considered—an impertinence?"

"An impertinence?"

"My invitation, my letter to the palace. Did it cause offence?"

Something was moving in Miss de Vries's eyes. Something uneasy. She was doubting herself.

"Good heavens," said Hephzibah. "All approaches to the palace must be considered an offence. To request the attention of Their Royal Highnesses is an impertinence by its very nature. It cannot be helped. Now, tell me, I hear this is a costumed ball, correct?"

"Indeed."

"But that is too enchanting. As what shall you go? A Van Dyck? A masked temptress?"

Miss de Vries's smile grew colder. "I shall have to keep it a secret, Your Grace."

"But you must confide in *me*. I'm dying to know. Will you be a sorceress? A sea serpent? A succubus?"

Miss de Vries stared at her.

"Oh, don't let me torture you. I'm being such a *gorgon*. But tell me you'll make the papers. Did you go to the Devonshires' ball?"

"I did not."

"No? A pity. It's helpful to measure the competition, I find. People *bore* so easily. Have you hired Whitman for the entertainments?" Mrs. King had told her exactly how to put the question. Gently, gently, almost like it was nothing at all…

Miss de Vries frowned. "I've not heard of Whitman."

Whitman was one of Hephzibah's greatest gifts to Mrs. King: a costumier and impresario who came from the Rookery in Spitalfields, and who kept a splendid side business in pickpocketing. Between Whitman, Hephzibah and the Janes, there wasn't a music-hall troupe or traveling fair they couldn't hire for this job.

"Of course you haven't. He doesn't *advertise*." Hephzibah fiddled in her reticule, drew out a card. "I doubt you'd get him now. Not worth asking. Perhaps next year." She tossed the card on the table, then sipped her tea. "He does the most *stupendous* entertainments. And by the by, in case you're wondering, I *did* mention your ball to the Princess Victoria."

"You did?"

"But of course! She was dreadfully shocked."

Miss de Vries considered this. Said, slowly, "I do not think there is anything about it that should shock Her Royal Highness."

"Oh, but it's such a deliciously loathsome thing to do! To

hold a *ball*, when you're in full mourning, not even half. We're agog with it."

Miss de Vries's face was immobile.

"Have I said something amiss?" Hephzibah patted her on the hand. "*Don't* fret. It's a new century, dear. We're all ripe for a shake-up. And you needn't stand on ceremony about HRH. She's slipping down the pecking order every year, poor thing. One day you'll be able to drag her to any old bazaar or rose sale you like. I can't see her making any great marriage, can you?" Hephzibah shifted in her seat. "But for now, of course, things are managed *terribly*, particularly in her household."

"Of course."

"It's the question of *security* that really gets us all stirred up. We are living in such awfully violent times. Now, *if* you wanted to secure the royal presence, I would have to assure the household that there would be *exceptional* care taken for Her Royal Highness's safety."

Only Miss de Vries's knuckles, the faintest cracking of the skin, betrayed her interest. "Of course," she said.

"She does not, you understand, go out in society a great deal."

"I hear she's very close to the queen."

"Quite right," said Hephzibah severely, "and we forget, *all too often*, they are first and foremost a *family*. The first family in the land, bound as tightly in blood and bond as any—" she paused, casting around for the right words "—tradesman and his daughter."

Miss de Vries took this flank attack with a thin smile. "Indeed."

"So her safety is of paramount importance. We have our own policemen at the palace, you understand."

The moment stretched, longer and longer. And then, at last, Miss de Vries said, "They should feel free to look around, if it would help things."

"*Thank* you," said Hephzibah, setting her cup down with a

clatter. "If a few of your people clear out, give them a few rooms to stay in, then I am sure that would suffice."

Miss de Vries looked uncertain. "You mean…"

"On the night of your party. We would want our own men in the house."

Miss de Vries laid down her cup. "Is it *likely* that the princess will attend, Your Grace?"

Hephzibah drew on the strength of all duchesses past and present, the specters of great ladies living and dead.

She sat up straight and said, "Miss de Vries. I would no more presume to predict the movements of Her Royal Highness than to divine the direction of the winds. But I am willing to put in a word, *if* you're able to oblige me."

Miss de Vries's gaze narrowed, suspicious. "If I can, Your Grace."

Hephzibah smiled. "It's quite remarkable, the expenses people incur, ferrying Their Royal Highnesses from one engagement to another. If there's anything that can be done to ease the burden for us…"

Miss de Vries's face closed, as if she'd disappeared behind a screen.

"She'll hate it," Mrs. King had said, "being treated like a piggy bank. It's everything she despises. But she'll need to see a sign of weakness. She needs to feel she's in control."

"I am, of course, willing to defray expenses," Miss de Vries said coldly. "If that is necessary."

"Too kind," said Hephzibah. "And tell me," she said, getting to her feet, heart hammering, almost done. "Who else is coming? I've been asking and *asking*, and I can't for the *life* of me uncover a single soul who's accepted."

Two spots of color formed in Miss de Vries's cheeks, but she maintained her composure. "I shall have someone send you a list directly," she said.

Hephzibah leaned in, as close as she dared. "Leave it to me," she said. "I'll rustle up a good crowd for you. Everybody does *exactly* as I tell them."

She saw it for a second: the extraordinary relief and anger in Miss de Vries's eyes, the reminder that she had to simply *pay* her way to the top. "Thank you, Your Grace," she said in a low voice.

"Good day to you," Hephzibah shouted—and she got out of that room at top speed, so she could take a lungful of air, so she could *breathe*.

19

The day before the ball

Sunday dawned hotter than anyone could have expected. The air was thick and ripe, the scent of horse manure and cut grass wafting in from the park. The household was summoned to the servants' hall after church to hear their final instructions before the ball.

It unsettled Mrs. Bone to see how easily she'd been stitched into the pattern of the house. The precise *clicks* and *thunks* of the household routine began to sound in her head. The skin in between her fingers had first grown red, then itchy, and then cracked—but as the days passed it began healing, hardening over.

Danny's portrait loomed over her all day long. At first she avoided it. Then she couldn't help herself. Lines had formed around his eyes. Crevices dug right into the skin.

Nobody knows what my brother looked like when he was young, except me, she thought. It gave her a funny feeling in her heart.

"What did he like to eat?" she asked Cook one day. She wanted a little slice of Danny, an insight. She wanted to know what he'd *become*.

Cook pressed her fingers together and gave a beatific smile. "Cheese soufflé," she said, heavily. "He liked that a *great* deal."

That didn't tell her much. Nobody did reveal anything here. Shepherd in particular was impossible to nail down. Once Mrs. Bone tried to follow him on his evening rounds, but he was too fast for her. He slid through a side door, somewhere near the Oval Drawing Room, and disappeared. She guessed she'd find him in the Boiserie, but he wasn't there, and even when she crept upstairs to wait in the vast, dark expanse of the ballroom, she didn't catch him. Clearly, he covered his tracks when he moved.

New girls had been arriving every day, hired on to help prepare for the ball. It seemed the more orders that came downstairs—different flowers, new drapes, fresh paint, another electrolier—the more servants Mr. Shepherd employed. He was looking increasingly harassed. Cook loved it. She glided out of the shadows, notes tucked up her sleeve, and gave the new arrivals her interminable tour. One of the girls gave her a wary glance. "I'm not staying," she said, as if to ward off any pleasantries. "I'm going for a shop job. Just took this to fill the gap." Cook's eyes gleamed at that. She took half an hour instructing the girl on the proper use of the napkin press.

Shop jobs. Factories. Offices. The clever girls, those with their wits about them, would come and go, wheeling upward, outward, away from this house. Mrs. Bone sometimes looked at Sue—quiet, with pale pockmarked skin—and worried. Some people liked having silent, frightened little creatures around. Thinking about this gave Mrs. Bone a strange feeling, a prickling sensation down the whole length of her spine. At night she smelled the sweet, sugary scent coming off the girl's skin and remembered her own little Susan, and her heart tightened.

Nobody had come knocking on their door again.

"Stand up straight, Sue," she muttered now. The girl had her hands shoved in her apron pockets. She'd get a hump, slouching like that.

"Yes, Mrs. Bone," Sue muttered back.

Mr. Shepherd said nothing during the briefing. He sat enthroned in his chair at the head of the kitchen table. The kitchen maids had no time to be briefed: they were running late, passing pans covertly down a line. William, the footman, read out everybody's duties. He looked gray, as if he hadn't slept.

Cook broke into Mrs. Bone's thoughts, breath hot in her ear. "And where are those two?" she said.

"Eh?"

"Them *Janes*."

Cook had been stewing on the Janes for days, the indignity of them, their very existence. She'd whipped herself into a frenzy about it. It was the peculiarity of them, she said—their odd looks, those daft expressions. The fact that they were allowed to share their own room. Cook didn't like this one jot. Sisters could cause trouble if they weren't separated, she said. "Who let them get away with that? Not Mr. Shepherd. I doubt he even knows about it. I should tell him."

"Go on, then," said Mrs. Bone, and flicked a bit of dry skin away under the table.

"I should ask him what he *means* by it. He ought to be ashamed of himself. And so should they! Not that they will be, for all the trouble they give me, *staring* at me all day, marching around like *they're* the ladies and *we're* the skivvies, as if I weren't the single most necessary person in this household, specially—"

"Hush, Cook," whispered Mrs. Bone.

"Who is talking?" said Mr. Shepherd. "There must be silence!"

I'll silence you, thought Mrs. Bone. *I'll stick flaming pokers in your eyes.*

Cook waved her hand, voice pious. "It's them *Janes*, Mr. Shepherd. We was just saying they're not here. They're missing all the orders."

Shepherd seemed annoyed. "But they must join us at once. Someone must fetch them."

"I'll go," said Mrs. Bone, unpeeling herself from the wall. She knew exactly where the Janes were. They were sweeping the guest suites, which never had any guests, hauling the contents into packing crates. They'd suggested to Mr. Shepherd that it would be sensible to put things in safekeeping before the ball. Clever girls. Getting a nice head start on the job. Eminently sensible.

She caught William's eye as she scuttled past. He didn't just look gray—he looked as if he'd had the blood entirely drained out of him. He was more handsome when he was unhappy. It was almost interesting. She held his gaze for half a second and raised her eyes, just a fraction, to jolt him, to say, *What's got your goat?*

He merely frowned, lost in thought.

A bell tinkled in the distance. All eyes went to the bell board, an intake of breath. They were picturing Madam, no doubt. Wispy, wreathed in black muslin, cooking up orders. Shepherd looked quite white in the face.

Lovely, thought Mrs. Bone. She wanted everyone nice and rattled.

She ignored her own nerves as they scampered all over her skin.

Sunday afternoon arrived. The Park Lane servants went off duty, meeting their sisters and cousins and gentlemen callers, and the women gathered to go over the plan together for the final time. They squeezed into a six-seater pleasure boat, two giant wheels crashing through the water, the Janes pumping hard on the pedals. Mrs. King sat in the front seat, studying the horizon.

Alice had pulled her hat low over her eyes, and Hephzibah had brought a colossal parasol that threatened to decapitate someone.

It made Winnie feel unusually bad-tempered. Her fatigue and nervous energy were catching up with her. She'd been meeting foreign agents all morning on Mrs. Bone's behalf, and her mind was spinning with Danckerts and Cuyps and Sèvres china and Joshua Reynolds. "I want the biggest sales lined up first," Mrs. King had told her. "We can't be managing fifty auctions. I need to know who's going to put cash down quickly, first night we're on the market."

And so Winnie had sat in the parlor at Tilney Street, discussing prices, guarded by Mrs. Bone's grim-faced cousins. She wore a veil during negotiations, and sat on one side of a screen painted with voluptuous nudes. She had to scramble, writing up all her notes, making sure she hadn't made any errors. By the time they went out to the park to meet the others, she was feeling entirely flustered.

"Sleep," she said now, clearing her throat for attention. "Sleep is the important thing. You'll want to be razor-sharp tomorrow." She leaned forward, prodded Hephzibah. "You especially."

Hephzibah swung her parasol in Winnie's direction. "I won't sleep a wink," she said. "It's far too hot." She pointed at Winnie. "*You're* the one who needs her beauty sleep."

I won't rise to that, Winnie thought. "Remember, Hephzibah, you've got to roll in to the ball early, to keep an eye on the arrivals and get Miss de Vries moving."

"Shall I be given supper?"

Winnie sighed. "If you make enough of a fuss, I suppose. Introduce her to Mrs. Bone's men, make sure Miss de Vries thinks they're Buckingham Palace policemen, and then get to work upstairs."

Hephzibah frowned. "Can't you make this thing go any faster, girls?"

The Janes thumped the pedals, and the boat roared ahead,

churning the water. Winnie could see other boaters looking around in displeasure, rocking on the waves. The motion was making her feel queasy. She tapped Alice's arm. "Parker. You'll head upstairs to sew Miss de Vries into her costume. Take your time about it. You want her strained, harassed, and running late."

Alice looked troubled, running her hand through the murky water. "I can't *force* her to do anything."

Mrs. King smiled into the distance. "You'll be fine."

And that was all.

How did she do it? Winnie wondered. *How could she be so smooth, so certain?* Winnie had to clench and unclench her hands when she spoke, consulting her notes. But Mrs. King was different. She held the vision in her head. Look in her eyes long enough and you began to see it yourself, lights glinting in the dark.

Mrs. Bone said, wrinkling her brow, "Now listen. I've been looking at our crates. You need to do something about them. They're so heavy they'll make the whole house shake when you winch them down."

"We've oiled the pulley," said Jane-one.

Jane-two nodded. "And we'll have mats on the floor, to take the landing. We've measured everything, even Madam's bed."

"Hmm," said Mrs. Bone. "If you say so, my Janes."

Winnie wished *she* had the knack for convincing Mrs. Bone of something so easily.

"Her *bed*?" said Alice, looking worried. "Do you plan to take her *with* you, while she's sleeping?"

Jane-one sniffed. "As long as we're very careful with the angles, as long as we can get it hooked up nice and easy, and it doesn't swing too much…"

Alice scrutinized Mrs. King. "You're not serious."

"I'm finding this very dull," muttered Hephzibah, lowering her parasol.

"Hephzibah, please," said Winnie.

Alice raised her voice. "Dinah…"

"Not Dinah," Mrs. King replied. "*Mrs. King.* Unless you're going to gag Madam with chloroform or tie her up or sell her to a kidnapper for ransom, that won't work. She'll catch us, she'll see everything, she'll know exactly what's going on."

Winnie studied Alice with concern. The girl had gone pink in the cheeks, speaking so boldly. But Mrs. King was unruffled. "Of course she'll catch us."

Alice paled. "What on earth do you mean?"

Mrs. King tilted her face to the sun, tipping the brim of her hat. "We'll talk about it tomorrow."

"Tomorrow, tomorrow, tomorrow," said Mrs. Bone. "It's all happening tomorrow, isn't it?"

"Yes," said Mrs. King mildly, "it is."

"Tell me now, please." Alice looked strained.

"Winnie," said Mrs. King, very calmly. "Carry on." She turned back to face the trees.

Alice's voice shook slightly. "No. I refuse to go on."

"She refuses," said Jane-two.

"Not complying," said Jane-one. "Throw her in the lake."

"Girls…"

"I'll throw *you* in the lake, you beasts—"

Winnie didn't like the way the wind was blowing. "Ladies, please…"

"I'll wring your necks, all of your necks," exclaimed Mrs. Bone. "I've been up since four o'clock this morning throwing out the slops, spit-polishing the utensils, scrubbing Cook's undies…"

The Janes pedaled madly, hurtling around the edge of the boating lake.

"I hope I'm not going to miss my dinner," said Hephzibah with an enormous sigh.

Winnie felt her patience start to snap. "Of course you won't."

"You say that, but it's past teatime already."

"Ladies, let's move on," said Winnie.

"Move on? I can't *think* when I'm this famished."

"Then go and sing for your supper," said Winnie, rounding on her. "Or whatever it is you do to pay for your subsistence."

"I pay for my *subsistence* with my *talent*," said Hephzibah. "A *rare* talent, as well you know!"

Winnie's forbearance reached the end of its limits. She couldn't help herself. "A rare talent? Hardly. We all know how your sort of actress makes her living. Oldest profession in the book."

The Janes stopped pedaling. The boat slowed, careening toward the bank.

Mrs. Bone's eyebrows shot up. Alice's glance flashed sideways, and Mrs. King frowned.

Hephzibah's expression cracked open, color racing up her neck, exposed.

"Well, now," said Mrs. Bone. "Fancy that."

The women studied Hephzibah.

Winnie felt her skin growing suddenly warm. "I…" she began.

As the Janes steered the boat to the riverbank, Mrs. King's voice cut through the air. "Winnie," she said. "Get out."

Shame rose within her. "Hephzibah…"

"Out," said Mrs. King again. "You know the rules. *If you need to make someone feel small, so that you can feel tall…*"

Mrs. Bone recited the rest. "*Then, my goodness, my dear, you're no person at all.* Quite right. I taught you that myself. You should all listen to that, my girls."

Winnie rose from the boat. It rocked dangerously beneath her. It would have been better if she had fallen in the water.

20

The night before the ball
10:00 p.m.

Shepherd had left orders for everyone to get to bed early, in anticipation of the ball. *Hurry up, hurry up*, Mrs. Bone thought, urging the house to go to sleep. Her first tranche of men were coming in tonight, an advance guard, ready for the main action. They'd be winched up to the roof, fully installed in the attics by dawn, their movements padded by Winnie's Turkish carpets. She glanced at the ceiling and imagined how it would smell, forty men crouched and waiting: sweaty feet, the air thick with whisky, piss warming gently in buckets. She would have gone up there herself, if only they didn't lock the doors at night. Mrs. Bone liked to inspect her troops before battle. It gave them a good kick.

Sue was at the washbasin, picking dirt out of her nails. She did this in secret, when she assumed Mrs. Bone wasn't looking, as if a little coal was something of which to be ashamed.

"Hurry along, Sue," Mrs. Bone said for the third time.

"It's hot," whispered Sue. She was wiping her face with a damp flannel, over and over.

"Better than the cold, my girl," said Mrs. Bone. "Better than your toes falling off. Get into bed."

Sue was taking an *age*, and the air was curdling like milk.

When the knock came, it startled her. A hard thump, fist against wood, not friendly.

Sue froze, hands on the basin.

"Who's that, then?" said Mrs. Bone as she hurried to the door, swung it open.

That boy was there, that weasel-faced little rat.

"What*choo* doing?" said Mrs. Bone. "Get away with you. Coming up here. These are the ladies' quarters."

"You're wanted, Sue," he said, not looking at Mrs. Bone.

And in that moment Mrs. Bone understood, and she was revolted. She had lived long enough to understand that look. Whether from an old man or a young one, a rich man or a poor one, there was a certain sort of summons you gave a girl that wasn't right at all.

Here, in Danny's house?

It wasn't disbelief. It was something clicking into place.

Here, same as everywhere.

Mrs. Bone was always a very pragmatic sort of lady. She assessed trades coolly, dispassionately: she weighed them on the scales and picked the most lucrative ones every time. But there was one business she wouldn't touch.

She pictured Danny, the gleam of his curls. Felt her flesh crawling.

"Sue's sick," she said.

The boy frowned. "I was told to fetch her."

"Tell 'em she's sick, and tell 'em I told you so, and tell 'em I said it was for the best."

She stared at him levelly. "Trust me."

He stared back. Calculating.

"Fine," he said.

He didn't waste time. He turned and ran away, back to who-

ever had sent him, heels echoing as he went. And he didn't lock
their door.

Mrs. Bone closed the door. She leaned against it, hands behind her back, tightly clasped.

"Anyone asked for you before?" Better to ask straight out, not
to fudge the question.

There was a silence. Sue shook her head. And then she spoke,
in a voice that sounded hard, snapped off at the edges. "But he
told me to get ready," she said, nodding to the door, meaning
the boy. "He said someone might ask for me tonight."

Mrs. Bone made her expression appear unruffled, unbothered.
"Stuff and nonsense. What's anyone going to want with a goose
like you?" She went to the bed, fingers shaking, and wrenched
down the covers. "You come to me if he speaks to you again."
She snapped her fingers. "Bed, Sue. Get in."

She looked again at the floorboards, the nicks and scratches
and marks, and wondered how many girls had been dragging
their bed across the floor to bar the door.

11:00 p.m.

Alice felt an ache right in the middle of her back. It was radiating outward, all her muscles contracting. She was sitting half-
stooped at the worktable, all the lights burning overhead, forcing
herself to keep going. This was the hardest, fiddliest, most ex-
hausting part of the job: doing the embroidery all along the
bodice and the sleeves and the back. She could have finished it
in a heartbeat if she didn't care about the results, if she thought
that hardly anyone would notice it. But she cared too much; she
cared enormously. Madam had such excellent powers of observation. She'd see any faults at once. She'd see the best bits, too.
"You'll be handsomely rewarded," she'd said.

That was incentive enough to go on.

She heard a footstep, the heavy sweep of the door as it opened. "Alice?"

Alice started, dropping the thread. She ran a hasty hand through her hair, trying to smooth herself. She could only imagine how she looked: greasy faced and pinched.

"Madam," she said, pushing back her chair.

"No, don't get up."

Miss de Vries had dressed for compline in plain black satin, buttoned all the way up to the chin, her hair swept up under a coif. She wore a black veil tight to the face, so that the embroidery crawled all over her cheeks. She was holding on tight to her prayer book. She peered at the dress from afar, almost with suspicion.

"Will it be ready in time?" she asked.

That was the worst question, the one Alice feared the most. She considered telling the truth, discarded it. "Of course," she said, trying to make her voice bright. It sounded more like a caw.

Madam put a hand to her jaw, prodding it, as if testing the weight and pressure of her cheeks underneath her veil. "Come with me to chapel," she said, "if you like." She gave Alice a dry look. "You can pray to the patron saint of seamstresses, if there is one."

Alice felt herself reddening at this, and she hesitated. Then she lifted her chin. "Very well, Madam." Her skin skittered as she said it. *Winnie and Mrs. King would approve of this*, she told herself. She was simply keeping Madam under closer observation. Although she wondered, sometimes, why Mrs. King was so intent on *tracking* Miss de Vries. There was something bloodthirsty about it, like stalking a fox or a deer. It was the reason she'd rejected the dress, when Madam offered it to her. It was one thing to *watch* the mistress. To sew for her, dress her. It was a different thing altogether to take gifts, slip into her clothes, try on her skin. Alice would have accepted Madam's entire wardrobe with pleasure. Her things were sumptuous, exquisitely crafted. But something had made Alice hesitate.

Now Alice and Miss de Vries sat together in the chapel, candles flickering, brass fixtures swinging gently from the ceiling. The chaplain had gone long ago: they were left to their own private prayers. The light was golden and hazy, wisped with smoke. It felt to Alice that they were sitting in a dark jewel box: onyx pillars, creamy marble edged with gilt, arched and pointed like blades. Golden angels glared down from the walls.

Alice wound her hands together, closed her eyes. *Lord*, she prayed, *You must protect me.* She was a whole week late to repay her debt. What did it mean, if you ignored a debt collector's summons, if you simply buried your head in the sand? Did the interest accumulate by the hour or by the minute? She pictured the debt collectors trailing her, extending a length of wire from their sleeves, ready to slice her throat…

Pull yourself together, she ordered herself. All she needed to do was make it through tomorrow and to the end of the week. Then she'd earn her fee and have enough to pay her debt and any interest on top. Surely they wouldn't exact any further punishment against her.

Going out on the boat had shaken her. She'd tried to hide behind Hephzibah's parasol. *Chin up*, she told herself. Men couldn't simply come and snatch her off the street. But her whole body had been on alert. She wanted this job done, finished forever. She wanted to eradicate this constant, creeping sense of dread.

Miss de Vries shifted in her tiny pew. "How's the mood below stairs?" she asked.

"I'm sure it's all going well, Madam," she said. A mealy-mouthed sort of response. Although, really, how on earth was she to know? She was locked away in the dressing room, spending her days negotiating yards of black crepe.

"They're getting in a twist about the preparations, I suppose." Miss de Vries's lips looked very dark under her lace, as if she'd rubbed a little stain into them. It gave them a fullness, a rawness, that was not there before.

Alice swallowed. "Who is, Madam?"

"Everybody below stairs."

Miss de Vries threw her prayer book aside. It fell with a thud to the tiled floor. She got to her feet, facing the altar. "And I suppose you're getting tired of life here, too," she said, voice short. "You'll be wanting to move on."

The light wobbled. Alice rose slowly. She was clumsier than Madam: her skirts bunched around her boots. "Not in the least."

Miss de Vries turned. She rubbed her forehead with her fist. "But what of your ambitions?" she said. "Or don't you have any?"

There was a sting to the words. Alice observed it. It made her own feelings prickle.

"I'm quite content here," she said stiffly.

"Content?"

"I'm very happy with my position, Madam."

Something darkened in Miss de Vries's gaze. She was keyed up about something. It was sharpening her, giving her new points and angles.

"You understand *I* shall be leaving soon?" she said, voice cold. "I expect to be engaged before the week is out."

Alice took this in. The air in the chapel felt thick, crafty. "Then I should offer my congratulations, Madam," she said, with care.

Miss de Vries's eyes came around quickly. "Hmm," she said. "Yes, you should." And then, with a tiny frown, she added, "You're a sharp girl, aren't you, Alice?"

Alice swallowed. "I don't know, Madam."

"Keen-eyed. Eyes like a *hawk,* I'd say." Madam gave a hard smile. "You've observed all of *my* movements."

There was something needling Alice's skin, sounding a silent alarm. She said nothing.

Miss de Vries raised an eyebrow. Lifted her arm, indicated the fabric in her sleeves. "I mean my gestures, the precise gradient of my limbs. To make my costume."

"Oh," said Alice, on an out breath. "Yes."

Miss de Vries smiled, expression flat. "In normal circumstances I never keep a personal maid. I find it so tedious, having one person around me all day. But I am considering making an exception. If I take control of a new household, I shall need to have the right people in my camp. Watchful sorts, girls who can report back to me candidly. To provide eyes in the back of my head, as it were." She held Alice's stare. "You'd do splendidly."

Far in the distance, through the thick chapel walls, Alice could hear a motor making its way around the edge of the park.

"I'm not sure, Madam," she said. "I'm not sure I have the skills."

"Well, do you understand hair? Paints and powders?"

"No," Alice said. She felt a tiny bead of sweat forming on her neck.

"And what of foreign tongues?"

"Tongues?"

"Yes, have you any? French? German?"

Alice shook her head, wordless.

"And no Italian, I suppose. More's the pity. I'd take you with me on honeymoon of course." She closed her eyes. "Florence, naturally. It would be expected." She opened her eyes. "Have you ever seen a picture of the Grand Hotel?"

Miss de Vries flipped open her prayer book, pulled out a picture postcard of a modern, brash-looking building, inscribed Grand Hotel Baglioni. "Charming, isn't it? The principal suites are supposed to be very fine indeed. And of course I'd have a connecting room for you, next door." She paused, as if weighing her words. "You'd live in the same style as me," she said, "in all my residences."

Alice could feel something shifting underfoot, like quicksand, sucking her in. It wasn't an entirely unpleasurable sensation. She forced her mind away from it. "But shouldn't you be sorry," she said, "to leave this house?"

Miss de Vries gave her a long look. Then she turned her face up to the painted angels, expression dead. "Naturally I shall," she said. "It will be the most enormous wrench."

There was something so darkly coiled within her tone that it made Alice shiver.

"I have none of the qualifications you need," she said weakly.

"I could instruct you, if you wish. Create a pearl from scratch." The swaying lamplight illuminated Miss de Vries's pale skin, throwing her veil into sharp relief. "You have a gift, when it comes to dressmaking. You may as well round out your advantages. Make the most of yourself, while you can."

Alice pictured Mrs. King's face in her mind, dark-eyed and worried. She knew the safest reply. *Very kind of you to suggest it, Madam. Something to think about, Madam. Do allow me to consider your kind invitation, Madam.* Tomorrow night this job would be over and done with and Alice would vanish from Park Lane forever. So it had been planned; so it *had* to be.

"Very kind of you to suggest it, Madam," she said, and imagined Mrs. King's expression relaxing in her mind.

Miss de Vries pressed her lips together, face tightening. It made Alice feel a twist of regret—a quick and guilty sensation, something to try to ignore, but *there*: absolutely there.

21

The night before the ball
1:30 a.m.

Mrs. Bone waited until Sue fell asleep, and then she opened the bedroom door. She didn't care if someone caught her in the passage. She was going to confront Mrs. King, come hell or high water.

She nearly ran down to the bottom of the garden. The whole place was alive with silent activity, men streaming over the walls. They bent double as they crossed in front of the house, ducking behind pillars and urns. Mrs. Bone saw them crawling up the pale, blank face of the house on rope ladders. In normal circumstances she would have watched with grim satisfaction, praying that the moon stayed behind the clouds. But she had bigger problems now. The air was sticky, clinging to her scalp.

Mrs. King was standing with Winnie by one of the pools at the bottom of the garden, concealed by trellises and vines. They started at the sight of Mrs. Bone.

"You," Mrs. Bone said. "I want a word." Her lungs felt too tight. She banged her chest with a fist, trying to knock them into order. "The girls," she said. "What's happening to the girls?"

Winnie paled. Her eyes widened.

Mrs. Bone jabbed Mrs. King's arm with her finger. "I know a bad business when I see it. I can smell it a mile off. I'm not a fool. Someone's using these girls. Getting 'em out of bed at all hours. I *know* what that means." Mrs. Bone jabbed her again, harder. "You brought me in here under false pretenses."

Winnie sucked in her breath. "No, Mrs. Bone."

"I've been making a fool of myself, crawling around on my hands and knees, wiping everyone's arses. You should have *told* me what I was getting into. It's sick; it's rotten. I've never let myself get anywhere *near* this sort of business."

At first Mrs. King looked entirely nonplussed. But then something moved in her eyes, a slow and creeping fear.

It made Mrs. Bone clench her fists. "What sort of house was you running here?" she said.

Winnie raised a hand. "Please don't," she said, voice constricted. "Don't put this on Mrs. King. She doesn't know."

"Doesn't know *what*?" said Mrs. King, voice taut.

Mrs. Bone let out a short bark of laughter. "What sort of person doesn't *know* what's going on under her own roof?"

"Winnie?" said Mrs. King.

Winnie sagged against the wall, closing her eyes. "I only found out three years ago."

"Found out *what*?"

"Girls," said Mrs. Bone. "They've been *meddling* with the girls."

Mrs. King's face went very still. She took this in, assessed it. Clearly, she understood what that word meant, what *meddling* was: of course she did. Everyone did.

"No," she said, her voice growing cold. "That's not correct."

Mrs. Bone snapped her fingers at Winnie. "You. Tell us. What do *you* know?"

Winnie rubbed her hand over her face. Her voice was low, hoarse. "I was here. I mean…here, in the garden. The mews house has a loft above it. There's a little staircase that comes down to the stables. They used to keep a carriage there, but it's empty now. I saw a man, someone I didn't recognize. He had a beautiful coat on. It was… I don't know. Seal gray. Sealskin."

She took a shuddering breath. "It was very smooth, like silk. I thought: Oh, what a *lovely* coat." She paused, frowning. "He was walking a girl down the stairs. I mean, he had his hand on her shoulder. He was pressing her down. Pushing her along. Like he was shoving her out. I knew at once it was wrong. I mean, my whole body felt it."

Mrs. King watched her the whole time she was speaking. Her face changed, grew ashen.

"It was Ida," said Winnie. "One of the kitchen girls. And I didn't know the man at all."

Mrs. Bone knew that mews house. She'd seen it every time she crossed the yard. Pale gray plasterwork, ivy beginning to climb the walls. One small window.

"How old?" she said.

"I don't know."

"How old, Winnie?" said Mrs. King, voice hard.

"Not old, not old enough. She looked…" Winnie screwed up her face. "Sick. As if he'd made her sick. She looked like she was going to…to throw up."

Silence. Mrs. Bone absorbed this, felt the knowledge shifting in her gut.

Mrs. King asked, "Did they see you?"

"No."

"What happened to that girl?"

Winnie clasped her hands together. Didn't reply.

Mrs. King took a step closer. "Winnie."

Winnie squeezed her eyes shut, as if to hide from it. "Shepherd told me one of the housemaids had given notice. That I'd better let the agency know. I must have asked him who it was. Just to…test him. And he must have told me—he must have said it was Ida." Winnie looked at the ceiling. "He just told me as if it was nothing, as if it meant nothing at all."

"Shepherd," said Mrs. Bone. Her mind was working quickly. "Mr. Shepherd. So Danny might not have known, either. He might not have had a thing to do with it."

Winnie lowered her voice. "Oh, he knew."

Mrs. Bone pictured her house in Deal. The treasures she'd stockpiled. The banker's order from her brother, the foundations of her whole fortune. She began chuckling, pain crisscrossing her breast. "What a set of stupid girls," she said, crooking a finger at Mrs. King. "Here's one." Pointed to Winnie. "Here's another." Pointed to herself. Dug her nails into her palm. "Here's a third."

Mrs. King stared back at her. Then at Winnie. "You never told me."

Winnie looked agonized. But Mrs. Bone didn't have any patience for that.

"Who else?" she said. "Who else knew? Mr. Doggett? *Cook?*"

Winnie shook her head again. "You don't understand. You can't understand what it was like in this place. It wasn't *there*, not on the surface of things. It was…" She tried to find the words. "It was *underneath* everything."

"And what about our fine lady mistress? Did she notice girls coming and going? Or was she as dense as you?"

Mrs. King's face closed up. "Winnie?" she said.

Winnie ran her hands through her hair. "I don't know—I've never known. It's… She was…"

"What?"

"She was always friends with them. With the girls in the house."

"Friends?"

"Yes, friends." Winnie reached for Mrs. King. "*You* remember what it was like up there, in the schoolroom, before Madam came out. Just the tutors, and the governesses, and the dance mistress. Mr. de Vries let her make friends below stairs." She closed her eyes again. "I thought it was such a *kindness*," she whispered.

"Friends?" said Mrs. Bone.

Winnie nodded, voice strained. "It seemed…natural. That a girl would want to make friends with other girls. To learn about their lives. Understand where they came from. Share a little schooling."

"Earn them an afternoon off," said Mrs. King quietly.

"And those girls took liberties. Grew cheeky. Felt they were favored. I always chalked it up to a lapse in discipline. The master allowing indulgences, just to favor Miss de Vries."

Mrs. Bone dragged her gaze back from the house. "Clever, really. A neat way to put the girls at ease. I daresay he needed them to be comfortable upstairs."

Mrs. Bone felt a shudder pass through her. "*Does* Miss de Vries know?"

Winnie simply shook her head. "It's like I said. You can't… you can't *tell*. It's not *spoken* of."

"Who was the man, then? The man in the gray coat."

"I never found out."

"Never asked, you mean."

"He would have been a gentleman of means," said Mrs. King. "He would have paid well for the visit."

"Danny didn't need more money."

"Money isn't everything," said Mrs. King. "It isn't influence."

Mrs. Bone knew that. She understood patronage. A corkscrew chain of favors. Tastes, pleasures, likes, fancies. Powders, perfumes, poppies. And in the night, behind rich drapes, with oil lamps: girls. Dancing girls, chorus girls, waifs and strays. You had to know where to find them, how to train them, how to get rid of them. Mrs. Bone didn't just avoid that business. She took in plenty of those girls, over the years. All those Janes.

She suddenly addressed Mrs. King. "No one ever came for *you*, did they?"

Winnie straightened, her eyes fierce. "Never. I shared a room with her the whole time. I wouldn't have let them. I looked after you."

There was something heated, something desperate, in the way she said it.

Mrs. King said, voice grave. "And you, Winnie? You were all right?"

Winnie's eyes flickered back and forth. "Yes," she said, quickly. "Yes, *I* was fine."

"What about our fine lady duchess?" said Mrs. Bone, quietly.

"Hephzibah?" said Mrs. King. Her eyes widened at that, shocked. It was rare to ever see that look upon her face.

Winnie opened her mouth, shut it again. Shook her head.

Mrs. Bone crossed her arms. "That's clear enough to me."

Mrs. King said soberly, "And me."

They looked at one another. "Something needs to be done about this," said Mrs. Bone.

"Something needs to be *done*?" Winnie's voice went up a notch. "You think I haven't tried? I went to Shepherd. I went to the master."

"What happened?"

"I said I'd discovered something perfectly dreadful."

"What did he say?" Mrs. Bone asked, fearing the answer.

Winnie laughed, a bitter sound. "He told me not to be so *disagreeable*. The next day, I was given my papers. I was out of Park Lane barely an hour after that. No character, no wages."

It wasn't easy to read Mrs. King's expression through the gloom. But Mrs. Bone had heard enough. Her heart was pounding in her chest. "Well?" she said. "I want answers. I want *solutions* to this."

"We have our solution," said Mrs. King. She averted her gaze from Winnie, reached out and tugged an ivy leaf from the wall. Ripped it up, piece by piece. "We get to work."

Later, when the women had gone, Mrs. King examined her own feelings. Her heartbeat had accelerated. She studied it, measuring time. Until now, her plan had felt kaleidoscopic, shiny but fractured, made of a million tiny pieces. But now it had stilled, had become a frozen, glittering thing. It had precise dimensions, like a diamond. It had its own force, a pull. The sensation made her feel weightless, without bonds or limits.

Her mouth tasted like metal. Her blood was shouting orders at her, *Fix it, fix it, put it right.*

22

The day of the ball

The twenty-sixth of June. Dawn came, hot and heady. Park Lane dragged itself awake, forming its usual cluttered assemblage of curves and chimneys and striped awnings, and began to shimmer in the heat. Dust was already rising in billowing clouds as carts and motor vans stopped with deliveries. The de Vries house had become a hive of activity.

One of the under-footmen wedged open the tradesmen's door, ticking visitors off a list, a long line of men carrying goods. Crates of wine, huge vases of lilies, hosepipes, boxes of linen. A newspaperman watched from the pavement and scribbled notes.

Mrs. Bone elbowed past him. "Bugger off," she muttered.

She shrank behind an urn once she entered the hall. Miss de Vries was already on the move, flanked by Mr. Shepherd, William, the footman, and a string of housemaids. The house had taken on a new sort of brilliance. The surfaces had been cleared, and huge flower screens raised against the walls—crimson roses, orchids, delphiniums, a volcanic cascade of red peonies. The housemaids had worked for days polishing the marble to a terrific toothy shine.

Mrs. Bone was sweating. But her niece looked cool as she surveyed the arrangements, a cloud of black muslin. Her waist had been drawn in dangerously tight.

"And, Mr. Shepherd, there's something delicate I'd like you to keep your eye on..."

The butler motioned the other servants away, but Mrs. Bone slipped behind the ornate railings of the staircase, concealed by flowers and glass butterflies. She listened hard but caught only a fragment of the discussion.

"...in the garden, speaking to William."

"I shall confront him myself. And I'll call the constable if she's seen again, Madam."

"No. I'll speak to William myself."

Mrs. Bone looked at the footman, standing stony faced across the hall, oblivious to the fact that he was being discussed.

"One more thing."

The girl's voice was like honey. Mrs. Bone's senses prickled.

"Have you had any luck in your searches?"

Something curious happened to Shepherd's face at the question. It closed down. "I'm doing my very best, Madam."

It was hard to see Miss de Vries's expression from this angle. But there was something dangerous in the level of her chin.

"I hope you are," she said, and then she moved on, the chill moving with her.

~

Later, sneaking out to the mews lane for a smoke, Mrs. Bone nearly jumped out of her skin.

"Archie?" she whispered, disbelieving.

Her cousin was lurking under the guttering, fiddling with

his mustache. He looked panicked. "It's *true*," he said. "You've gone and lost your head. Look at the *state* of you."

"What in heaven's name are you doing here, bothering me? Who's minding the shop?" He smelled of new cologne—orange flower and spices. *Who's paying for* that? she wondered.

"We've got trouble."

"What sort of trouble?"

"The shop's gone."

Mrs. Bone felt her pulse jumping in her neck. "What do you mean," she said, very slowly, "'the shop's gone'?"

"It was Mr. Murphy's boys, first thing this morning, before the stalls were even out. They sent a rock through the front window."

Mrs. Bone shut her eyes. "That's just larks."

Archie frowned. "Larks? Mrs. Bone, that was a starting shot, clear as day."

"Where's the ledger?"

He patted his overcoat. "Got it. But we had to leave the rest."

"Leave?"

"We'd already boarded up the back windows. We knew something was coming—you could smell something fishy all week. We put locks on the back office, but they'll get through those, no trouble. Same with the rooms upstairs."

My hidey-hole, thought Mrs. Bone, heart tightening. She grabbed Archie with both hands, shook him. "You ought to be up there seeing them off, not down here talking to me."

He wrestled himself free. "You ought to be up there seeing them off *yourself*," he said hotly. "They wouldn't have come if you'd been at home. But everyone knows Mrs. Bone's absent without leave."

"Get down to the bloody factory, lock the gates, get a dozen men on patrol."

"A dozen men? All our bloody men are down *here*, Mrs.

Bone." He took a breath. "And they won't stay put if they know we're in trouble."

Mrs. Bone squared up to him. "Then you'd better hold your tongue, hadn't you?"

Archie let out a rattling sigh. "Men need their wages, Mrs. Bone."

"We'll pay 'em this week. We'll pay 'em tomorrow."

"We've got debts up to our eyeballs. We can't be paying anyone anything, not till *this* harebrained job's settled." He fixed her with a grim expression. "*If* it's settled. We might need to go to Mr. Murphy, call a truce, seek a loan. What's your fee on this job?"

She straightened. "Two-sevenths," she said, stoutly. "And I'm not asking Mr. Murphy for tuppence."

Archie was doing the calculations in his head. "Net or gross receipts?"

She paused.

"Mrs. Bone?"

"Net."

Archie shook his head. "That's not enough." He gave her a careful look. "You signed a contract?"

She wanted to box his ears. "I always sign a contract," she said, voice stiff.

"There's ways out of that."

She summoned her brother then. She did what Danny would have done. She rose up on the balls of her feet, pressed a fingernail to Archie's face. Scratched the surface of his skin, ever so gently. Traced his eye socket. Said, voice low, "Don't be telling me how to run my affairs, Archibald. And next time Mr. Murphy comes around, get out the guns."

She exerted a tiny bit of pressure, imagining his nerves and muscles tingling underneath.

"Mrs. Bone. If we don't have the cash, and our men get spooked…"

"Not a word more, Archie. To anyone. You got that?"

He nodded, silent.

"Then *off* you go."

She hurried back into the house, thoughts swirling, not liking this one bit. Two portions of the net receipts suddenly didn't seem like much money at all.

A crowd began to form outside the house. By tea-time, there was a crush on both sides of the street. Shepherd put men on the pavement to guard the front porch.

Miss de Vries did her rounds. She couldn't sit still: she had to watch the transformation. It was like watching the house grow a new skin. Huge boards had been set down across the garden, a vast and slippery deck. The supper tables had been placed under the cypress trees, branches strung with lights. *They could catch fire*, she thought, glancing upward. The whole place could go up in flames.

After mass she changed her clothes. "Alice can do it," she said when Iris came up to help her with her dress. Alice looked scared, but she nodded, and dressed Miss de Vries gently, barely touching her skin. Miss de Vries put on her deepest mourning, layering herself in serge and black taffeta, her waist strapped with black velveteen. Her veil was thickly embroidered and came all the way down to her waist. She felt the heat rising in her skin as she descended to the garden, white lilies in her hand.

"Dear Papa," she said so that the gaggle of newspapermen could hear her. "How we miss you."

She knelt outside the mausoleum, and laid the lilies at his grave. The flashbulbs burned the air, shocking the pigeons into flight. The picture would make the papers. She'd counted on that.

Virtue displayed, she went back upstairs and put on her tea gown.

"Good, Alice," she said, inspecting her buttons, her clasps. The girl hadn't missed a single one. "That will be all."

Alice gave her a long, pale stare—and went away.

The late-afternoon post was due. Miss de Vries was hungry for it, couldn't bear to wait any longer. Slowly, slowly, hour by hour, cards had begun landing in the front hall. First the Rutlands. Then Lady Tweedmouth. Lady Londonderry's circle was quick to follow. Mr. Menzies sent his thanks. So did Lady Fitzmaurice and Lord Athlumney. It was happening. Apparently, the Duchess of Montagu had done her best work. They were coming.

From her bedroom she could hear the distant, whispering sound of the girls rubbing the parquet, could smell the wafts of vinegar coming from the glass in the ballroom. She kept the door open. She would have ordered up a cigarette if she didn't fear fouling her breath.

There was a knock at the door. She heard William's voice, right on schedule. "Post, Madam."

"Come," she said.

He was tense—she knew that. There had been a shift in his mood in recent days. He'd been keeping his distance. She could always sense these things.

He laid the platter on the table.

She could see one of the envelopes bore a dark red crest. Her heart started beating faster.

Papa had always taught her the art of patience. Of suppressing one's whims, curtailing one's deepest desires.

I would make a fine ascetic, she thought dryly. *I would make a splendid nun.*

"William," she said. "You must tell me. *Was* there something between you and Mrs. King?"

The air tilted. His expression became guarded.

People said that William was very beautiful. They praised her for it, as if she had something to do with it, as if she'd won him at an auction. Perhaps she had. But his eyes had no effect on her.

"I only ask," she said, "for the sake of the household. I am accountable for its reputation."

He stood there, trussed up in cream silk and his afternoon livery, groomed and manicured. He flushed. "Do you mind, Madam, if I keep my counsel on that matter?"

"Yes," she said lightly, "I do." She stretched, reaching for the post tray. "You were spotted with Mrs. King in the garden the other day. *Not* a very sensible thing to do, given your recent indiscretions."

His voice was tight. "Spotted by whom, Madam?"

She flipped the envelopes over, picked up the smallest one first, the most uninteresting. "That's not a denial."

He said nothing.

She glanced up. "By me, if you must know." She took out the card:

So pleased to accept,
Yours &c,
Captain and Mrs. C. Fox-Willoughby.

"I'm forever looking out of the window and seeing things I oughtn't."

His eyes became blank, indecipherable. *Good*, she thought. *He's rattled.*

"Will that be all, Madam?"

"No, I don't think so."

Next envelope.

She smiled. "I have a proposition for you."

He said nothing. She approved of that, too. It was best to remain composed in the face of disagreeable things. "I may soon find myself," she said, "in need of a new household. You take my meaning?"

William's eyes narrowed, just a fraction. "I did hear that Lord Ashley is coming tonight, Madam."

"Too clever of you. Yes, he is. And it has come to my attention that Lord Ashley does not keep a butler on Brook Street. Rather a deficiency, to my mind. One I'd take care to correct."

He didn't say the obvious thing. He didn't ask, *What about Shepherd?* He had clearly guessed the answer. Shepherd belonged to her father, and the world was ticking on. It needed new people. New energy.

"I suppose I'd better think about it, Madam," he said.

She shook her head. "No, you'd better tell me this instant."

His face darkened. She saw it: his pride, wounded. It pleased her immensely. Men were like that: so easy to prick.

"What's the matter?" she said softly. "Have you made other plans?"

Footsteps. The door opened. One of the under-footmen peered in. "Madam," he said. "Lady Montagu has just arrived."

Miss de Vries felt a jolt. "So early?"

"Yes'm."

"Very well." She rose. "That'll be all, William."

He gave her another long look, pressed his lips together, as if making up his mind about something. "Very good, Madam," he said, and backed out of the room.

She laughed to herself. He'd come crawling back the following morning. She swiped the heaviest envelope from the pile before she went. She wanted to be alone, unobserved, when she opened it. She touched the wax seal with trembling hands. Tore open the paper.

…to advise you with pleasure that Her Royal Highness is minded to answer your request in the AFFIRMATIVE, and that you may expect the Equerry and her principal Lady of the Bedchamber to attend you at…

The light was falling gently through the window. *I am touched by grace*, she thought, heart leaping. *I am on my way to victory…*

Shepherd made a beeline for her in the front hall. "Her Grace simply *turned up*, Madam. We had no idea…"

Miss de Vries waved him back. "Never mind that now. Can we get her some early supper?"

"I'll bring up the consommé."

There was something entirely right about the air. Everything was scented with orchids. "Is Lord Ashley coming soon?"

"We haven't had word yet."

She wrinkled her nose, not liking the dry smell of Mr. Shepherd's breath. "Very well. Take me to Her Grace."

23

6:00 p.m.
Six hours to go

Hephzibah studied her costume in the looking glass. She'd encrusted herself in paste jewels, adorned herself with feathers. She wore gigantic hoop skirts, and a wig teased and curled several feet into the air. She looked as if she'd been painted pink, the punch-colored satin clinging to her skin. *I am a bird of paradise*, she told herself, hands shaking. *I am the sensation of my age.*

She heard that voice, hard and cold. "Your Grace. I hope something isn't the matter?"

Hephzibah took a breath, right from the gut, and whirled around. "I always arrive as early as *possible* for a ball," she said, her words ringing out across the dining room. "I love every *minute* of a party."

The ball wasn't due to begin until nine o'clock. The full robbery itself wouldn't commence until midnight, per the plan. By any measure, Hephzibah had arrived impossibly early. But she needed to be in position, ready to steer her first guests into the house. It meant holding character, without pause, for hours.

Hephzibah's hands began to shake even more, and she fanned herself violently to hide it.

Miss de Vries glanced at the clock, raised an eyebrow. But Mrs. King was right. This girl had been trained well. She was a consummate professional. "I am glad you are here, Your Grace," she said. "I owe you a great debt of gratitude for your attendance."

Hephzibah started. "Oh." And then, recovering, said, "Then you may kiss my hand, if you wish."

Miss de Vries smiled, a flat-eyed, reptilian expression. "And your costume is simply marvelous."

"I am the French queen," Hephzibah said. "A wayward, wanton she-devil, one who brings revolution and fire. I am death! I am destruction! I hope I keep my head on!" Hephzibah felt her wig bobbing. "I will station myself here, to ensure we can properly receive Her Royal Highness. I have received every indication that she will be with us this evening. Her detectives will be arriving at any moment."

Hope, a little flash of it, dawned upon Miss de Vries's face.

"Yes," she said, voice low. "I already received the message."

Hephzibah didn't know what to make of this. She supposed Alice Parker had gone to Miss de Vries first and told her mistress that the princess was coming.

"Excellent," she said. "Then follow me, my sweet hostess, and we shall meet them!"

❧

A group of men, fresh shaven and quick eyed, stood in a louche group at the edge of the hall. This was Mrs. Bone's second tranche of foot soldiers. Hephzibah glimpsed Mrs. Bone concealing herself behind a pillar.

"Your Grace," said the first man. "We're here to have a quick look around."

"*Splendid,*" said Hephzibah.

Miss de Vries scanned them, her expression unreadable. "You are members of the constabulary?" she said.

"Sure, we are," said the first with a lilt.

Miss de Vries's eyes narrowed. And then she looked at Hephzibah.

Hephzibah beamed, a rictus grin that made her cheeks ache. Sweat beaded its way down the back of her neck.

"By all means, gentlemen," said Miss de Vries.

They didn't waste a moment. They flowed out and around her, up the stairs and through the house. The place was flooded with Mrs. Bone's troops in minutes.

Mrs. Bone sighed with relief as her men slipped past. She'd sneaked away to make sure they arrived safely: she always liked to oversee a big delivery. And they didn't seem spooked. They were all working to plan. Everything was simply fine. *Finally,* she thought, *we're off.* All day she'd felt like a horse pawing the ground behind the gate. She needed to get on now, be in motion. She was clutching a pair of vases, her fingers twitching.

"What are *you* up to?"

Mrs. Bone jumped. Cook had appeared behind her.

Of course you're *here,* Mrs. Bone thought, *creeping and crawling around, scratching your arse and getting in my business when you should be looking after the young ones, protecting them, keeping them safe...*

"Hadn't you better stay below stairs, Cook?" muttered Mrs. Bone. "Isn't there something for you to be doing?"

"If *you're* allowed to sneak a peek upstairs, then I'm quite sure *I* am," said Cook in a comfortable whisper, leaning on the pillar, not hidden at all. "Would you look at that one—she's trussed up like a turkey, ain't she?"

Hephzibah was standing at a distance. They could hear Miss

de Vries as she said, "I'm afraid I shall have to take my leave of you, Your Grace. I've yet to change into my costume."

Hephzibah turned, in full view of Cook. "As you wish, Miss de Vries," Hephzibah said. "I shall gather my strength in expectation of the dancing."

"Oh," said Cook, an expulsion of breath. "I *know* her."

Mrs. Bone felt her chest tighten. She shoved her vase at Cook. "Give me a hand with this. It needs taking down to the courtyard."

It was always going to happen. There was always going to be one of the servants, one of the old guard, who'd remember that scullery girl. Mrs. Bone almost let out a bitter laugh. Of course it would be Cook. She stepped out from behind the pillar, staring desperately at the back of Hephzibah's head, trying to telegraph a message through the air: *Get out of the way, get yourself hidden, quick.*

Miss de Vries heard the words, and looked straight at Cook.

Mrs. Bone froze. She knew what should happen. What would happen, in any normal circumstance. Miss de Vries would frown, glance around for a footman, or Mr. Shepherd, someone who could clear Cook out of the way. But she didn't. She just studied Cook, curious, and then slowly—oh, dreadfully slowly—turned back to Hephzibah.

Hephzibah's gaze widened, sensing crisis. And later Mrs. Bone thought, if it weren't for Hephzibah's courage, her magnificence, if she weren't such a powdered and painted sort of heathen, they wouldn't have made it through the night at all.

Hephzibah tilted her head toward Miss de Vries and said, in a confidential whisper, "You would seem to have a rather eager sort of woman working for you there."

It felt to Mrs. Bone that the air screwed itself up. She forced the vase into Cook's hands, feeling light-headed. "Move," she whispered in her ear. "Now." She saw Hephzibah moving on, unconcerned. Felt Cook go rigid, color racing into her cheeks.

"Sorry, mum, sorry, m'lady," she said, dipping a curtsey, the vase slipping into her hands.

"And off we go," muttered Mrs. Bone, getting her by the elbow. "*Off* we go."

"I…"

"*Now*, Cook."

Yes, go, go, go, she thought, *run.* She dragged Cook away, feeling eyes on her back, ice racing after them through the floor.

Cook said, "I just thought…for a second. It was odd… I thought she looked like…"

Mrs. Bone banged open the door, got them out of the hall. "Here," she said, shoving another vase at Cook. "You'd best take that and all." Feints and distractions were the only things that ever worked on Cook.

Cook scowled at Mrs. Bone, said in a dangerous voice, "You want to watch your tongue. Who made you queen of the castle?"

"The Lord himself," Mrs. Bone said, although she was breathing fast, her heart hammering. "And you'll thank me later. But would you *listen*, Cook? There's something awful I need to tell you…"

24

Five hours to go

Alice had slipped out for her break, checking over her shoulder every second. Winnie met her on the corner of Mount Street, a purple veil covering her face. The slump in her shoulders made her look exhausted.

"I don't have long," Alice muttered. "Can we make it quick?"

Winnie lifted her veil, checking they weren't being observed. Her skin looked gray, her eyes worried. "Fine. Talk me through the plan. I need to make sure you're on top of the details."

Alice dug her hands in her pockets, looked nervily down the road. "It's like we said. I'll make a fuss. Kick up a hullabaloo, get Madam downstairs so Mrs. Bone's men can start on the third floor."

Winnie shook her head. "No. That's not in your nature. And Miss de Vries will *know* your nature. She'll have worked you out already."

Miss de Vries shimmered in Alice's mind. She yearned to get back to the costume, to correct it, to make the last adjustments.

She couldn't wait to fix it to Madam's skin. She tried to conceal all this with a shaky smile.

"I've only been working here five minutes," she said.

"You think that matters? Miss de Vries is an excellent judge of character. She'll know if you're behaving strangely."

Alice pictured Miss de Vries's eyes. Gray, changeable, penetrating her. *Was* she behaving strangely? All Alice's emotions felt entirely strange. "Fine. Tell me what to do."

"You tell me."

Alice began to sweat. She had been given the easiest job of any of them, and that made her even more anxious. *Watch Madam.* That's all she had to do. Just watch her. Nothing more than that. If she got this wrong, she'd have failed them all, ruined the whole enterprise. She felt sick.

"Alice?"

"I suppose I'd…feel badly about things. Being a snitch, I mean. I'd be hemming and hawing about whether to say anything."

"Good, that sounds right."

"I'd say, *I don't wish to cast any aspersions…*"

"Hm."

"All right, I'd say, *I don't want to cause any trouble.*"

"Better." Winnie squeezed her arm. "And you should look guilty. Go red, if you can."

"I can't make myself do that."

"Picture Miss de Vries trying to skin you alive."

Alice paled. That idea gave her a quick, hard kick of pain—something altogether unexpected. She released her breath. "Look here, Winnie, I don't see how I can do it. She's impossible to control. There's no earthly way I can get her downstairs."

Winnie gave her a nervy smile. "Certainly you can. You're doing marvelously. Now, once she's finished in the servants' hall, you *must* trail her. Stay on her all night—indoors, outdoors, everywhere. Mrs. Bone's men won't go near her rooms until the last possible moment, for safety's sake. The second we give you the word, bring her to us—wherever you are, no matter what's happening. *Make* her come."

Alice had been over and over this part of the plan. "I'll try."

"Alice, what's up? You look terribly pale."

Alice shook her head. "Nothing."

"I told you: Mrs. King's awfully pleased. She trusts you implicitly."

"Who does? Mrs. King, or Madam?"

Winnie frowned. "Mrs. King, naturally." Winnie paused. Then said, with care, "How are things, with Miss de Vries?"

Alice felt a wave of unease. "Fine. I mean, splendid." Was that right? "I hardly know. She's up at five. She spends her morning on her letters and the papers. Reads from two till teatime. Then it's dinner, bed. Not much to tell you, really." Alice laughed, a hollow sound.

Winnie studied her, silent. "She's a very captivating person," she said.

Alice looked away. "If you say so."

"I do say so. She can be terribly charming. Perceptive. Good sense of humor. You're new here, so you're easily susceptible to it."

"Oh, naturally, I'm everybody's chump." Alice's own anger caught her off guard. She swallowed it. "I don't mean to be rude," she added. "Perhaps it's…the strain."

"Then I suggest you take a deep breath," Winnie said seriously, looking down at her watch. "Because it's time for you to start singing, little bird."

Alice wished very badly then to say something, to unburden herself, to say, *Help me.* Miss de Vries wasn't *charming.* She wasn't *captivating.* She and Alice didn't speak as friends would; there wasn't any laughter or gossip between them. It was different, a sort of keen, fizzing fellowship.

The kind that made her heart flip over in her chest.

The Janes moved fast, carrying a huge tray, laden with a mountain of boxes concealed by a white cloth. The chauffeur was
wrestling with the hose. It was chugging hard, filling the courtyard with water. "What's all that, then?" he called, clocking
them.

"Cakes!" they shouted as they barreled into the house.

They weren't cakes. They were Parenty smoke machines, and
they rattled dreadfully in their boxes.

"I wish this *were* cake," murmured Jane-two as they slid carefully into the electric lift.

"Don't start, Moira," said Jane-one.

They glided upward, otherwise unobserved.

It was remarkably easy to make trouble. Mrs. Bone had spoken
a little word in Cook's ear—just as planned—and the kitchen
had descended into chaos, as predicted. Cook was at the center
of it all, wooden spoon aloft.

"You heard 'em!" she said, pointing at Mr. Shepherd.

Mr. Shepherd had paled, hands raised, trying to soothe the
uproar. "Ladies," he called, over their voices, "now is *not* the
moment for dissension in our ranks."

Cook lifted the wooden spoon higher. "We can't work safely in
these circumstances, Mr. Shepherd. *You've* got to make a decision."

Mrs. Bone was watching all this with an eyebrow cocked.
Easy, she thought. *You wind 'em up, give a few sharp twists, and
off they go…*

Cook saw her. "There she is. Ask her yourself, Mr. Shepherd!"

The butler turned to Mrs. Bone, perspiring. "Well? What is
this all about?"

"Tell him!" said Cook, hot with indignation, jabbing the spoon. "Tell him what you told me."

Mrs. Bone wrung her hands, made a hangdog face. "It's the princess's policemen, Mr. Shepherd. They've been ogling us ladies, giving us marks out of ten!" She cast a sideways look at Cook. "It was filthy!"

"You *see*, Mr. Shepherd," said Cook, triumphant, eyes shining. "They even eyed up the old *daily woman*."

Mr. Shepherd goggled at them.

"Oh, yes, Mr. Shepherd," said Mrs. Bone, jutting out her hip. "And they touched me. Here. And here."

Mr. Shepherd averted his eyes. "Now, ladies…"

Cook raised a finger. "It don't matter what you do. You can call 'em bobbies, you can send 'em up to Buckingham Palace, you can put 'em in uniform, you can give 'em any airs and graces you like. It don't make a difference, if they're *Irish*."

"Cook…"

"Irish, Mr. Shepherd! *Known* philanderers!"

William moved in, right behind Mrs. Bone, smelling delicious. "What's happening here, then?" he murmured.

Mrs. Bone wound her fingers together. "I dursn't say."

Cook pressed her hand to her heart, voice dropping to a harsh whisper. "And *what*, I'd like to know, are Their Majesties doing bringing *philanderers* into their house to guard their daughters? We might as well put them princesses up for sale to the highest bidder. They can call Maud *Bawd*."

"Cook, enough," said Mr. Shepherd, agonized.

"No Irish!" said Cook, and the spoon went back up in the air. *"No Irish!"*

"Enough," said Shepherd. His eye swept over the crowd, landed on William. "Show the princess's men out to the mews house. Get them some refreshments, with my compliments."

"Compliments, Mr. Shepherd?" gasped Cook.

"And tell them to stay out of the kitchen, and *well* out of the way of the ladies."

"Ooh, I think I'm getting a bruise on me hip, Cook," said Mrs. Bone. "They pinched me *that* hard."

"Go!" roared Mr. Shepherd.

Good. Mrs. Bone wanted a squadron of men near the back gate, ready to keep the road clear when required.

Cook turned, irate. "But what about Mr. Doggett, Mr. Shepherd? He won't want his mews house being overrun by—"

Mr. Shepherd flapped her away. "Mr. Doggett is helping up here. William, you sort things out."

"Yes, Mr. Shepherd."

"I want everyone *back* to work."

Cook gathered her bevy of girls around her. She crossed her arms, eyebrows knit together. "He didn't ought to do that," she said as Mr. Shepherd retreated. "Madam won't like the idea of strangers sitting out in the garden. They might unlock the back gate."

Mrs. Bone didn't care for this line of thinking in the least. "Oh, you're a regular detective, ain't you?" she said. "Got your magnifying glass in your apron, have you? Got your police whistle?"

The kitchen girls gaped at her. Mrs. Bone scowled at them. She'd be out of this house soon enough. She was very nearly done being a humble worm. "Ah, shut your mouths. And one of you can help me with these pails."

Cook aimed a frigid stare in her direction. "Help yourself," she said, and spun on her heel.

⟶

The Janes had started packing the guest suites on the second floor—and they assumed they had the place to themselves. Their laundry baskets were already heaving with ornaments. Their system was smooth. Lift one thing, wrap it with tissue paper, drop it in the basket. They were steady, focused. They didn't even hear the door open.

"Oi. What are you doing?"

The girls whipped round. There was a shadow on the wall.

Jane-two's stomach contracted as she saw one of the house-parlormaids in the doorway, eyes on stalks.

"Putting stuff in safekeeping," said Jane-one, without missing a beat. "Give us a hand, would you?"

"Mr. Shepherd said guest suites. Not *all* the suites."

"I'll tell him you slowed us down, if you like."

The house-parlormaid stiffened at that. "I've only got five minutes."

"That's all we need."

Jane-two wished she had her logbook with her. Risks made her want to sneeze.

"I don't like this," she murmured.

"*Hush,*" said Jane-one.

25

Four hours to go

The crowd outside was growing restless, waiting for the great folk to arrive. They were like moths to a flame: men after a day at work, dressed in their shirtsleeves, women brandishing paper fans. Didn't they have homes to go to? Lives to lead?

No more than I do, thought Winnie. She hadn't slept for two days. Her hands were shaking, yet she had planned this moment with precision, and in the end it went exactly as she had pictured. Her own imagination could spin things out of thin air. And it needed to. She had everything to prove. Hephzibah was avoiding her. No doubt Mrs. King was, too. The revelation about the girls had changed something between them, twisted the plan, given it new and dark dimensions.

Winnie was dressed as Isis, sister-wife of Osiris. She rode down Park Lane in procession, atop a gilt-licked pyramid mounted on wheels, accompanied by a huge quantity of Mrs. Bone's hired men, who were done up in grease paint and the tunics Winnie had sewn for them. They were preceded by two lines of camels, hired from Mr. Sanger's circus, restless and golden, drawn by two dozen men in overalls with ropes looped to their waists. The other men carried drums, resounding with each step. Above it all, Winnie stood in white sequins, shimmering, her hands outstretched.

The crowd gasped, delighted. The traffic ground to a halt in every direction.

Winnie closed her eyes. She could feel sweat on her brow, but she didn't dare touch her paint. The crowd applauded her, whooping. Winnie concentrated all her energies on being a queen. It wasn't very easy to stay upright. The pyramid rumbled and rattled beneath her. She willed herself, *Don't fall, don't fall.* The structure was hollow inside, full of shelves and compartments. And more men, not seen: the relief party. She pictured them clutching the handles, wincing at every jolt in the road.

The other entertainments came tripping along behind her: jugglers and fire-eaters and dancing-girls with hoops. Men with accordions, angels carrying bells. The whole thing was splendid and discordant, as loud and extravagant as they could get it.

Her throat tightened as she finally descended from the pyramid.

"Here," she whispered, collaring a man in a white tunic. "Can you take a message to Mrs. King for me?"

"About what?"

"Just say, *Something's up with the little bird.*"

"She'll understand?"

"Just tell her." Winnie hadn't liked Alice's expression earlier. There was something working in the girl's mind, something Winnie couldn't easily interpret. It sounded the alarm in Winnie's head. She needed a second opinion.

Mrs. Bone's man looked at her in disapproval. "You realize you're not *really* a queen?"

She ignored that. The men guarded her across the pavement, under the porch, through the gigantic front door. She had known she would falter when she smelled the inside of the house again. Wax on wood. Vinegar on glass. Those scents lingered over something vast and rotten underneath.

In you go, she told herself, and brought her warriors into the house with her.

─◆─

The bell board was painted a dark shade of forest green, surmounted with gleaming brass bells, gilded labels naming the rooms: Mr. de Vries's Study. Mr. de Vries's Bathroom. The Boiserie. The Dining Room. The Oval Drawing Room. The Ballroom.

One of the bells set up a furious ringing.

"Alice?" a voice called. "Madam's ready for you."

Alice shot another glance at the bell board. She could see the brass shimmering, the clapper still vibrating.

Miss de Vries's Dressing Room.

"Coming," Alice said, smoothing her apron.

─◆─

Miss de Vries met Mr. Lockwood in Papa's bathroom. She expected results, and she intended to get them. She had already emerged from the water, wrapped herself up, was entirely decent. But her skin was still damp and flushed, and his eyebrows went up when he saw her.

"In here, Miss de Vries?" he said. "Really?"

The walls were the darkest oak, rubbed to an impossible shine, inlaid with a hundred mirrors and grotesque wood carvings. He eyed them now, wrinkling his nose at the nudes, the ivory statues, the phallic water jugs.

She pulled her shawl over her shoulders. "I wanted to speak in private. Have you finished the negotiations?"

He sighed. "Lady Ashley's people are reviewing the finer points of the jointure."

"They were doing that three days ago."

"And they may well be doing it three days hence, Miss de Vries. Or longer."

Miss de Vries emptied the water jug, watching the water explode against the sides of the sink. "I want this business concluded tonight."

Lockwood set his mouth in a grim line. "So do we all. But these matters take time."

Miss de Vries turned, faced him straight on. "I need surety, Mr. Lockwood," she said. "I need to make progress. I can't wait forever."

"You can wait three days."

"Perhaps I can, but I won't. Give them till midnight, or I'm closing the negotiations."

Lockwood closed his eyes. "You don't mean that."

She smiled. "No, I don't mean that. But you'll tell them I do." She adjusted her mantle.

"I shall need a sweetener if I'm to turn the screws."

"No sweeteners. You've made far too many concessions already."

He tilted his head. "To Lady Ashley, perhaps. But you're seeking a different quarry. Lord Ashley has his own particular weak spots."

Miss de Vries rubbed her fist against the mirrored glass, clearing the steam, examining herself. "Then press them. Press any one you like."

"It's not so much about pressing." Lockwood's voice was soft. "It's more about...*presenting*." Lockwood smiled, eyes dead and unreadable. She felt a tingle in her skin.

"You mean a gift."

"Yes."

It had been coming for days. She'd felt Ashley hovering

around it when he came for tea, and Lockwood had picked it up at once, his little lizard tongue flickering all over it. Tasting it for salty bits, for blood.

"I see," she said.

"In normal circumstances I'd discuss this with your dear papa, but…"

She looked at him, silent.

He raised an eyebrow. "Miss de Vries?"

"Yes?" Her skin was hot, getting hotter. She'd never come this close to the business before. Never all the way to the brink.

He held her gaze. "Have you a name in mind?"

Alice took the stairs, not the lift. The hall was filling with early guests, the least important people, and the house churned and eddied beneath her. The marble glimmered as she passed, and in it she saw her reflection, a nervy little ghost hurrying upstairs.

I could run away, she thought. *I could get on a steamer. I could jump off a bridge, for that matter.*

Pull yourself together, she told herself.

Miss de Vries was already undressing, unpeeling her robe, freeing her hair. She looked pink, vulnerable in the lamplight. It twisted Alice's heart.

"Yes?" Miss de Vries said, voice tense.

"It's me, Madam," said Alice, trying to keep steady. "I've come to sew you into your costume."

Madam was nimble, like a wolf. She came across the room, hard, quick steps, arms out. "Unbutton me," she said. "How swiftly can you do it?"

Her face was gleaming, rubbed with creams, yesterday's fatigue smoothed away. Alice began unfastening Miss de Vries's gown, her fingers fumbling.

"Hurry."

"I have to be careful," Alice said, and then added, "Madam."

Miss de Vries wriggled out of Alice's hands, vanished behind the screen, revealing a flash of whalebone corsetry as she went.

"Come and help," she said, and crooked a finger, beckoning.

The bird women sat on benches in the corner of the park, scattering bits of stale bread on the ground. Mrs. King sat with them, hat tilted over her eyes, throwing her own scraps to the pigeons. She listened to the old women's chatter, secretive and girlish, and felt the evening thickening with heat. She waited there, keeping the de Vries residence in the corner of her eye, gathering her strength for the night ahead.

Big motors came rolling around the corner of Park Lane. She counted the minutes in her head, then clapped her fingers at the birds. They rose into the air, up and away, flying around in a circle. That's what she'd wanted. To feel her own power. To be a magician.

The birds returned, settled, and she got up from the bench. She began to advance, feeling her blood pumping, crossing the sultry expanse of the park.

Mrs. King faced the house, reckoning with it. Miss de Vries's bedroom suite was above the winter garden. It had a big picture window, wreathed in muslins, blurring the figures within. Alice would be there now, doing exactly what was expected of her. Everything was ticking along beautifully. It couldn't fail.

Motors and carriages clogged the street all the way to Hyde Park Corner in one direction, and up to Oxford Street in the other. Mrs. King could hear the shrill cry of a constable's whistle. There were people moving, swarming toward the house. Winnie's golden pyramid remained gleaming, tremendous, abandoned in the middle of the road, a magnificent obstacle to all and sundry.

The tradesmen's door to the de Vries residence was opening

and closing every thirty seconds. Mrs. King joined a troupe of waiters, their voices raised in laughter, jackets pristine. She passed with them through the door, entirely unnoticed.

✦

Alice brought out the dress, carefully folded.

Miss de Vries rose from her couch, hands outstretched. "Marvelous," she said softly, running a finger down its crusted edges. She looked up at Alice, frowned. "It's better than I expected."

Alice felt her heart expanding. She kept her eyes down. "It's not so hard when you've got a pattern," she said, trying to sound offhand.

"But you didn't have a pattern," Miss de Vries said.

Alice blushed. "No."

Miss de Vries studied her for a moment. Something passed between them through the air, something unspoken, caught just underneath a breath. Then Miss de Vries said, "All right. Help me in."

The rush and movement of the fabric. Pale flesh. The air was tight here, lamps burning low. Miss de Vries clutched Alice's shoulder for balance. They were playing drums outside, and the beat matched Alice's pulse.

"Get this buckle, would you?"

"Yes, Madam."

She fixed it. Miss de Vries's breathing had quickened. It must have been the anticipation, the excitement, the promise of the night to come.

"Alice," she said. There was something tight in her tone, as if she were readying herself to ask something, give an order.

Now was the moment. Alice's mouth was dry. She spoke before Miss de Vries could.

"Madam," she said, "there's something I need to tell you…"

26

Miss de Vries moved fast, chains clinking lightly as she held her headdress in place. Alice hurried after her, watching how the dress moved. It had an armored structure around the waist, and yet it still flowed with a ferocious sort of grace. "I wasn't sure whether to say anything, Madam. But, knowing how many people will be here tonight, I thought perhaps it was best…" Winnie would have approved of that, she thought, feeling sick. She was following the plan perfectly. But it made her feel as if her rib cage were being squeezed. Her nerves were dancing in her skin.

Miss de Vries's tone was hard. "I'll be the judge of that." She was walking so quickly, faster than Alice could have expected, hurtling out of the room and toward the stairs.

When Alice had told her, Miss de Vries had clenched her hands, digging her nails into her palms, as if to punish herself. As if she *expected* treachery in her household, as if she'd been waiting for it all along. She'd hastened to her dressing table,

yanking open the drawers, rummaging inside, searching, real-
izing what was missing.

She'd turned to Alice, face pale. "You're right. It's gone."

She was angry, but the anger was operating somewhere deeper
than Alice had seen before, something right down at the base of
the bone. She could hear it in the roughness of Miss de Vries's
voice. "I cannot stand it," she said. "Being *preyed* on like this."

Alice said, feeling a prickling in her spine, "I should go and
fetch Mr. Shepherd, Madam. Really, I should have gone to him
first…"

It was the right move to make.

"Shepherd is a fool. He won't fix a thing. These are my *personal possessions*." She waved Alice away. "I'm going down to the
servants' hall myself."

They'd counted on this. They needed her downstairs, dragging the household with her, holding everyone there while the
attic doors were softly opened, and Mrs. Bone's men began trickling downstairs. They hastened toward the lift, and Alice looked
over Miss de Vries's shoulder. Stifling a gasp, she spotted the
Janes on a pair of stepladders in one of the adjoining bedrooms.
The door must have swung open. They were right on their
tiptoes, lifting the huge, brocade drapes clean from their rails.

"I'd best come down with you, Madam," Alice said, voice rising. "To back you up." She squeezed herself into the lift, blocking the Janes from view. "Down we go," she said, breath tight,
punching the button.

⤙

Later, Mrs. Bone would remember the moment, the fear and
the thrill, when her niece came below stairs.

She was sideswiping a bread roll, stuffing it in her mouth,
trying to fill her belly before someone shoved another mop and

bucket in her direction. Then she felt it, the faintest tremor over-head. Footsteps, quick ones.

Here we go, she thought. *It's happening.*

She rubbed her fist over her mouth, wiping away the crumbs. Swallowed. Cook was at the stove, closely encircled by her girls. The other servants were fighting to get past one another, im-peded by the constant crush. There was a terrific hullabaloo, a medley of banging tins, shouts, wild bursts of laughter, a good deal of it aided and abetted by her own men in their costumes.

Mrs. Bone took a breath, flexed her fingers, kept her eyes straight ahead.

It was a voice at the door that broke through the din. Low, furious. "Mr. *Shepherd.*"

He was on the other side of the kitchen, but he turned at once—everyone did. The room slowed as Miss de Vries swept in.

There was a terrible falling-away of noise as Madam came to a standstill, gleaming with jet ornaments, bedecked in black with a gigantic beaded headdress, wearing no sort of mourning they'd ever seen on a lady before.

It was Mr. Shepherd who spoke first, who had to speak. "Madam?" he said, voice going up a note.

Miss de Vries snapped her fingers for someone. "Alice. Who was it?"

And there was young Alice, creeping out from Madam's shadow. She looked gray in the face. *Good girl,* thought Mrs. Bone. It was all coming together.

"Mrs. Bone," said Alice, in an undertone.

"Mrs. Bone," Miss de Vries repeated. "Where are you?"

You wouldn't credit it, Mrs. Bone thought. *Danny's little girl hav-ing a voice like that. Where did it come from, in such a laced-up body?*

"Here, mum," Mrs. Bone said, raising her hand.

She felt like the Lord himself, the way the crowd parted for her. She ignored the trembling in her hand, looked straight into

Miss de Vries's eyes. They were swampy, impossible to read. Mrs. Bone wondered, *Do mine look like that?*

"Anything the matter?" she said, bright as a button.

It was about to begin. Mrs. King watched the guests swarming in.

They came in crocodile formation, leaving their opera cloaks and mantles and shawls behind in their motors. They entered with flushed faces, feasting their eyes on the house and on each other. They wore ruffs, headdresses, sleeves the size of hot-air balloons, hoopskirts, powdered wigs, boots with curled toes—really, London knew how to do a costumed ball. In several cases they were already three sheets to the wind. *Good,* thought Mrs. King.

She had changed into her own costume in a tent in the garden, alongside the other entertainments. A Roman tunic-dress of white cotton, the waist armored and plated in gold, a scarlet cloak thrown over the shoulders. White patent leather boots, gold buckles, toes plated with metal. She echoed when she moved. Mr. Whitman himself had dressed her.

"Can you breathe?" he murmured as he fastened her mask. It was made of copper, light and beveled, the metal warm against her skin.

"Perfectly," she told him. She didn't need to look at herself in the glass. She buttoned her gloves, hearing the crack of new leather.

"Our fine empress," Mr. Whitman said, and he sent her on her way.

The orchestra had taken up position in the ballroom, playing a waltz at full tilt. Buglers and trumpeters stood at the top of the stairs, blasting an intermittent tattoo every time a clutch of guests reached the saloon floor. The band in the street pounded their drums, sounding cowbells and gongs for good measure, and the whole thing made Mrs. King's head ache. *Even better,* she thought.

The air was perfumed so thickly with orchids that the scent got stuck in the back of her throat. The gigantic wall of red peonies rose all the way up the stairs.

"Mrs. King?" One of the waiters they'd hired had glided up to her, eyes averted.

"Yes?"

"Message for you, from one of the ladies."

"Go on."

"She says, 'You've got something up your little bird.'"

"I beg your pardon?"

"That's the message, Mrs. King."

She ignored it: she'd spotted William by the ballroom doors, as straight-backed as a Beefeater, brushed and shimmering in white tie and tails. His eyes were blank. *How do we do it?* Mrs. King wondered. It almost bewildered her. The bowing and scraping and the chores that made mincemeat of your dignity: carrying trays, answering call bells. You unraveled yourself, polishing butter knives, waiting for something to happen to your life. It had felt like a stomach punch when she turned thirty-five. *I'm never, never, ever going backward,* she told herself. She would be like a shark: forward motion or death, nothing else.

"Nice stockings," she said, sidling up to William.

His eyes widened. She wondered if he would struggle to recognize her voice, muffled behind her mask, but he knew her at once. He controlled his expression, but his tone betrayed his astonishment. "Dinah?" he said.

"Don't make a fuss," she murmured, standing close. She could feel the heat of him, and she knew he could feel hers.

"What are you *doing* here?"

"I might need the tiniest little favor from you tonight."

"*You* might need... Dinah, what on *earth?*"

She kept her face on the crowd, her body as motionless as a Roman soldier. "Ask me no questions—I'll tell you no lies."

Will was silent, stony faced.

Then he said, voice even lower, "I might be getting out. Madam's offered me a new job."

Mrs. King felt the cut. She said coolly, "That doesn't sound like getting out to me."

"Getting out of Park Lane, I mean. Going with her to her new household."

"Her new what?"

"Her *married* household."

Mrs. King took a breath. "I see." She couldn't keep the bitterness from her voice.

"And what do you mean, 'favor'?" said William with a slight frown.

"What?"

"You said you need a favor." He half turned to her. She could smell him: tar soap on his neck, the rough scent of wax. "What is it?"

Mrs. King had longed to be free. At liberty to put things straight, to order and corral and bend the world. To make corrections where corrections were required. It made her feel vast and enormous inside, as if her soul were built like a cathedral: a great and mighty project, reaching for the divine. To risk that now would be impossible.

"Never mind," she said. "You've got other things on your mind."

She turned and left. She didn't touch him, although she yearned for it. He said something, but she didn't wait. She didn't want to hear.

Mrs. King took the *grand escalier* downstairs, slicing through the crowd in sleek white and gold. The other women were dressed as Eleanor of Aquitaine, Marguerite de Valois, Mary Queen of Scots—beruffed, beribboned, trussed up in lace. There was even an extraordinarily elderly lady who'd come as the great Palmyrene queen, Zenobia herself, stitched from head to toe in green velvet, bearing a gigantic headdress that looked set to snap her neck. She was held up by two men in seal-gray cloaks. *Seal gray*, thought Mrs. King. It reminded her of men visiting the mews house, men paying calls on girls. It made her clench her fists.

But there was one person there in plain dress. She saw the flash of silvery hair, a gentleman in dark tails, forging his own path through the crowd.

Just as she had predicted.

She was quicker than he was. She met him at the bottom of the stairs, putting a gloved hand out to bar his way. Lawyers never liked to be impeded. They were forever pressing on, counting minutes, charging hours. "Mr. Lockwood," she said.

She saw him transition out of his private thoughts, arrange his public face. It was so much easier to watch people, to really watch them, when they couldn't assess your own expression in return.

"To whom do I owe the pleasure?" he said with a perfect and wolfish smile.

She didn't play with him. "Mrs. King."

The manners fell away. They simply dissolved. Something hard and brutal entered his face. "Mrs. *King*," he said, taking in her gloves, her tunic. His lip curled. Perhaps he remembered her choosing the name. She'd done it on his instructions. "Good heavens."

She didn't move. He glanced up the stairs, judging the crush. Down here the noise was growing into a roar, hundreds of people staggering through the porch and entering the front hall. She knew what he was thinking: what can people see, what can people hear, what reason will they construct for this discussion, when will the risks show themselves? She rattled through a similar list herself, every moment.

He smiled, eyes running over her mask. "Miss de Vries mentioned to me that you had made an unwelcome visit. She charged me to keep an eye out for you. I must confess I thought she was overreacting."

"Foolish of you," said Mrs. King. "For here I am. You've caught me."

She was Jonah inside the whale. She was stepping right into the heart of the matter.

He snapped his fingers, and two younger men hurried over. They were dressed as dominoes. Clerks, she guessed, his own little entourage. Evidently, Lockwood liked having his own people in the house, too. "Accompany us to the library," he said to them. "And guard the door."

They gawked at Mrs. King. Then they saw Mr. Lockwood's hand touch her elbow, and they squared up.

"I think we should have a private discussion," Lockwood said.

"I agree," she replied, lifting her mask.

"May I?" he said. He offered his arm. He wasn't her equal—he would never countenance that notion—but he could pretend to be civil.

"No," she said, and they walked upstairs, men at her back—trapped, as intended.

27

Three hours to go

The ball had begun. But the lady of the house was still below stairs, just where they wanted her. Mrs. Bone was being held in the butler's pantry, and the chauffeur barred the door. Mrs. King had been very clear about this. *Let them interrogate you as long as they want. We need them down in the servants' hall, so the men can pack up the old nurseries.* Mrs. Bone pictured rocking horses creaking as they were lifted onto runners, gigantic dolls blinking as they were turned upside down. The nursery was a forlorn sort of place, preserved in aspic: too big, too bleached. The wallpaper was metal colored, a bleak and relentless pattern. The whole place had given Mrs. Bone the shivers. She was glad it was being packed away.

"Alice, tell Mr. Shepherd what you told me," Miss de Vries said, her face glinting in the lamplight.

Alice kept things brief. "I saw her," she said, pointing at Mrs. Bone, "selling silver spoons to a man in the street. She had them hidden in her apron."

So far so good. Mrs. Bone tutted loudly. "I was cleaning them."

"No, she was not," said Alice.

Mrs. Bone shook her fist, per her stage directions. "Rot!"

"Madam, I had no idea," began Mr. Shepherd.

"That's what's troubling me, Shepherd."

Mr. Shepherd went very red in the face then. He gripped Mrs. Bone by the shoulder. His fingers felt surprisingly dense. "Tell us at once," he said, and his breath smelled, soured by wine. "Are you a thief?"

She wrenched herself away. "Yes, I helped myself to a fork or two," she said. "What of it?"

Silence, but for Mr. Shepherd's intake of breath.

"There's plenty of cutlery going spare. *She* sits upstairs and has dinner by herself every night—" Mrs. Bone gestured at Miss de Vries, whose eyes were like steel "—using one little cheese knife, one little butter knife, and don't even get me *started* on the spoons. And yet here we are, counting 'em, polishing 'em like our lives depend on it. I took a couple to make something *useful* out of 'em. Who cares?"

"Someone call for the constable," Mr. Shepherd exclaimed, "to apprehend this wicked woman."

Wicked? Mrs. Bone thought, staring at him. I'm *not the wicked one.*

Shepherd knew about the girls. He had to know. He was the one with the keys. Mrs. Bone pictured him, disappearing into the bowels of the house at night, concealing his movements. Bowing to a gentleman slipping through the garden door. Pocketing a little tip for himself.

Wicked, Mrs. Bone thought again, mind hardening.

They'd planned for Mrs. Bone to grow wild with fear, to distract them all with hysterics. But when it came to it, she did the more satisfying thing. She locked her hand into a fist, and she punched Mr. Shepherd straight in the mouth. Knuckles met bone. Hot, clean justice.

"Aaah," he cried, reeling back.

A gasp went up from the servants watching at the open doorway.

"Get— Call the constable—" Mr. Shepherd's voice was muffled, hand pressed to his lip. He had blood on his fingers.

Alice spoke quickly, as rehearsed. "A constable? With the princess on her way to the house, and a pack of detectives sitting out in the yard? Are you mad? But look here…" Alice fished something out of her pocket. "I found *this* in her room."

She held up a silver watch, sparkling dimly in the light. Mrs. Bone recognized it by those narrow letters engraved on the underside: WdV.

Miss de Vries showed immense restraint. She didn't reach for the watch. But something crossed her face. Something hard and furious.

"Alice is right," she said calmly.

The others stilled.

"Don't send for the constable until tomorrow morning. We can't afford any disturbances tonight. Take this woman upstairs and lock her in her room. And go and wash your face, Shepherd. You look a fright." Miss de Vries turned to Mrs. Bone, expression rigid. "You might have thought you could do what you like here," she said in a deadly voice, "but you can't."

Mrs. Bone was transfixed. Anger was coming off that girl in waves, but it was controlled, harnessed. She'd only lost a watch. An old silver watch, and a couple of teaspoons. Her fury was all out of proportion.

But she understood it entirely. She pictured Mr. Murphy's men finding their way into her hidey-hole, rifling through her drawers, sniffing her peach-colored tea gown. It made her feel unsteady. The same would happen to this house: it would be carved up, sliced into bits, profits *shared*. Extracted from its current ownership. Taken out of the family.

It prickled at her. A tiny, wicked thought. This house belonged to O'Flynns. It belonged to her blood. The notion had been circling all day at the back of her mind. It had been there for weeks, if she was honest about it. It was her loan that bought Danny his ticket to Cape Colony, his ticket to his new life. It was *her* cash, earned from her own jobs, that got him going in the first place. Just like it was *her* cash that had got this job on the move. *My carts*, she thought. *My vans. My men. My loans. My Daimler. My* Janes.

Lucky sevens. Two equal portions. Just two. It made her teeth ache. It made her feel like she'd been punched in the face. Like Mrs. King was laughing at her, curls gleaming, eyes dancing...

Mrs. Bone knew what envy felt like. She recognized the low burn, the rage that existed deep in her gut. It was far too easy to get lost in it. She forced her mind to come back to the room. Miss de Vries was gathering her skirts, her costume shimmering darkly. She sent her voice down the hall so that all the servants would hear her.

"Don't ever touch my things," she said.

Hephzibah didn't enjoy parties. Never had. They gave her the willies. But she knew she'd never be at a ball like this again. She held on to her wig with one hand. Her skirts ballooned around her, taking up space, sweeping the floor. People stared.

"I know," she said, raising her glass. "I look *marvelous*."

Naturally she had business to take care of. Once the ball was underway, she'd begun surreptitiously gathering her actresses, sending them circling around the ballroom, knocking over drinks, upsetting supper plates, causing confusion. "Movement," Winnie had said when they were going over the program for the evening. "We must have constant and *immediate* movement. We need people away from the windows, eyes on the entertainment. We've got ropes going up the eastern side of the house. We can't have anyone spotting that."

"I've got it," Hephzibah had said. Winnie had made her apologies half a dozen times, but Hephzibah still wouldn't meet her eye. "Don't fuss."

There was no delay to the dancing, no wallflowers spoiling the mood: Hephzibah's actresses saw to that.

I might join in, Hephzibah thought, a splendid fog descending over her vision. She saw her men leading women to the ballroom floor, music swelling. They looked like sea anemones, billowing into each other's arms, pulsing. It was a waltz, a fast one. It made the blood start pumping in the veins.

I need more champagne, she decided. *And more jelly.*

She spied a boy gawking at her from the corner of the room. A lamp-trimmer, she assumed, or an urchin kept for running errands. He had a pointed, weaselly face, and he was keeping himself carefully out of view from the other servants. In the normal course of events, Hephzibah might have flicked him half a crown for trying his luck upstairs. But this wasn't the time for unkempt boys to be scuttling around the house. They'd made no allowances in the plan for that. And she didn't like the way he was staring at her.

One of Hephzibah's actresses came whirling past, a profusion of taffeta and silks. "*Goodness* gracious!" she cried, throwing her champagne glass to the floor, where it shattered in all directions. "Enough chaos for you, dear?" she muttered to Hephzibah as the waiters hurried to clean it up, the dancers surging around them.

The boy's eyes narrowed. *Have I been rumbled?* Hephzibah wondered, with a prickling of alarm.

"Boy!" she exclaimed, sidestepping the actress. "Fetch me a drink!"

Perhaps her voice came out a little louder than she'd intended. An under-footman or a waiter glided up, tray in hand. "Madam," he said, blocking her path.

She dodged. "That little boy can fetch it for me," she said. "He needs teaching a lesson. He made a face at me. He is a cheeky rodent."

I never, mouthed the boy.

"Tell him…tell him to go down to the kitchen and fetch me a…cold flannel!"

Oh, I do feel a little dizzy, she thought. Perhaps it was the heat. Or the champagne. Surely she could leave her actresses to manage things, just for a moment. "Here, help me," she said, lurching forward, grabbing the boy by his shoulder. He wriggled furiously underneath her. "Get me to a chair."

The footmen had glanced at each other, then at the crowd. "Help Her Grace into the Boiserie," one said to the boy. "I'll bring her a glass of water."

It was very hard keeping a hold on these people. They moved so quickly, in such unexpected directions, sidling around the edge of rooms. She looked for her beautiful waltzing troublemakers. But they were gone, sucked into the heat and noise of the ballroom.

"Don't move a muscle," she said to the boy. "Don't even think about leaving me unattended." *I need to decide what to do with you*, she thought.

He squirmed, nearly spitting. "Mr. Shepherd," he called.

Hephzibah felt her body go on alert.

She hadn't seen him downstairs. The footmen had opened the front door, seated her, escorted her to the dining room, brought her wine. Not Shepherd. She'd been braced for him. It had to happen—she had to see him; it was inevitable. *It was like pulling a tooth*, she told herself. A necessary and shocking pain that would subside as quickly as it came. That was what she wanted. Something sharp and clean.

But he hadn't appeared. She began to hope, to believe, that he wouldn't. This was an enormous house, full of hundreds of people. It was possible that they might never cross paths again.

The last time she'd gone to see Mr. Shepherd, she'd nearly slipped on the parquet. Not for nothing did she hate that floor. Eighteen years ago, and she'd been hurrying to the stairs, skidding, nearly falling on her face. She couldn't stand the smell of beeswax, to this day.

Shepherd had done what he always did. He took his report. He had a way of asking questions without using the necessary words. It didn't make it any less revolting. It made it worse, as if the discussion were being bleached. She recalled the scratch of his pencil, the feeling of nausea, as if someone were shoving their fingers down her throat.

She left Park Lane that night. The scullery maid called Dolly Brown gobbled herself up. She dissolved, disappeared. She would never come back.

Sometimes, when things were very painful, it was best to draw back. Hephzibah did that now. She didn't let go of the lamp-boy, but she leaned away from the door. She could see Shepherd on the other side of it.

Evidently, he had been hurrying in the other direction, and he didn't look at all pleased to be waylaid. He peered across the room, spotting her. Hephzibah heard him speaking to the footman, sotto voce, flustered. "Who is…?"

"Hephzibah Grandcourt," she said, standing, facing him fully. "That is my name."

The early hours of a ball were a febrile, anxious affair. Things could swing in two directions. Dull or magnificent. There was nothing in between. When Winnie entered the house, leaving her pyramid glittering in the road, she made for the garden, where the most eye-catching entertainments would be held. She stepped nervously onto her raft, balancing precariously, the hosepipes chugging as they flooded the courtyard that had been turned into the Nile. She could see her own painted reflection in the scabbards and spears of the other entertainers. The court-yard walls glittered with lights.

"Miss de Vries," someone called from the terrace. "*You* must be the first to cross the Nile."

Applause went up, a delighted crowd appearing at the top of the steps. The barges, which were rafts joined up with painted and gilded chairs, bobbed merrily on the surface. There was a dank smell to the air: too much tepid water in a confined space.

"If I must," said Miss de Vries, emerging from the crowd. She looked pale but calm, Queen Cleopatra from head to toe, corseted and decked in black crepe, her jet ornaments swinging danger-ously as she moved.

"I am Isis," Winnie said, throat dry, paddling the raft toward the steps.

She didn't like being near Miss de Vries. Never had. She learned that lesson on her last day in the house. Her mistress was then just twenty. She still had some plumpness in her cheeks then. She hadn't yet begun to reduce, to slough off her excess, to drain her body of blood. But her eyes were as old as the hills, just like her father's. Maids came and went, and it made Win-nie feel sick. They hadn't been going off and getting shop work, like Mr. Shepherd said.

"Doesn't it seem odd to you, Madam?" she had said when she mentioned it.

Miss de Vries had stared at her, face blank. She didn't even speak. She didn't say, *I've no notion what you mean.* Did she know or not? There was some silent, unsayable, unseeable thing in this house—and the utter wrongness of it made Winnie's skin crawl.

The barge trembled now upon the water. Miss de Vries turned, not recognizing Winnie, seeing only the painted face, the sapphire gems, the white sequins.

"Get ready," said Winnie as Isis, and extended a hand. "I have come to deliver you to your death."

But Miss de Vries took another hand, stepped onto a barge of her own. "Very nice," she said vaguely, and floated away.

Cheers went up, and the waves lapped sorrowfully at the edge of Winnie's boat. *Oh, I shall empty this house*, she thought. *I shall strip the meat right down to the bones.*

28

Two hours to go

Alice checked the clock. She'd checked it several times already, watching the minute hand inching forward. Time to ready Mrs. Bone's men in the mews yard. They'd need to be opening the back gates soon.

She picked her way through the boxes in the dressing room. Fresh wares had been delivered that morning. Bolts of white satin, stretches of Honiton lace. Linens, and velvet gowns, jet-crusted parasols. Madam was already assembling her trousseau, in expectation of her engagement. Alice pictured herself holding one of the parasols, skin bronzed by the sun. Dressed in white lawn, holding a purse full of money. A lady's companion, far from England, entirely sheltered by her mistress. Living in a fine suite, with every luxury, near Madam herself. Madam, with her edges softened, her drapery growing more gentle, more tractable, by the day.

Stop it, Alice told herself. Her thoughts were developing dangerous, sinuous lines.

She went downstairs, trying to keep a steady pace. She knew exactly what she had to do. Winnie had drilled it into her. The back stairs were frenzied, men running up and down from the garden with trays from the kitchens. *The mews*, she reminded herself. *Go to the mews.*

She slipped out through the garden door, making sure she hadn't been observed. It felt cooler out there, on the other side of the wall. The city rumbled in the distance. She peered down the lane. Out there, around the corner, poised and waiting, were a hundred van drivers ready to descend upon the house and begin the almighty clearance.

A figure moved at the end of the lane. Someone was watching her from the shallow arch in the middle of the lane. He separated himself from the shadows, a sliver of darkness.

A man.

One of the entertainers, a woman in a silver dress, hoisted on painted stilts, peered down at Winnie. They were on the terrace, the house looming behind them. Winnie was surveying the crowd, eyes peeled for any disturbances, any problems. There were none. It made her heart thrum with excitement. "That's good paint," the woman said, reaching down and touching Winnie's forehead.

Winnie dodged. "Thanks."

She was keeping her back to the wall. Miss de Vries moved from guest to guest, managing things perfectly. Shaking hands, exchanging a whisper, squeezing an arm, admiring a gown. One man stayed on her tail.

"Don't stare—you'll make them blush," said the woman on stilts.

"Pardon?"

"At *those* two. The lovebirds." Stilts pointed at Miss de Vries. "We've got a bet on it. A proposal, under the fireworks, before the night is over."

Winnie squinted, studying the young man accompanying Miss de Vries. He'd dressed as Charles the First, with a wide-brimmed hat adorned with feathers. He had a dangerous-looking jaw. A bored, laconic expression.

"Lord Ashley, of course," said Stilts, confidentially. "Busy Hands, we call him. It's all right for me—I'm up here, out of his way." She hiked off, gargantuan legs rippling beneath her dress. "You might not be so lucky!"

Winnie's mind clouded over. Lord Ashley wasn't watching Miss de Vries. He was talking to the maids, all in uniform, arrayed on the terrace. They giggled, humoring him, pretending to be amazed by the entertainments. Only pretending, though. They were beyond exhausted. You could see it in their shoulders. Fatigue in the soul, something chronic. A few pounds a year and a scrag of mutton at Christmas—that's all they had to look forward to.

She felt her chest tightening.

Miss de Vries checked a tiny wristwatch affixed to her costume. It caught the light, a sparkling flash. She said something briefly to Lord Ashley, catching his attention. He turned sharply, treading on her gown. Nobody else noticed, but Winnie saw. He pinned Miss de Vries to the spot and she looked down, a flash of annoyance. The dress had torn.

Lord Ashley moved on, not caring. *They don't look much like lovebirds to me*, thought Winnie.

Miss de Vries stayed motionless for a moment, inspecting her train. Then she gathered herself, rearranged the crepe folds and moved toward the house.

She did it so subtly that the crowd barely parted for her: she was simply there one moment and then gone the next.

Winnie thought, *Someone needs to follow her.*

And then she thought, *Why isn't Alice here?*

The Janes were sweating now, wrapping delicate furniture with dust sheets, binding everything together with string. Glossy wood, a lot of walnut, Queen Anne cabinets with a hundred gleaming brass latches.

"What would you go as?" Jane-two said.

"Eh?" said Jane-one.

"To a fancy-dress ball."

"Like this one?"

Jane-two nodded.

Jane-one thought about it. "I wouldn't."

"I would."

"As what?"

Jane-two considered it. "Helen of Troy."

Jane-one snorted. "Oh, very good. Here's your wooden horse."

She rolled the next box, filled to the brim with treasures, along the tracks they'd laid down the corridor, and ran a quick hand through her hair. *Don't stop*, she told herself. *Not even for a minute.* She didn't need to look at the clock. She knew what it would say. Midnight was fast approaching. "We need to speed up," she muttered.

Alice had recognized the man in the mews lane the second she saw him. He had come without his usual companion. For some reason this made her more afraid, not less. One man, alone, without constraints, with his shirt collar loosened. Even debt collectors felt the heat, she thought, smothering a desperate bubble of laughter.

Usually he showed perfect courtesy, and tipped his hat. But

tonight he wasn't wearing a hat at all. He looked bigger than before, and the lamp shone on his bald head.

She searched for his hands, but they were shoved into his pockets.

He let out a breath when he saw her. This, too, made her feel weak. It was a tiny gesture, a little huff of...what? Anger? He was impatient to get this job done, sorted, over with.

She could see he had something concealed in his pocket. A lead pipe or a rope or a knife: her imagination unraveled all the possibilities, fear rattling through her chest.

"You're late on your payment," he said.

Alice ran her eyes down the lane. She looked over her shoulder, back into the yard. No one there. No one who could help.

She didn't hesitate. She didn't think. She turned and ran, straight back to the mews house. *Run*, said her body, *run and hide*.

She scurried through the lower offices, dodging the waiters and footmen. *Think*, she urged herself. *Think, think,* think.

"Alice?"

A face looked around the corner of the kitchen passage. It sent a jolt through her skin: she gasped.

It was one of the under-footmen. He gave Alice a quizzical expression. "Steady on. Madam just asked for you. She's gone and torn her gown. Run upstairs and fix it for her, will you?"

Madam. Alice's mind was whirring. *Yes: Madam.* Someone fierce, someone in *charge*, someone who could offer immediate protection...

Alice could feel her chest tightening, worse than being laced. The under-footman's frown deepened. "What are you waiting for? Go!"

29

M r. Lockwood kept Mrs. King waiting for the best part of an hour. She didn't let this rile her. She held herself upright and calm, in one of the vast wing-backed chairs in the corner of the library. It was such a good place for a private conversation. The walls were muffled by the bookcases, layers of vellum and gold-stamped leather. Mrs. King could hear the guests as if through water, a distant roar.

Mr. Lockwood sat opposite, ignoring her, writing a letter. His patience equaled hers.

Mrs. King's women didn't know she'd come up here. This conversation formed no part of their plan. It was part of *her* plan only. Mrs. King had one clear objective. To make sure, *absolutely* sure, that she hadn't missed a vital piece of information, before the house was emptied. She was turning over rocks, inspecting any number of maggots.

At last, she asked, "What are you writing, Mr. Lockwood?"

"I thought you'd never ask," he murmured in reply. He blotted the paper, pursed his lips, swiveled it to face her. "It is an affidavit," he said. His smile was fixed, immovable.

Mrs. King's face grew warm as she read the words he'd put in her mouth. A groveling promise not to trouble the house of de Vries with any lies, scandal, shame of any sort...

She lifted her eyes to meet Lockwood's.

"I presume you're here for your own advantage," he said. "To discomfit your former mistress. To exact payment." He tilted his head. "Or do you have an extraordinary and secret design, of which I'm quite unaware?"

Mrs. King smiled inwardly at that. But she kept her expression closed. "I will not sign this."

"I am willing to discuss...arrangements. Compensation. If that's what it takes, to..." He paused, as if choosing the best phrasing. "Send you on your way."

Mrs. King pushed the paper back toward him. "Perhaps you might give me some information instead."

"I'm sure I don't have any information for you."

"Dear me," said Mrs. King. "I haven't told you what I want yet."

He tutted with impatience. "Really, I cannot tell you how tedious I find this business. It's one thing to smooth over a gentleman's indiscretions. It's quite another to find them popping up and causing trouble. Although I've seen it before, of course. Dying men are always troubled by their bastards."

Mrs. King looked over Mr. Lockwood, the soft parts of him, the pale ghost-white skin at his throat. "I'm nobody's bastard," she said evenly.

"Good gracious, I wish you'd put that in writing. Better still, sign the affidavit saying so."

Mrs. King studied him. "Mr. de Vries had a very lengthy discussion with me before he died."

Mr. Lockwood's eyes glittered. "*Did* he? I thought you might say that. Did he make you all sorts of fantastical promises? Offer cash gifts and special heirlooms? *Do* tell me. I must have missed them in his letter of wishes." He held her gaze. "His will doesn't mention *you* at all."

"You don't think my testimony matters?"

"No, I do not. Nor would a court of law."

"Well, we're not in court, Mr. Lockwood. We needn't pick and choose what we call admissible."

"Indeed not. Though, if we were, you'd need a witness. Have you one of those? Was someone with you during this scintillating conversation?"

Mrs. King felt a prickle of annoyance. "No," she said flatly, revealing no emotion.

Mr. Lockwood closed his eyes again, just for a moment. "Well," he said, in a weary voice, "then really we've nothing further to discuss."

Mrs. King touched the affidavit with her fingernail. "I'm perfectly happy to put my name to *something*, Mr. Lockwood. It's just the *tone* of this paper I can't abide. All this talk of slander, of libel, of scandal. Not my cup of tea at all. Let's work up something more straightforward, and I'll sign it in a heartbeat."

The air shifted. He smelled danger. "Oh?"

"Write me a few lines now, if you like," said Mrs. King. "Something like, 'I am not the bastard child of Wilhelm de Vries. I never thought I was. I never heard the same.'"

She saw a muscle leaping at the corner of his mouth.

"Shall I fetch a pen and ink?" she said, pleasant.

"I'm not sure," he said, "that I trust you, Mrs. King."

"Heavens, I'm as honest as the day. You needn't worry about that. And while we're talking about *truth* telling, I had one little, tiny question. It's somewhat related." She took care with the next words. This was the heart of the matter. "Do you have my father's marriage certificate?"

Lockwood's back stiffened. She saw his brow crease. Confusion.

"Mr. Lockwood?"

Silence. She'd got him off-balance. "Do you, or don't you?" she said. "You ought to have *all* the family papers."

Lockwood took a small breath. Then he said, "What do you mean?"

"Dear me. I suppose I shall have to go back to the register office again."

"Whatever do you want to do that for?"

Mrs. King had two choices. She could rile him for the fun of it, but that could lead to unpredictable outcomes. She could play for time, but that would test her own patience, too. She decided to rile him.

"That's a conversation I'd rather have with Miss de Vries."

"Why?" His eyes were glued to hers.

"It's a personal matter."

He leaned back in his chair, weighing that. There was something coarse in Mr. Lockwood, underneath his gloss and gleam. You could tell by looking at his hands. Calloused, with blackened nails.

"I'd advise you to talk to me," he said.

Mrs. King smiled. "No."

Then Mr. Lockwood got up. "Tell me at once," he said, voice low. There was a tiny bit of spittle at the edge of his mouth. It glistened.

"Be calm, Lockwood," she said.

He stepped closer. "Mind your manners. I'll ask you again." He licked his lips, a quick, reptilian move.

Mrs. King could feel her lungs expanding, contracting, entirely steady. Mr. Lockwood bent over and put his arms on her chair.

"Don't do that, Mr. Lockwood," said Mrs. King. His breath was too sweet. It smelled of vanilla and honey. It turned her stomach.

"Then answer my question."

"I really won't."

His front teeth were very straight and even. But she could see the ones at the back, a jumble of black and silver. "Do you want me to drag it out of you?" he said.

Mrs. King stared at him. "I wouldn't advise it."

"Stand up." He reached out and grabbed her arm.

Mrs. King shoved him hard in the chest. He stumbled backward, eyes widening in shock.

She rose smoothly from her chair and backhanded him across the face. It was the sort of blow they delivered in the workhouse, or the asylum. Clean, powerful, without emotion. She heard the crack.

Mr. Lockwood tripped, as she knew he would, and fell to the floor. It always surprised Mrs. King how easily men fell over. Even wiry, compact people like Mr. Lockwood. They never saw it coming.

He flailed for a moment, grubby hands out.

"Up you get," said Mrs. King. "Before someone comes in and sees you brought so low."

She watched him take a moment, recover, propel himself upward onto the balls of his feet. He crouched there, fury in his eyes.

There was a *click* at the door, a sudden rush of light and noise. A whiff of ferns, of orchids. A low voice cut through the air.

"Mrs. King."

Miss de Vries stood framed by the light in the hall. The ball was a bonfire of heat and color and noise behind her. Mr. Lockwood rose, turning crimson.

Mrs. King stayed where she was, entirely ready.

Now they could really get down to business.

"Sit down, Mr. Lockwood," said Miss de Vries, black crepe rustling. She adjusted her skirts, hiding the rip in the cloudy black concoction that formed her train. "You seem out of sorts."

Miss de Vries looked well, thought Mrs. King. Skin luminescent. Hair burned to the color of sand. There was strength in her gaze: confidence radiating outward, a certain supremacy.

Her presence in the room felt like a weight. It made the boards strain beneath her.

Mrs. King smiled. "Mr. Lockwood got himself in a temper, I'm afraid."

"I didn't ask you to speak, Mrs. King," Miss de Vries said.

"I'll speak when I care to," said Mrs. King evenly. "And what brings you upstairs? Did someone mention I was here?"

"I've got eyes in the back of my head," said Miss de Vries, and she crossed her arms.

One of those clerks, then, thought Mrs. King. *Good*. If they hadn't summoned the lady of the house, as she had predicted they would, then she would have gone and found Miss de Vries herself. She'd been waiting to have this conversation for weeks.

"Well," Mrs. King said. "It's good to see you. I never did get to take my leave."

"Miss de Vries," began Mr. Lockwood, face pale, but she lifted a finger.

There was a long pause, a running heartbeat in the air. Miss de Vries stepped close, pressed her fingers to Mrs. King's copper mask. "Extraordinary," she said.

It was then that Mrs. King saw Miss de Vries's dress for the first time. It startled her how luxuriant it was, how delicately it had been crafted, how powdery the crepe appeared. She hadn't realized Alice possessed such skill.

Or such dedication.

"Walk with me, Mrs. King," said Miss de Vries.

Mrs. King considered her options. She could refuse, try to pin Miss de Vries to her chair, interrogate her. But Miss de Vries was far stronger than Lockwood: she was at least as strong as Mrs. King. Better to play her gently, unspool things little by little.

"Very well," said Mrs. King.

Miss de Vries opened the door, and the noise swelled, a sudden blare of horns from the orchestra.

The ball roared in delight, beckoning them into its midst.

Every room on this floor had great sliding doors, and these had all been thrown open. The ballroom stretched the whole length of the house, and it seemed to Mrs. King that she could see all her people in motion, that she could *feel* them simply packed to the rafters. She sensed the Janes wheeling crates through the guest suites upstairs, knew Mrs. Bone's "policemen" were playing lookout at the back gate, spotted the waiters pouring out dangerous quantities of champagne, clocked Hephzibah's actresses running rings around the bishops and barristers. The *real* guests were red in the face, already inebriated. They bowed to Miss de Vries as she passed.

"Don't you look *marvelous*?"

"Cleopatra, too clever!"

"Thank you," murmured Miss de Vries, extending her hand one way, then another. The paintings hanging outside the saloon loomed over them all. Blue oils, men in powdered wigs, trees bent in a storm. Mrs. King spotted guests picking at the gilt-work, estimating the value. *I could tell you the price*, she thought. Winnie had costed them up, the buyers primed and ready. They were of near-incalculable value, and yet they looked dull and dreary beside the flower arches and the walls hung with silks. A palm tree the size of an omnibus lapped at them gently. It was beaded with sweat, teardrops running all the way down the trunk.

Mrs. King wasn't one for hanging about. She saw Miss de Vries's eyes on the clock, too. "Shall we get down to it?" she asked.

Miss de Vries nodded, curt. "Yes."

"Your father spoke to me just before he died. I imagine he spoke to you, too."

Miss de Vries quickened a half step. "He did."

There was no tension in Miss de Vries's face. No expression at all. Dangerous, that. The women paused on the threshold of the ballroom and together they surveyed the room, their triumph.

The crowd was immense, and the air smelled of musk and perfume and sweat. The walls were a fresh shade of salmon pink, glazed and gleaming under the electroliers. The waltz unfurled in loops and swirls, dancers orbiting the room in perfect formation. Miss de Vries's eyes shimmered. Mrs. King had to hand it to her. This had to be the greatest ball of the season.

Lockwood approached. Cleared his throat. "Mrs. King is willing to swear that she is *not* Mr. de Vries's daughter," he said, under his breath.

"Illegitimate daughter," said Mrs. King, with a smile. She was interested to see how Madam would react.

Miss de Vries didn't make a sound. But her face tightened, a little twist of irritation. It aged her. She caught eyes with a group of men huddled near the door, dressed like Cavaliers and Roundheads. They lifted their hats with a flourish, and she inclined her head in response.

Mr. Lockwood gave a nervous laugh. "It's *good* news, Miss de Vries."

"I need a drink," Miss de Vries said. "Do you, Mrs. King?"

Mrs. King pondered this. Was it cruel, having this conversation now, tonight—*here?* In public? Perhaps. But she perceived a sparkle of provocation in Miss de Vries's eyes.

"I really do," Mrs. King said.

Miss de Vries moved slowly, her costume rippling. The refreshments had been set out in the anteroom, an abundance of lemonade, iced sherbet, wafers, bonbons. She picked two glasses of champagne from a tray and handed one to Mrs. King.

"Go on, then," said Miss de Vries, sipping from her glass. She closed her eyes as she did it. Swallowed. "I can see you're simply *itching* to say something to me. The floor is yours. Speak."

Mrs. King studied her own champagne, tiny bubbles splitting, bursting, one by one. "I had everything upside down," she said.

"And so did you. Your father pulled the wool over our eyes." The music surged, and the dancers shifted, too. "We've lived our lives back to front. You must have thought me an awful woman. Here in this house, taking your wages, with nothing but shame hanging over me."

Miss de Vries was silent for a long moment. And then she said, "I did think that."

"I don't blame you. I thought the same myself. I thought, what have I been *doing* here all this time? But I was always curious, you see. I always sensed there was something else going on. And you're a clever girl. You must have clocked it, too."

There was a wall around Miss de Vries, an airlessness. "I've no notion what you're talking about."

"Of course you do. You know your father's secrets as well as anyone. You know he was a sham. You know he'd been married before."

30

Two months earlier

The house was more quiet than usual. It had been muffled and cushioned to ensure the master wasn't disturbed, to aid his sleep. Mr. Shepherd was waiting at the entrance to the bedroom as Mrs. King approached, hands clasped.

"Good evening, Mrs. King." Somber tone.

"Good evening, Mr. Shepherd," said Mrs. King. And then, when Mr. Shepherd didn't move aside, "He sent for me."

"I'm sure I don't know why. He needs his rest. What's this about, Mrs. King?"

Mrs. King felt her patience waning. She didn't have the energy to coax and manage Mr. Shepherd anymore. "It's my birthday," she said, reaching around Mr. Shepherd, opening the door. "I daresay he wants to give me my present."

The room had changed the moment he'd returned from the Continent. A decline that was never to be reversed. The windows were shuttered, the tables covered with all the paraphernalia of a sickroom: pillboxes and towels and bowls ready for the nurse to collect. There was a sulfurous smell in the air. She wondered if the master had brought it with him from the gaming tables and watering holes of the spa towns.

She made herself look at the bed.

Mr. de Vries was lying there, propped up with silk cushions, curtains pulled back. Even from a distance, she could hear his breathing, the grating sound of his lungs.

"Good evening, sir," she said.

His eyes were closed, but he took a breath, a painful little sip of air. "Come here."

Evidently, he wasn't going to waste words. Mrs. King crossed the room. The carpets absorbed her footsteps; she moved completely without sound.

"Your present," he said, resting his hand on a prayer book, there beside him on the bed.

His fingers were thin, very nearly elegant. But there was something gross about them, encrusted with rings, prominent knuckles, hairs sprouting at odd angles. Hands for touching, prodding, peeling back layers. Fingers that carried disease under the nails.

She didn't touch the book. Someone would bring it down later. Pile it with the others, by her door.

"Thank you," she said—because it seemed like a kindness, because it didn't cause anyone any harm.

"I wrote a letter," he said, hoarse. "If you want to know the truth."

She felt her body grow very still. "What?"

"It's in the house," he said. "The letter."

Later she tried to recall the moment, to pinpoint what she had felt. Surprise? Curiosity? It was a wriggle in her gut, certainly, but it was more like—unease. He was being economical with words, and so was she. It took care, and skill, and precision, not to say too much. And looking at him lying there, flat against the pillows, she felt something cold entering her heart. *He's on the edge*, she realized. *He's dealing with the final things.*

"What letter?" she asked, at length.

His eyes flickered at that. He still had it: the taste for a game, the nose for a tease.

"Find it," he said, "and you'll know, won't you?"

She yearned to move toward him, and she wanted to creep away, all at the same time. As if blood spoke to blood, repelling and seeking in equal measure.

"Are you comfortable?" she said, at last.

She asked because she was curious. She wondered what it felt like to be there, right on the brink. Because surely this *was* the end? Surely they were very near it now? You only had to measure the shrinking line of his neck, see the way the weight had fallen away from his cheeks. His movements were growing slower and slower, the degradation unstoppable.

He let out a shallow breath. His eyes moved toward the blur of the medicine cabinet, the bowls, the pillboxes.

"I'm *bored*," he whispered.

She loathed him in that moment, but she wanted to laugh, too. *I would be bored*, she thought. *Oh, I would be so bored by it, dying.*

Straightening, she said, "Tell me about this letter."

"It's about your poor mother," he replied, barely a whisper.

Mrs. King felt her body turn quite still.

It was extraordinary, wasn't it, how easily people could shock you? Even if she counted up all the years she'd been here, all the hours and minutes and seconds—and she could count them, she felt sometimes that she simply held them all in her mind, like little slots marked up with luggage labels—then she still couldn't think of a time he'd mentioned Mother. In his house, in his world, this world that she had entered, Mother didn't exist. Lockwood had impressed as much upon her, the first day she arrived.

She felt a frisson pass through her skin. "What on earth do you mean?" she said, voice low.

There was something building in her chest, something dangerously akin to fear. Because she knew how games worked.

There had to be a delicious little bit of irony, a slice of pain. Someone had to lose for someone else to win.

Mrs. King knew she was a bastard, an indiscretion, a stain. She'd folded that away inside herself long ago. This had to be something different.

"This is yours," he said. He lifted a finger, barely half an inch. "All this."

To Mr. de Vries, an inch could cover oceans, prairies, great sweeping tracts of land. Silver. Gold. Mountains, studded with diamonds. So many possessions, held under his name, in his empire. She should have been confused. Dizzy with the scope of it, uncomprehending. But she felt only nausea, deep in her gut. She understood at once. *Ha-ha*, she thought, dully. A twist, a ruse, right at the end.

"You were *married* to Mother."

He didn't nod. He didn't shake his head. He just stared at her.

Mother always said she was a widow. Mrs. King never gave it any credence. She'd imagined Mother as a nervy, scattered girl, already in the family way. She'd had a fancy man, Danny O'Flynn: slick curled, a fast talker, causing trouble in the neighborhood. "He gave all the girls a ring," Mrs. Bone once said, dourly. "To appease the neighbors."

Mrs. King had understood that. Appearances mattered enormously. They were everybody's first line of defense. But once Dinah entered that house, she pieced things together: the oddness of her situation, the funds supplied to keep Mother in hospital. Mr. de Vries had fathered a bastard, same as a thousand men before, same as a thousand men would after. She had a stain upon her, and always would.

Hadn't she?

The notion that Mother had been telling the truth, that she was a widow in law as well as in sentiment, was like being hooked in the stomach. The guilt—that Mrs. King had never considered it, hadn't even *thought* to believe her—took her breath away.

"Why are you telling me this now?" she asked.

He didn't answer that. He lay there, breathing, watching her with a peculiar light in his eyes.

"Find the letter," he said. "And then tell anyone you like."

❦

That night, Mrs. King began the search for the letter. *Start at the top of the house*, she decided. *The attics.*

But the house was impossible. It bested her, every time she approached it. It was comprised entirely of compartments, of secret boxes, of tight containers. Jars, hatboxes, packing crates, vases, bookcases, writing desks, picture frames, looking glasses, false-backed cupboards, bedrooms, bedposts, bed frames...

She needed to make a more thorough inspection.

The plan came as her plans always did: in colors and shapes, not words. But this was bigger, grander, than anything she'd imagined before. It was cloudy, gauzy: she saw gilt and glass. Hot faces and men shrieking in confusion.

She went up to see Madam with the menus, as usual. While Mr. de Vries had been on the Continent, they'd fallen out of the habit. Now he was back, the routine returned, too.

"Soufflé," Madam had said, edgily. "Speak to Nurse to see what Father wants."

Mrs. King had put her pen away.

"Is there something else?" Miss de Vries said.

She doesn't know, thought Mrs. King.

She could read Madam. She could see the girl working hard, at all times, superintending her thoughts and feelings. She seemed weary: her father's return was like a storm cloud hanging over her head. But she didn't realize the truth.

"No, nothing else," said Mrs. King. She left off the *Madam*.

Mrs. King sat on her knowledge, concealing it. It was like walking around with a mortar bomb under her skirts. *I refuse to be rushed*, she told herself. *I need to plan.* She sensed the master growing impatient, yearning for her to commence warfare. She refused to oblige him.

Of course it occurred to her that he might have been lying. Playing an almighty game, telling her a fairy story, only to shred it to pieces when she was entirely sucked in. *If* he'd married Mother, then there had to be *real* evidence. She drew up a list of churches, scattered all over the East End, and began inspecting the marriage registers on Sunday afternoons. She took her Gladstone bag with her notebook, magnifying glass, blotter and good pens so that she could make notes. She dipped into her own savings and gave the rectors a healthy dollop of cash for the collection plate, so they didn't ask any questions.

There was no evidence of a wedding. But of course they could have used false names. Indeed it was almost certain they would have done. The O'Flynns must have disapproved of Mother. They were a family who formed strategic alliances with greengrocers and pawnbrokers and ironmongers. They didn't marry loose-screwed, weak-brained girls—and that's how they would have seen Mother. Even Mrs. Bone never hinted, never suggested for a *second* that Danny had made a true marriage. She would have torn him down from his glorious perch in a heartbeat, if she had.

Lucky for Danny O'Flynn. So easy to vanish, remold himself just the way he pleased. Mrs. King pictured him assessing his options, shuffling them idly like a deck of cards. She wished she didn't recognize the trait.

Two days later, she heard his bell ringing. A summons for Madam. The master wanted to speak to his daughter.

Whatever passed between them Mrs. King never knew. Miss de Vries came downstairs, went to her own rooms, without saying a word to anyone. She didn't send for any supper; she gave no orders at all. Mrs. King sat in her own small sitting room, waiting. She could feel something coiled in the house, a storm about to break.

Their father died that night. A sudden deterioration, entirely expected in a consumptive case like this one, said the physician later. The news broke like a river forcing its way through a dam. Mrs. King felt it rolling downstairs, floor by floor, the electroliers seething and spitting, the servants turning pale as they received the intelligence. The dinner service was suspended, the under-footmen stood about with their mouths open. Cook took to her bed. You could even hear the horses growing agitated in the yard. Mr. Lockwood and the other lawyers descended upon the house, papers out, pens aloft, issuing memoranda. The nurse cleared away all the pillboxes and bowls and towels, her trolley rattling all the way down the passage of the bedroom floor. Everyone heard Mr. Shepherd moaning, keening, from the butler's pantry.

Miss de Vries remained in her room.

Mrs. King counted out the black armbands, one by one. *This is it*, she thought, blood thrumming. Truthfully, she didn't know what *it* was. It felt too enormous, too unimaginable to piece together. Possession of this house, of all it contained, whistled through her mind.

The wording in the will was precise. It caused no comment. "I leave everything, my whole estate, to my true and legitimate daughter."

Clever, thought Mrs. King, when she heard, anger rushing through her veins. *Clever, clever, a lovely trick, a lovely game.* Of course the lawyers didn't remark upon such straightforward phraseology. Madam didn't question it; nobody said a word at all. They felt they understood the natural order of things. It was up to Mrs. King to correct them.

She gave herself an order.

Strip the house. Take *every* box, *every* drawer: shake them, search them, root it out. *Find* that letter.

Once Alice was in post, once Winnie was in on the job, she went to the men's quarters. She'd only have one chance to investigate those. It was the worst place for a woman to enter, if she wanted to keep her reputation. Mr. de Vries had always been so *particular* about his servants' morals. Prayer books for birthday presents, church every Sunday, prayers at breakfast. The women slept on one side of the house, the men on the other. Even Mrs. King and William had never attempted to cross that divide. Although when she asked him, he agreed to keep the door to the men's quarters unlocked. "But *why*?" he'd asked, deeply puzzled. "What on earth do you need?"

She ignored that. Troubles had a way of multiplying when other people became involved. But of course she *did* involve him; she did get him in trouble. Someone was sitting on a chair near William's door, kicking his heels. A little rodent-faced boy, keeping an eye out for intruders. Mrs. King knew the rules. She knew there was a risk that she'd be caught, and she went up there anyway. It was her warning shot, a signal to anybody that might need to hear it.

"What*choo* doing up here, Mrs. King?" the boy had asked. "Visiting a fancy man?"

She had been acutely conscious of her body, its stillness. Her blood, mixed by her mother and her father. The danger within her, the currents she'd inherited from both.

She had stared the boy down, stared him right down to his bones, but he didn't run away. Of course he ratted on her, went squealing to Mr. Shepherd. Mrs. King didn't complete her search of the men's quarters, and she didn't sleep that night. She felt invisible cracks running through the house, felt the walls riven from top to toe, blood pounding in her chest.

Cheated, she thought. *I've been cheated out of my rights.*

She was the rightful inheritress. She always had been. And yet she'd been put in a frilly cap and a starched collar, trained to answer bells and take orders. To sit, stay, be silent. And she had allowed it. She had *permitted* it to be done. It made her as angry with herself as with the world.

The following morning she faced Mr. Shepherd. Being dismissed didn't frighten her. She was ready for it. Her plans required her to be *outside* the house, at liberty to circle it, correct it, tilt it, push it all the way over. Besides, she recognized her dismissal for what it was: a shot being fired right back at her. A message from Madam: *Get out*.

It pleased her. It gave her exactly what she needed. Permission to do her worst.

31

Now

"You know he'd been married before," said Mrs. King. Miss de Vries said nothing. She sipped her champagne.

"I suppose he had the same set of choices as all the other men who take secret wives." Mrs. King counted on her fingers. "Come clean. Start running. Or say nothing. He picked the last option, didn't he? Even *Lockwood* didn't know." She smiled, a pitying glance. "Men like him, they so nearly get away with things. But then they let the cat out of the bag. It's as if they *want* to be caught. As if they can't help themselves."

Miss de Vries raised her chin to the ceiling. She pressed her lips together.

"And he unburdened himself, didn't he?" continued Mrs. King. "On his nearest and dearest, his own flesh and blood, his own kith and kin. On you and me."

She'd looked forward to this moment, regardless of the risk. It would have been more prudent to keep her counsel, stay out of sight. But the urge to face Miss de Vries, bring everything out in the open, was too great. Besides, she had one fear, one deep concern. Had Mr. de Vries told his other daughter of the letter? Had *she* found it? If Miss de Vries had destroyed it, then Mrs. King needed to know.

Mrs. King wished Miss de Vries would show something in her face, her eyes. But Miss de Vries didn't. Her voice was entirely controlled. "I'm famished. Let's eat."

She moved faster this time, champagne sloshing in her glass, and she tucked her hand into the crook of Mrs. King's elbow. Lockwood sprang, following.

The supper room was on the other side of the ballroom, opening onto the balcony, steps hurtling down to the garden. Lights leaping in the trees. Walls gagged with white silk. The tables had been laid out Parisian style on long buffets. Fowls sliced and stacked on silver dishes. Fruit plunged in bowls of ice. Mrs. King touched a peach, felt the chill like a burn.

Miss de Vries took a knife. Picked a sliver of meat.

"Anything else to tell me, Mrs. King?"

"No."

Miss de Vries tilted the knife in the air. "Clearly, you've taken leave of your senses." Her eyes were bright.

"I haven't," said Mrs. King, taking a moment, watching her temper. "As well you know."

"Prove it," Miss de Vries said.

"Prove what?"

"What you said. What he told you."

Mrs. King felt a quiver in her stomach. "So you accept he told me *something*."

Silence.

"Well, I can't," Mrs. King said. "I didn't write anything down. I've no witnesses. I'd rather know what he told *you*."

Miss de Vries looked away. "Me?"

She needed to be pushed, to be provoked. "Come now,

Madam," said Mrs. King. "Tell me all about it. Tell me how it feels. Knowing that your father could be so spiteful."

The noise from the ballroom surged and crashed over them like a wave. Miss de Vries's expression changed. The words wounded her. But she simply shrugged.

"He wasn't spiteful. One says *spiteful* things by accident. When one can't hold one's tongue." She considered her knife, studied the reflection. "This was entirely deliberate. Papa sent for me. Directly after you, I expect. He told me he had *a little something to tell me*." Her mouth twisted. "Just a *little* thing."

Mrs. King felt her chest thrumming. *Go on*, she thought, goading Miss de Vries with her mind. Lockwood took one step closer. He was looking at Miss de Vries oddly, recalculating her.

"He told me he'd made a *mistake*," Miss de Vries said.

Lockwood went very still.

"A mistake?" said Mrs. King.

"He told me he'd fathered a child. I said that wasn't any concern of mine."

Silence. Mrs. King allowed this to sit between them for a long moment.

It was strange, so enormously strange, to hear Miss de Vries speak of this matter at all. Mrs. King tried to picture the conversation between Miss de Vries and her father: a daughter's dawning comprehension, the shimmer of betrayal. "It must have been a shock," Mrs. King said, more gently. Miss de Vries's eyes turned on her, a flicker of derision.

"Hardly. We've been paying your mother off for years. Hospital bills do stack up, you know. They send receipts." She took a short, tight breath.

Mrs. King had never seen Miss de Vries express pain. Even when she was small, she never cried; she was trained too well for that. But this was pain: that's exactly what it was. Mrs. King recognized it at once. She understood what it was to deduce something enormous, something that turned the world back to front. She felt a searing sense of kinship with Miss de Vries in that moment.

It made her ask the next question bluntly, not sidestepping it, not winding her way in. "Did he mention a letter?"

Miss de Vries turned, light shivering. "Papa spoke a lot of *nonsense*," she said.

It wasn't a denial.

Mrs. King stepped forward. "I'll guess what he said, then. He got himself worked up. Said he couldn't keep a secret. Wouldn't meet his Maker without reconciling his affairs."

Miss de Vries considered this. "No," she said, reaching for a pear, polishing it idly against her dark sleeves.

"No?"

"He wasn't thinking of his *soul*, Mrs. King. He was thinking of…" She shook her head again, a smile playing on her lips, something strangely close to disgust. "He was thinking of his *future*."

She began peeling the pear. Her motions were faultless. She handled the blade with such dexterity, such absolute precision. Mrs. King couldn't help but recognize that trait too.

"His future," Mrs. King repeated.

"His name, his precious *name*, that wonderful thing he'd made for himself."

Mrs. King frowned. "But there was no risk of anyone forgetting that."

Miss de Vries's eyes widened. She took a step back, let out a mocking laugh. "No risk?" She raised her hands. "But that's too splendid! You *are* like him. Just as dense and self-involved as he was." Her face darkened. "You think all this will last forever? This place, this house? The name 'de Vries'?" She gave Mrs. King a long look. "It'll be gone by next Whitsun, if I've anything to do with it."

Mrs. King studied her. In that moment, she remembered the girl Miss de Vries had been. In the days when she still lived in the schoolroom, when she wore her hair loose and wild, when her skin was scuffed and greasy. When she was still being trained, when the governess was strapping rods to her back and shoving marbles in her mouth. Eyes hard and bright and furious, all angles and points, voice unsteady.

"I see," Mrs. King said. She reached for Miss de Vries. She wanted to touch her, to cross the divide. There had always been a pane of glass between them: they had preserved it perfectly. "I understand."

Miss de Vries drew back, a swift movement. She balanced the knife between her fingers, and said, with something approaching a laugh, "D'you know what he told me? 'You've got it the wrong way round. Mrs. King's the one with rights on *you*.'"

Lockwood's mouth went slack, aghast. Guests tripped into the supper room, making for the buffet tables, voices shrill on the air. Miss de Vries stood upright, her carriage perfect, ignoring them. Eyes on Mrs. King, skewering her, anger coursing.

Mrs. King remembered what Mr. de Vries had said: *Tell anyone you like.* Urging Mrs. King to do it. Longing for her to destroy his other daughter. "He wanted to punish you."

"Yes."

"For wanting to be married."

"For wanting to be *free*."

"And?" said Mrs. King, gently. "What did you say?"

Miss de Vries laid down the knife. "I said, 'I don't want to talk about it.' He didn't like that. I'd never spoken to him like that before. He started coughing."

A dark flash in her eyes.

"Did he?" said Mrs. King.

"Yes. He couldn't speak. I thought the nurse would come; he was making such a racket. But you know how it is upstairs. You can't hear a thing when the doors are closed."

The guests were helping themselves to cold cuts, to pieces of ham, to slices of tongue. They gave Miss de Vries sidelong looks, trying to identify Mrs. King. Lockwood smiled at them, his face glassy and pale, moving to obstruct their view. *His* mind was working furiously: Mrs. King knew the signs. He had the faintest sheen on the surface of his skin, looking around for his clerks, debating whether he needed witnesses.

Mrs. King turned to her sister. Miss de Vries *was* that, after all. Formed of the same materials. An equal, when all was said and done. "He didn't say anything else to you?" she asked.

Miss de Vries smiled. "Not another word."

She folded her hands. So neat, so tidy. The scrag ends of the matter chopped off and swept out of sight. *Too clean*, Mrs. King thought.

Then Miss de Vries added, voice low, "I should have got rid of you years ago. I should have taken better care."

Mrs. King shrugged. She did it to hide her anger. "Perhaps I should have got rid of *you*."

She saw Miss de Vries react. Pleasure, a vicious bite. The urge to fight.

"Me?"

"We could have done it. The girls and I."

Miss de Vries paused. A tiny frown appeared on her forehead. She didn't understand. "The girls?" she repeated.

"Any number of girls, from the sound of things," said Mrs. King, voice low.

She felt Mr. Lockwood grow still beside them. And she saw Miss de Vries grow even stiller, her face shuttering up.

"Do you know about that, Madam?"

Something strange happened in that careful, watchful gaze.

"Don't," she said, voice taut.

Her eyes went sideways, a single rapid glance, to Mr. Lockwood—and then away again. But Mrs. King understood at once. It was fear. Miss de Vries had buried her father, and she wanted everything about him to stay hidden deep, deep in the ground.

Mr. Lockwood raised his hand to his mouth, touched his bruised lip. "I would take care, Mrs. King," he said.

It made Mrs. King laugh in anger. "Of what?" she said, turning to look fully at him.

His mouth worked a little, choosing insults, jettisoning them. "Everything," he said, voice heavy.

Miss de Vries took a tiny step backward, away from this. The crowd circling the supper tables had thickened, spiraling, growing closer. Lockwood didn't seem calm. He was calculating everything, fingers fluttering, eyes going to the ballroom, signaling to his clerks. Mrs. King wondered something, in that moment. Perhaps Madam wasn't the enemy here? Her fortune might be the greatest adversary of all. It was bigger than both of them, a hurricane all its own. It had been drawn in vast and sweeping lines, great mercantile interests spinning outward, wild, battering the world. But at the center, in the very middle of it all, there was always a calm eye, watching. The Lockwoods and the Shepherds of the world. When they moved, the storm moved with them.

"*You* should take care," said Mrs. King to Mr. Lockwood.

Miss de Vries was silent, or silenced, face immobile. Lockwood ignored Mrs. King entirely.

Then a voice pierced the moment.

"Madam?"

One of the under-footmen had crossed the supper room, oblivious to the tension in the air around his mistress. "Your dress, Madam," he said. "I've brought the sewing maid."

Miss de Vries's gaze shifted downward, remembering. She reached for her train, unfolded the pleats, revealed the rip in the fabric. "Yes," she said, voice low. "Yes, fix it."

Mrs. King felt the room slowing. A figure emerged from the crowd. Pale faced, strained looking.

Alice.

Mrs. King didn't miss a beat. She controlled her face, looked sharply away. She could feel Alice staring back at her. *Don't*, she thought, *don't* look *at me*. This was the worst moment to be brought together. It was too dangerous.

Miss de Vries was shielded a little from the view of the crowd. "Here," she murmured, snapping her fingers for Alice, pointing at the spoiled inches of her gown. "Down here."

Mr. Lockwood was watching Alice. "Ah, yes," he said. "The little sewing maid."

He looked at Miss de Vries, and she looked back at him sharply.

Mrs. King spotted it. It made her skin burn.

"You have a rare talent, young lady," said Mr. Lockwood as Alice bent, needle in hand, to study Miss de Vries's gown. "You must come and tell me how you came by it."

Alice's eyes came up fast. She tried to smile, expression scattered, unraveling. She was panicking. It made her look entirely like Mother.

No, thought Mrs. King. Pain: right in her chest.

Miss de Vries kept her eyes fixed on the wall.

"Sir?"

The clerks circled them, still dressed as dominoes. Their costumes seemed ghastly, not fanciful. They had Mrs. King cornered.

"Escort this person outside," said Mr. Lockwood, casting a quick, backward look at Mrs. King. "At once."

Miss de Vries's voice was tight. "But are we clear on our position?"

Lockwood took a moment to answer, but then he squared his shoulders. "This discussion has revealed nothing but circumstantial evidence and gossip."

The clerks surrounded Mrs. King.

"Wait," she said, reaching for Alice. But the crowd moved, swallowing her up, pinning Mrs. King to the spot.

In that split second when Alice disappeared from view, Mrs.

King felt a weight dropping in her stomach. She had told her women they were equals in this, one and all.

And she'd just fed one of them to the wolves.

Miss de Vries stayed behind her protective wall, her cage of men. "I am going to fix my gown, and take care of my guests, Mrs. King," she said, voice dangerous. "I don't expect to see you again."

32

One hour to go

Mrs. Bone sat in her bedroom, waiting for one of the women to come and get her out. How long could it take to clear the old nurseries? She strained her ears, studying the ceiling. She knew her men were leaving the attics, per their instructions. The heat was gathering, billowing up through the house, through the soles of her feet, racing to her scalp.

She wished she hadn't been left alone. Her thoughts were preying on her. It was the tiredness, the anticipation—that was all. But the question kept needling her: what use was earning two-sevenths of anything when you could earn the whole lot? She remembered what Archie had said. *There are ways of getting out of a contract…*

"Could I?" she wondered out loud.

Emptying this house was one thing. Taking Danny's *whole* beautiful kingdom was something else altogether. The mines in South Africa, the estates in North America, the holdings in shipping and brewing and steel and gold. They made the house on Park Lane look like nothing. There might be a way to do it. She'd need to take over this whole job. Make a firm negotiation with her niece, Miss de Vries. To carve up the empire between them, in suitable fashion. It deserved to stay on the right side of the family.

Every part of it.

She felt sickened.

This house was built on rotten foundations. So was Danny's whole empire. You didn't get loans that big without leverage. You didn't rise to the top of the tree without treading on a million lesser folk along the way, without ruining other people's lives. Mrs. Bone pictured Sue, and the girls who came before her. Her own fortune was tainted by association.

So was her blood.

Begone, you green-eyed monster, she told herself, shuddering. Now wasn't the moment for jealousy. It was time for absolution.

Sniff.

She was up like a shot. "Who's that?"

She peered through the keyhole. Pale eyes goggled back at her.

"Sue," Mrs. Bone said, taking a breath.

The girl spoke in a whisper. "I can help!" she said.

Mr. Lockwood was clearly furious, but he smiled. "It's unconscionable," he said, drawing Miss de Vries into one of the anterooms, away from the main crowd, "that you should not have apprised me of all this."

"Why?" said Miss de Vries. She halted, feeling the heft and weight of the ballroom beyond. Alice and the under-footman hung back, watching her, listening. "What difference would it make to tell you?"

He stared at her, disbelieving. He lowered his voice. "You understand how this works? You *entrust* me with your affairs.

Your interests are my interests. As you rise, so do we all. That is the compact between us." His face was flushed. "There wasn't a single detail of his affairs that your father didn't share with me."

Miss de Vries didn't bother lowering her voice. "Weren't you listening, Lockwood? My father didn't entrust anything to you at all." She smiled at him. "Perhaps he meant to dispose of your counsel."

Lockwood's expression twisted. He was about as indebted to the house of de Vries as any man could be.

"Send Lord Ashley to me," she said.

"What?"

"I don't see that *you're* making any progress with him. I shall have to take matters into my own hands."

"Into your own..." Lockwood's eyes widened. "You can't be serious."

She pressed her face into his, not caring if the other servants saw her do it. "Why not?" she said, hating him, exhausted by him. "Why *not?*"

The bruise on his lip was turning an ugly color. She wished she'd given it to him herself.

She snapped her fingers for Alice. "Come." She felt rather than saw, her maid obeying her, edging closer, reaching out to fix the final threads on her dress. She could smell the faintest tang of sweat rising from the girl's neck. It gave Miss de Vries a shooting feeling of relief. Here, at least, was someone she could depend on. She wanted Alice near. Not with Lockwood. Not anywhere near Lord Ashley.

The emotion startled her: she tried to swipe it away. She glanced down at her dress. "Have you fixed it?"

Alice looked pale. Clearly, the heat and excitement of the evening had gone to her head. She opened her mouth, as if to say something. Then she shut it again, nodded. The rip had been mended; the dress was perfect.

Miss de Vries was ready.

Lord Ashley was still in the garden, joshing with ministers and clerics and dour old judges, poking them in the chest, tugging on their doublets and robes. His own gaggle of lordly friends followed him, tittering, approving every gibe. He was in good spirits. This seemed promising. The garden felt sweaty, swampish, anticipation on the air.

"My lord," Miss de Vries said, pitching her voice up a note. "I abandoned you. Forgive me."

He turned, appraising her, and gave her a curt, quick bow from the neck. Miss de Vries felt a burst of fierce satisfaction.

"You are forgiven," he said, a little spot of color rising in his cheeks.

He can't talk to women, she thought. This pleased her. This confirmed what all her senses were telling her: she was in charge.

"Gentlemen," she said to the others, "perhaps you might excuse us?"

They hesitated. Lord Ashley's eyes whipped sideways, looking for someone: his lawyers, or hers. "The lady deserves a chaperone," he said, with a leery sort of gallantry.

As if you could seduce me, she thought with an inward laugh, but she kept her expression solemn. "You're very good to think of it." She turned to the oldest, most wizened-looking man she could find. "Your Honor. You will accompany us if we take a turn about the garden, won't you?"

The judge's lip wobbled, but he nodded—*certainly, certainly*—and the others stepped away, dissolving into the crowd. The judge grinned at them, a filmy, toothy smile.

"Lord Ashley," said Miss de Vries, locking her arm into his, tugging him into motion, "I would be honored to be your wife."

It was like punching him. It made her feel as if she lived at the dockyard, as if she'd rubbed chalk on her fists. It was exactly what Papa would do: a clean, fast cut. She sensed his recoil.

"There's no dignity in poverty," she added, voice lower. "And I won't wait all season to close this matter. You must answer me at once."

His body went rigid beside her. "*We* do not discuss this," he said.

She made her face gentle. If anyone were watching them, they would have fancied he had just paid her a beautiful compliment. She led him along the terrace, feeling the weight and density of him. It was like dragging a mountain rock. "I will not permit your mother to manage this matter. This should be your choice, yours alone."

She stole a glance at him. Surprise crossed his face. "My mother?" he said. "She has nothing to do with this at all."

Miss de Vries understood, in that moment, how this game was played. He really believed his wishes were his own, that his thoughts were of his own design. His people had managed things to make him believe that it was so. He cocked his head at her.

"Of course you understand that you must submit to me, if we press ahead?" he said. "You must obey me, in everything."

If she had been a superstitious person, she might have crossed her fingers behind her back. "Naturally," she said. "My vows will make sufficient provision for that."

He chuckled, the tension leaving his face. *Changeable*, she noted. *Inclined to take things as a conquest. Not a bad temperament, perhaps.*

"Then come," he said, "and dance. My people will settle the smaller details."

He was only fractionally taller than she was. At that height she could look directly at his forehead, pierce his skull, read his mind. Victory surged within her. "Your Honor, thank you," she said, inclining her head toward the judge.

"My *dears*," he said, in raptures, stretching his hands out to them. "My deepest congratulations."

Hephzibah had been in the Boiserie this entire time, gathering herself. Mr. Shepherd hadn't understood her when she'd told him her name. It meant nothing to him. And in any case her mouth had become so dry, so sticky, that she'd garbled the words. *I'm foaming at the lips*, she thought. *They'll have to cut out my tongue.*

But the urchin, who had likely never been to a theater in his life, who would likely never earn enough to even contemplate purchasing a ticket, had gaped up at her. "*What* did choo say?" he'd asked.

She'd gazed down at him, vision blurring. He had dark, hungry-looking eyes. She had seen boys like him causing trouble outside the Paragon, scrabbling and kicking one another in the dust. You could always count on one to pick up a playbill with mocking laughter, strutting about in imitation of the powdered, laced-up lady in the illustration.

She pressed a shaking finger to his lips. She could feel things slipping out of her control.

"This lady," Mr. Shepherd had said before he departed, "is clearly not at all well. Someone fetch the physician."

"No," she said, trying to make her voice steady. She did feel pain, seeing him. But it wasn't like pulling a tooth, after all. It was like an open wound, fresh and bitter. "Leave me be."

He did leave. He retreated, distracted, rubbing his swollen-looking lip, and left her in the Boiserie.

"You'd best sit down," the boy muttered. "*My lady.*"

"What do you want?" she said, scrunching his sleeve in her fist. "To keep your mouth shut?"

He hesitated.

"Too slow," she said. "Say one word and I'll have you strung up on a lamppost."

His eyes went black.

Hephzibah exhaled, looked out of the window. *Not long now,* she thought. It was nearly done, nearly finished. She'd nearly made it. Best to stay here, she decided, where she couldn't set off any further suspicions. Her actresses would manage without her for now. *You're just having a little rest*, she told herself, trying to steady her nerves. Don't *run away*.

The Boiserie was positioned above the front porch, its windows bowed, facing the park. An enormous motor, bigger even than the Daimler, drew up slowly beside the curb.

Who's that? Hephzibah wondered, peering down.

A figure in a dark suit leaped from the passenger seat, hurried around, waving the crowd back. Reached for the door, unfastened it.

A gaunt woman in a squashed orange turban emerged.

Someone of quality, Hephzibah mused. You could spy old money a mile off. Delicious-looking silk. Not a moth hole anywhere. A viscountess, perhaps. She liked to say *viscountess*. It pleased her lolling tongue.

"What?" grunted the boy.

"Silence," ordered Hephzibah.

But then the turban moved, and the woman bent to say something to the other person sitting inside the motor, and suddenly the world became very still. It turned on its axis no more; it made no revolutions; it came to a terrible halt.

For it was clear to Hephzibah, as it was clear to those people on the pavement, that this motor car was altogether too grand, too anonymous, to contain any ordinary person. It had curtains drawn down over the windows. The tassels were bobbing, gleaming gold. Hephzibah felt the thrill passing through the crowd. Saw the traffic slowing.

Surely not, Hephzibah thought. *Not possible. Not the…*

The viscountess in the orange turban stepped back. And slowly, back straight, she descended into a curtsey. The crowd sighed with anticipation.

Hephzibah was transfixed. Someone else began to emerge from the motor. Hair glossed and folded, dark with wax. A neck bound tight with a choker, as if the pearls had been sewn directly into the skin, flesh jeweled from chin to clavicle. No costume, not even a nod to one. But a sash, royal blue, cutting straight across the shoulder. It blazed up at Hephzibah.

So did a face. A familiar face. One you saw on picture post-cards. Long and angular. Thick brows. Heavy lidded, heavy jawed.

Hephzibah felt her fingers trembling. "Ah," she said to the boy lightly, as if she didn't care. "The Princess Victoria is here, after all."

Her mind began racing. *How, how, how on earth…?*

Hephzibah staggered to the door of the Boiserie. Looked out at the saloon, at the open doors to the ballroom. The noise and the fug of champagne on the air hit her in a rush.

You're the greatest actress you know, she told herself. *The best. So*, act.

33

Ten minutes to go

Miss de Vries let her neck fall back, spine arching. Lord Ashley's fingers were digging into her shoulder blade, his nails scratching black muslin. She kept one fist on her train, taking care not to trip. The electroliers were popping and spitting overhead, and the crowd roared with pleasure as they swept past. Lord Ashley had led her inside to dance, as the news of their engagement swept through the house.

"They're offering us their congratulations," she said in Lord Ashley's ear as he hurtled her backward into the center of the room. Up close, she could see his curls were slick with grease, darker than his usual white blond. The waltz was the fastest of the night, the orchestra red-faced and exhausted.

"Get your skirts out of the way," he huffed, wrenching her waist.

He wants to show off to the crowd, she thought. The room was spinning around them, all roaring salmon-painted pillars and the tang of sweat. But Miss de Vries made out two figures moving ponderously in her direction.

Shepherd and Lockwood, making a beeline for her.

She smiled, radiant, laughing, for the crowd. "May we stop," she said, catching her breath, "my lord?"

His hands came away so fast he nearly dropped her. He turned, arms aloft, hair askew, and the best families in London cheered for him. She tried not to stumble.

Shepherd was on her, Lockwood right behind. "Her Royal Highness is here, Madam."

"What? Where?"

"Her motor just pulled up at the front door."

Lockwood still looked pale. "Excellent news, Miss de Vries."

"Where's Lady Montagu?" she asked.

Shepherd frowned. "Indisposed, Madam. We took her to the Boiserie to——"

"Ah, there she is," said Miss de Vries. She saw a familiar gleam of pink satin, hoop skirts lurching through the crowd. A powdered wig bobbed furiously in the air. "Come."

They all followed the duchess, who was half running down the *grand escalier.*

Hephzibah thanked God for her hoop skirts. They kept people at arm's length. Everyone caught up with her at the foot of the stairs, a perfect traffic jam. There was Miss de Vries, descending behind her, butler and lawyer at her side. In the opposite direction, she saw the Princess Victoria's people, clustered at the front porch, waiting for someone to come and receive them. *Oh, Lord,* she thought.

"Lady Montagu?"

Miss de Vries was moving toward her at double speed.

Hephzibah turned. *I refuse to be rushed,* she said to herself, trying to blink her dizziness away. Men stood under the portico. *Real policemen,* she realized, feeling sick.

"Miss de Vries!" she said. "Splendid, you're here."

Guests on the right, guests on the left. No way out. Could

you be arrested for fraud? Naturally. But on the spot, without clear charges? Hephzibah's mind spun like a loose wheel about to fall off. She wished, in this moment, that she had someone solid beside her, someone to reassure her.

Winnie would help her, if she were here.

Buck up, Hephzibah, she told herself. *Buck* up*, do*.

Miss de Vries frowned. "Aren't you going to meet the princess, Your Grace?"

Hephzibah summoned all the severity she could muster. "*You are the lady of this house, Miss de Vries*," she said. "Her Royal Highness is waiting for *you*." She threw her arm wide, as if to say, *Do hurry up*.

Hephzibah had never been trained to be a lady. She'd never been schooled in dance, posture, elocution. She'd refined herself on her own, for the stage—keeping her wits about her, her eyes open, watching other people, *learning how to do it*: how to *live*, how to *be*. But Miss de Vries *had* been trained. Belts and chokers and laces and straps on her flesh. She was alert, ready, all the time.

She gave Hephzibah a hard, penetrating stare.

Hephzibah dug her fingernails into her palms, made her face smooth. She raised an eyebrow.

Another second and she would have failed. Miss de Vries would have seen a line of sweat creeping out from under her wig. She would have smelled the acrid scent rising off Hephzibah's body. Fear. Hephzibah could already smell it on herself.

But Mr. Shepherd leaned forward, worried, eyes on the clock. Hephzibah saw the saliva on his lips. "Madam..."

"Yes," said Miss de Vries briefly, and moved on.

Hephzibah followed. She had no choice.

Oh, God, she thought. *Oh*, God.

Winnie should have known something was about to go wrong. Everything had been too simple. From her vantage point, patrolling the terrace, she had watched Hephzibah's people herding the crowd, shifting them eastward then westward, keeping them entirely distracted as ropes began rippling down the eastern side of the house. The plan had been immaculate; everything was progressing without a hitch. She'd begun to feel her heart thump with surety, with unshakable confidence.

But suddenly one of the waiters snapped his fingers. "Get those beasts out of their boxes."

Slowly, the French doors at the top of the terrace opened. Winnie saw movement, a crowd emerging from inside the house. And she felt something change in the atmosphere, a thrill passing through the company assembled in the garden below.

Miss de Vries was at the front of the party issuing down the terrace steps, and she'd removed her headdress. It made her look small, like a jet-painted icon. Next to her walked a woman of no very remarkable height, maybe in her late thirties, maybe forty, with a bright blue sash across her shoulder. She was being steered along a sort of tidal line of people, catching them like driftwood: guests, hangers-on, people crumpling into curtseys as she passed them. She looked almost like…

Princess Victoria, said a voice in Winnie's head.

She almost laughed in disbelief.

They had spoken of a letter. An invitation sent to the royal household. But it was a fairy story, a tale spun by Hephzibah. They'd filtered Miss de Vries's post, checked it every hour. No card ever left Park Lane for the palace. Hephzibah had rehearsed what she'd say to Miss de Vries, when she finally scampered out of the house: the princess had a royal headache, she was royally indisposed, terribly sorry, what a *shame*…

And yet they'd missed something. A letter *had* gone. Unmistakably, undoubtedly, it had. For here stood a princess of the United Kingdom, in all her state and glory, decked almost carelessly with diamonds, surrounded by courtiers, palace officials, equerries, men in dark overcoats who looked unmistakably like detectives. Clearly, news of this spectacular, unparalleled ball had spread like wildfire; it had billowed out of their control.

Where's Hephzibah? she wondered, growing cold. She should have been controlling this crowd.

"All right, love, watch out behind you."

A hand pulled her aside. Winnie smelled something hot and pungent on the air, the whiff of matted fur. Heard the heavy clop of hooves. The decking shuddered. In any other circumstances she might have laughed. But now she felt only panic. Mr. Sanger's camels came plodding out to greet Cleopatra and the princess. Applause rose up around them.

She saw Miss de Vries leaning in to say something to the princess, something humble, something reverent. She saw Lord Ashley beside her, his face jubilant, jaw glinting under the lights.

This wasn't in the plan. If Hephzibah had been rumbled, if the actresses weren't being directed, if Mrs. Bone's "policemen" were caught out... Risks began hurtling toward her like comets. She had no contingencies for this.

I need Mrs. King, thought Winnie. *I need Mrs. King right* now.

Hephzibah stayed with the princess's people. There was nowhere else she *could* go. The viscountess in the orange turban, the lady-in-waiting who'd ushered the princess from her motor car, had eyes everywhere. She sniffed a little as the crowd edged closer.

"I'm not sure Her Royal Highness can meet *all* these people," Hephzibah heard her say to Miss de Vries.

These people were the next-door neighbors: wool makers and soap manufacturers and bankers. Men dressed as centurions, their wives dressed as Celtic queens. The better class of guest, the ministers and members of the diplomatic corps and the bishops, were all staying at the far end of the terrace. They feasted contentedly on the grape tower, knowing the princess would be steered in their direction.

Miss de Vries flushed, cutting the introductions short. "We must show you the entertainments, ma'am."

The princess allowed herself to be maneuvered firmly toward the gardens, people goggling at her from the stairs. The lady-in-waiting with the orange turban coughed incessantly into her gloved hand.

You need to take control of this, Hephzibah instructed herself, *before something goes wrong. "Darling,"* she said, reaching for the orange turban. *"Here* you are, at last."

The lady-in-waiting jumped, startled. She half turned, her passage obstructed by Hephzibah's skirts. She peered upward, eyes bleary. Hephzibah towered over her, jeweled, powdered, bewigged.

The viscountess frowned. "Who are you?" she said.

That beautiful golden-eyed footman was nearby. He cast a sharp look in Hephzibah's direction. "Lady Montagu," he said, voice clear. "May I help you through the crowd?"

The lady in the orange turban sighed. "Lady…? Oh, *Bea*," she said. "For heaven's sake. You startled me." She coughed again, fingers fluttering for a handkerchief.

Hephzibah felt her lungs tightening.

"D'you know, someone said: you'll never guess, it's too funny, Beatrice *Montagu* is going to this party. I told them I didn't believe it. I said Bea Montagu hasn't gone to a ball once this *century*, and she's hardly likely to go to this one." She linked arms with Hephzibah. "But *here* you are. What possessed you? Was Charles being too infuriating? Heavens, look at your costume. I wouldn't have recognized you. When in Rome, I suppose. Aren't these people simply too marvelous? *Such* a lot of vultures."

Hephzibah squeezed the viscountess's arm in return. "Wait till you see what's coming," she whispered. "We'll be talking about it for *years*."

"Will we really?" said the viscountess with a sigh, tucking her handkerchief into her sleeve. "How tedious."

To the garden they went.

I'm doing it, Hephzibah realized, her courage rising. *I'm winning here.*

She wondered about sending for another champagne.

Winnie was searching the gardens for Mrs. King. She could hear the guests talking among themselves, ogling the proceedings.

"Did they really have the *circus* in ancient Egypt?"

"Oh, naturally! And Punch and Judy shows."

"And clowns!"

"And tightrope walkers!"

"Don't be beastly. It must have cost her the earth."

"Ashley's footing the bill for that now."

"Quite right."

"Quite ghastly, you mean. Can you imagine that girl running Fairhurst? *Poor* Lady Ashley."

"Poor nothing. Just think of the weekend parties. The trapeze artists! The dancing girls!"

"The *camels*, darling!"

They broke off into laughter, reaching for more wine.

"Oi," said a voice at Winnie's ear.

She turned and started. Behind her, eyes narrowed, stood one of Mrs. Bone's men. His jaw was clenched. Winnie backed behind the marquee. "What are you doing?" she muttered.

"We're off."

"What?"

"We're getting out. This place is swarming with peelers."

Winnie looked around, searching for Mrs. King. "Nonsense," she said. "Everything is simply fine. Go back inside."

"Can't." He nodded at the distant figure of the princess, moving slowly through the crowd. "Not now *she's* here."

"Then you'll need to improvise." Winnie held his stare. "You don't leave this house until Mrs. King gives the word."

For a second she feared he might refuse to obey her, might tell her to go and fetch Mrs. King. *I would if I could*, she thought desperately.

But then he nodded again, a quick, smart little duck of the chin. "Yes, ma'am."

Equals, Winnie said to herself, almost in disbelief. *We're all equals…*

Mrs. King was frog-marched downstairs by Lockwood's clerks. "I can see myself out," she said angrily, shaking their hands off her arm.

"Mr. Lockwood said—"

"Hang Mr. Lockwood," said Mrs. King. But they steered her through the front hall, avoiding a huge crowd of guests that seemed to be processing toward the garden. Mrs. King couldn't see who had arrived. She felt the mob rolling, not steered, not marshaled. Evidently, Hephzibah was busy elsewhere. A sudden fear pulled on Mrs. King's heart. She was *required* here: to direct things. But she needed to get to Alice first.

Dunce, she thought, directing all her anger on herself. *Idiot.* Even the *Janes* had sensed a risk with Alice, but not her. She was incapable of understanding other people's feelings. She always had been.

It was clear at once what had happened. She'd seen the way Alice had bent her head toward Miss de Vries, yearning toward her, fixing that awful, splendid gown. She'd been snared. Alice wasn't a canary. She was a mouse, right in the trap. Lockwood was sizing her up. Mrs. King's instincts told her everything she needed to know. She felt sick, frightened.

"Off you go," said the clerks, disposing of her on the front step, very nearly pushing her into the road. She didn't talk back: she hurtled to the tradesmen's entrance, trying to double back inside before they spotted her. This time it was harder to get in: there were crates of wine obstructing the door, waiters smoking. She had to push her way through the crowd of servants, speeding up the servants' staircase, panting.

The sound of the orchestra grew duller as she reached the second floor. There was a door half-open, letting in a soft breeze. Mrs. King nudged it open with her toe.

Empty.

I should have planned *for this*, she thought. She should have made arrangements to extract Alice from the household's clutches if needed.

Nothing mattered, Mrs. King thought, if Alice was lost. She'd abandoned Mother when she entered this house. Allowed her to be restrained, hidden away, forgotten—because it was *easier*, more convenient for *everyone*.

She wouldn't let that happen to Alice, too. She refused—on her honor, as a sister, she *refused*.

"Winnie?"

Jane-two emerged from the shrubbery. The princess was up on the terrace. The fire-eaters were sending sparks into the sky to the sound of applause. Winnie had been circling the crowd of guests, searching for Hephzibah, for Mrs. King, for *somebody* who could agree what they should do.

"Good heavens," said Winnie. "What are you doing in there?" She waved the answer away. "Never mind now. Have you seen Mrs. King?"

Jane-two frowned. "I have examined the lane. The police-men—the real policemen. They're watching her." She nodded across the garden, toward the princess. "Not the back gate. It's a clear run to the road. We should launch the operation while we have the advantage." She stared at Winnie, who was rooted to the spot. "Someone needs to give the order."

Winnie looked at all those people thronging the garden, sway-ing dangerously near the edge of the Nile. Lights spilling from the ballroom, shapes whirling past the windows. Braziers being lit, and the fire-eater taking one last gulp of his flame, the crowd bellowing in delight. She saw candlelight flickering in the attic windows.

From the house, from every floor, she heard the chimes. Midnight.

I have my voice, she thought.

"Then go," she said.

34

Midnight
Go-time

Winnie burst into the kitchen. She'd never seen it like this before. The whole place was alive and breathing, filled with smoke and noise and people in perpetual motion. The waiters circled her, trays gleaming, boots ringing on the flagstones. The air smelled of wine and goose fat and dripping.

It was time to find Shepherd, get the keys, recover Mrs. Bone. Shepherd was propped up against the long table in the servants' hall, supported by his train of bootboys, mopping his brow, glugging a glass of sherry. He adjusted his waistcoat. Winnie watched him clipping and unclipping his keys. In the end it wasn't difficult to do, and she didn't hesitate. She approached him, followed by an acrobat and three waiters, thankful for her disguise. Cook was bawling at the French chef. The kitchen maids were running in circles around Cook. The waiters were smuggling bottles of wine to one another under the table. In other words: chaos, the kind they'd prayed for. Winnie reached for Mr. Shepherd's keys and plucked them lightly from his belt.

He sensed it. Winnie backed away and saw him reeling. There was a crowd all around him. He patted his waist, let out a noise. Bent down. "Here, get out of my way, I've dropped my…"

As Winnie rounded the corner, she broke into a run. She'd lost her breath, every scrap of it, by the time she reached the servants' quarters. She counted the doors, looking for Mrs. Bone's. She fiddled with the keys, tested the lock.

In a second she heard Mrs. Bone's voice. "Who's there?"

"It's Winnie. Wait a moment. I'm just trying to work out which—"

"I am *so* glad you have come for us," she said, high and forced. She rapped on the door, stopping Winnie midbreath.

"Us?" said Winnie.

"*Behind* you."

Winnie spun round. Saw a figure shrinking from her gaze, right at the end of the passage.

Mrs. Bone's whisper came through the door. "Our Sue has been telling me some very *interesting* things."

Winnie heard a rustling sound. A sheet of paper sliding under the door. She picked it up. Saw a lot of neat, handwritten lines.

A list of names.

Winnie found the right key, unlocked the door. Mrs. Bone was on her in a second. "About bloody time. Third floor sorted?"

Winnie was hardly thinking of the third floor now. "Mrs. Bone. *What is this girl doing here?*"

Mrs. Bone shook her head. "You're not paying attention." She jabbed the paper. "Don't you see what this is?"

"We need this girl *out* of the way, Mrs. Bone."

"This *girl's* our good-luck charm. She's our little *jewel.*" She snatched the paper out of Winnie's hand, waved it in front of her face. "Wasn't you *reading* it properly?"

Winnie studied it, comprehension dawning. Ordinary, everyday names. Agnes, Sylvie, Molly, Eunice… Each with a gentleman marked in the margin, with dates, with times…

"Got it? We can take this to the police. Or the papers. Get Danny's people where it hurts. Their *reputation*. You can't do a thing without that. We could bring his whole bloody *empire* down."

"But Mrs. King says…"

"Hang Mrs. King."

"Mrs. Bone," said Winnie, grabbing her arm. "You remember our instructions. No clever ideas. No deviations. None at *all*."

Mrs. Bone's nostrils flared. "You had your chance to fix things here. What good did that do? *Something* needs to be done for those girls."

Winnie pictured the housemaids standing out on the terrace. Caps, aprons, embroidered fringes, pleats and ruffles. She shook her head, dots dancing in front of her eyes. She looked again at the paper.

"Very well," she said, feeling Mrs. Bone's eyes boring into her. "Very *well*. We'll manage this between us."

Mrs. Bone's mouth was set in a determined line. "Good for you," she said, as much to herself as to Winnie. Then she turned to Sue. "You, put your apron on. We've got housekeeping to do."

Alice was hiding in Miss de Vries's dressing room, a safe and familiar place: high in the house, far away from the man in the mews yard, far away from anyone. She knew what was expected of her: to glue herself to Madam, to trail her like a hound. But when she closed the dressing-room door, she felt the compression in the air, the sturdy *thunk* of the door, and she knew she was staying put. It wasn't safe outside.

She'd only been standing there for a minute when she heard movement in the bedroom. Footsteps as stealthy as her own. It wasn't Madam. *She* moved briskly, without a care in the world. Alice backed hurriedly into the closet, crouching to the floor, holding her breath.

"Alice?"

Alice knew the voice at once. Mrs. King. Then came shame, a great roll of it, the awful realization that she was cowering here like an animal in a trap. A weak thing, beyond useless.

The footsteps stilled. Silence. And then another soft *click*, the door handle turning, and a pool of oily light oozing across the carpet.

She couldn't see her sister. But she could feel her gaze sweeping the room. Alice held her breath.

Seconds passed. She yearned for Mrs. King to enter. To excavate her, rescue her.

The door didn't creak. It was too well oiled for that. But the air sighed, the oily light contracted, and there was a heavy *thunk* as it closed once more.

***

Miss de Vries had the honor of bringing the princess up to the supper room. The waiters were setting out jellies and fondants. *Bring me red meat*, thought Miss de Vries. *Bring me blood*. She felt as if she were approaching the altar, ready to be transformed. The air felt thick and heady with cologne and scent. An equerry pulled out a chair for her. Its pommels gleamed, and it looked almost like a throne.

Miss de Vries wondered how many people were watching her. She could feel it, something greedy in the atmosphere. They were waiting for her to show herself up. To fail. She gripped her fork, smiled, biting the favorite part of her lip, tasting the blood.

Up close you could see the veins in the princess's skin. It gave her a blueish aspect. The eyes were less striking in reality than in photographs—smaller, filmy looking. Her mouth drooped a little at the sides. *She looks like her father*, thought Miss de Vries, and it gave her a curious feeling in her stomach.

"Ma'am." A confident voice, right behind her. A hand on the back of her chair, jolting it.

The lady-in-waiting with the orange turban smiled. "Ashley. Naughty *you*. Late again."

Miss de Vries turned. She'd left Lord Ashley in the garden, hoped they would have given him enough wine to distract him. This was *her* ascendance. She wished to enjoy it by herself, before she was pinned to his arm forever. But he didn't seem distracted. He lowered his chin, and for an extraordinary second she thought he was going to kiss her on the head. But he was only bowing to the Princess Victoria.

"Forgive me," said Lord Ashley with a smile, and slipped into his seat.

He didn't look at her. Didn't say a word. Didn't ask her permission to join, didn't thank her for the food. He grabbed his fork as if seated at his own table.

The princess retreated into her own head, eyes down. The ladies all made a graceful turn left, and commenced conversation with their neighbors. Of course they all knew each other; it was effortless for them. Miss de Vries found herself seated beside a spindly and decrepit colonel, who was fussing with his handkerchief and inspecting the forks, saying not a word. Someone had altered the table plan without seeking her authority: someone from the royal household, perhaps. Or Lord Ashley. Miss de Vries stared at the wall in enforced silence, feeling a flush rising up her neck, suddenly out of her depth. The crowd stood panting at the door to the supper room.

This is my triumph, she reminded herself firmly, feeling ravenous, eating nothing.

Meanwhile, the Janes were consulting the instruction labels ironed into their petticoats. This was the most delicate part of the operation: sweeping the rooms in the public parts of the house. They got to work on the library, with Hephzibah's decoy guests stationed right outside, guarding the door. Mrs. Bone's men, still dressed in their tunics, stood on extendable ladders, handing books down the line and stacking them in towers. It was taking longer than Winnie had calculated.

"Come on," muttered Jane-one, her eyes fixed on the clock.

"What time is it?" said Jane-two.

"Don't ask."

The men heard. Fear, the first true prickle of it, shimmered across the room.

Someone dropped a book. Jane-one saw it happen. It simply slipped from a man's hand, toppling into a tower of leather-bound volumes already on the floor.

She knew what would follow. Her mind unspooled it, several seconds ahead. The first tower fell into the next. *Dominoes.*

The men looked on, aghast, as the towers crumbled. Jane-one felt the tremor as hundreds upon hundreds of books hit the bare floor. It was a rumble she could feel in all directions, passing through the walls.

"Lock that door," she said. "Right now."

A fist hammered on the library door. "Open up!"

One of the footmen, thought Jane-one. They'd heard a commotion in the library and come running, pushing past Hephzibah's actresses. She pressed her finger to her lips. The men all stared at her, pale and sweating. They were trapped. Books lay scattered on the floor around them.

Silence outside. "Hello?" the footman said, uncertain. "Everything all right?"

Jane-one pressed her finger to the keyhole so he couldn't peer in. She used her other hand to point to the window. Mouthed to Jane-two.

Perch act.

Jane-two frowned. *You're not serious.*

Got another idea?

Jane-two considered this, quite seriously. Then sighed. Marched to the window, hauled it open. Reached out, feeling for the drainpipe.

Glanced back over her shoulder. Mouthed, *Two minutes.*

Jane-one motioned one of the men to cover the keyhole. Tiptoed to the center of the room. Twirled a finger in the air.

At first the men didn't understand. Then she kicked off her shoes, pulled her apron over her head, unbuttoned her black twill dress. Their mouths dropped open.

She stood there in her chemise and her bloomers.

The men turned around in a hurry.

Jane-one felt a tingling in her muscles, and began her stretches.

35

1:00 a.m.

Hephzibah had a new problem. There was a man heading upstairs.

She recognized the ashen gleam to his hair from the old days. The family lawyer. Mr. Lockwood.

As soon as the princess had gone in for supper, he'd slipped away from the royal party. Hephzibah had watched him beetling toward the stairs. She'd planted several of her best people by the banister to head off any real guests who tried to leave the saloon floor, but the crush was too great—they couldn't waylay him.

No, no.

She hastened after him.

He took the stairs two at a time, as if he were in a hurry. Hephzibah had to cling on to the banister to stop herself from tumbling over. "Sir!" she exclaimed, voice going up a notch.

He didn't hear her. He rounded the stairs and disappeared.

Her first thought was, *He's fetching something for Miss de Vries.* But *her* bedroom was at the front of the house, facing the park.

And Lockwood had turned the other way, toward the enormous suite above the ballroom.

He had entered Mr. de Vries's bedroom.

Her heart plunged when she saw Mrs. Bone's men marching over from the other end of the house, ready to start clearing Mr. de Vries's suite of its possessions. She hoisted her skirts and legged it along the passage.

The double doors were open. The lights were burning dimly in the gigantic suite beyond. Lockwood was already in there.

The men frowned at her, halting.

"Do as I do," she said, breathless.

She pressed herself behind the half-open door, skirts to the wall. The lawyer didn't seem to notice that half the objects in the room were sitting under dust sheets, or atop packing crates. He was crouching by the bureau, opening drawers, rifling inside, closing them again.

Searching for something.

One of the men leaned over her shoulder. His breath smelled very faintly of beer. He had a terrifyingly muscular forearm. "We need him *out* of there," he said.

Hephzibah scanned the insurance contract in her mind. No gags, no blindfolds. But there was nothing about *scaring* people…

"Death!" she cried, throwing open the sliding doors. "Destruction! Doom!"

Lockwood started nearly out of his skin, lurching backward. Hephzibah strode across the bare floorboards, sequins scattering as she went.

"Good *Lord*," Lockwood said, face reddening in annoyance. He had a nasty bruise on his top lip.

"We will deliver you to your *doom!*" she cried.

The men got it: they were sharp lads. They formed a tight circle, leering at Lockwood, their thighs greased and hairy underneath their tunics. "Doom!" they grunted.

"Really, Your Grace," Lockwood said, "the entertainments should stay *downstairs*."

"Come with us!" boomed Hephzibah. "To my den of—" she considered this "—of terror!"

"Terror!" echoed the men.

They were still in a ring around him, and began dragging him lockstep toward the door.

"Good gracious," exclaimed Lockwood. "Your Grace, I…" He found himself being pulled bodily from the room. "Would you…would you get *out…of…my way*."

"He goes *of his own volition*," said Hephzibah loudly, as if the insurers were crawling around in the rafters. Lockwood was borne out of the room, leaving the bureau drawers wide open.

It seemed he hadn't discovered what he was looking for.

Sliding down the drainpipe, Jane-two found a pair of gentlemen locked in intimate conversation in the shrubbery. They were real guests, costumed, and they were both wearing perfectly enormous ruffs, which seemed to have become unusually tangled.

"*Excuse* me," said Jane-two, rummaging in the undergrowth, searching for her extendable pole.

"You shouldn't sneak up on people like that," said one of the men, straightening his doublet and hose.

"Sneaky is as sneaky does," said Jane-two severely. "And your codpiece is showing."

She grabbed hold of the fire-eater on the way back inside. He was on their team, naturally. She'd drilled him herself. "Keep the crowd on *that* side of the garden," she told him. "Anyone comes near me, you blow your torch at them."

The fire-eater had wonderful eyes, crystalline blue, and a

honeyed way with words. He inspected her bloomers. "Sweet Moira, my treasure, my angel! A word from you, and I die!"

"Don't die," said Jane-two. "Just blow."

***

Jane-one heard the screams from the garden below, and peeped out of the window. There was a roar, a great lick of fire, and she saw the crowd scattering across the garden. *Come* on, she thought, hearing another loud knock at the door.

And there, looming out of the dark, was the extendable pole.

"You lot, down the drainpipe," she said.

"Down the *what*?"

"And you two—" she picked the quickest, most dexterous pair "—start passing me books."

She was up on the windowsill in a heartbeat. She sensed Jane-two far beneath her, steady as a rock, holding the pole upright. She swung onto it, clenching her thighs.

"Down you go," she said to the men. "We don't have all night."

You had to give Mrs. Bone's men credit. They had nerve. They were shimmying down the drainpipe, catching books in the circus nets, in no time.

Three minutes later, she climbed back in and opened the library door.

The footmen stood outside, looking scandalized. They tried to peer past her, but she blocked the view.

"I wouldn't," she said, shaking her head. "Guests. In flagrante delicto."

"What was *you* doing in there, then?"

Jane-one fixed them with a dead stare. "Protecting my virtue."

She left them to stew and speculate and press their ears to the door.

Time was running out.

The princess was tired. This seemed to have been ordained by the viscountess or her equerries, and she rose from her seat, attendants collecting cloaks and gloves and furs. To have held the royal presence in this house for nigh on two hours was an extraordinary achievement. The whole enormous party began drifting toward the *grand escalier*, like day-trippers trudging across a beach, and Miss de Vries accompanied the princess. Conversation was impossible. Her Royal Highness kept a wall around her. *I do that, too*, thought Miss de Vries.

The orchestra fell quiet, the crowd drew back, and there was a burst of riotous applause. The band began playing the national anthem, half a measure too fast, and the princess looked around, temporarily nonplussed.

She caught Miss de Vries's eye. "I congratulate you on your engagement," she said, over the music.

"Thank you, ma'am," she muttered, bowing her head.

The anthem died just as it was getting into full swing, and the princess's people began shoving the onlookers, beating a path to the door. The princess herself glanced over Miss de Vries's shoulder. Lord Ashley was fighting his own way down the stairs behind them, hat skewed, plumes bobbing.

"You would be better off alone," the princess said.

Her accent was tucked into the recesses of her throat, and she spoke without emotion—as if she didn't care how her words would be received. It was a breathtakingly offensive thing to say. It silenced Miss de Vries altogether.

"Ma'am," said the viscountess, turban swaying, "this way…"

The princess moved on, offering no thanks, no farewell. Evidently, her mind had turned to bed, and the groaning, dusty, glorious heights of Buckingham Palace. There was a flash of diamonds, a firework *pop* in the garden, a collective flurry of bows and curtseys as the royal presence left Park Lane. Through the crush, Miss de Vries saw the big motor car roll away from the curb. A roar went up in the front hall, men and women peeling off their gloves, letting out enormous sighs of relief, shouting for more champagne. The band began hammering the drums. There was a bang as a flashbulb went out in one of the electroliers, and people screamed in delight. Miss de Vries felt her neighbors crushing her, touching her, all over her.

She didn't budge.

Lord Ashley bounded up the front steps, saying in a careless voice to Miss de Vries, "Christ, what a drag that must have been for ma'am. At least you had me here. She wouldn't have said a word otherwise."

The world grew dark. Miss de Vries could feel her father's eyes on her back, his portrait looming over her at its usual furious angle. In that moment she loathed Lord Ashley. She urged herself not to let the feeling take root. Anything less than joy would count as failure.

There was a gleam of pink satin, a scent of almonds and rose water. Lady Montagu was hurrying past. "Terrible headache, must dash, forgive, forgive… Splendid evening, goodnight to you all!"

Miss de Vries felt a hand on her elbow. Lockwood, bruised and angry eyed. "Thank his lordship for the dance," he said. "It will be expected."

Lord Ashley was throwing back his head and bellowing with laughter, rubbing his thighs, making an obscene joke.

She didn't wish to thank him. He should have been thanking *her*, for saving him. "No," she replied. Ashley was taking her triumph, polluting it, making it his own. "I'm going to bed."

Lockwood's eyes narrowed. "There are still a good many people to speak to…"

"I've concluded all my business. And I'm tired."

She looked at Lord Ashley, then looked away. She tried to summon up the sweet tang of success. It tasted bitter. She made for the stairs, the scarlet peonies raging overhead, and she didn't glance back.

36

2:00 a.m.

Without Mrs. King, Winnie was going to have to manage the next step herself. She was at the other side of the house, in the guest suites on the second floor. She put the box of matches back in her pocket and peered at the smoke machine, wiping the sweat from her brow. The Janes started stuffing sheets around the bedroom door frame, bunging up the cracks, to contain the smoke. Not that there seemed to be much smoke at all.

"How long will it take?" Winnie asked. The machines were working, pistons pumping, air bubbling in the water towers. But the cigarettes were releasing only little wisps of smoke.

"We come back every couple of minutes to replace the cigarettes," said Jane-two. "And we've checked the gauges. They're set to double."

"None of that means anything to me."

"It means you should get ready," said Jane-one firmly.

Alice had slipped into Miss de Vries's bedroom. She envisioned the other women looking for her, growing angry when they couldn't find her. She pictured Mrs. King's face, her disappointment, confusion. Alice's nerves were skimming through her skin, fingers trembling. She moved like a mouse, zigzagging, touching Miss de Vries's bureau—because it was something cool, something solid. Her crucifix felt hot, sweaty, the chain scratching her throat. She was tempted to throw it out of the window. What use was it now?

She heard a soft tread from the passage. It made her start, swing around. The big bedroom doors rolled slowly back.

Miss de Vries stood silhouetted in the lamplight. It made Alice squint, put a hand to her eyes. The movement must have alerted Miss de Vries to her presence. She heard her say, on an outward breath, "Ah."

Miss de Vries stayed standing on the other side of the bed. The sight of her, so familiar, made Alice's heart start pelting. She knew every inch of Madam, every line: every nick and hollow. She'd watched her long enough. *Good*, she thought, mind racing. *Keep her here. Keep her with you, away from everyone else. Just as Mrs. King would have wanted.*

But it wasn't Mrs. King's orders that made her cross the carpet. It wasn't because of the *plan*. It was something different, circling deeper in her gut.

For once Miss de Vries's expression was easy to read. Anger. Alice felt it in her own body, too. It enraged her, that she should be so frightened, that she should be *made* to feel so.

"Whatever are you doing up here?" said Miss de Vries.

"I...felt unwell," said Alice. "I didn't want to cause a fuss."

Miss de Vries took a half step backward. "You should go to

your own room, not mine." Her headdress glittered; her shoulders were pale in the light. "Are you feeling faint?"

Alice didn't move. "Yes," she said.

"Then sit down, for heaven's sake. I'll send someone to help you."

"No," said Alice, voice rising. "Don't. Please."

Miss de Vries stared at her. Something was working in her mind, and it was hard to interpret. She raised a hand to her forehead. Her movements seemed fractious, edgy: there was something crackling in the atmosphere around her. "I hope you're not going to be disagreeable. I've had a very long evening."

She was still close enough that Alice could smell her. A stinging scent, something bitter, something burned. It clung to the silvery white-blond sheen of her hair.

"Madam," said Alice, taking a breath. "Your costume."

A pause. Miss de Vries's eyes darted to meet hers. "What of it?"

Alice made sure her voice didn't sound weak. "Are you pleased with it?"

Miss de Vries looked startled. She regarded herself in the long looking glass. She was a column of black crepe and jet ornaments, her train pooling behind her like oil.

"*Pleased* with it?" she said. She shook out her wrists, almost nervous.

Alice gathered her courage. "You said, Madam, that I should be rewarded. For my work. That I should be paid."

Miss de Vries went still.

"Paid?" she said.

Alice imagined the man in the mews yard in her mind's eye. *Finish this*, she told herself. *Finish it, get it done, get out.* It was not part of the plan. It was entirely in contravention of it. "Yes, Madam."

Miss de Vries did something strange then. She closed her eyes. "You want to be *paid*." She began chuckling, a low and troubling sound. "I see. Of course. How entirely predictable."

Alice felt her skin growing hot. She wanted to step backward, but she held her ground. "I'm very grateful to you, for giving me the opportunity."

"Are you? You don't seem it." Miss de Vries's eyes shimmered in the half light. Her voice hardened. "What of my other offer? What of that?"

Alice hesitated. She felt the pull in her gut, the temptation. "I'm not cut out to be a lady's maid, Madam."

Miss de Vries's eyes were bright, fierce. "I'm offering you something far better. You would be my *companion*. I would show you the world. Florence, New York. You'd have a *salary*, since that's so important to you."

That word *companion*. It made Alice's heart flicker. "I'd be no *use*, Madam," she said. "I've nothing you need."

"Need has nothing to do with it," said Miss de Vries, voice rough. "I *need* nothing. I *wish* to keep you. You understand?"

The ball might have been taking place a hundred miles away. The roar was distant, contained beneath sediment and rock.

"Keep me?" said Alice, trying to laugh. "You can't *keep* me."

Miss de Vries's expression changed. "Whyever not?" she said. "Shouldn't you like it?"

Her voice was strained.

Miss de Vries was very close, then. It was possible to make out the beating of her pulse. There was something heightened, hectic about it. It matched the rhythm of Alice's own.

Miss de Vries reached for Alice. Her touch wasn't cool. It transmitted heat. Alice saw Madam's lips: soft, faintly touched with wine.

Would she like it? Alice wondered. The room held its breath.

Miss de Vries's eyes widened, as if checking herself. It was an expression Alice had never seen on Madam's face before. Uncertainty: delicate, shivering in the heat.

Alice reached out to touch the most brittle parts of Madam's dress, around the shoulders. She alone knew where the joins were, where the clasps could be found. It was her strength that loosened them.

Miss de Vries closed her eyes. But she didn't move. She inched closer, the tiniest, clearest fraction.

Alice went further. She closed the breach between them. She kissed her mistress, the air wreathed with orchids, lamplight flickering overhead.

Winnie stood back from the smoke machines, her nostrils burning. Her scalp was slick with sweat. Her hands shone with greasepaint.

Now, she thought. *Now.*

The Janes nodded.

Winnie pulled air into her lungs, opened one of the doors, and let loose a cry. "Fire!" she shouted.

Her voice came out as a croak. "Fire, fire!" Figures appeared at the foot of the stairs and she hauled the doors open fully.

Smoke billowed out around her. Blueish, stinking, sweet— far more than she could have hoped for. She covered her mouth and ran down the stairs, arms aloft.

"Fire!" she cried.

The Janes followed Winnie downstairs. They observed the pleasing majesty of it all. Footmen running. Noses turning upward. Disbelief. The orchestra falling silent, waltz frozen midspin.

"Fire, fire!" yelled a voice.

And then it was real, the fear. It unfurled itself like a ribbon. The guests were like starlings in flight, a drunken, frightened rush of powdered hair and crooked crowns and ermine trains.

Jane-two tested her voice. "Fire!" she bellowed. "Everybody out!"

"Oh, give over," muttered Jane-one, pressing a hand to her ear.

Together they worked the crowd: pushing, shoving, scaring, very nearly ramming people down the stairs. Mrs. Bone's men, the ones dressed as guests, helped. "Out, out, out," they chanted, and it was remarkable to see the world obey them, growing increasingly frightened. "I'm choking!" cried one. "Smoke! It's in my lungs!"

By the time they reached the front porch, they could hear Lord Ashley. Clearly, he was the worst sort of person in a crisis, bellowing orders for horses, buckets, hoses, causing even more confusion than before. Jane-one observed the chaos on the pavement, countesses calling for their husbands, ministers calling for each other, and a hundred motors jammed at every junction.

"They need to call for the fire brigade!" exclaimed Lord Ashley. "Now!"

"They have," replied Mr. Lockwood. "I'm sure of it."

"That bloody *pyramid*," said Ashley. "It's blocking the *bloody road*."

Jane-one spotted the lamp-boy lurking by the railings. He had a weasely, toothy look about him.

"You, boy," said Lockwood, reaching for him. "Run to the fire station."

"Sir, there's people inside. Upstairs. I can see 'em moving around…"

Lockwood shook him. "Aren't you listening? Get them to send the engines."

A window opened, and one of Mrs. Bone's men looked out, waving his arms, scaring back the crowd.

"Who's that?" said Ashley. "Who's inside?"

"Get back, get away from the house!" the man was shouting. A cry went up, and people began backing away, into the street, making for the park. "We'll get the drapes down!"

Lord Ashley shouted up at them. "Quick, men, that's it! Get those curtains off their rails!"

Jane-one heard Mr. Lockwood say slowly, "Where is Miss de Vries?"

~

Winnie came into the hall. "Ready?" murmured one of the men, peering upward.

A pulley above them was wheeling madly, taking the long chain with it. The pulleys had been looped onto the iron braces underneath the glass dome. They held a platform, operating like a gigantic version of the electric lift, wide enough to shift half a dozen big crates between the ground floor and the upper floors of the house. Their faces showed the strain of holding all the ropes. The dome shimmered over the front hall.

Please, God, let it hold, she thought. She could almost feel the glass quaking.

"Someone give the word," said the first man.

Winnie's mind scrambled. Plans, papers, schematics, diagrams, calculations, machinery, pulleys, inventories and ledgers. Hired hands and fences. Prices marked up in the ledger. Tricks, tales, lies, glorious acts of make-believe. Puzzle pieces, carved up and scattered by Mrs. King for them to piece together. Games for women.

It's not a game to me, Winnie thought.

In her dreams, she had seen Mr. de Vries, and she had chased him through long, white, glistening corridors, longing to catch him and trip him and drag him to the ground. It had woken her last night, hot and panting, sheets twisted. This part of the job was supposed to be the end of the story. Emptying the house, taking the world's breath away, that was the *point* of it all. To bring everyone low, to the same awful level.

And then what?

She had *one* plan, one laughable plan. *A hat shop*, she thought in disbelief. *I wanted to open a* hat shop.

It wasn't enough; it wasn't nearly sufficient. Mrs. Bone's list burned in her mind.

If just one of those girls had made *friends*, then they wouldn't have got into trouble. Shepherd couldn't have picked them off. But when you were alone, you could be unstitched, you could have your lining ripped out.

"Go, then," she said, raising her hand, giving the order.

The men nodded, eyed each other, braced themselves. And in a silent, perfect rush, the crates began descending to the floor of the hall, ready to be ferried to the garden and the mews lane beyond.

Winnie unfolded Mrs. Bone's list from her pocket. She needed to find Hephzibah, and start putting things right.

～

Hephzibah had changed costume on Tilney Street, removing her wig and returning to the house in a gigantic veil and a plain cotton dress. She directed her people with skill. "Moving," she reminded them subtly, *"keep everybody moving."* A footman fired up another brazier. The neighbors had sent out supplies: Brook House delivered a dozen trestle tables and Stanhope House provided several crates of wine. The ball had been transposed entirely to the park: the crowd was not disposed to disperse.

"Would you look at those women," said Lord Ashley, three feet from Hephzibah. Girls from the circus, wearing long tights and ruffs, were dancing between the trees, undulating, wheeling past on giant hoops. "Splendid."

The guests—both Miss de Vries's and Mrs. King's—had begun dancing barefoot on the grass, throwing their hands aloft, rapturous with the sheer pleasure-seeking gaiety of it all. Only at the de Vries house, the most vulgar house in London.

Mr. Lockwood was studying the house, puzzled. "There's no fire," he said.

"No fire?" exclaimed Hephzibah, feeling a rush of panic. "I *saw* it myself!"

Nearby stood the head footman, eyes watchful. He had his hands behind his back. Lord Ashley reached out and shook him by the arm. It startled him: his face wrinkled with displeasure. "Go and look for your mistress," said Lord Ashley. "Make sure she's safe."

No, don't, thought Hephzibah. But he bowed, and marched toward the house.

37

2:30 a.m.

"Did someone shout *fire*?" said Miss de Vries, reaching for the bedpost.

"I expect it's a false alarm," muttered Alice. Noises were coming from the road or the park, distant and muffled.

Miss de Vries moved. "I'll go and see. Fetch my dressing gown."

Alice grabbed Miss de Vries's hand. "Don't," she said. "It might not be safe." She found Madam's skin to be dry and cracked around the knuckles. It had ridges and corrugations as if soap had chapped it, burned it. This made her seem more breakable, more delicate.

Madam gazed back at her, eyes dark. She let out a long, shaky breath, but did not reply.

"I'll go," Alice said, kissing her hand. "You wait here."

She slipped between the gap in the drapes, closed them tightly behind her. She could hear Miss de Vries shifting, pulling her rich sheets around her, not following. The carpets sucked at Alice's feet, silky air wrapping itself around her throat. She looked around the room, hands trembling, taking in all the familiar and wonderful things: the polished walnut table, the gigantic looking glass, the escritoire. The bureau was winking at her, locks sparkling. The whole room was telling her what to do.

Mrs. King approached the bedroom suites just as Alice slipped through Miss de Vries's door. Mrs. King was at the far end of the passage, and she turned when she heard the roll and *click* of the sliding doors, saw a figure hurtling away down the stairs.

"Alice," she breathed. She didn't dare call out her name, for fear of discovery.

Mrs. King ran silently down the passage. She wouldn't permit Alice to be alone in this house one moment longer. Lockwood, Shepherd—she could not let them touch her. Corruption started on the surface of the skin. Dirt in the fingernails, nicks and cuts, flesh bubbling, hardening over. It needed to be treated quickly, with carbolic and gauze, before the rot could set in. The thought of Alice being taken, priced up, sold, made Mrs. King's lungs burn.

Alice was fast. She vanished down the servants' staircase, and Mrs. King had to double her pace. She felt the riptide of the job in motion, this thing of her own creation: it vibrated in the walls as she descended through the house. The hiss of the pulleys, the whoosh of the crates, the creak and hum of wires. She dodged the crowd of Mrs. Bone's men wheeling trolleys down the garden, entered the sultry garden and glimpsed Alice in the distance, racing for the mews house, her apron winking in the dark. Mrs. King could see men on the roof, on rope ladders, winching up the drainpipe. They crawled over the house like insects. It was miraculous. But immaterial, if Alice were in danger.

"*Dinah.*"

A hand reached out, catching her arm.

She saw the gleam of golden eyes.

"No," cried Mrs. King, staggering to a halt. Her voice carried on the air as Alice disappeared around the corner, into the night. The men around her, dragging crates, stopped dead.

They all stared.

And William, wide-eyed, amazed, held on to her.

⟡

Winnie carried the Inventory like a priestess with a prayer book, moving through the public apartments, watching as they were skinned. The house thrummed around her, sweltering, in never-ending motion. Things weren't going the way she'd planned.

She imagined the house would simply divest itself of its treasures, that it would be glad to give them up. It wasn't.

Men swarmed the stairs, tripping over ramps and cables. Several boxes nearly went flying. Winnie's heart was in her throat, checking for nicks and cuts and bruises on the walls. She'd impressed this on everyone: it was essential that the house was left entirely undamaged.

"Careful," she begged them, and when they ignored her, she raised her voice: *"Take care."*

"Yes'm," they murmured.

It was such a long time since anybody had obeyed Winnie without demur. The pleasure increased every time she tested her power. "Carry on," she said.

She counted items. Tapestries, peeled from the walls. Cushions, blankets, eiderdowns, tassels, testers, sent off in chutes. Paintings, swinging out through the windows. And then someone let out a frightened roar. Winnie felt a rush of air, massive velocity. A grand piano came plummeting through the air toward them.

"Wire!" she breathed, pointing, cold fear in her throat.

The men scrambled, hurling themselves on the ropes. There was a dreadful *crack* as the cables tautened, the platform lurching, the piano lid swinging open with a bang.

Awestruck silence, three dozen faces. The piano swung madly, braced to its platform, creaking. It was safe.

The grotesque things came, too: the stag's head and the stuffed bears. Chairs, footstools, small couches, side tables, urns the size of full-grown men. Mrs. Bone burst out of the saloon, a tiger-skin rug draped over her shoulders.

"Come on, you Janes!" she shouted. "Let's be having you!"

Don't close your eyes, Winnie ordered herself. The Janes had fixed a pair of swings under the dome. The greatest art pieces were all up here: the painted panels and triptychs and angels. You could go up on a ladder, take them down one by one, if you had half a day to spare. The men broke off what they were doing to watch. Winnie didn't scold them. She clasped her fingers together, pressed her hands to her heart.

"Don't worry," said Mrs. Bone thinly. "My Janes can do anything."

Winnie felt her stomach looping as the girls climbed up onto their perches. Slowly they began to swing. The men gazed, transfixed. There was something unutterably lovely about it when Jane-one let go, forming a giant curve, slicing through the air.

Up Jane-one went, a reverse dive, landing perfectly on the ledge just underneath the dome. She couldn't have had more than two inches to land on. Didn't pause. Lifted a frame from the wall. Didn't turn. Leaped backward into the air, gilt gleaming as she fell. Jane-two swung out from the other side, caught her by the feet. Together they swung toward the French doors. Out went the painting, a straight throw, to the nets and waiting hands beyond.

Back to their perches. And this time Jane-two was off.

It's happening, Winnie thought. She felt an extraordinary sense of rightness, of purpose. Perhaps it was hubris.

"Can they go any faster?" she asked Mrs. Bone.

Did the girls hear? Jane-two was lifting a diptych from the wall. Its hinges creaked as she did so. Its illuminated boards must have swung open as she lifted off, affecting her balance, breaking her dive. Winnie gasped as she slipped from her swing.

A cry, piercing the silence. Jane-one, already launching off from her swing. A shriek from Jane-two as the diptych and gravity pulled her toward the marble floor.

Winnie couldn't help it. She closed her eyes.

"Aah..." grunted Mrs. Bone, rigid beside her.

Winnie opened her eyes.

Jane-one had latched her ankles to the second swing. She had swung out to grab Jane-two. The girls were dangling together, the diptych hovering—safely—above the floor.

"Faster, my arse," said Mrs. Bone, clutching Winnie's arm.

Out in the garden, Mrs. King shook William's hand away. Mrs. Bone's men circled them, eyes dark.

"You shouldn't *be* here," Mrs. King gasped.

He stood back. "You think I don't know *that*?" His eyes flashed. "I've been watching your lot all night. You think I don't know what it means when half a dozen packing crates go up in the lift for no reason? When half the guests keep sending me off for more wine and then tip it straight out of the window? When someone comes down shouting *'Fire!'* because she's having a fag?"

The men drew closer.

"For heaven's sake, Dinah," William said. "What do you need?"

Her heart tilted. It was gratitude. It ran right through her.

"Well?"

"Give us a hand," she said, letting out her breath. "I need to find my sister."

She turned and ran.

Alice had raced to the park.

She crossed Rotten Row, her boots leaving footprints in the sand. She didn't bother to scuff them over. Who cared if she left tracks now? She could hear the crowd of guests gathered outside the house, on the wide stretch of grass opposite Stanhope Gate. She wasn't going anywhere near it.

She remembered Winnie's instructions. There were only four exits from the house. Front door. Tradesman's. Mews gate. Garden door. She picked the mews gate.

She *was* followed, of course. As she knew she would be. She sensed it first, the tingling in her skin. A twig cracking underfoot.

That voice.

"You got it?" The debt collector, dry and hoarse, as if he was longing for a drink, as if he'd lost the last remnants of his patience.

Ten feet away, said her mind.

"I said, *Have you got it?*"

She turned. A plane tree soared above him, boughs reaching for the heavens. He must have taken a great arching loop across the park to intercept her.

She approached him slowly. "How much do I owe?" she asked.

She unbuttoned her apron. Her uniform made her look so useless, so small. She didn't feel special; she didn't feel like a soldier anymore. She rifled in her pocket.

He named the sum. It almost made her laugh in despair. The price for her salvation. The cost of betrayal. Was that it? Would her fear simply vanish when she'd paid her debt? She held the money in her apron.

When she'd left Madam's bed she'd opened the bureau. Rummaged as silently as she could, among the silk stockings and envelopes containing banknotes and cash. She knew which drawer

to open: she'd seen it opened many times before. She knew exactly where Miss de Vries kept her personal funds.

Behind her, a figure moved between the trees. "Don't go
anywhere near her."

The man whirled round. So did Alice. In that moment Alice's
shame bloomed: the night opened up around her, all-seeing.

"Dinah," she breathed, agonized.

For there was Mrs. King: panting, gloves off, hat tilted at
a vicious angle. Clearly, she'd come running, tracking Alice
across the park.

"I mean it," Mrs. King said. "Get *away* from her." She was
holding a knife.

The man studied the knife. He looked at Alice. "Who's this?"
he asked, raising an eyebrow.

Alice shook her head, raised her hands. "Dinah, don't. It's
nothing—it's fine."

Mrs. King's eyes flashed in the gloom. "It's not *fine*," she said.
Her voice sounded throttled, scared. She didn't sound herself at
all. She turned to the debt collector. "Who *are* you?"

"I'll do you the courtesy of telling you to clear off," the man
said. "And I'll only say it once."

Alice had never seen her sister do it. She'd only heard about it.
The neighbors said that Dinah could be violent. That she could
make grown men weep. Alice had never been able to credit it.
And yet now, as Mrs. King stepped quickly toward the debt
collector, she understood. It was like watching a demon, a soft-
footed sort of devil. Mrs. King sheathed her knife and came at
him without a hint of fear. She drove into him, white gloves
balled into fists.

"Ah—" said the man. He flailed, righting himself, reaching
into his pocket. Alice saw the dull gleam of silver, the black eye
facing her.

A pistol.

The park swayed, a gust of wind roaring through the trees. Mrs. King staggered.

Calmly, breathing fast, the man centered himself. His arm was steady.

"You shouldn't have done that," he said.

He lifted his pistol.

"I've got the money!" Alice's voice was strangled. She drew out a fistful of banknotes from her apron, keeping her eyes only on the gun. "Here, here. See? You can count it. Take what I owe."

Slowly, he came to her. He smelled ripe, as if he needed to bathe, but his overcoat still carried the faintest whiff of gardenias. "Show me."

He kept the pistol on Mrs. King and Alice unfolded banknotes with shaking hands. He sniffed, held out his hand. Folded it all away in the lining of his coat.

"This was a bad business," he said, staring her in the eye. "You're lucky."

He swiveled the pistol away. Tipped a finger to Mrs. King. "Good day to you."

Alice didn't watch him trudging away through the trees. She felt no relief. She closed her eyes. The plane trees were whispering, worrying, overhead.

She heard Mrs. King's voice, tight, and from a distance. "Alice," she said. "Are you safe?"

"Dinah," she said. "I've been in trouble."

At last, Miss de Vries got out of bed. It was a sound that did it. An echo of something, crystalline and pure, at the outermost edges of her consciousness.

A cry.

She ran a hand across the rippled surface of her sheets, instincts stirring.

When she rolled the bedroom doors back, the air around her felt as if it had been hollowed out, immeasurably expanded. The lights were burning, same as always, in the passage. But she saw the wrongness at once. The floor: glossy black paint, obsidian smooth. It made her dizzy. Someone had taken up her splendid carpets. They'd left only the bare, stained boards underneath.

She touched the floor with a toe. Cold.

Movement below. Footsteps, hundreds of them, unmistakable. But no voices.

She stepped out into the passage.

38

3:00 a.m.

Winnie surveyed the courtyard. It was still filled with water, the abandoned rafts bobbing worriedly on the surface of the Nile. The garden was alive with activity, and she could hear a racket building in the mews: coaches and wheelbarrows and pony traps and boys with panniers over their shoulders. Cart after cart after cart was rattling away from Park Lane, out of sight of Hyde Park, taking the side streets and mews lanes and alleys of Mayfair. Enormous motors stood at the gates, spiriting the angels and triptychs and diptychs into the night. Winnie saw their agents observing proceedings from the gate. The whole underworld was out tonight.

She came back to the hall. The Janes appeared, limping.

"How much more time do you need?"

"Five minutes."

Winnie tried to be calm. "Five *more*?" She had hoped they could be away by three. It had seemed very nearly impossible that they would keep the crowd in the park for even ninety minutes, even with their pyramid and their vans carefully blocking the junctions. "Give Alice the word. Let's get Madam downstairs."

"We haven't seen Alice for hours."

"Then *find* her. We need her to go and fetch—"

An out-of-breath, a voice above them: *"Ah."*

Winnie turned, looked upward, and there stood Miss de Vries, motionless above them.

Miss de Vries had descended through her house the way she always did, passing the ballroom and the saloon, absorbing the great sweep of the *grand escalier.*

She looked down at the front hall. She didn't gasp. Later she was glad she didn't show that sign of weakness. But, really, it was because the air was sucked from her lungs. The silence, the vastness, the emptiness, took her breath away.

The light was too bright, the white marble too brilliant. The height of the hall seemed almost obscene, cathedral like, glistening. Ropes hanging from the roof. Sweat on the air.

She understood. Everything had been stolen from her.

It is extraordinary what the human brain can comprehend, what new realities it can absorb. *It had always been unlikely,* she thought, *that she would be allowed to control this place, whether she loved it or not.* This life had been fleeting, transitory. Only half-real, all along. She remembered how angry she had been, a few hours earlier, when that awful woman stole Papa's old watch. A watch: a tiny thing. Nothing. She felt the urge to laugh: a hollow, dreadful sensation.

Then it burned away. She went all the way down the stairs, slowly.

Footsteps. A figure among many more, winking and glinting, beneath her.

Isis, painted, sequined, clambering on top of a box. A huge

crate, at the foot of the *grand escalier*. "I told you," the figure said to Miss de Vries, "that I would deliver you to your death."

Miss de Vries had rung the bell when she'd awoken. Not the usual bell, the one that sounded in the servants' hall. The emergency bell, the brass button in her father's bedroom, the one that rang in Mr. Shepherd's room.

But nobody had come. The house was empty.

"I will call for the constable," she said, because she had to say something; she had to test her voice. It had risen; it very nearly wavered. "I will call for him at once!"

❧

But Mrs. Bone had the constable. Three of her biggest men had him pinned to the ground, ignoring his grunts and moans. She stroked his hair, whispering, "*And* one silver muffineer, all noted, all recorded. So if you *must* run and get help, you'll run *awfully* slowly, won't you?"

❧

Winnie watched Miss de Vries treading toward her, slow as a lioness, tongue running over her teeth.

Delay her, thought Winnie. *Before she kills me.*

"We would like to propose an arrangement," Winnie said.

Silence.

Then, that voice. Low, careful. "'We'?"

Winnie said nothing more.

Miss de Vries said, heavier, "What arrangement?"

Winnie stood up straight. "The property in this house has disappeared. It's done and cannot be undone. It can never be recovered, at least not by you."

Miss de Vries stared up at her, face masklike. Her eyes were like a cat's, opaque and glassy.

"We have not touched your room. Although we have monitored most carefully what is contained within it. If you comply with our wishes, we will permit you to keep the contents of your trousseau, and we will preserve confidentiality over the circumstances of your—defenestration."

"What are your wishes?"

Winnie shifted. She had expected more resistance from Miss de Vries.

"First: demolish this house."

Silence.

Then: "Why?"

"It causes pain. It is a blight on you. It has harmed many others. I think you sense this." Winnie paused. Then said, making her voice stronger: "Take it down. It must not burden anyone again."

"What else?" The same cold voice, the same expression.

"We expect your complete withdrawal from society. You understand why. We cannot take any risks."

"What risks do you fear?"

Winnie studied her. "A repetition of the crimes committed here."

She saw that sharp and whittled mind working hard. A flash of fear, avoiding something. It vanished as quickly as it appeared.

"Anything else?" said Miss de Vries.

Winnie shook her head. "No."

"What do I need to do?"

"Keep your guests at bay. We'll finish up here." Winnie folded her hands.

Risks were everything, in games. That's what Mrs. King said. It wasn't like rolling a dice or flipping a coin. These odds were many-sided: they could land any number of ways. Winnie hadn't liked that one bit. She'd reasoned with Mrs. King, argued with her: *She'll call the constable, she'll call for the footmen, she'll have us arrested, she'll never permit it…*

Winnie remembered that Mrs. King had shaken her head. "She *will* permit it," she'd said. "She'll look at her options. She'll consider them all." She added, with a grim smile, "I can predict exactly what she'll do."

Winnie had been nearly despairing. But she saw those lights dancing in Mrs. King's eyes. She didn't argue.

Miss de Vries's silence indicated that she was conducting internal deliberations. If she recognized Winnie's voice, if it triggered a memory, or understanding, then she didn't show it. She showed nothing at all.

"I have a personal fund," she said, at last. "Emergency reserves, which sit outside the household accounts." She paused. "I will need to keep that money."

Winnie hadn't bargained for this. Mrs. King had not discussed it with her. *How much money could there be?* she wondered. Enough to form a dowry, or a new household? Enough to make a deal with the devil?

"Keep my things," said Miss de Vries, "but give me my independence."

It stirred Winnie, to hear those words. She couldn't help it. "Very well," she said. "Do we have your agreement?"

Miss de Vries remained silent. Then she said, "What have you done with my father's portrait?"

Winnie looked around, chest contracting. Mrs. Bone, hidden at the back of the throng, shouted, "We've thrown it on the rubbish heap."

Miss de Vries surveyed the ranks of silent men, her eyes passing over Mrs. Bone without even a flicker.

"I comply," she said. She moved like a wraith, still clad in black mourning silks, making for the front porch.

"Go," Winnie breathed, to the others. And then, louder: *"Go."*

39

4:00 a.m.

Hephzibah watched it play out from the pavement. Miss de Vries emerged from the house, shoulders bare, eyes on the crowd. A cry went up: *"Are you safe? The fire!"*

"There is no fire," she said to those near at hand. "And no cause for alarm. Everybody should go home."

Disbelief and confusion rippled out across the crowd. It was strange, thought Hephzibah, watching Miss de Vries: this tiny creature, guarding the front porch. It was the men who tried to push their way in first. Shepherd. Then Lord Ashley. But she held her hands to the door frame, a small smile on her face, barring the way. Hephzibah couldn't hear what Lord Ashley said. She only saw what everybody else witnessed, too. His betrothed didn't bow to him, didn't bend: she sent him on his way.

Mr. Lockwood was next. He knifed his way across the pavement. But Hephzibah was on him. "No, no," she murmured, gripping his arm. He swung around, startled. "Come with me."

He resisted. "What on earth?" He shook her off.

"I can assure you," she said, keeping her voice low, "it will be worth your client's while."

Earlier, while the crowds were surging outside the house, Winnie had grabbed Hephzibah. She'd given her the paper, pressed it right into her hands. "We're going to put this right," she'd said. She was out of breath, eyes fierce, clinging to the Inventory. "I promise you. On my honor."

Hephzibah had unfolded the paper, reading the names: *Eunice, Eileen, Ada...* It had stopped the breath in her throat. "When?" she had said, voice dry.

"Now," Winnie had said. "We're going to fix it *now.*"

So Hephzibah led Mr. Lockwood to Tilney Street. The dessert trolley was laden high with trifles. They smelled sour, as if they'd begun curdling in the heat. She closed the door behind Mr. Lockwood with a firm and uncompromising *click.* "What on earth," he said, "is this all *about*?"

Hephzibah kept her hand over her veil. She took a piece of paper from her sleeve. "Crawl over here," she said with disdain, "and have a read of this."

He took it from her outstretched hand, scanned it carefully, from top to bottom. She guessed lawyers always did that with pieces of paper. "It's a copy," she warned him. "Don't bother doing anything silly with it."

Clearly, it required a whole long minute for him to comprehend it, to really take it in, line by line. Name by name. "What do you want?" he said at last, looking up, face ashen.

Hephzibah leaned forward. She felt something uncoiling inside her. It wasn't glee; it wasn't giddiness. It was tiredness. Fatigue, bone-deep. Grief: for herself, and all the others.

"Never underestimate the kitchen girls, Mr. Lockwood," she said. "They've got brains the same as anyone. They see *everyone* coming and going."

Miss de Vries stayed at the front door for a very long time. People kept coming. "Miss de Vries, are you quite all right? Miss de Vries, are you quite well?" She ignored them. She examined the stained glass and tried to close her ears to the noises behind her. She wondered idly whether they might tell her they had finished. They didn't, of course. The sound of footsteps simply faded until there was nothing left, and she was alone in her vast and desolate home.

She went straight to the second floor. The chill shocked her: the ballroom was like an icehouse, all the windows to the garden thrown open to the morning breeze. She searched for signs of damage, but there were none. Everything she owned had disappeared without a trace. She felt the queer urge to laugh, to howl.

Her bedroom was as they had promised: untouched. Only the bureau had been disturbed. She went to it. First job: to gather her personal funds.

The top drawer was empty.

She reached into the compartment, as if the banknotes had magically shrunk, as if someone had kindly rolled them up for her.

It wasn't pain she felt. It was something different. She sat down on her vast and rumpled bed.

Miss de Vries had been betrayed before, by Papa, but that had felt different altogether, a burning sensation in her heart, her skin, as if she'd been dipped in white spirit. Now she felt only short of breath, as if squeezed into an airless box.

I consider this arrangement terminated, she thought, and went back downstairs.

She stayed indoors, sitting on the *grand escalier*, and waited for Lockwood to return. She heard Cook haranguing him on his way through the door. "Is Madam ruined, sir?" she cried. "Will we be paid?"

Miss de Vries couldn't catch his response. He slammed the door, the echo reverberating through the house. He looked ghastly. Gray, and drawn, and yet strangely wild-eyed. *Vulture*. He was loving this. Chaos meant more work for him, for his kind.

"I need you to go to Lady Ashley," she said, not bothering with greetings.

He jumped. Perhaps he expected her to be upstairs, lying in a swoon.

"Why?" he asked, eschewing pleasantries, too.

"I want to ensure everything is proceeding as planned."

"Everything relating to…"

She turned the full force of her stare onto him. "My marriage."

"I am not sure this is the best time for that."

"No day like today, Mr. Lockwood."

"You were very terse with Lord Ashley," he said. "You denied him entry to this house."

"It's my house. It's my prerogative."

"You barred his way. In public. Everyone saw you do it."

"Can anyone possibly blame me? I have suffered the most enormous shock."

"You don't seem shocked," he said.

"Go and see Lady Ashley," she ordered. "Go and do it now."

He gave her a long, strange look, almost as if he were sizing her up, deciding where to hang her. He said, "A lady residing very near this house has certain papers in her possession. Papers documenting visitors to this house."

"Visitors?"

He didn't reply.

At first she didn't understand. And then she saw the way he pressed his lips together, taking the utmost care not to speak a word before she did.

"Ah," she said. She felt the world tilting, turning, getting ready to drag her under its wheels.

He said, "You'll need a lawyer, of course."

Dawn arrived, sleepless, cloudy and unreal. By nine o'clock a stream of lawyers had crammed themselves into the empty, echoing winter garden. They'd come out of the drains like rats running toward a carcass. Miss de Vries hovered beside Lockwood.

"I'm innocent," she said.

Lockwood said nothing. No one had accused her of anything. But she knew someone was drafting the story, drawing up the terms. A tale of girls, and gentlemen who enjoyed them, and those who aided and abetted it all...

"I'm *innocent*," she said again, and surveyed all the gray-faced, gray-suited men ranged out before her. "I've harmed no one. I know nothing."

Lockwood made his face a mask. "About...?"

Miss de Vries wished then very badly to be alone. She stood up from her seat, and went to the vast bay windows overlooking the park. Lockwood moved away from her, as if she were infectious, as if she carried plague.

She put her hands on the window ledge and surveyed the road. In the old days Papa would drive up in his carriage, and later in his gigantic motor car, and she would wave to him. He'd squash his hat down over his head, pretending not to see her. It made her laugh in delight. He was always playing jokes and games. All the things she loved, when she was small. Before she understood that he wasn't joking. That he wasn't looking, that he hardly thought of her at all.

It would have been easier if she felt any self-pity. If she felt the urge to weep. It might have made her able to exist inside her own skin. But the only thing she felt was dread.

Nothing had changed yet. Lockwood was grim-faced but clear. Any question of illegal business would need to be properly charged, and in due course clear the courts, and the implicated parties had the best attorneys in London. Yes, there would be newspapermen outside the house from dawn to dusk, and inspectors pouring in from Scotland Yard, and not a single neighbor would call on her. The house would be tainted by gossip, speculation, all things horrid. But surely it would pass?

"Go for a walk," said Lockwood. "Let the neighbors see you. No use hiding away indoors."

Why not? She still had her chauffeur, and her motor, and her faithful footman. And her trousseau, come to that. She picked out the crepe with jet. Alice never did take it, she supposed, throat tightening. The girl had vanished. She remembered the pressure of Alice's fingers, the scent of her skin, and she felt something hollowing in her chest. She put on her gloves, and a hat, and William walked behind her down the road, saying nothing.

A small, rackety motor carriage drew up beside them, incognito—and evidently, by design. She saw the dark maroon-colored leather, stains all over the silverwork. *Everything is tarnished*, she thought, laughing inwardly. *Everything in the world is spoiled.*

"Lord Ashley," she said, voice steady. She was astonished to see him. If she were him, she would have stayed home. She would have preserved the greatest possible distance from this house, for safety, for reputation.

William was watching her. He put out a hand to her, a tiny bit of kindness.

She brushed him away and stepped into Lord Ashley's motor with a smile.

Lord Ashley wore a dangerous expression as he steered the Victoriette. He didn't ask her how she was, what she was feeling. Didn't speak a word about the house, or what had happened to it, at all.

"Fancy chap you had carrying your things, there."

"William?" she asked.

"Tall sort of fellow. Don't much like the way he looks at you."

"I hardly notice him."

"I wouldn't let a wife of mine keep a handsome chap like that around the house. You'll have to get used to potbellied pigs if you plan on making a decent marriage."

If? She pressed her lips together, controlling herself.

"Your man Lockwood came to see Mother this morning."

Miss de Vries grew still. "Did he?" she said, looking out at the park.

"What's all this about a list?"

The carriage rattled as it took the hard turn at Hyde Park Corner. Miss de Vries remained silent. But he waited for her to speak.

"List?" she said, at last, throat dry.

"I'm not on it," he said, giving her a sideways glance. "Naturally."

It astonished her, his boldness, his breathtaking confidence.

"And your man Lockwood says he'll make sure it stays that way. He wanted to offer his help."

"Help?" She couldn't avoid the sharpness in her tone. "He'll put conditions on you for that."

"We've put conditions on *him*. Mother's strict about things like this. We don't want any taint on the family, no suggestion *we're* covering anything up." He gave her a fast look. "We've all heard rumors about your father's funny business. Somebody should go to the police."

Miss de Vries turned, clutching the side of the carriage. "Why on earth," she said, "would you want to do that?"

"It's my duty," he said smoothly, "as a Christian."

He arrowed the carriage into the park, hurtling over rough ground. "I expect Lockwood'll come and tell you the rest himself. We've torn up the contract. With you, that is." He braked, hard, and Miss de Vries felt her stomach jolting.

He turned, expression as flat as she could make her own. "Thought I'd do the decent thing and tell you myself."

Lockwood was waiting for her in the front hall. He hadn't removed his gloves. "Miss de Vries, I regret to tell you, I think I must withdraw my counsel."

She wanted to press her thumbs into his throat, stop him from breathing. She knew she could do it. "*You'll* survive," she said, "won't you? You loathsome little cockroach."

Lockwood grimaced and raised a hand, silencing her. "Ah, Shepherd."

A door had opened. Mr. Shepherd lumbered slowly in. He glanced at Lockwood, then his mistress. "Keys," he said.

The air chilled.

"What?" said Miss de Vries.

Shepherd's mouth was working furiously, eyes ablaze. "Keys, miss. I'll need to take your keys, for safekeeping. While the police are looking into everything."

To her credit, she told herself later, she didn't act as though the wind had just been knocked out of her sails. She put her hand in her pocket. "I only have this one," she said, plucking her single key, the one that was for the garden door. "As well you know."

She bent her knees a little, and then she threw it across the hall. It hit the marble with a gentle clang, skidding past Shepherd's feet.

"Fetch," she said, with disdain.

This wasn't over, she promised herself, hands shaking. This wasn't the end.

40

The day after the ball

That night the women had a feast. Not in Tilney Street, but in the docks, in Mrs. Bone's inventions room, cuckoo clocks hooting at them every hour.

There was a queer energy to the air. The first proceeds were already coming in, rushing like dark water through underground tunnels. They came faster than Mrs. Bone could tally them, orders running like wildfire back and forth across the wires, steamer routes, trains, the express—to Paris, Marseille, Kristiania, Venice, Prague. Mrs. Bone had ordered game pie, and boned capon, and cutlets and peas, and chicken in aspic. She gave them melon and green figs, and ribbon jelly, and an amber-colored sponge cake at least a foot high. There were candied oranges and a dish with ices, and a basket of greengages and meringues.

"Too much," said Hephzibah, clutching her stomach. "I thought you were a skinflint, Mrs. Bone."

"I can get more," said Mrs. Bone, eyes flashing. "I'll get as much as you like!" She knew her largesse was almost indecent, but she felt the need to do it.

Mrs. King had sat with her, studying the books. "Two lots of lucky sevens for you," she murmured. "Less your advance. We'll hold my share back for now."

Mrs. Bone had flushed, trying to cover her shame. "One share will do nicely," she said. "A great fortune doesn't suit me. It sends me around the bend. In fact," she added, "give another portion to my Janes. They'll make better use of it than me."

She couldn't believe she had done it. But the second she had, it felt unutterably right. She told the Janes to burn their uniforms. She wanted them to buy opera coats, and furs, and parasols, and patent-leather boots. She sent one of her men under cover to a department store to buy them a pair of hats. They were shaped like boats and were crammed with white roses. They wore them at the dinner table. "You're my *best* girls," she said, holding them close, feeling teary.

"Thanks, Mrs. Bone," they replied, unmoved.

Alice sat between them. They'd edged their chairs aside, making a little room for her.

"Thanks," she said in a whisper. She'd gone pale when Winnie spoke of her own triumphant negotiation with Miss de Vries.

"But I took it," Alice said, voice hoarse. "I *took* Madam's money."

The silence was dreadful. Winnie's expression grew taut. Mrs. King opened her mouth—to protect her sister, to smooth things over. But Jane-two spoke first, eyes solemn. "You did what was necessary for your own preservation," she said to Alice. "There is honor in that."

Mrs. King touched Winnie's arm. "Miss de Vries would have reneged on the bargain anyway. She wants to be great. She doesn't want to be free."

"You don't know that," Winnie said.

Mrs. King looked grim faced. "I do."

"I'll pay Madam back," said Alice, agonized. "I promise."

"Turns out you've got some pluck, after all," said Jane-one to Alice, forking her jelly. "Good for you."

"Pluck?" said Winnie, pulling herself together, pointing to Hephzibah. "Talk about *pluck*. I've never seen such fine acting in my life."

Hephzibah went as pink as her ball gown and threw a shaky smile at Winnie.

Mrs. King sat ramrod straight, eating nothing.

At last, Mrs. Bone leaned over. "Well? What's the matter with you?"

"Nothing."

"Don't 'nothing' me."

"Something's missing," said Mrs. King. "That's all."

She had been through every item. They came to her for inspection, one by one, carried or hauled or dragged out from under dustcloths. Painstaking, brutal work.

The letter wasn't there.

Had it ever been? she wondered. She pictured Mr. de Vries's watery gaze. It could have been another trick, a lie, sickbed delirium…

She sat on an upturned crate in the yard as the sun went down over the factory, and ran her hands through her hair.

A small voice said, "All right?"

Alice had been watching her, keeping her distance, as if uncertain about Mrs. King's mood.

Mrs. King roused herself. She stood up. Went to her sister, grasped her by the shoulders. "It's a funny world, this," she said. "Don't let it get to you."

Her sister gave it back at her. "Don't let it get to *you*."

Mrs. Bone had given each of them a bedroom, armored, bunkered, almost without light. "Lie low," she'd said. "Don't move a muscle. I need three days to shift the best stuff. And a week to get rid of the rest."

They obeyed her. Mrs. Bone knew what she was doing.

Mrs. King faced the wall, ancient bedsprings creaking beneath her, and examined her feelings. She was rich already, and soon to be richer still, but she felt empty.

Failure.

It trickled down her spine.

Someone knocked softly on the door. She turned. "Come."

The door opened, letting in an orangey gleam of light. Winnie was in a long nightdress, her hair in paper curlers. Hephzibah had done it for her.

"Can I come in?"

Mrs. King felt like refusing. "Of course."

Winnie closed the door, tiptoed across the room. She sat beside Mrs. King on the bed, almost gingerly. "Dinah."

"Yes."

"You remember what I told you? When we first started all this?"

Mrs. King looked at her.

"That you need to talk to me. To consult me. To tell me what's going on."

"Nothing's going on, Win. It's finished. We did it." Mrs. King heard her voice, dead cold.

Winnie gave her a long and searching look. Then she said, "Come on. Buck up."

Mrs. King felt her heart tightening at the words. They were like an echo, a reminder of those first unfamiliar nights in Park Lane, twenty years ago. Sitting up in that tiny room at the top of the house, trying to understand what she'd done. That she'd left her mother, sister, her whole life behind—for what? For a mysterious benefactor, the sort every girl craved. She remembered all the things *not* spoken, not explained, not answered, when she asked, "Why have I come here?" But Lockwood had put a stop to all that. "No questions," he told her. "Just be grateful." She remembered Winnie staring at her, earnest eyed, knowing nothing. "Buck up," she'd said, with a gentle smile. "Do."

"I had some papers," she said. "Expenses. The menus for the ball." She paused. "Letters."

Shepherd had watched her do it. He'd been with her, in her housekeeper's room. He'd watched her throw them on the fire. And with them, folded with the order bills and receipts and notes for the ball, were the letters to Mother. The letters she never sent. The ones saying sorry, sending love, things impossible to say in person.

Had the packet felt heavier than before? Even fractionally? Had someone put another letter in beside them, tucked away?

She'd *burned* it all. She remembered the ribbon dissolving, turning to ash.

"What do you mean? What letters?" said Winnie, puzzled.

Mrs. King did something she'd never done before. She leaned forward, arms rigid at her side, and laid her head on Winnie's shoulder. She felt as if she could not sit up straight any longer.

"Dinah," said Winnie, as if frightened for her. "Oh, Dinah."

The night loomed vast and black around them.

Three days later

The lawyers were emerging from an office in the City, near Middle Temple. Mrs. King had gone with William to keep them under observation. Offers had started coming in overnight. Mrs. Bone's spies reported that there had been several bids made to take over the de Vries empire. All the major magnates were naming hideously low sums, promising to mop up the de Vries family debts—sweeping the Kimberley mines under their control, divesting the gold holdings and the North American territories, selling off the shipping positions. It would ruin everything that Mr. de Vries had left behind. It would leave hardly anything to inherit. Mrs. King sounded the order silently in her head: *Find the letter.*

Madam didn't arrive; she didn't object. Nobody knew where she'd gone. Some said the country, some said to jail. The house on Park Lane was swarming with detectives, men in trench coats with any number of questions, examining the locks and windows, trying to fathom the biggest burglary they'd ever seen in their lives. One or two were there on more sensitive business. Looking for the kitchen maids, to ask the most delicate questions. But most of the servants had scattered, giving up any hope of getting their wages.

"You were right," William said. "About getting out."

Mrs. King tilted her hat. "Now you tell me."

He sighed. "I've been pigheaded."

She remembered the moment he'd offered her that ring. Cut grass, the park, the stink of the house lingering on them as she told him: "No." It should have happened at night. By the river, in their secret corners of the city.

"So have I," she said.

A crowd of gentlemen came hurtling past, papers under their arms. Mrs. King lowered the brim of her hat.

He put his hand out to her. She stood there, and looked at him, and then she took it. She squeezed his fingers. Not an answer, but something.

"When?" he said. He meant, *When will we see each other again?*

There was an enormous motor car behind her, a Daimler. Vast and rumbling gently. She longed to keep hold of his hand, not let go. But she repressed this. Too soon. Not safe. Nothing was *settled.*

"I'm taking myself out of circulation for a while," she said stolidly. She withdrew her hand from his, denying herself the comfort of it. "But I'll let you know."

Outside the post office, Alice saw the newspapers tied up with string, stacked on the pavement. They were all carrying the same story, the one that grew wilder by the day: the greatest robbery of the age, the biggest search in history...

She glanced over her shoulder. She half expected to glimpse a man waiting for her at the end of the lane. Her nostrils were flared and ready, searching for an unsettling hint of gardenias.

No one there.

She entered the post office.

It cost a lot of money to send a postcard to Florence. It cost even more to wire a large sum to a foreign bank. She chose the one opposite the Grand Hotel.

"No message," she said. "No need."

She felt lighter once it was done. She felt free.

Alice met her sister the next morning, at dawn, five minutes from the Mile End Road. The light was creeping up, birds sounding their chorus. The cemetery smelled fresh, clean, not grim at all.

Mrs. King came in a white dress, not black or navy. She looked strangely loose, untethered, hair swept over her shoulders. There was a fierce color in her cheeks. Alice wondered if she'd been out all night, just walking.

"Where is it?" Mrs. King said.

Alice took her to the grave. She adjusted her crucifix. "It's very peaceful, isn't it?"

"Don't be morbid, Alice."

Alice put her hands in her pockets. "Want a moment by yourself?"

"Yes."

Mrs. King stood there for a long time, staring down at the tombstone. The breeze pulled on her skirts and from a distance it made her appear almost small, like a little girl. Alice had to turn away.

Afterward they walked together through the graves.

"I'm going abroad," Alice said.

"Good," said Mrs. King. There was a calmness about her. "I might need to do the same."

"I mean, *really* abroad. To America, if I can manage it. To take in the latest fashions."

"You can manage it." Mrs. King looked at her seriously. "You can do anything you like."

Alice considered very carefully what she wanted to say. "I wish Mother had been able to see the ocean," she said. "I wish she'd been able to do anything at all." The thought carried its own pain: dull, right in the center of the chest, immovable. Mrs. King nodded, lips pressed together. Evidently, she felt it, too.

"Shall we write to one another?" Alice said.

Mrs. King stopped. Straightened her cuffs. "Would you like that?"

Alice laughed, feeling her nerves. "I don't know. We're family. I suppose we ought to be in touch."

Mrs. King reached out and touched her on the arm. "Write if you want to," she said.

Alice kissed Mrs. King gently on the cheek. Her sister didn't feel like marble anymore. She had warm skin, warm as any other human's, warm as Alice's own.

"You're marvelous," she said, solemnly, meaning it.

Mrs. King laughed, startled. "Heavens," she said. "I'm not." Something shifted in her expression, something dark. "How can I be? Knowing who I come from?"

She meant her father. Alice hesitated. The women were skirting around it, avoiding it. This topic felt too enormous, too dangerous, to discuss. They were both waiting for Mrs. King to set it out for them, explain what it meant, tell them what they were supposed to think. And yet she hadn't done so. She seemed to have turned inward, growing fretful, as if there were something constantly on her mind.

Alice was still trying to compose the right reply when Mrs. King pulled away. Her eyes were on the gravestones behind Alice. A small temple had been erected there, a flashy memorial.

"What is it?" Alice said.

Mrs. King closed her eyes. "I need to see Mr. Shepherd."

41

Winnie had to tell the conductor to stop at her station. It was hardly a station at all—it was more like a halt. The train would have steamed right through otherwise. It took nearly two hours to get there from London. "I want the slow train," she told them in the ticket office. She wanted to watch the countryside unfolding at its own pace. She wanted to be sure that she'd picked the right spot.

She took a seat in a first-class carriage. Important journeys deserved suitable investment. They also deserved expensive millinery. *I can't make a good hat*, she told herself stolidly, *but I can* buy *one*. She purchased a slanted-cartwheel hat with magenta tips, a big boxy centerpiece, and rosettes all around the brim. It made her look a little like a banker and a little like a prize pony. It was quite something.

She wondered if they would treat her differently at the station and, of course, they didn't. She could have stood in the middle of the terminus throwing banknotes up into the air, and people would have ignored her. She was still herself. She wasn't the queen.

"All right, madam?" said the conductor as she stepped down onto the platform.

"Yes, thank you," she said, feeling her rosettes flapping, but he was back up on his plate, raising his hand to the guard, and the train was already huffing into motion. When the last carriage had turned the corner the noise suddenly died away, and there was only birdsong left behind.

Winnie unpinned her hat and felt the sun on her neck. "This is the right place," she said out loud, testing the fact.

She'd copied out the particulars, but she didn't need to check them: she'd committed them to memory. Take a right at the station, follow the road till it comes to a fork, then head uphill.

I trust myself, she thought, setting off down the lane. *I know where I'm going.*

A horse chestnut stood sentinel at the gate. The breeze lifted its boughs and the house peeped through, a flash of pale blue and white, a twinkling of diamond panes.

Winnie fetched a key from the neighbor. "No, don't come with me. I'll judge the place better myself."

The neighbor wore a marvelously hefty jersey, and tiny wire-rimmed spectacles. She gave Winnie a shrewd, appraising look—and smiled. She had very large teeth. They seemed to indicate great strength.

"Of course."

Winnie examined the bedrooms first. Judged how big they were, how comfortable they'd be, how private. Made herself ignore the gentle curves of the garden, the yellow scattering of cowslips, the dense and lovely tangle of the hedgerows. She had to be very sensible about this. She measured the cupboards and the closets. She counted Sue's list of names. The ones she'd kept her eye on, the ones she knew were in trouble. The ones who'd left Park Lane in a hurry, without explanation, in the night. The ones who might need a place to stay.

"It's a long list," Mrs. King had said when she looked at it.

Winnie had taken her hand gingerly. "If you ever want any-where yourself, you only need to ask."

Mrs. King had returned the pressure in her fingers. "Thanks," she said.

Winnie marched back to the neighbor's house. The woman opened the door, frowning over her spectacles. "You're taking it?"

"I live quietly," Winnie said, "but I shall have people visit-ing from time to time. Ladies. People needing sanctuary. To get back on their feet. I shan't want any trouble about it. No gossip."

The woman considered this, twirling the latchkey around her finger. She had bookcases in the hall, and there were pam-phlets and newspapers piled high by the door. She looked at Winnie with understanding. "Just what we need around here," she said. "Tea?"

A week after the ball

Hephzibah did what you should do when you come into a great fortune. She ordered champagne. Then she ordered some more.

It was one of those nights when her chest tightened so badly that she feared her heart might stop beating, when the walls rat-tled and zigzagged around her. This still happened to her. She'd hoped it would end when the Park Lane job was finished. The others were so happy, so exhilarated: Winnie was brimming with purpose. All right for *her*. Hephzibah sat by herself in a restaurant like a woman of dubious means and then she walked home alone. How she managed it she didn't know.

In the morning she had a deeply strange experience. She awoke outside her body, floating over it, as if suspended by fine threads from the ceiling. She didn't think she'd died. She just thought she'd been given the opportunity to inspect herself. At first it frightened her; she wanted to screw her eyes shut.

But then she looked.

She saw her body, gray skinned and greasepainted, mouth open. But, all things considered, she appeared remarkably well. She'd lain down with some care, stiff as a board, before passing out.

I'm lovely, she observed with interest. *I'm sweet looking.*

She floated up there, full of wonder, and then she woke up.

Shame was the usual sensation in the mornings. But that day she felt only a faint curiosity, a sort of scientific interest in herself. She touched her hair, that mountainous, chestnut-rich, glowing structure, and felt proud of it.

She was *here*. She had survived—she was surviving—despite everything.

How clever I am, she thought. *How remarkable. I love being me.*

This realization meant something. That morning she went for a walk in the park, wearing her rich brown cape and carrying a pink umbrella, and when she came home she went searching for a pencil. It took her ages, and she had to turn out half her closets to find any notepaper. Writing was hard, almost painful, and the letters were nearly illegible. But the words came.

What is this? she wondered, staring at what she'd written. *A novel? A letter? A confession?*

A play, she decided. *I* will *write a play.*

She slept that night as she had not slept in years. It strengthened her immensely. She woke with a splendid appetite and treated herself to an enormous breakfast.

She thought about the Paragon. Did she miss it?

I'd build a very good theater, she thought. *I'd run it splendidly. I'd run it better than anyone.*

She reached for her pencil and did the sums.

Mrs. Bone had had a grueling seven days, totting up the accounts. The figures were eye watering, stupendous, unbelievable. Archie began paying off her debts, handing out wages, spreading the word: Mrs. Bone was back in business. *Big* business. The other major families looked on in awe. At the end of the week, Mr. Murphy called in at the factory, bringing the keys to the pawnshop. He crept into her parlor, pale faced, on his knees. He kissed her hand.

"I don't forgive you," Mrs. Bone said, digging her nails into his flesh, and sent him out of the room. Her men dealt with him outside in the yard.

On the last day of accounting she did something very important. She made a quiet adjustment to their books, the only little bit of skimming she ever did, and popped a banker's order in an envelope. She put the envelope in her bag and took the omnibus to Lisson Grove.

Mrs. Bone knew how to find people. She did it her usual way, by instinct. Constable first, then the man running the pie shop. Then down the back lanes, where the girls were hanging out laundry. She could hear little voices chanting rhymes. Could smell the drains, a fractionally different scent here, as if the water were harder in this part of town.

These people stared at her, an oddity, a curio, but they sent her in the right direction. She located a dark and miserable house at the end of the road. The stairs were set at a worrying slant, as if the foundations were having a joke at the owner's expense.

"Sue?" Mrs. Bone said, banging on the door.

There was a long wait. And then a footstep, a creak of the hinges. A face peered around.

Those eyes! Big and utterly scared.

"Here you go, little goose," said Mrs. Bone, shoving her hand through the door, holding out an envelope. "Your fee."

Sue goggled at her. "My what?" she said. Her voice was husky.

"You know what for," Mrs. Bone said, folding her arms. "Don't pretend you don't. I pay well when people hold their tongues." She nodded at the envelope. "Open it."

Park Lane, at dusk.

"Aha."

Mrs. King lowered her binoculars. "Seen him?"

"Upstairs window."

She and Mrs. Bone took the ladder and scaled the garden wall. Midnight came. Then one o'clock. Then two. The world grew quiet, shifted its dimensions.

Mrs. Bone coughed into the crook of her elbow.

"You can still go home, Mrs. Bone."

Mrs. Bone snuffled. "Look here, I need to say something. I thought… I thought they were *pretending* to be married—I never thought that Danny would have *ever*…"

"Don't trouble yourself," Mrs. King replied gently.

Mrs. Bone shook her head, closed her eyes. "You never should have gone into that house."

There was a great deal Mrs. King could have said in response to that. Any number of people might have altered things for her. They didn't: because Mr. de Vries was a rich man, and being rich was a virtue—it carried all before it. Even Mrs. Bone must have believed that, on some level.

"I daresay you're right," Mrs. King said. No need to cause a fuss. "Now look sharp. I'm going to get him."

Mrs. King crossed the garden, made for the house. She guessed where Shepherd would be. In the master's old room. She picked up a handful of stones, aimed for the balustrade on the second floor. Her aim was straight and true. One pebble. Then another.

It didn't take long. She heard the scrape of wood. A window opening. Saw a pale and flickering light.

"Mr. Shepherd," she called up. "It's Mrs. King."

The garden was dark and hollow all around her. The light wobbled above her, fearful. She wondered what it was like for Shepherd, living alone inside the house. Someone had to guard it till it could be sold. He was the most natural candidate. She wondered if he slept on the floor, his cheek against cold marble. She wondered if he licked the walls.

The window juddered closed. The lamplight died.

He was coming downstairs.

It took him a while. At last, she heard the distant *click* of the French doors, saw a lamplit figure in a greatcoat picking his way down the steps. He'd lost weight in the past few weeks.

He looked like a priest no longer. Nor even a butler. He looked more like what he was. A pimp, or a pimp's agent, living on the underside of the world.

"Evening," she said.

Mrs. Bone stayed in the shadows.

Mr. Shepherd wound his fingers together. His voice was as oily as it ever was. "Mrs. King," he said. "What a pleasant surprise."

She closed her eyes for a moment, picturing the darkest nights on Park Lane, imagining it as it must have been. Shepherd, bolting the garden door. Weak light spilling out of the mews house. A girl cutting through the dark garden, unsteady on her feet. The ghost-white gleam of her apron against the black.

"You've got something I want, Shepherd."

The realization had come to Mrs. King when she was standing in the cemetery, thinking of her father. The mausoleum behind Alice was huge and vulgar, a festival of funereal gloom.

It had made her think at once of Park Lane.

A microscopic sneer came into Mr. Shepherd's eyes. He shifted the lamp from one hand to another, light wobbling. "I doubt that."

"You know where the letter is."

Shepherd said nothing. His eyes blazed at her.

"I know my father gave it to you," Mrs. King said. "Entrusted it to you, I should say. You were utterly loyal to him. You're the only one who was."

Shepherd lifted his chin. But he didn't say, *I don't know what you're talking about.*

"But you didn't do as you were told. You can't have done. Because you didn't give it to me. You must have been *ordered* to do so. But you disobeyed that order. You thought you knew best. You couldn't possibly let me see any proof of my rights."

Shepherd had a belligerent look in his eyes. "I don't have time for all this. I've a household to manage."

"Doesn't seem like it. No mistress. And, come to that, why doesn't *she* have the letter? You should have gone straight to her when your old master died."

The lamplight gleamed. Shepherd said nothing.

"Did you want to punish her? Did you feel her pushing you out?"

Shepherd pressed his lips together.

Mrs. King nodded. "So you hated me, you hated her, you hated *both* his daughters. What a sorry little creature you are, Shepherd." She smiled. "I suppose you put that letter somewhere nobody would find it."

It would be easy to get Shepherd by the scruff of his neck. They could shake him, the whole soggy mass of him, rattle his bones. Mrs. King could kick him to the ground, break his jaw. The temptation was very strong. She felt it galloping through her.

"I've been through every inch of this house," she said. "I've opened every cupboard, knocked on every wall. This isn't a castle. There are no secret passages. No hidden panels. No strongrooms, no vaults."

Mrs. Bone emerged from the gloom. Shepherd's eyes widened. "You wicked woman," he said, recognizing her.

"Wicked is as wicked does, Mr. Shepherd," said Mrs. Bone levelly.

"It's in his coffin, isn't it?" said Mrs. King.

There was a little flash of defiance in his eyes. He still didn't respect her. He loathed her. It was his weakness. He flexed his hands, as if he meant to do something with them: push her away, punch her…

"I'll break your fingers," Mrs. King said. "You wouldn't be able to use them again. Believe me."

"I put it in his *coat*," he said, at last.

Mrs. King felt the night yawning open around her. *She was right*. Of course, Shepherd had taken charge of the master, helped the undertakers to dress him. He did the most sensible thing in the world, inserting a flimsy little bit of paper into a pocket where nobody else could find it.

"And *you* can't get it," he added with a vicious little smile.

"Can't I?" said Mrs. King.

Mrs. Bone put her fingers to her mouth, and whistled.

Movement at the foot of the garden. The *clack* of ladders being put against the walls. Figures scaling the mews house. Black shapes dropping to the ground. Men streaming up the path, encircling them. Hoods covering their faces, pickaxes and shovels in hand.

Body snatchers.

Fear dawned in Mr. Shepherd's eyes.

"Keys please, Mr. Shepherd," Mrs. King said.

The mausoleum seemed to tremble in the lamplight. Shepherd put his hand into his pocket. Just his everyday pocket, not a secret place, not the lining of his coat. He lifted out the little key, delicately ridged, like the edge of a tooth. "You wouldn't," he said.

Mrs. Bone plucked it from Shepherd's grasp. "*She* won't. *You* will. Give him a shovel, lads."

The men had got him by the arms—they had him pinned to the spot. His mouth fell open.

Mrs. King took the key from Mrs. Bone, stepped into the little portico at the front of the mausoleum. She pressed her fingers to the cold metal door. Felt around for the keyhole.

The others waited at a distance, holding their breath.

The key clicked in the lock. Recently oiled.

The door swung open.

Cool air. She braced herself for a bad smell, but of course there wasn't one. No leaves, no twigs on the ground. The crypt was undisturbed. Quiet and somber, with the gigantic marble tomb looming out of the darkness. She reached out and touched it. Angels, kneeling.

She felt a rush of fear in her gut. *I'm going to see him again*, she thought.

"Bring the ax," she called.

Shepherd tried to run. She heard the scuffle, his grunt as he tripped, was knocked to the ground.

Mrs. King turned. She felt O'Flynn blood churning inside her. "Come," she said.

They'd snatched the lamp from his hands. The light swayed violently, and she saw his shock, the desperation in his eyes. Mrs. Bone kicked him forward.

Mrs. King caught her eye. "How long will it take?"

Mrs. Bone peered in. "That's a lot of marble."

The men lifted their axes and chisels.

She could see it as it would be, grotesque and monstrous. The tomb smashed open, great hunks of marble scattered on the floor, the casket dragged onto the steps. Splintered wood. Hands avoiding flesh. Fiddling with a waistcoat, using a knife to open up the seams. Mrs. King still kept good knives upon her person.

All that, to find a scrap of paper.

She could guess what the letter would say. A few lines. Some formalities.

I write this on Friday the fifth of May, in the year nineteen hundred and five, in sound mind, and desirous only to promulgate the truth, that I did lawfully marry Catherine Mary Ashe in...

There would follow the name of the church, St. Anne's in Limehouse, or Christ Church Spitalfields, or St. Mary's in Whitechapel. And the date, and the names they used on the marriage register. The lawyers and courts could pick over it all they liked.

A scrap of paper.

Her father's empire, not yet sold off, still intact...

The angels knelt before her. This was a dreadful place to be buried. Lonely, forgotten. *It's where they'd bury me*, she realized, *if I lived here.* She pictured her own casket being placed into the family tomb. *Family*, she thought, feeling cold. She reached for the lamp and bent down, studying the brass plaque.

It was blank.

No name, she realized. Did he run out of time? Or didn't he know what to call himself? Did he mistrust de Vries at the very end? She didn't care to know. She had no desire to understand him anymore, at all.

She breathed out. "Leave it," she said.

Mrs. Bone grabbed her by the arm. "You won't get a thing without proof, Dinah."

Mrs. King turned from the mausoleum. She heard Mr. Shepherd's ragged breathing. The house was empty. The most important things had been corrected.

"I don't need anything else," she said.

42

Nine months later

"It's her," said Winnie.

"Sure?" said Mrs. King.

Mrs. King and Winnie were standing on Bond Street, outside a dressmaker's shop.

Winnie didn't answer. Her expression said it all. *Yes.*

"*Mind* yourself," said a flash-looking woman, crashing through the door, barging into Winnie. Mrs. King peered through the glass. One of the seamstresses was coming out of the back room, carrying a bolt of fabric in her arms.

Yes, it was her. It didn't matter what she wore, or how she disguised herself; it was undoubtedly and absolutely Miss de Vries. Or whatever she'd transformed herself into, with her hair cropped and dyed and pinned so that you could see the whole stiff line of her neck.

"Wait here," said Mrs. King. And she opened the door.

Miss de Vries looked up at the sound of the bell. Her eyes were flat. She didn't recognize Mrs. King at first. It wasn't play-act-ing: she really had no idea who Mrs. King was. *I've transformed,* thought Mrs. King, with interest. She was wearing a bright mustard-colored coat, something cheerful for the winter, trimmed with furs and lace. It was a bit much, she admitted, glancing at herself in the glass.

"Yes?" Miss de Vries said.

She didn't say, *Madam*. Evidently, that was beyond her. She was wearing a dull green dress, with some rather weary-looking embroidery along the sleeves, strangely shapeless and unbound.

"Look where you've ended up," Mrs. King said with a smile. "Who'd have thought it?"

It hadn't been easy, tracking down Miss de Vries. Mrs. King read the newspapers, which told her nothing, and Mrs. Bone talked to every servant she knew, which told her even less. They were all agog about Park Lane, loving a salacious story, talking of filthy perversions, girls being squirreled from house to house. It exhausted Mrs. King. It missed the point altogether.

They assumed she must have left London, perhaps even England. Mrs. King could picture her on the Continent, propping up the gaming tables. She was still her father's daughter, after all, no matter what side of the sheets. But then Winnie caught word from her old contacts in the garment business: there was a queer, hoity-toity girl making trouble in a shop on Bond Street.

"They told me she's a devilish hard worker," said Winnie.

"A seamstress?" said Mrs. King. "Not likely."

"Apprentice," said Winnie. "I think it's worth a look."

And so they came. The shop was on the south side of Bond Street. Remarkably close to Park Lane. A ten-minute walk, if you cut through the side streets. But Winnie was right: it was Miss de Vries, with those familiar cold, gray eyes. They narrowed now in recognition. "I'm busy," she said, but her voice was uncertain.

She seemed stooped, somehow: smaller. Mrs. King felt a sudden urge to straighten her, correct her posture. The feeling gave her pause.

"Have you come to laugh at me?" Miss de Vries said finally.

"Not in the least."

"I could laugh at *you*. You look a fright."

Mrs. King examined her sleeves. She'd bought this coat to please Mrs. Bone, who had developed a mad love of furs and ruffles and violent patterns. "This was very expensive," she said mildly.

"Good for you," Miss de Vries said, without emotion.

Her hands looked chapped and sore: the way Alice's always had.

She's come down in the world, thought Mrs. King. *She's become one of us.* It didn't feel like a triumph. It felt like a great injustice.

"Who made you so hard?" she said. "Our father? Or did you do it yourself?"

It was evident Miss de Vries didn't wish to answer this. She wasn't willing to plumb those depths for any person, for any reason. She said, voice rough, "You're hardly gentle in *your* methods, Mrs. King."

Mrs. King smiled at this. "You'd have done the same," she said. "You'd have taken any action required to get what belonged to you."

Miss de Vries didn't move. The fight didn't leave her eyes, but it shifted. It retreated into the back of her head.

"You *did* take action," Mrs. King said. "Didn't you?"

This thought had circled in her mind almost the instant she heard that the old master had died. Miss de Vries looked at her cautiously. Her expression changed altogether. It was a deeply strange look: almost shy.

"No," she said, and her voice sounded quite different, too. The faint flush in her cheeks, the little glow of something self-congratulatory, told Mrs. King that she was lying.

"I would understand," Mrs. King said, "if you had."

She meant it. She remembered standing in Mr. de Vries's bedroom. Silken pillows, bursting with goose feathers. Tawny light, clinging to everything. Mr. de Vries flailing, struggling. Miss de Vries, small as she was, had always been densely constructed. She could have easily pressed a pillow down, muffled any noises, stolen the breath from her father's lungs. To stop him repeating that slander: *Mrs. King has rights on you.*

"If I were you," said Mrs. King softly, "I would start looking to make some new friends. Protection. In case anyone else works it out."

Miss de Vries disliked this: it showed in her face. "I don't need protection," she said.

"I can help you."

"How?"

Mrs. King reached into her coat, drew out a small silver watch. The letters flashed at them: WdV. Miss de Vries took a tiny breath.

"Sell it," Mrs. King said. "If you like. It's an heirloom. It will have enormous value."

"You're mad," Miss de Vries replied. "I could report you."

Chairs scraped in the room at the back of the shop. The girls were getting up from the workbench, ready for their lunch.

Mrs. King held out the watch, but Miss de Vries remained motionless.

Mrs. King felt a quiver of irritation. *Move*, she thought. *Fight me. Say something.* She'd taken such care over her costume, over her appearance, wanting to communicate something: strength, honor. Clearly, she transmitted nothing to Miss de Vries. She carried no currency at all.

"Take it," she said. "I wish you would. You deserve something."

Miss de Vries shook her head. "I'd rather bet on myself," she said.

Bets, games, risks, odds: long ones, short ones. Mrs. King could see the light sparkling in Miss de Vries's eyes, and she looked so entirely like their father that it twisted her in the gut.

But if Mr. de Vries were present in the room, as a specter or a memory, he made almost no impression; he was very nearly forgotten. His name would die; it would simply fade away.

"Fair enough," said Mrs. King.

What had she expected? That they would talk, that they would speak of their own betrayals, and compare notes? Mrs. King could see it, almost: the two of them, ladies of an equal height and temperament, taking a brisk walk together around the park. Mrs. King realized that she had come here to find a sister, but there wasn't one to be found.

She reached into her pocket. Drew out an envelope. "This isn't from me," she said. "And it's not a gift."

Alice had given her the instructions. Indeed, she'd purchased all the tickets. The train to the coast, the cabin for the crossing from Plymouth, the trains from France to Italy. "Don't say anything," she'd said to Mrs. King. "Just give them to her."

Miss de Vries took the envelope, puzzled. She didn't open it. This didn't surprise Mrs. King. She wouldn't have done so, either—not in public, not under observation.

She said, simply, "Good day."

And then she left the shop, not looking back, not even for a moment.

43

June 1906

Mrs. King waved her hands to clear the dust from the air. She looked across the street. She could see secretaries, lawyers, men from the auction house, all huddled on the pavement. A lot of top hats gleaming.

"We've got all the ghouls out today," said a voice.

Mrs. King turned, heart lifting. There was Mrs. Bone, leaning against the railings. Beside her stood a bicycle with a basket so large it made Mrs. King start laughing. "What d'you want that for?" she asked. "Have you stolen a ham?"

"Wouldn't you like to know!"

"Tell me you didn't ride that here."

"I've got to keep my joints going!"

Mrs. King hugged her. She did it before Mrs. Bone could protest or pull away.

"You've gone soft," Mrs. Bone said, voice muffled.

"And you've turned into a lady." Mrs. King straightened, stepped back. "What's that smell? French perfume?"

Mrs. Bone scowled. "Fix your veil, girl."

Mrs. King adjusted the Russian netting tied under her chin. She knew her face was perfectly concealed. "Thanks."

Mrs. Bone reached for her, a sudden move. Her fingers were gentle. "Listen. I don't like interfering in people's business. And I won't be used as a go-between."

"All right. Where is he?"

Mrs. Bone tilted her head, a quick sideways jerk, and Mrs. King looked over her shoulder. She felt her heart expanding. "Good. Clear off for a bit, would you?"

She raised a hand, a solemn gesture, and William—at a distance, hat pulled low over his eyes, raised his slowly in return.

"Let me know, won't you?" Mrs. Bone said, squinting up at the de Vries residence. A worried look entered her eyes. "What you decide."

William came across the grass toward her: straight, purposeful strides. Mrs. Bone scuttled away, her bicycle jolting as she went, and disappeared into the trees.

Mrs. King spoke first. "I didn't put a call out for any hired hands."

William tipped his hat. "How about sweethearts?"

"Not advertising for those, either."

"Well, fair enough."

"Look at it," she said, pointing to the house.

He followed her gaze. White plasterwork, pillars. The great bow windows, the awnings. The huge heft and height of it.

"Smartest house in London," Mrs. King said.

"They do say that."

"And up for sale, too."

The auctioneers were fanning themselves in the heat.

William's voice was cautious. "Right."

Mrs. King felt the warm breeze coming across the park, heard the roar and grind of the traffic coming around the bend. Saw the fierce glitter of the windows.

Then William said, "I thought we'd meet sooner."

"I told you: I had to take myself out of circulation." She smiled through her veil. "Temporarily."

He touched her arm, and her heartbeat accelerated. She'd taken care, such enormous care, to stay away from him. She did it to preserve her safety, and his. But now, at last, she felt herself bending. She had missed him, and she let herself feel it, the tingle as it passed through her chest, her skin.

"Hmm." There were questions William could ask, whole barrel loads of them, but he didn't. She loved him for that. He said only, "I don't want you to think I'm coming for your money."

Mrs. King folded her hands. "Money? Who says I've got money?"

She felt the weight of her hat, piled high with roses. The expensive lace at her throat, the ruby on her little finger.

His expression narrowed. "Dinah. What they're saying about the girls…" He studied her face. "Did you know?"

"Did you?"

He considered this. "No. But I don't feel any better for it."

"Then you'd better repent, same as me. Let's talk to the vultures."

For the first time she could remember, a whole crowd of gentlemen lifted their hats as she approached. She had an appointment, after all. She imagined she looked strange to them. A lady, but an anomaly. Tightly buckled. Lips the color of garnets. She'd given them a false name, of course. She tightened her veil.

The house was calm and still. It seemed to her that something made of brick and white plaster and sandstone couldn't really harm anyone. It possessed neither good powers nor bad. It possessed nothing at all—it *was* nothing. Yet still it possessed a certain pull. A small temptation. She had to test herself, just to see if she was making the right choices.

"Would you like to go inside?" said a gentleman, putting his top hat back on.

She nodded. "Alone."

She entered through the porch, not the tradesman's entrance. Not the garden door. Not through the mews. The front door.

"Will you wait for me?" she said to William in a low voice.

"Long as you want," he replied, and she felt the pressure of his fingers. She left him on the front step.

She walked through the house by herself. She allowed herself to touch everything, the marble and the iron. Someone had opened all the windows, and the air was cycling around and around, a tumbling and scattering of particles. The house smelled different. Clean.

She hadn't been entirely truthful with Miss de Vries. There was one thing left in the house, a wooden box, concealed in a recess behind the old housekeeper's room. She winced, reaching for it, struggling to draw it out. She had to brush all the dust off her sleeve.

"Dinah?" She heard William's voice calling her from a distance. It seemed to her that the floors were thrumming beneath her, that there was a high whistle in the air.

She came outside, carrying the box under her arm. She heard the gentle rumble of a motor, her own vast and splendid Rolls waiting for her by the curb. The men in top hats all peered at her, expectant. She could afford this place, she supposed. If she spent everything she'd earned, every last penny.

William came to her, squeezed her arm. "All right?" he said.

"Do you want it?" she asked, meaning *the house.*

He went quiet then. "Do *you*?" he asked.

She shook her head, serious. "No."

She lifted the veil. Looped her fingers into the crook of his elbow. Kissed him.

He kissed her back.

The auctioneer stared at them, agog. "Not for me, I think," she said to him, gently.

William laughed, a low chuckle. She felt the warmth of him, his nearness. "Come on," she said.

The house shimmered behind her. She felt a flicker of doubt, the briefest tug of desire, but then it unraveled. Winnie and Hephzibah were having her over for luncheon. Alice had sailed back from New York. The Janes were unveiling their new patent for a miraculous suction cleaner. It was going to be an entirely busy afternoon.

They climbed into her Rolls. As they pulled away from the curb, she settled the box on her knees.

"What's that?" said William, beside her.

She rubbed it with her gloves, removing the dust. Unfastened the clasp. Folded back the velvet. Studied her knives.

Mrs. King lifted them out, one by one, inspecting them. She didn't do it to impress William, although she knew he would be impressed, but just to make the point. She kept good knives. She took excellent care of them. She was ready for anything.

They roared away down Park Lane and left the house behind.

★ ★ ★ ★ ★

AUTHOR'S NOTE

It's a strange and wonderful thing to be sending a story out into the world for the very first time: a long-held dream, of course, and a tad daunting too. So, allow me first to say the most enormous thank you to you for joining me in the world of *The Housekeepers*. I hope you enjoyed it, and I'd love to tell you more about how it came to be.

I think all writers have core stories they come back to time and again: settings, conflicts, and dreams luring them to the keyboard, even when writing (and finishing!) a novel seems almost insurmountable. I love books full of big houses, broken families, loyal friendships, and wild ambitions—textured with all the glorious sights, scents, and sounds of the past.

When I started *The Housekeepers*, I was itching to write a novel set in the early 1900s. I had in mind those big hats and house parties of popular imagination: vast, sweeping croquet lawns; gilded sunsets; that notion of the United Kingdom gorging on one great dollop of luxury before going to war. Of course both hindsight and intelligent historiography have given us a more nuanced view of the era, capturing innumerable shifting forces—social change, new technologies, political conflict, war. On May 12, 1905, as we imagine Mrs. King plotting the first steps of her audacious robbery, Emmeline Pankhurst was leading the suffragettes to their first protest at Westminster. On June 27, as we picture our gang celebrating a job well done, feasting on fine wine and chicken in aspic, soldiers were rebelling aboard the Battleship Potemkin. That uprising followed hot on the heels of the First Russian Revolution in January of that year. In other words, change was afoot, and not all that glittered was gold.

So here was a perfect, glamorous, complicated setting; a world to revel in. But what about the story? I'd always adored the slick engineering of a juicy heist plot and was longing to try to write one of my own. I was washing the dishes—apt, in hindsight!—when it occurred to me that the marbled drawing rooms and glittering saloons of Edwardian London had all the gumption and gloss of a Las Vegas casino, and could make the perfect backdrop for a high-stakes heist. My mind's eye turned slowly to a green baize door, and a cast of servants began sidling out of the shadows, each with their own desire for revenge…

The Housekeepers is a work of fiction, but the Park Lane mansion at the heart of this story is inspired by a string of extraordinary houses that once stood all around the wealthiest parts of West London. Outside the present-day Dorchester Hotel on Park Lane, you can still glimpse Stanhope House, turreted and gargoyled, commissioned by soap manufacturer Robert William Hudson in 1899. It once faced 25 Park Lane, a luxury townhouse built for Barney Barnato, a music-hall actor who made an eyewatering fortune in diamond mining before dying mysteriously at sea. These were homes built for powerful men, containing the most decadent and costly treasures, attended by a seemingly endless supply of obedient servants. And the thrill and joy of writing this novel was to imagine what might have happened if some of the women working below stairs had decided to claim some of that privilege for themselves.

Books like *The Lost Mansions of Mayfair* by Oliver Bradbury and *The Rise of the Nouveaux Riches* by J. Mordaunt Crook, which bring the excesses and the financial forces in high society to life in quite brilliant detail, were so helpful to me when I was designing Mr. de Vries's gargantuan mansion and empire. So too were the archives of the *Illustrated London News*, which carefully itemized British politician and socialite Sir Philip Sassoon's collection of furnishings and *objets d'art* on Park Lane and provided me with a deliciously tangible sense of the riches stored in houses such as these. Isabella Beeton provided immaculate instructions for cleaning picture frames. And I'm forever indebted to List-Verse for surfacing my favorite discovery, the bizarre Parenty Smoke Machine. Here, in fact, I must beg the reader's leniency and ask you to assume that in the world of this novel, Winnie was able to buy these bonkers contraptions in bulk, at very thrifty wholesale prices, and use them to simulate a fire convincing enough to send Miss de Vries's guests hurtling out of the house. Here and elsewhere my rendering of 1905 takes liberties with the historical record in service of my story, and of course any mistakes and errors are mine. For example, the Duchess of Montagu in this novel is a fictional figure, the Montagu dukedom having been extinguished in the late eighteenth century. I have adjusted the daily weather forecast for my own purposes, and while George Sanger might really have been able to loan camels from his legendary circus, shadowy figures such as Mr. Whitman exist only in the universe of Mrs. King.

One further note: In the world of *The Housekeepers*, decadence and opulence are built on the back of reprehensible actions and corruption. There is no suggestion that any historical figures who inspired aspects of Mr. de Vries and his agents were involved in the kinds of abuse and exploitation uncovered in this novel. But I am indebted to authors like Julia Laite, whose brilliant book *The Disappearance of Lydia Harvey* is just one poignant and incisive account of the very real dangers faced by young women entering the service trade at the turn of the century.

And now I am sending Mrs. King and her gang off into the sunset, or their next enterprise. Their fierce desire to imprint themselves upon the world, to right the wrongs they see around them, and to make the most of the ride—ideally on the trapeze!—have made this book the most extraordinary joy to write. For that, I love them—and I thank you for taking the time to read their story, and mine.

I'd love to stay in touch and hear what you think. Do reach out via Twitter or Instagram (@AlexHayBooks) or via www. alexhaybooks.com. And one day I must tell you one of the stories left untold from the world of *The Housekeepers*—a whole galaxy of lady con-artists, dastardly impresarios, and runaway maids…

Alex Hay

ACKNOWLEDGMENTS

So many people have helped to bring *The Housekeepers* into the world, so please indulge me as I try and thank as many of them as possible…

Colossal thanks to my agent, Alice Lutyens. Dream-maker, straight-talker, story guru, you have given so much of your formidable skill and care to this book and to me, and I'm so grateful. Sincere thanks to Shanika Hyslop for amazing support at the start of this mad and joyful ride, and to the whole superstar team at Curtis Brown—with special appreciation to Luke Speed, Anna Weguelin, and Theo Roberts for taking Mrs. King to L.A. and beyond.

Enormous thanks to my phenomenal editors, Frankie Edwards at Headline and Melanie Fried at Graydon House. Your tireless reading, ingenious suggestions, and unfailing good humor made the editorial process such a collaborative and creative joy. Frankie, thank you for piloting everyone on "Team Housekeepers" with such vision, imagination, and skill; you simply got this book, and me, from day one, and have made this such a special experience. Melanie, enormous thanks for your incredible guidance and discerning eye, which strengthened this book immeasurably; it's been such a pleasure! Singular thanks to Jessie Goetzinger-Hall for your amazing input and the most excellent (and motivating) correspondence. Thanks to Samantha Stewart and Greg Stephenson for meticulous copyediting, and to Shan Morley Jones, Nikki Sinclair, Leigh Teetzel, Sasha Regehr, and Erin Moore for amazing proofreading.

At Headline, epic thanks must be given to: Rebecca Folland, Flora McMichael, Grace McCrum, and everyone in Rights; Becky Bader, Chris Keith-Wright, and everyone in Sales; Caitlin Raynor for publicity; Lucy Hall for marketing; Hannah Cawse for audio; Louise Rothwell for production. Thank you to Mari Evans, Jennifer Doyle, and Sherise Hobbs for the warmest of welcomes and for your support. At Graydon House, special thanks to Diane Lavoie and Ambur Hostyn for marketing, Heather Connor, Sophie James, and Leah Morse for publicity, and all those in the sales, production, and subrights departments who worked behind the scenes to support *The Housekeepers* so brilliantly. Thank you to Andrew Smither and Quinn Banting for designing the most beautiful covers. So much creativity, energy, and talent has gone into launching *The Housekeepers* from publishers in territories around the world, and I'm so grateful to everyone involved.

To the matchless community of authors, book bloggers, reviewers, and early readers who have shown early support for *The Housekeepers*—thank you so very much!

To Wendy Bough and the Caledonia Novel Award—being longlisted for the 2022 prize boosted *The Housekeepers* in ways I couldn't have imagined, and made all the difference; thank you.

To everyone at Curtis Brown Creative: thank you. Heartfelt and fondest thanks to Anna Davis for astute and generous advice over the years; to Norah Perkins for early encouragement; to the incomparable Erin Kelly for such kindness and inspiration; to Katie Smart; and to my beloved CBC classmates for great dinners, wonderful friendship, and for reading multiple books/ ideas/emails/urgent Whatsapp queries about how to use Track Changes over the years.

To my cherished Apple Owls/Dancing Toads—Amy, Anneka, Fran, Sacha—I love you beyond the telling of it, and thank you from the bottom of my heart for cheering me along on this journey. Special thanks to Richard, fellow resident of the Towers, for such solidarity and encouragement over the years.

Immeasurable thanks to my wonderful mother (and marvelous writer) Dale Frances Hay. You've inspired, encouraged and supported me in ways too numerous to count or name, so I shall just say the most sincere thank you, with all my love.

And finally, and with a swelling heart and all the love in the world, thank you to my wonderful husband, Tom. You've been at my side, literally and figuratively, the whole time I was writing this book. Your questions and advice strengthened *The Housekeepers* before it even went out on submission, and your patience and kindness and support meant the world during those nervous days/weeks/months/years waiting to see if it would all pay off. Thank you for cracking open the prosecco when it was needed most: a Perfect Moment that wouldn't have meant nearly as much without you there. Thanks, buddy—I love you.